Trieste

Daša Drndić

TRANSLATED FROM THE CROATIAN BY
Ellen Elias-Bursać

MARINER BOOKS
HOUGHTON MIFFLIN HARCOURT
BOSTON   NEW YORK

First Mariner Books edition 2015
Copyright 2007 © by Daša Drndić and Fraktura
English translation copyright © 2012 by Ellen Elias-Bursać

www.hmhco.com

First published in Croatian as *Sonnenschein* in 2007
First published in Great Britain in 2012 by MacLehose Press, an imprint of Quercus

Library of Congress Cataloging-in-Publication Data
Drndić, Daša, date. author.
[Sonnenschein. English]
Trieste / Daša Drndić ; translated from the Croatian by Ellen Elias-Bursać. — First U.S. edition.
pages cm
ISBN 978-0-547-72514-7 (hardback)
ISBN 978-0-544-53850-4 (pbk.)
I. Elias-Bursać, Ellen, translator. II. Title.
PG1619.14.R58S6613 2014
891.8'235 — DC23
2013044258

Printed in the United States of America
DOC 10 9 8 7 6 5 4 3 2 1

This book is a work of fiction. Names, characters, businesses, organizations, places, and events are either the product of the author's imagination or are used fictitiously. For example, the early life of Haya Tedeschi is based on an account by Frank Gent of the life of Fulvia Schiff and her family ("My Mother's Story," 1996). The affair with an S.S. officer and subsequent birth of a son are fiction. In reality the Schiffs fled from Sicily to Albania in 1938, and lived there for six years, when they returned to Italy via Yugoslavia, Hungary, and Austria. Fulvia Schiff met a British soldier, Frank Dennis Gent, in Milan in 1945. She returned with him to England — where they still live — married, and had six children.

A single moment suffices to unlock the secrets of life,
and the key to all secrets is History and only History,
that eternal repetition and the beautiful name of horror.

— Jorge Luis Borges

For sixty-two years she has been waiting.

She sits and rocks by a tall window in a room on the third floor of an Austro-Hungarian building in the old part of Old Gorizia. The rocking chair is old and, as she rocks, it whimpers.

Is that the chair whimpering or is it me? she asks the deep emptiness, which, like every emptiness, spreads its putrid cloak in all directions to draw her in, her, the woman rocking, to swallow her, blanket her, swamp her, envelop her, ready her for the rubbish heap where the emptiness, her emptiness, is piling the corpses, already stiffened, of the past. She sits in front of her old-fashioned darkened window, her breathing shallow, halting (as if she were sobbing, but she isn't) and at first she tries to get rid of the stench of stale air around her, waving her hand as if shooing away flies, then to her face, as if splashing it or brushing cobwebs from her lashes. Foul breath (whose? whose?) fills the room, rising to a raging torrent and she knows she must arrange the pebbles around her gravestone, now, just in case, in case he doesn't come, in case he does, after she has been expecting him for sixty-two years.

He will come.

> *I will come.*

She hears voices where there are none. Her voices are dead. All the same, she converses with the voices of the dead, she quibbles with them, sometimes she slumps limply into their arms and they whisper to her and guide her through landscapes she has forgotten. There are times when events boil over in her mind and then her thoughts become an avenue of statues, granite, marble, stone statues, plaster figures that do nothing but move their lips and tremble. This must be borne. Without the voices she is alone, trapped in her own skull that grows softer and more vulnerable by the day, like the skull of a newborn, in which her brain, already somewhat mummified, pulses wearily in the murky liquid, slowly, like her heart; after all, everything is diminishing. Her eyes are small and fill readily with tears. She summons non-existent voices, the voices that have left her, summons them to replenish her abandonment.

By her feet there is a big red basket, reaching to her knees. From the basket she takes out her life and hangs it on the imaginary clothes line of reality. She takes out letters, some of them more than a hundred years old, photographs, postcards, newspaper clippings, magazines, and leafs through them, she thumbs through the pile of lifeless paper and then sorts it yet again, this time on the floor, or on the desk by the window. She arranges her existence. She is the embodiment of her ancestors, her kin, her faith, the cities and towns where she has lived, her time, fat sweeping time like one of those gigantic cakes which master chefs of the little towns of *Mitteleuropa* bake for popular festivities on squares, and then she takes it and she swallows it and hoards it, walls herself in, and all of that now rots and decomposes inside her.

She is wildly calm. She listens to a sermon for dirty ears and drapes herself in the histories of others, here in the spacious room in the old building at Via Aprica 47, in Gorica, known as Gorizia in Italian, Görz in German, and Gurize in the Friulian dialect, in a miniature cosmos at the foot of the Alps, where the River Isonzo, or Soča, joins the River Vipava, at the borders of fallen empires.

Her story is a small one, one of innumerable stories about encounters, about the traces preserved of human contact. She knows this, just as she knows that Earth can slumber until all these stories of the world are arranged in a vast cosmic patchwork which will wrap around it. And until then history, reality's phantom, will continue to unravel, chop, take to pieces, snatch patches of the universe and sew them into its own death shroud. She knows that without her story the job will be incomplete, just as she knows that there is no end, that the end reaches on to eternity, beyond existence. She knows that the end is madness, as Umberto Saba once told her while he was in hospital here, in Gorizia, in Dr Basaglia's ward perhaps, or maybe it was in Trieste with Dr Weiss. She knows that the end is a dream from which there is no waking. And the shortcuts she takes, the quickest ways to get from one place to the next, are often nearly impassable, truly goats' paths. These shortcuts may stir her nostalgia for those long, straight, rectilinear, provincial roads, also something Umberto Saba told her then, so she sweeps away the underbrush of her memory now, memories for which she cannot say whether they even sank to the threshold of memory, or are still in the present, set aside, stored, tucked away. It is along these overgrown shortcuts that she walks. She knows there is no such thing as coincidence; there is no such thing as the famous brick which falls on a person's head; there are links – and resolve – of which we seem to be unaware, for which we search.

She sits and rocks, her silence is unbearable.

It is Monday, 3 July, 2006.

HURRY UP PLEASE IT'S TIME

Her name is Haya Tedeschi. She was born on 9 February, 1923, in Gorizia. Her documents state that she was baptized on 8 April of that same year, in 1923, by Father Aldo Boschin who, of course, she does not remember, just as she has no memory of her godmother, Margherita Collenz. There is also a baptism celebrated by Don Carlo Baubela. Baubela is a German name. She meets Don Carlo Baubela in the autumn of 1944 when he is already old and hunched over and, spreading the fragrance of incense and tobacco with his half-frozen, trembling hands, he gives his blessing. Gorizia is a charming little town. There have been interesting histories in Gorizia, little family histories, like this one of hers. She never met many of the members of her family. She has never even heard of quite a few of them. Her mother's and her father's families are large. There are, there were, families in Gorizia with tangled stories, but their stories do not matter, despite the way history has been trailing them along with it for centuries, just as rapids sweep along broken branches wrenched free of the shore, and the carcasses of livestock, their bellies bloated, cows, their eyes glassy, tailless rats, corpses with their throats slit, and suicides. There were no suicides in her family. Or if there were, no-one ever spoke of them to her.

There were several well-known people who lived in Gorizia and committed suicide. Many people passed through Gorizia on the run. Some stayed, some were taken away. Of these some were Jews, some were Gentiles. Of these, some were poets, philosophers and painters. Women and men. The most famous person to commit suicide in Gorizia was Carlo Michelstaedter.

Her mother's name was Ada Baar . . .

It took her years to assemble the information from which she tailored her mangled family tree and learned who was what to whom. For a long time now she has had no-one to ask. Those who remain are few, and their memories are blotted, full of gaps, covered with the black stamps of oblivion or contention and like little islands engulfed in towering flames – they shimmer, elusive. The dead voices of her ancestors shudder, whimper, well up from the corners of the room, from the floor, the ceiling, they creep in through the Venetian blinds and hum history just beyond her reach.

She has no idea what her ancestors looked like. There is no proof. Nothing remains.

The Baar Family

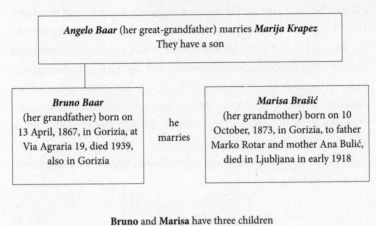

Angelo Baar (her great-grandfather) marries **Marija Krapez**
They have a son

Bruno Baar
(her grandfather) born on 13 April, 1867, in Gorizia, at Via Agraria 19, died 1939, also in Gorizia

he marries

Marisa Brašić
(her grandmother) born on 10 October, 1873, in Gorizia, to father Marko Rotar and mother Ana Bulić, died in Ljubljana in early 1918

Bruno and **Marisa** have three children

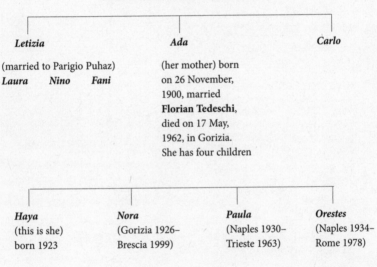

Letizia

(married to Parigio Puhaz)
Laura *Nino* *Fani*

Ada

(her mother) born on 26 November, 1900, married **Florian Tedeschi**, died on 17 May, 1962, in Gorizia. She has four children

Carlo

Haya
(this is she)
born 1923

Nora
(Gorizia 1926–Brescia 1999)

Paula
(Naples 1930–Trieste 1963)

Orestes
(Naples 1934–Rome 1978)

The Tedeschi Family

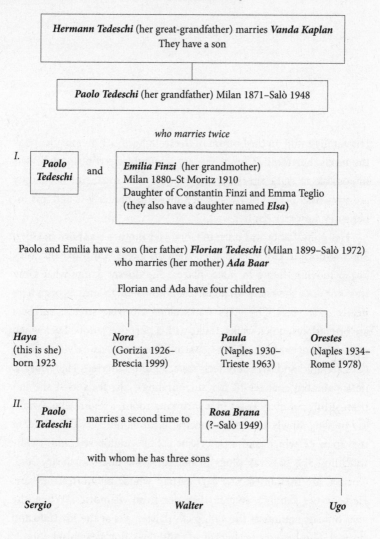

Hermann Tedeschi (her great-grandfather) marries **Vanda Kaplan**
They have a son

Paolo Tedeschi (her grandfather) Milan 1871–Salò 1948

who marries twice

I.

Paolo Tedeschi and **Emilia Finzi** (her grandmother)
Milan 1880–St Moritz 1910
Daughter of Constantin Finzi and Emma Teglio
(they also have a daughter named **Elsa**)

Paolo and Emilia have a son (her father) **Florian Tedeschi** (Milan 1899–Salò 1972)
who marries (her mother) **Ada Baar**

Florian and Ada have four children

Haya
(this is she)
born 1923

Nora
(Gorizia 1926–
Brescia 1999)

Paula
(Naples 1930–
Trieste 1963)

Orestes
(Naples 1934–
Rome 1978)

II.

Paolo Tedeschi marries a second time to **Rosa Brana**
(?–Salò 1949)

with whom he has three sons

Sergio   **Walter**   **Ugo**

Her family rattle on the bottom of the trough (of her memory). Today the limbs, her family's branches, are so jumbled, so dislocated, it is impossible to settle on their whereabouts. The organs of her family are strewn all over. The lives of her ancestors matter less and less for her story, however, for her wait.

Her grandfather was born in Görz. Her mother was born in Görz. She was born in Gorizia/Gorica. When the Great War broke out, they began moving, living in many places. She doesn't know what Görz was, nor does she know what Gorizia is now though she has been here nearly sixty years. She takes walks along Gorizia's streets, but hers are brief forays, quick walks, walks with a purpose, jaunts. Even when she takes longer strolls, when her strolls are more leisurely (when the days are mild and her room feels stale, a humid inertia), Haya doesn't notice the big changes in her surroundings. She feels as if she has been sitting for sixty years in a shrinking room, a room whose walls are moving slowly inward to meet at a miniature surface, a line, at the apex of which she sits, crushed. She cannot see, nor is she watching. She has wax plugs in her ears. She does not hear. Görz, Gorizia, are memories. She isn't certain whose memories they are. Hers or her family's. Maybe they are fresh memories. When she goes out she squints at the sun, picks daisies, sits at the Joy Café and smokes. She has not let herself go. She does not wear black. She is not forever rocking back and forth. All is as it should be. She has a television. She has little memories, darting memories, fragmented. She sways on the threads of the past. On the threads of history. She swings on a spider's web. She is very light. Around her, in her, now is quiet. Gorizia has a history, she has a history. The days are so old.

Sometimes she dreams

she is dragging her mother in a plastic sack. she is dragging her by the legs. she wants to hide her. one of her mother's legs snaps off. her mother is dead, but she says, hide that leg, bury it near the stationery shop at the intersection of seminario *and* ascoli; *take the rest to rose valley, that is what she says*

Her grandfather, grandmother and mother are born as subjects of the Habsburg Monarchy to which their ancestors came long before, from Spain, she thinks. She is born in Italy. They speak German, Italian and Slovenian, mostly Italian. Grandmother Marisa was a Slovene, as was her great-grandmother, Marija. Both died young. Her family did not mix much with others in terms of race and nationality, yet they became mixed. Today all her ancestors are jumbled, impossible to disentangle.

An oft-thumbed family booklet, a guidebook of sorts from 1780 that Haya Tedeschi keeps on the desk by the window with a dozen old volumes and several pamphlets, says that Görz or Goritz is an ancient city on the banks of the River Lizono, situated in Gorizia, in a small province by the name of Friuli, a possession of the House of Austria. Sovereignty over the Gorizia Habsburgs is lost between 1508 and 1509 when the Venetians rule the town, building it into a fortification, only to lose it during the Napoleonic Wars, when it becomes part of the Illyrian provinces. The castle (1780) still dominates Gorizia. In the second half of the eighteenth century, the guidebook says, a synagogue was built there, suggesting the influx of a colourful community. Gorizia lies about thirty kilometres to the north of Aquileia and, according to the guidebook, some seventy kilometres north of Venice. The town of Gorizia is in a wooded area, not far from a road that ran, in Roman times, from Aquileia to Emona. The name of the town appears first in a document dated 28 April, 1001 ("*quae sclavonica lingua vocatur Goritia*"), with which Emperor Otto III makes a gift of the fort and settlement to Patriarch Giovanni II and Verihen Eppenstein, the Count of Friuli. Today, the guidebook says, Gorizia is an archbishopric with jurisdiction over the bishoprics of Trieste, Trento, Como and Pedena.

Her grandfather Bruno Baar fights in the Austrian Army during World War One. His half-brother Roberto Golombek, a student in Vienna at the time, opens a dentistry office there at Weinberggasse 16 in 1924. Roberto moves to Great Britain in 1939 and gets a job at a sardine factory, so that between 1943 and 1945 the Baar family, while still living at Via Favetti 13 in Gorizia, is supplied, who knows how, with vast quantities of salted sardines, thanks to which they survive the bleakest years of World War Two.

As of May 1915, Italy is no longer neutral. It has not been granted Trentino, the Southern Tyrol and Istria by Austria-Hungary, which it had demanded in return for staying on the sidelines. Rarely does war leave anyone on the sidelines. Hence, affronted, Italy conducts *secret* talks with the Triple Entente, after which it crosses over and joins them. Invariably there are conflicting sides in any war. The Great War was a conflict between two sides led by the selfsame purpose. To conquer the world. For themselves. For one side. When it enters the war on the side of the Triple Entente, Italy asks again for: Trentino, Trieste, the Slovenian coastline, Istria, a part of Dalmatia and Albania, as well as the right to the Turkish provinces of Adalia and Smyrna, expansion of the colonies in Africa, and so forth. Italy asks for a great deal. What is not granted after World War One, Italy strives to make up for in the next war. Wars are games on a grand scale. Self-indulgent young men move little lead soldiers around on many-coloured maps. They draw in the gains. Then they go to bed. The maps hover in the sky like paper aeroplanes, then settle over cities, fields, mountains and rivers. They cover people, figurines, which the great strategians then shift elsewhere, move here, there, along with their houses and their stupid dreams. The maps of the unbridled military leaders cover what was there, bury the past. When the game is done, the warriors rest. Then historians step up to fashion false-hoods out of the heartless games of those who are never satiated. A new past is written which the new military leaders then draw on to new maps so the game will never end.

Italy joins the Triple Entente. A new front is created – the Italian front. Major battles are fought along the Soča. The Soča flows through

Gorica, Gorizia, Görz, Goritz. The Soča, the Isonzo, is a river of a vivid turquoise hue. In its river bed it holds a history which eludes historians. The Soča is a river much like a person. Quiet one moment, raging the next. When it rages, it is mighty. When it is quiet, it sings. The Italians wage four terrible battles in 1915 along the Soča. In the Sixth Battle of the Soča (there are eleven or twelve all told), in 1916, the Italians finally capture Gorizia. They shout *Viva! Evviva Italia!* The Soča is red. Blinded. The rains tell it, we will heal your wounds. The rains push fiercely into the Soča, like lovers gone wild. The Soča is silent. The muddy and bloodstained waters rise, but the rains do not rinse them clean. On the river bottom roll bones which, like a huge baby's rattle, disturb its dreams. To this day.

The Soča is a flowing archive of history, a warehouse of wars and love, of legends and myths. It is a coronary artery nourishing the banks. It holds its internal organs in so that they do not spill over. It is a miraculous ray of the cosmos in which endurance shimmers. It is webbed with bridges that summon, like outspread arms, to an embrace. As Ungaretti writes: *Questo è l'Isonzo / e qui meglio / mi sono riconosciuto / docile fibre / dell'universo . . .*

In early July 1906, avid hunter Archduke Franz Ferdinand reluctantly sets down his gun and abandons his favourite castle at Konopište. The castle is nestled in a dense pine wood in central Bohemia surrounded by bountiful hunting grounds. It is lined inside with precious leather and mahogany, and furnished with a host of Ferdinand's hunting trophies. Ferdinand was fondest of hunting bison. On two hunting expeditions to Poland he nearly wiped out the European bison as a species. The castle is in fact a noble and precious animal cemetery. At Konopište the thousands of post-mortem remains of Ferdinand's victims have been meticulously stuffed and arranged in glass cases. Their heads hang on all the walls, and there are many walls at Konopište; the teeth and tusks, devotedly repaired and polished by local dentists, are displayed on cushions of purple velvet and set out in little cases of lead crystal with decorations carved to fit. In addition to the hunting trophies, the castle at Konopište is overstuffed with furniture that František carts back from his also beloved Villa d'Este. He also keeps his weapons there. He has a cache of all kinds of armour, a total of 4,618 pieces. Aside from his fondness for bison, Ferdinand has a special affection for St George, so he also collects 3,750 little sculptures of the Christian martyr slaying the "dragon". Archduke Ferdinand is a serious collector. He collects antiques, paintings by naïve "masters", village furniture, all sorts of big and little utilitarian and useless objects of ceramics, stone and minerals, stained glass, watches and medals.

The castle is surrounded by a spacious, well-tended rose garden visited by guests and horticulture experts. When they see the roses, each of them sighs, *aaah.* Among the roses stand many Renaissance sculptures.

Thirty-five years later the castle at Konopište caught the eye of high-ranking S.S. officials, who turned it into an S.S. vacation centre. Hitler had most of Ferdinand's collection transferred to the Wehrmacht Museum in Prague. He also saw to it that the remaining 72,712 exhibits were shipped off to Vienna so that "after the war" he could have them brought to his private museum in Linz, which had not yet been built. Before they moved into Konopište, the Nazis ordered that the castle be painted black inside and out.

So Franz Ferdinand leaves the Konopište hunting grounds for Vienna where he boards the Woheiner Bahn (the Venice–Trieste line) and stops at the railway bridge in the town of Solkan/Salcano. Actually, he stops in a ravine through which the Soča/Isonzo river runs, not far from Gorizia (Nova Gorica today) on the Slovenian–Italian border, which has nearly disappeared in the new, certainly historical, birth of yet another empire – Europe. A brass band is playing, the banners and flags of the Austro-Hungarian Monarchy are flying, the black and yellow flag, by then somewhat outdated, the Ausgleich flag – the flag of the Compromise of 1867 – and the merchant marine, red-white-green flag with its two crowns, the banner for war – the Kriegsflagge – which would vanish not even eight years later, in 1915.

It is Thursday. The sky is clear. Now and then a small blackbird wings by, quickly, like a restless eye. From the cool shade under the bridge wafts a breeze with the fragrance of wilting linden blossoms, fresh pine shoots on the branches, the moss and cold water. On flows the Soča, serene and pure, its breathing even and deep.

Most of the people in the crowd are children, because school is out for the summer. The children wave because they are children, they have no feel for history. Precisely ten years later, on this very spot, these same children dig into their trenches, crawl across the mud, then disappear in the Soča, and images of that ceremonial summer day break through the raging rapids of the emerald "holy waters" like fireflies, like a lullaby, like an echo, and slip in under their eyelids whispering "Farewell" in at least five languages. With their dying breath, they call out to their mothers *Mutti, mama! Mamma mia, oh mamma! Majko! Anyuka, anyuka! Mamusiu! Maminka!* The birds won't fly. The birds will drop. A black rain of birds will become the Soča death shroud.

Escorted by members of his family, Franz Ferdinand disembarks, shakes hands with the builders, waves to the assembled crowd, smiles, then goes over to the railing of the marvellous white bridge carved from 4,533 stone blocks of Karst limestone and looks at the gleaming river. Rudolf Jaussner, the architect, and Leopold Orley, the engineer, do not hide their pride and exhilaration. Franz Ferdinand looks into the River Soča/Isonzo and has no notion of the number of pledges of love and passionate promises that have been flung into its waters while it rose, angrily overflowing its banks, powerless to prevent incursions into its sky. It took Jaussner and Orley nearly two years to make the miracle happen: the largest arched railway bridge ever raised over a river. Five thousand tons of stone were built into the bridge; the central arch, completed in only eighteen days, has a span of eighty-five metres, unheard of until then.

And so it is that the famed Transalpina railway line is inaugurated: a route that would connect the coastline, actually Trieste, to Austria. The Monarchy needed a direct link to its southernmost provinces. The Monarchy had no wish to travel through alien territory, such as Udine. The Monarchy felt complete until the territories it possessed began to seem inadequate so it wanted more; until it lost what it had already had. Today the old Meridionale line passes through the main Gorizia railway station, built in the second half of the nineteenth century. The trains which stop in Gorizia are half-empty. As if Gorizia is still healing from the wounds of the war. Nova Gorica is left with the Transalpina line. At the border between Nova Gorica and Gorizia there is a museum in which they preserve small, nameless histories. On what used to be a "solid border" slicing Gorizia, cake-like, into two unequal parts, on that "solid border" today there is a square around which everyone is permitted to walk. Beyond the square, in both halves of the sliced city, there still rises a wall of air.

His Highness Franz Ferdinand and the Duchess of Hohenberg, Sophie Chotek, cross Solkan Bridge for the last time on the evening of Tuesday, 23 June, 1914. The husband and wife have boarded the Transalpina in Vienna, bound for Trieste. The windows of their compartment are open. It is June, so the perfume of the linden trees is in the air. Sophie hums the Blue Danube waltz, and Franz says to her, *Perhaps one day they will write a song for this little river, too.* Sophie says, *I don't think so. This is a small river, unimportant and unknown.* Franz says, *That may not always be so.* Sophie and Franz toast each other's health with a glass of first-rate, chilled Tokay. They do not know it, but their hearts beat the way the Soča is flowing, just then, at Solkan Bridge.

On Wednesday, 24 June, Franz boards the warship *Viribus Unitis*. Despite a shiver of fear, he wants to believe that the "united forces" will truly protect his empire. But the nerve of European history has already been flayed. Italy and Austria are ever closer in an embrace of mutual loathing. A new ethics of misunderstanding is born. The "legacy of bitterness" between Austria and Italy mushrooms into one of the most acute instances of European nationalistic intolerance, a sort of negative *folie à deux*, a hatred embraced by both sides, and its web snares Germany and France, Greece and Turkey, America and Russia, Vietnam and Cambodia, Croatia and Serbia . . . The white stain of reason.

On a smaller vessel František then sails up the River Neretva to the town of Metković, continues by train to Mostar, and briefly to

Ilidža, where Sophie is waiting for him. On Friday and Saturday, 26 and 27 June, the Archduke takes part in a mountain exercise, near Sarajevo, of the 15th and 16th Military Corps, but it is already becoming clear that every attempt to create a new beginning, even Ferdinand's, will lead to an end, just as every end holds a beginning. As the story goes, after he was hit, the Archduke whispered with relief to his adjutant, *God brooks no challenges. A higher power has once again imposed the order I was no longer able to sustain.* In July 1914, Franz Ferdinand and Sophie travel aboard the *Viribus Unitis*, the same Austro-Hungarian warship on which they arrived, but this time in coffins. In September 1914, the Russian Chief of Staff publishes a *Map of the Future Europe*, which is remarkably like the one drawn up later, in 1945. The bullet with which Princip shot Ferdinand is preserved at Konopište.

It is 25 May, 1915. The last passenger train crosses Solkan Bridge on its way from Vienna to Trieste. Solkan Bridge is battered, bombed, repaired and then hit again by a barrage of fire, and over it roll batteries, columns of soldiers of opposing armies march over it until 1918 – the Austro-Germans and the Italians. Bruno Baar marches, too.

In the bloodiest of all eleven or twelve battles waged along the Soča, the Sixth, fought from 5 August to 17 August, 1916, Italy opens the way through to Trieste. In the embrace of its lavish gardens and palaces, shielded by mountain ranges, with the Vipava and the Soča as a diamond necklace on its bosom, Gorizia, a little Homburg, a treacherous copy of Baden-Baden, would for many years to come fail to draw the Austrian aristocracy as it had once drawn them during the hot summer months.

General Cadorna lines up twenty-two Italian divisions along the Soča on 5 August, 1916. On the other shore, nine divisions of weary and dispirited Austro-Hungarian troops await the order to attack, most of them too young and too old for warfare.

Bruno Baar is forty-nine. He has a pot belly, three children and a wife who bakes cakes for the Austrian soldiers. He has a winery in which he no longer makes wine. He has a collection of the latest seventy-eights, to which he is not able, just then, to listen, so he dreams of them as he marches along the flooding banks of the Soča, humming "*La donna è mobile*", because he adores Caruso. Meanwhile, his Marisa, swaying on dented high heels, carries walnut crescents to the brothel for the Austro-Hungarian officers, and imagines that she is Bice Adami bringing the audience in Milan to their feet with her rendition of "*Voi lo sapete*", accompanied by the piano. Marisa Baar, *née* Brašić, does her best to sing soprano, but without success, her voice is coarsened by harsh tobacco. A droplet of summer rain falls on her eyelash, where it lingers, making a miniature crystal ball which reflects her future. Marisa Baar sings "*Voi lo sapete*" without an inkling that Bice Adami will long outlive her.

Cadorna begins the battle with a diversionary artillery volley on 6 August, 1916. He places two infantry units to the south on the Monfalcone side with two corps each as decoys. Cadorna's ruse does not work. The Austrian units do not budge. As it was, Count Franz Conrad von Hötzendorf had already cut back the number of troops along the Soča front in order to bolster his offensive near Trentino. Hence Cadorna swiftly deploys his troops from Trentino by train (on the Transalpina line) to the Soča. Fierce fighting, dangerously out of control, begins two days later in Oslavia and on Podgora Mountain, when Cadorna captures the peak of Mount Sabatino. Units of the 12th Italian Division march into Gorizia on 8 August. The Italian Army crosses the Soča the next day under a barrage of fire. Holding their guns high over their heads as if they were carrying children, as if they were greeting the sky, the soldiers plunge into the river singing the Garibaldi hymn:

Si scopron le tombe, si levano i morti
i martiri nostri son tutti risorti!
Le spade nel pugno, gli allori alle chiome,
la fiamma ed il nome d'Italia nel cor:
corriamo, corriamo! Sù, giovani schiere,
sù al vento per tutte le nostre bandiere.
Sù tutti col ferro, sù tutti col foco,

sù tutti col nome d'Italia nel cor.
Va' fuori d'Italia,
va' fuori ch'è l'ora!
Va' fuori d'Italia,
va' fuori o stranier!

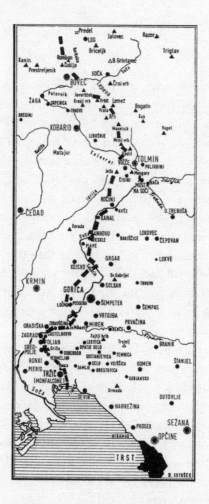

Later people will sing other songs. Mostly women will sing, and mostly they will sing a song with the refrain, "*O, Gorizia, tu sei maledetta*".

O Go- ri- zia tu sei ma- le- det- ta....

Austrian shrapnel whistles, churning the drunken Soča into a pool of green-blue foam. Then a terrible silence settles in, pierced by the sun's sharp rays, and a vast crimson veil dances on the Soča, wet and sticky and thick. The army bugles sound the signal to charge and the grey uniforms line up in a protective firewall. This living wall, resembling insects with their wings plucked, howls *Avanti Savoia!* The stone bridge over the Soča has been hit the day before. Engineers ready the railway bridge over which the railway line runs from Milan and Udine to Gorizia and Trieste. The Italian fighting batteries, now in tatters and gashes, gallop over to the other side, firing at the Austrians, who fall back. Following the soldiers under a forest of spears are the Carabinieri, the Alpini, the Bersaglieri, the infantry and the cavalry. As far as one side is concerned, Gorizia is taken. For the others, Gorizia has fallen.

Bruno Baar scrambles up a hill and watches the battle, hidden behind the scratchy trunk of a hundred-year-old pine tree on which someone has carved a heart. They seem to him like idle children who have chosen to split into two camps separated by a slender thread. As if on both sides of the thread these children are lying flat on their stomachs, puffing, and the thread rises into the air, twists into a snake and falls like a waft to the ground. *That thread is the border*, Bruno Baar says. *It will always twist and turn.* Then he says, *I'll go and turn myself in.*

Twenty thousand Italian soldiers are killed at the Sixth Battle of the Soča and 31,000 of them disappear or are captured. The Italians take 19,000 soldiers of the Austro-Hungarian Army prisoner. They capture sixty-seven pieces of artillery weaponry and a heap of mines and machine guns. The Austrian losses come to 71,000 men, some of whom are killed, some missing in action and some taken prisoner. The tally of casualties for all twelve battles along the Soča for the Italians is 1,205,000, and for the Austrians, 1,291,000.

The losses of the Kingdom of Italy on the Austro-Hungarian front in World War One are: 650,000 killed, 947,000 wounded, 600,000 taken prisoner or missing in action; 2,197,000 victims in total.

The losses for the Austro-Hungarian Monarchy on the Italian front are: 1,200,000 killed, 3,620,000 wounded and 2,200,000 taken prisoner or missing in action; a total of 7,200,000 people are casualties one way or another.

Later, a medal was designed to commemorate the taking of Gorizia. It was awarded to the bravest, both those who survived and those who were killed. The ones who went missing in action were unable to receive the medal. These men missing in action are a big problem, one cannot simply go missing. Turn into nothing. The missing are a problem because they turn up sooner or later. They come back. No matter when, no matter in what shape, they return, whether in someone else's body, in someone's voice, they always leave a trace. When they come back they are a nuisance, because the medals have already been doled out. The medal for valour at the Sixth Battle of the Soča is an important medal. It is a testament to the battle over the only corridor that led out of Italy into Austro-Hungary. The largest number of Italian medals was given to fighters of the 45th Infantry Division, because the most fighters were killed in the 45th Infantry Division. At the Soča. In the Soča. A local Gorizia resident, Castellucci, "designed" the medal. Today there are few such medals on the market. They are rare, so their value is rising. Collectors pay €50 and more for one. Precisely as much as a forgotten life is worth. Along with the medals, there are souvenirs and mementos of the battles along the Soča. Genuine souvenirs and those of more recent vintage. For instance, a twenty-centimetre-high, nickel-plated vase made from an eighty-millimetre shell, with etchings on it of towers and a gateway, describes the march into Gorizia.

These vases are inscribed with the words *Ricordo im Gorizia* and *Ricordo di Gorizia*, and Bruno Baar keeps his in a display case as if they were trophies. Here:

This is for the sake of remembrance. Medals and souvenirs in general. For those who have the time to remember. Remembering is best done in old age. Life is calmer then. Because fresh memories are not, in fact, memories at all, they are happenings. Except in old age memories become deceptive, distorted, and it is difficult to determine whether these (old-age) memories have ever been real.

Bruno Baar does not write home from the front. He has no time to write. He returns soon after he leaves. He says: *One should adapt.* He says this in Italian, because now he is speaking Italian more often and forgetting his German.

Many write. Many never return. Many go missing. That is why their letters have been preserved. Today some letters are sold at auctions, like the medals and the souvenirs.

> *I did not go missing. I am a journalist. I report from the theatre of war. I arrived in Gorizia in 1916, accompanied by Sig. Ugo Ojetti,* well-known

---

* Ugo Ojetti (1871–1946), a writer and art historian. Founder and editor of the journals *Dedalo* (1920–33), *Pegaso* (1929–33), *Pan* (1933–5); occasional editor of the paper *Corriere della Sera* and their art and literary critic of many years. He wrote short stories, novels, humourist commentary, and compiled anthologies. A traditionalist. A member of the Fascist Party since its inception. Fascism attracts a number of Italian intellectuals. Later they say they saw the light and left the Party. Luigi Pirandello joins in 1923, receives the Nobel Prize for Literature in 1934; Curzio Malaparte joins in 1921, quits in 1931. Malaparte's real name is Kurt Erich Suckert. In March 1925 at the Congress of Fascist Intellectuals held in Bologna, their Manifesto is signed by Luigi Barzini, Antonio Beltramelli, Francesco Coppola, Enrico Corradini, Carlo Foà, Filippo Tommaso Marinetti, Curzio Malaparte, Ugo

Florentine fine arts and literary critic. Ojetti was
assigned the task of protecting historical monu-
ments and art works in the war zones.

Yes, for we live in a country of contemporaries who
have no ancestors or heirs, because they have no
memory. When we die, everything dies with us.

Here is Brother Giorgio, the regiment chaplain,
a handsome man. Tall, broad-shouldered, with a
warm smile and unusually temperamental, down-
to-earth views. I am almost certain he joined the
fray. I happen to know thousands of priests and
monks who fought in the Italian Army; many were

Ojetti, Massimo Bontempelli, Salvatore Di Giacomo, C. E. Opo, Serbio Panunzio, Alberto Panzini, Camillo Pellizi, Ildebrando Pizzetti, Enrico Prampolini, Ardengo Soffici, Ugo Spirito, Gioacchino Volpe and others. The Italian Academy is founded in 1926. The President is Guglielmo Marconi, who from 1930 on, three years before Hitler comes into power and eight years before Mussolini's racial laws are adopted, systematically prevents Jewish candidates from being accepted into the Italian Academy, marking their names with the capital letter "E" (*Ebreo*: Jew).

Among the members of the Academy are composers Pietro Mascagni, Ottorino Respighi and Umberto Giordano, scientist Enrico Fermi, writers Giovanni Papini, Antonio Beltramelli, Alfredo Panzini, Luigi Pirandello, Ugo Ojetti and Filippo Tommaso Marinetti, painters Achile Funi and Giulio Aristide Sartorio, historian Gioacchino Volpe and religious historian Raffaele Pettazzoni, sculptor Adolfo Wildt, art critic Emilio Cecchi, and musician Ildebrando Pizzetti. All of them enjoy a sizeable monthly stipend. They travel first class on trains for free. People address them as "Your Excellency". They appear at public ceremonies in the robes of the Academy, and carry ornamental swords.

A law is passed in 1926 banning Italian women from teaching philosophy, history, Italian language and literature, and Greek and Latin in secondary schools.

killed. That is as it should be, no matter what the Pope says and the faith preaches. So it is, too, in journalism. If you do not intend to lie, the truth is never relative.

It poured with rain during my stay in Gorizia. The largest city hotel was closed, so we dined at a more modest spot, La Posta. They served us our food in the kitchen because an Austrian shell had fallen on the dining room just before we got there. We had a fine meal: minestrone, mutton with vegetables, pudding and fruit. We drank excellent vintage Austrian wine. There aren't wines like those any more. And finally, coffee the likes of which hadn't been had in Europe since the beginning of the war. While we were eating, Italian and Austrian batteries exchanged salutations over the city.

We crossed the Isonzo and arrived at the Friuli heights. The sun broke through the leaden grey clouds and lit the blazing bastion of the Karst. Beyond it lay Trieste, the Italian city of longing. But before the longing of the Italians can be fulfilled, the Karst will bleed for years and years to come.

Much later Bruno Baar tells his grandchildren, he tells Ada Baar, Tedeschi by marriage, what it was like on the Soča, because his grandchildren are always pestering him, *What did you do in the war, Grandfather?* And because his children, too, ask, *What did you do in the war, Father?*

There was fighting for a second mountain, for Sabatino, Bruno Baar tells them. *We were living then at Via Romagna 8. We had a beautiful view of the Isonzo. There were gardens and trees all around the house, lush greenery. Gorizia had been captured with caution, so it wouldn't be damaged, because everyone was counting on the town, the Italians and the Austrians, as they meant to come back once the war was over. So Gorizia was only bombed a little, for tactical reasons. People went on* living in Gorizia. *There were hospitals here and cafés, and the artillery was in the streets at the edge of town, and there were two brothels, one for soldiers and the other for officers. The nights got chilly in late summer. There was fighting going on in the mountains, on the other side of town. The metal railway bridge was battered by shells, the tunnel running along the Isonzo caved in. The avenue of trees on Corso Italia was unscathed. There were girls in town waiting for their soldiers. After the fighting there wasn't a single oak tree left standing on the mountain, no pine forest, nothing but tree stumps, trees split apart and the land torn up. I started making my Picolit and my Asti wines again.*

When I came back, Bruno Baar tells them, *sometimes in the dark we'd hear the troops marching under the window and guns going past pulled by motor-tractors. There was much traffic at night and many mules on the road with boxes of ammunition on each side of their pack-saddles and grey motor trucks that carried men. In the fall the rains came. The vineyards were thin and there were mists over the river and clouds on the mountain and the trucks splashed mud on the road and the troops were muddy and wet in their short capes. The king came through at times. He lived in Udine and came out this way to see how things were going, and things went very badly. With the rain came the cholera. But it was checked, and in the end only 7,000 soldiers died of it.*

Bruno Baar speaks, but again Haya asks him, *What did* you *do during the war, Grandfather?* And she says, *You are making all that up. That is Hemingway's story, not yours.*

A story is a story, says Bruno Baar. *It can be anyone's.*

But the story doesn't go like that. It meanders.

Bruno Baar does not engage in battle. Any battle. Ever.

So it is with war, Haya Tedeschi says. *There are civilians in war. They do not fight. Civilians live. Civilians do their best to go on as if nothing were happening. As if life were beautiful. As if they were children.*

Gorizia is still slowly coming into its own in 1916. It is shelled by the Austrian Army, by a stern parent castigating a wayward child.

They are children of Austria, my grandfather and grandmother and my mother are children of Austria. Later, Austria abandons its children and they have to adjust, right? asks Haya Tedeschi.

So the shells are falling. Bruno, Marisa, Letizia, Ada and little Carlo run down to the cellar every time the shelling starts, when flour and sugar begin spraying from the kitchen shelves and the stone floor becomes an airy dough for Marisa's crescent rolls and macaroons, over which the members of the household tiptoe, lightly, as if flying, as if on a cloud floating beyond time. It is October 1917 – 25 October, 1917 – when Caporetto wages the final, twelfth, battle of the Soča. Marisa sweeps Carlo up, but does not make it to the door. A bullet zings through the window, ricochets off the stone mortar and pestle, still green inside from the pesto ground in it the day before, and comes to rest in the belly of the pale-complexioned woman in a blue and black dress with white polka dots.

Marisa is taken to Laibach, where else? Gorizia, formerly the Nice of the Monarchy, is still only an island, a blotch on the no-longer-sumptuous thighs of the Empire. Marisa struggles, semi-conscious, for three months. Bruno sends packages, because the hospital telegraphs: FOOD NEEDED URGENTLY. Letizia, Ada and Carlo muck about in the cold kitchen under clouds of flour and sugar rain, as if playing in sand and mud, making white worms and little bread rolls like pigeon shit when it splats out of the sky on to one's arm, and these, nothing like Marisa's crescent rolls and macaroons, they send to Laibach, but Marisa is already dead. Decades later, when the wars are over, at the Military Archive in Ljubljana Haya finds a yellowed page from the local papers with a news item about the death of an unknown Slovenian woman, who "to her last breath" was calling out for her children, *Otroci moji! Otroci moji!* and for someone named Ada, while the nurses with their caps resembling the spread wings of swans were helpless to do anything but shake their heads, say *Hier spricht man Deutsch*, and fly away.

No-one comes to visit Marisa. None of her family is left in Gorizia. Bruno, Letizia, Ada and Carlo leave on a refugee march towards southern Italy. Marisa dies in early 1918. She is buried in a common grave for the nameless at the cemetery in Ljubljana.

We left, Bruno says. *We had to go to survive. Two hundred and twenty-five people died in the first seven months*, he says.

Carlo is given a bar of dark chocolate, because he is small, nine. The others are given a half-loaf of bread. The column of refugees is a long one. They all walk single file. It rains for days. The roads are mud-soaked. Their legs ache. Their feet blister. In front of Bruno walks a man with a thick bandage around his neck. A plaster collar, rigid and brown with clotted blood. Bruno asks him whether he is wounded, and the man wheezes and gesticulates. Bruno cannot understand what the injured man is saying. He asks again. The man wheezes terribly. *A bullet pierced his voice box*, says a woman in front of the wheezing man who is walking. There are ten badly wounded people in the column, they are on stretchers. They aren't moving. They do not move their heads. Maybe they are dead.

The column is setting off in the direction of Latisana, Udine, Padua, someone says. Bruno has no idea where. He is not familiar with Italy.

In Palmanova the streets teem with refugees. There is a great crush. They are all given cups of coffee. A woman lies, unconscious, in a wheelbarrow. The wheelbarrow is pushed by a boy. The wheelbarrow rocks, tips. *That woman will fall out*, Letizia says. *She'll fall out and people will step on her*, Ada says. The boy is wearing a brown, short-sleeved shirt. The rain pours down. *Wo ist Mama?* asks Carlo.

There is a huge cauldron of hot tea on the square. The cauldron sits on the square like a church, like a chapel. Around it gather muddy refugees in muddy tatters, silent. A German plane dips out of a grey cloud and hovers halfway up the sky. The plane sprays machine-gun fire through the crowd on the square. The soldiers and nurses keep doling out tea. A woman in a garden to the left of the square drops, and with her drops the child she is holding by the hand. The woman and child tumble among the wilting sunflowers, as if they are from Latisana, Latisana is full of sunflowers. The woman and child disappear behind the fence as if they are puppets in a puppet theatre, out of sight. The plane lands on the square, shot down by an Italian machine gun. The refugees step back from the tea cauldron. The pilot has been shot, too. He is a German pilot. Both his legs have bloomed like a bouquet of crimson roses whose petals are dropping in bunches, softly. A French soldier comes running over, shoves his face into the German pilot's face and howls *Vous êtes fou!* The French soldier saw the woman and child fall among the sunflowers, which is why he is shouting. The Italians pull the pilot from the cockpit. It is a small plane, a three-seater, so the cockpit is cramped. While the Italian soldiers pull out the German pilot with his crushed legs, the French soldier comes even closer and shoots the German pilot in the forehead. The women working for the Red Cross stop doling out the tea. Empty tea cups swing from slender hands in the air like silver balls on a Christmas tree. New refugees stream into the city. The city is crowded with refugees who will move on the next day. There are carts pulled by oxen, there are donkey carts, people jouncing in them, eyes open, apparently alive. Others cling to their bundles as if they were newborn babes. The column leaves the town. The battle-fields are not far off. There is shooting. An old, grey-haired village woman walks behind Bruno, straight and tall like a white flag on a mast, wrapped in serenity and severity. She trudges alone through mud that is getting deeper and thicker. *This is not going to end well*, she says. There are no more wounded in the column. Someone has unloaded them somewhere, at a hospital maybe. The rain comes pouring down. It is November 1917.

The road is blocked. The column crawls along for another three kilometres, then turns into a field all shiny with dampness and the wet. Someone says: *This is a strategic point.* Now the rain pelts. The field becomes a swamp. Bruno coughs. Carlo coughs. *The mud is slippery between my toes*, Ada says. There is no shelter, only the faraway sky. A doctor comes running out with his arms raised high, as if preparing to dive into the sea. *Non ho i medicinali per i feriti! Trovatemi i medicinali!* he shouts. Everyone is silent. The whole column is silent. *When will the Germans come?* asks Bruno. *Wann werden die Deutschen kommen?* No-one answers. Then an old man says: *Das da ist mein Haus. Wenn ich weggehe, werde ich alles verlieren. Aber bleiben kann ich nicht . . .* He gestures with an open hand, as if onstage, as if in some dramatic scene, he waves at a little grey hut over which the dark rainwater comes down so that the hut resembles a convict in a striped suit. The old man sobs.

Night falls. The column still has ten kilometres to Latisana. In Latisana the Baar family board a refugee train for Bologna, which takes them southward. Meanwhile, young men from the newly defunct Monarchy, children who have gone to fight for their own liberty, languish in prisoner-of-war camps all over Europe.

At the camp the Baar family eat cold mutton goulash, which puts them off mutton for the rest of their lives. The goulash is covered in a layer of shiny, whitish fat, a miniature skating rink for the camp fleas and lice, on which Ada traces out with her finger the Italian words she is learning, until the cold, fatty surface cracks and the dark-red liquid from underneath spurts up. Ada dreams of Marisa: *ada goes to the cemetery, she is happy she'll see mama marisa, she tells the flower seller, make me a big bouquet with lots of branches. the flower seller asks, why the branches? i'll leave them on a tree, ada says. mama comes down the hill over gorizia and shouts, wait for me, ada, wait for me!*

Ada is no longer a child. When she gets back to Gorizia she will be eighteen.

The Austrian and German camps scattered around the former Monarchy are also full of refugees and prisoners of war. The Italian boys mostly dream of food, just as all those who have lost their liberty dream of food. Some sleep on straw mattresses, some have sheets. They send home testimonies, little pieces of the puzzle that make up the panorama of history, edge pieces, corner pieces, without which the picture can never be framed. But History has no interest in frames. History wants to remain open. So that it can be filled in and multiply. Emanuele from Sigmundsherberg writes asking for chocolate, warm socks and tobacco, he complains of the frozen bread which cannot be sliced at fifteen degrees below zero. Gerolamo writes that they steal chickens, since all they are given is rice. From a camp in Celle, Antonio requests Maggi bouillon cubes, butter, thread, needles, buttons, a mirror and a comb. Sandro wants ten packs of cigarettes and two packages of Maryland tobacco, ricotta cheese and eggs, a kilo of white flour, three kilos of ravioli and twenty-five lire. In the Ostffyasszonyfa camp, Guido would like basil pesto, while Nicolà asks for black beans, figs and dried pears with a few walnuts. Antonio urgently requires a kilo of butter, tomato juice, twenty tubes of soup concentrate, grated cheese, two kilos of rigatoni, five cans of fruit salad, condensed milk, he wants cookies with hazelnuts, fresh sheep's cheese and a kilo of mostazzola. Aside from the jumpers Ruggero asks for, and the woollen socks, gloves, mufflers, a jacket and a cap (no smaller than a size 59), he craves dried mutton, while Luca from the lunatic asylum in Cogoleto writes out his existential hunger, his physiological and philosophical enlightenment, in broad strokes, asking for money, two pigs and a goat (for the milk), "because I am seriously ill". So food, the compelling huckster, illusion-maker of belonging, of being special, of survival, of *return*, of *redemption*, spreads out a bed in the tomb of nostalgia for our hunger, our folly, as cure and as a way out. We obediently make ourselves comfortable in that endlessly terrifying space of existence, seeking what we already have.

> *Is not your time*
> *as irreversible as that same river*
> *where Heraclitus, mirrored, saw the symbol*
> *of fleeting life? A marble slab awaits you*
> *which you will not read. On it, already written,*
> *the date, the city, and the epitaph.*
> *Other men too are only dreams of time,*
> *not indestructible bronze or burnished gold;*
> *the universe is, like you, a Proteus.*
> *Dark, you will enter the darkness that awaits you,*
> *doomed to the limits of your travelled time.*
> *Know that in some sense you are already dead.*

Borges

The war ends and what is left of the Baar family returns to Gorizia, to the new border rife with invisible malignant cells resembling particles of atomic dust. Along that border, as along all borders, deep into the soil is thrust the steel axis of a Ringelspiel, a merry-go-round, a lively carousel doomed to repeat eternally the invidious drama of family sagas. History – that lying, traitorous mother of life – continues, logorrhoeically, to spin its tiresome story, secretly dreaming up new borderlands one after another. And a border, like every long, deep wound, even if it heals and does not turn into a wellspring of putrid stench, is streaked with proud scar tissue that separates the living from the dead. A border is a "land" of spirits howling as they seek a form to assume.

Ada finds a job in a stationery shop at the intersection of Seminario and Ascoli streets, near to what was once the Jewish ghetto. It is a small shop. From the ceiling hangs the dead Monarchy, so through the little shop spreads the past, burning down just as sticks of oriental incense gradually snuff out, turning into small mounds of light-grey ash. The shop has something of everything: newspapers in Italian, German and Slovenian, red and yellow sweets in thick jars through which the sun shines, capturing the sweets in its everlasting, loving embrace, chains for pocket watches, cheap cologne, tobacco from every place imaginable, an assortment of baubles, chocolates, razors, buttons, threads, pocket mirrors, combs that tuck into the pocket of a military uniform. Florian Tedeschi certainly has reason enough to frequent such a shop.

Gorica is now Gorizia, rather than Görz. Thus, Ada's shop is visited more and more often by the soldier Florian Tedeschi, stationed at the garrison barracks on Via Trieste, at the east end of town, near the border with the Kingdom of Serbs, Croats and Slovenes.

The year is 1920. Politically and economically Italy is twisting and flapping like a flag snapping in a powerful gale. There are scuffles and clashes with police. Half a million workers take part in strikes that last nearly to the end of the year; 320 people are killed in the first six months. The harvest rots in the fields. The wine is bad. Ada has no idea of any of this, she thinks how she will unbraid her hair at precisely the moment when she catches sight of Florian Tedeschi crossing the street on his way to the door over which the little brass bell might announce the beginning of a new life, ding-a-ling. With her finger on the golden-yellow wooden countertop steeped in the fragrance of tobacco, the fragrance of honey and cherries, Ada traces out her future. A smile of close-held happiness and anticipation, rolled up in a ball, like the bell on the door, swings on her face. Though coming to them late, Ada is reading the plays, novels, poems and letters of Gabriele D'Annunzio, grand lover and seducer, a man barely five foot tall, a bald, one-eyed warrior with a little moustache like the tail of a frail swallow, a decadent with rotting teeth, a media manipulator, a pilot and a shyster, a cavalry officer, a champion of her Gorizia, a rumour addict and petty dictator, a Blackshirt. When the family comes home from the camp she happens upon all the books that had belonged to her mother Marisa who disappeared so mysteriously; there they are, untouched, on a shelf above the shelves with the walnuts and the flour for the macaroons. Under the counter in the shop, out of view, Ada leafs quickly through a life that will pass her by. With her free hand, as she reads, she crumbles a slice of *Gugelhupf* purchased at the neighbouring bakery owned by Frau Arughetti, who forgot to leave town. Elusive images flick through Ada's mind; she snatches at them, her breathing jagged, and the windows fog up at the La Gioia stationery shop in the winter evenings. For her – just as for virgins and mothers all over Italy into whose dark labyrinths of repressed lust strode that very same lover whom Paris greeted, ecstatically blind, arms and legs wide open – the borders between poetry and reality were erased with the smudge of a cheap eraser. Ada keeps the Toscanelli cigars, His favourites, in a special spot, under glass. Ah, all the actresses, duchesses, dancers; all the poets, journalists, singers and marquises whom He gets to know and love long after His first forays to local brothels at sixteen (when He pawned His grandfather's watch); ah, Teodolinde and Clemenze, and Giselda Zucconi, and Olga Ossani; Maria Luisa Casati Stampa, amasser of exotic animals and bizarre furniture; oh, Ida Rubinstein,

Isadora Duncan, the singer Olga Levi Brunner, and after her, the pianist Luisa Baccara, then wealthy American painter Romaine Goddard Brooks, who later comes out as a lesbian; then, oh Lord, celebrated Eleonora Duse; Elvira Natalia Fraternali Leoni, Contessa Natalia de Golubeff, who dies in 1941 from alcohol and poverty (for whom Ada, long since married to Tedeschi, cared not at all); Maria Gravina Cruyllas di Ramacca, mother of four sons who bears Gabriele a daughter, Renata; Giuseppina Mancini Giorgi, 1908, committed to a mental hospital; and just then, in 1920, Parisienne Amélie Mazoyer, still a hot item. Morphine addict Alessandra Carlotti di Rudinì, dubbed Nike, is another of them: after her brother and children die she takes her vows and dies a Carmelite in 1931. And Maria Harduin di Gallese was there all along, of course, as D'Annunzio's lawful wedded wife.

Ada reads *Il trionfo della morte*, *La figlia di Iorio*, *Canto novo*, *Il piacere*, *L'innocente*, *Terra vergine*, *Le primavera della mala pianta*, *Il fuoco*, so she has no time to read the newspapers, meanwhile in the little town of Fiume people are strutting around sporting their newly tailored black shirts, and D'Annunzio, "*il deputato della belezza*", recites his poems from a balcony, champagne flows under the blaze of fireworks, and syphilis spreads. In July 1920 rats come pouring out of the Trieste sewers: there are *squadristi* crawling all over the city. They set fire to the building of the Slovenian National Home. Agrarian Fascism is born. Trucks packed with *squadristi* come to villages at night, twenty of them, a hundred. Armed with guns and revolvers, they surround the houses of members of the Farmers' League and left-wing unionists and, systematically, one by one, order the head of each household to step out, and if they have to wait too long, they say: *Don't toy with us, we'll set fire to your home with your wife and children inside,* and then out he comes, and they tie him up, throw him into the truck, take him to a secluded spot and beat him senseless; then they leave him tied to a tree somewhere, unconscious and naked. Fascism sweeps the masses as if they were caught up at a football match. In her lovely light-blue jacket, in yellow stockings and petite yellow shoes, which many years later Florian will remember with longing, Ada often visits her lover at his barracks on Via Trieste on the east end of Gorizia, near the Yugoslav border. When she isn't reading D'Annunzio and when her bare bottom isn't rubbing against Florian's army blanket, Ada is out on a bicycle, for bicycling is a healthy sport because it strengthens the calves. And so it is that a new *joie de vivre* creeps into Ada's soul like a moth into a trunk of woollens. *Those were the happy days in my life of suffering*, Ada would say to Haya in 1943, and maybe in 1944, too.

Haya's father, Florian Tedeschi, comes from a wealthy and fully assimilated Jewish family, not like Haya's mother, Ada, who comes from a poor and altogether unassimilated Jewish family. Among Florian's ancestors there are experts on the Talmud, financiers, chemists, glass-cutters, sculptors, failed students, musicians, seafarers, collectors, anti-fascists and, fascists. Some of them are buried in cemeteries all over Italy, Catholic and Jewish cemeteries, while the bones of others were swept up into dancing clouds, dropping black pellets laden with grey dust, as fine as grimy confectioners' sugar. Some are here in Goriza, though not in Gorizia, but on the other side in Gorica, in a valley that isn't much of a valley, in a valley meant to be full of roses, and Haya Tedeschi doesn't remember any roses in that valley, because she hadn't buried any of her own there, because her mother said to her, it was in a dream but she did say to her, bury me in the Valley of Roses, in Valdirose, because Haya misplaced her mother Ada in death, just as she had lost her grandmother Marisa, whom she never met, what else could she do, she was young and there was a war on, besides, that's a Jewish cemetery with many small upright stones, by now old and aslant, chilled under damp moss like the amputated limbs of a body long since dead. And her dead, Haya's dead on her father's side, have not been buried in such cemeteries, Jewish cemeteries, for a long time, a hundred years or so. Haya Tedeschi knows that in Gorica, in Nova Gorica, a man named Wilhelm Tedeschi who died in 1891 was laid to rest. Born in Mannheim in 1837, he was a sculptor who gave painting lessons in Piran, Trieste and later Gorizia, yes, Gorizia, and before that in Pula, where his bust of Admiral Bourguignon may still be standing. In that family of Haya's, on Florian's side there are musicians and iron-casters, too, thank goodness, who create compositions of some sort for listening and viewing which are presumably meant to express beauty, though Haya doesn't understand of what kind. All trace, apparently, has been lost of those composers and the casters, too. So, while she waits in the old building at Via Aprica 47, while she shuffles through the cards of all those lives, lives that are sliding through her fingers as if she were playing solitaire, Haya shakes her head every so often and says, *We are a family with no traces.*

In 1922 Claudio Magris returns his protagonist Enrico Mreule, a professor of classical philology, from Patagonia to Gorizia. The K.u.K. Staatsgymnasium has been renamed the Liceo Vittorio Emanuele III. Professor Schubert-Soldern (whom Ada Baar also remembers) has left by then. He is in Austria with no nationality of any kind and is undecided about what to choose, after having lost two monarchies, now that Gorizia has become Italian and his native Prague is part of Czechoslovakia. Just possibly he is not discontent with life in the draughty vacuum created by the cyclones and anticyclones of history. Enrico arrives, others depart.

On 30 October, Fascism officially takes its seat on the throne.

At the Vittorio Emanuele III Gymnasium, Italian is taught by Nerina Slataper with whom Ada Baar begins going out for sweets to the pastry shop on Via Municipio every Wednesday evening after she shuts the stationery shop. That is when Nerina tells Ada of her brother Scipio, who died *near here, at Podgora, on 3 December, 1915, it seems so long ago, but it's as if it were yesterday,* Nerina says, *when an enemy Croat shot him with a fragmentation bullet from a distance of only a few metres, when the bullet plunged into his throat, blew him to pieces and killed him instantaneously*; then she gives Ada Scipio's slender volume *Il mio Carso*, published a few years earlier, which Ada reads immediately and the next Wednesday tells Nerina that *war has many truths, or perhaps no truths at all.* Nerina tells her how she and her friends Bianca Stuparich, Maria Schiller and Lucilla Luzzatto spent a full three years, *and the war was raging,* she says, *my brothers were at the front, Guido on one hill, Scipio on another,* she says, *they called us the "floral foursome"*, she says, recalling how in their Trieste house at Via Fabio Severo 45 (*I'll take you there one day to show you*, she says), how they spent three years sewing a tricolour, and how later, when the war was over, when the victory of the 39th Battalion and the 11th Regiment was being celebrated on 1 November, 1918, they had gone into the street and waved their flag and how the flag had billowed and how they had given it to the Bersaglieri.

Enrico Mreule says – or is it Claudio Magris?, Haya is no longer sure, time is melting in her mind like chocolate – *someone* says that Monsignore Fogar, their religious teacher and now the Bishop of Trieste, is doing as much as he can to protect Slavs from Fascist oppression and violence, but that the Slavs retreat behind an impenetrable wall, and he says that a Ceccutti, the only other lay teacher among the cassocks, is furious at the *squadristi*, who also gave his cousin the castor-oil treatment, and says that they who are furnishing the *squadristi* with money without dirtying their own hands, the big estate owners or top civil servants, are far worse than the *squadristi* themselves.

Gorizia is in a new phase of its coming of age. Who can say how many phases there have been since its beginnings? It is baulking and petulant, caught up in rebellion against its parents, who leave it, return, then leave it again. Different lives are taking tiny ballet steps (*petits pas*) in Gorizia. Some trip and stumble, cave in. For instance, the life of Enrico Mreule who walks around barefoot, like a sort of Christ figure, in order to buy off his destiny, or with an open umbrella, to shield himself from both his destiny and Gorizia, from its caprice with light and dark. Other lives drip. They make notches and grooves, the edges of which they erode and undermine. They make scars which gape into wounds and then heal over again. Yet other lives lie down, arms and legs spread wide, and let themselves be washed by the rains from the nearby mountains, they go back into the Soča.

Florian Tedeschi tells Ada Baar his brief history. He arranges and sets out his brief history, making space for the future, which will become Haya's past, which will be lost, which now, eighty-three years later, she searches for, arranges, orders, catalogues, this here, that there, something into the rubbish, something on to the desk by the window, to shine like a tiny light. Florian tells his story, and Haya is already wiggling in Ada's belly. Florian speaks about how his father Paolo Tedeschi marries Emilia Finzi, daughter to Emma Teglio and Constantin Finzi, all of them from the most prestigious Italian Jewish families. Some are annihilated and others are not. Some convert, others do not. Later, books are written about them and films are made, and Haya watches the films after all the horrors have supposedly passed. She watches, and then again she says, *There was a war on, what else could I do?* The Teglio family have an entire fishing empire today stretching across several continents, which were conquered, thank goodness, without war, circumventing war, despite war, thanks (?) to war. Florian has had word from time to time of Elsa Finzi,* his aunt, though he has never met her. She is always winging around the world in the company of remarkable women, particularly an Englishwoman named Sylvia Pankhurst and a German woman named Rosa Luxemburg, who also travels from one country to the next, and Elsa doesn't ask after him to see how things are going in the wasteland of Gorizia where he hasn't even adequate pocket money, let alone the wherewithal to start a family. Furthermore, Elsa Finzi is always up in arms about one thing or another, fighting for some kind of so-called equality for everyone, and it bothers him that she is alive while her sister, his mother Emilia, is not.

---

* *Elsa Finzi*, born in Genoa on 14 May, 1891. Arrested in the spring of 1942 with an anti-fascist group, including *Ferruccio Parri*. Accused of founding an anti-fascist association and of fomenting anti-fascist propaganda. After the trial, released on 24 November, 1942. *Ferruccio Parri*, Italian politician born in Pinerolo in 1890. Under fascism, persecuted and arrested. From 1926–33 held in internal exile. With Carlo Rosselli starts an organization which helps victims of fascism flee the country. From 1943 to 1945 a leader of the Italian partisan movement; a founder of the *Giustizia e libertà* partisan brigades. President of the coalition government in 1945, and until 1948 a deputy, then a senator. President of the League of Veterans of the Italian Resistance Movement. Dies in 1981 in Rome.

Ada listens and says, *That is a stupid sort of equality. Let's forget about Elsa Finzi*. And this Aunt Elsa of his, Florian Tedeschi says, is a show-off, as if her family coat of arms were special, but it isn't, it is a perfectly ordinary coat of arms, *a coat of arms like any other*, he says, *un albero di pepe fra due leoni*, and he can't remember whether the family of his father, Paolo Tedeschi, have a coat of arms, which wouldn't be bad if they did, and Ada asks, *Why weren't you circumcised?* And what is Elsa after, anyway? says Florian. She has a baby, but she won't marry, and besides, children irritate her, and Ada says, *Our child will be called Haya. If it is a boy his name will be Orestes,* and Florian says, *Orestes is a dangerous name.*

Haya remembers Elsa Finzi. She no longer recalls her funeral, which as far as she is concerned never happened, because Elsa only allowed the select to come, to attend the funeral, so around the grave stood a little cluster of senile former revolutionaries in rumpled trench coats, bedraggled partisans, that is what the papers wrote, so Haya did not go, and even if Elsa had permitted her to be there Haya wouldn't have gone; instead she would have sat as she is sitting now, locked in her locked-up world, waiting. Haya remembers Elsa's flat at Via Santa Maria alla Porta 11 in Milan. She remembers (from Nora's letters) that Elsa's husband throughout all of 1944 plies Ada with Pierrot absinthe (once she had wearied of the revolution Elsa did marry, after all, but someone else), and how in that year, 1944, her family in Milanino drank liqueurs instead of water, so they were cheery but ate very little, mostly carrots and cabbage, their bellies often ached and the bombs fell.

In the inside pocket of his uniform, one might say close to his heart, Florian keeps a sepia photograph, by now already creased, covered in a web of white lines through which stares a tight-lipped, black-haired woman. Emilia Finzi (Tedeschi by marriage) awaits her death in style. Barely thirty, she dies on 13 November, 1910, at St Moritz, the "magic mountain", at the Schatzalp sanatorium for wealthy patients afflicted by tuberculosis. She is buried at the Jewish cemetery in Milan. In a tin box resembling a miniature coffin, Florian keeps several more photographs and this postcard of the Schatzalp sanatorium, which Haya pats and says, *What a nice place for dying*.

O, i giorni felici, whispers Florian into the scant evidence left of what was once a crowded landscape of devastated memory. Yes, happy days. Back in 1904, in their De Dion-Bouton, Paolo and Emilia go for afternoon spins along village roads that run between two rows of sycamores, when the sun is mild and there is a gentle  breeze. Meanwhile, the servants make hot cocoa, bake amaretti, petits fours, from time to time the more dramatic *ganache* and obligatory *Linzertorte*, that delicate marvel, the work of Jindrak, an Austrian confectioner. In the evening, wearing a gown of emerald-green shantung with a high collar of black lace, Emilia reads *I promessi sposi* aloud yet again, first published, what a coincidence, in Gorizia, a distant and unknown place as far as she is concerned, in another empire. The Monarchy is mighty. Within it, from Voralberg in the west to the easternmost village of Bukovina (1,274 kilometres), from the smallest Czech town in the north to the Dalmatian fishing villages in the south (1,000 kilometres), order, serenity and a single currency reign. All across this great and happy land the same products and the same brands are distributed, the same food items of equal quality, with only the names adapted discreetly to the language of each of the peoples: in Hungary the Julius Meinl chain of shops is called Meinl Gyula, while Jules Verne becomes Verne Gyula; *Knödel* become *knedliky* in Czech; the *Wiener Schnitzel* is called *bečka* in Croatian and in Italian, *cotoletta Milanese*. The distant centres of the Monarchy, its balls, waltzes and its coaches, schnapps and *Sachertorte*, its painters and its imperial family, all this becomes intimate and dear in the provinces as soon as it is ever so slightly Italianized, Croaticized, Magyarized, Bohemianized; *die grosse glückliche Familie*, oh, happy days.

As a naval engineer, widower Paolo Tedeschi ventures to Libya, where he finishes installing some sort of electric generator, meanwhile sending his son Florian off to the Beretta boarding school on the western shore of Lake Garda, in the little town of Salò, which would become the seat of a small puppet Fascist state some twenty years later called Repubblica Sociale Italiana, otherwise known as Repubblica di Salò. On a visit to his boy, Paolo makes the acquaintance of Rosa Brana, a Catholic school teacher, and for the sake of peace in bed he relinquishes his Judaic faith in which he had not, to be fair, placed much stock to begin with. Meanwhile, Paolo goes bankrupt, so he and Rosa live off her modest income and have more children, three new Catholic children bearing the Jewish surname Tedeschi, who would, when the moment came (with the exception of Ugo, the flautist), first salute *alla Romana*, then shout *Sieg Heil*, and live until their deaths in the romantic little town of Salò on the shore of Lake Garda. Florian continues his schooling at the Collegio San Alessandro in Bergamo and grows a moustache. He enrols in the military academy in Rome in 1919, and off he goes in 1920 to do his military service, first in Mestre, then in Gorizia, where he meets the love of his life, Ada Baar. When Ada's bulging belly can no longer be concealed, Florian asks his father Paolo to bless the marriage, but Paolo declines. Ada is poor, she has no pedigree. Ada is a Jewish woman and screws extra-institutionally. Florian relinquishes his right to his mother's inheritance, which includes villas and factories, paintings and books, silver cutlery and money, hardly a negligible legacy, and marries Ada Baar the day before Haya is born, on 8 February, 1923. A new life begins.

Florian works at all kinds of jobs. He sells typewriters in Gorizia and then in the evenings on a 1915 model bicycle – precursor to today's mountain bike and designed by acclaimed Edoardo Bianchi for the Alpini and the Bersaglieri – he delivers his daily takings to the factory outside town, then he picks up copies of *Gazzeta dello Sport* and *Lo Sport Fascista*, and stops in at the Taverna I Due Leoni or, less frequently, at the Doppolavoro. He sips a glass of home-made red wine to relax. He listens to the news broadcasts people listen to in Gorizia at the time in the café bars and taverns, and he is indifferent to what he hears. Sundays, when he listens to a broadcast of a football game, Florian is far from indifferent, he is captivated. The tavern is lively and stifling. The customers wrangle, then quarrel and shout. Reporter Niccolò Carosio invents a new football language, much like the new culinary language Marinetti has already ushered in. Florian is a Juventus fan, though perhaps he shouldn't be. He begins to have second thoughts about football and "his" club after the World Cup in Italy in 1934, when Mussolini orders presidents of football clubs to be members of his political party. Leandro Arpinati holds the Italian football federation, the FIGC, in a stranglehold for years. In 1926, Il Duce pulls off the famous "*carta di Viareggio*" move, which means every team can take on only one foreign player per season; in 1927 every foreign player who is not a "son of Italy" (the homeland) is sent packing. After that there are almost no Hungarian players left on the Italian team, which Florian regrets, because they are his favourites. In 2006 Haya happens to be watching television when she sees Paolo di Canio take the defeat of his Lazio like a hero, greeting the Livorno players with the "Roman salute"; his fans wave their swastikas, the Livorno fans wave their red flags. *This never ends*, Haya says.

Haya is not fond of football.

Obsessed with radio equipment and radiophony in general, Florian gets a job in 1925 at a shop called Marconi. Florian listens to the speeches by Guglielmo Marconi, whom Mussolini, the best man at his wedding, names President of the Royal Academy of Italy. When Marconi weds his second wife Maria Cristina Bezzi-Scali in June 1927, Florian listens to the broadcast. While they are playing Wagner's wedding march, Il Duce's dog Pitini can be heard barking in the background. A year earlier, Florian also hears over the radio that Mussolini is introducing a tax on bachelors. *Lucky I have Ada*, he says.

Ada goes out into the nearby woods and picks mushrooms and sings the opera arias that come back to her. She goes to her stationery shop. Under the counter she reads various magazines, mostly ones with photographs. In *La Rivista Illustrata del Popolo d'Italia* an article about Margherita Sarfatti at the Venice Biennale XV catches her eye. Margherita Sarfatti praises a painting by Oskar Kokoschka. Several years later, two world leaders will declare that same painting to be degenerate. Ada regularly reads the monthly *Rivista delle Famiglie*, because it prints many articles dedicated to woman and her family, and family is everything to Ada: *Haya and Florian – my greatest riches*, she says. Haya has kept an issue from 1936, and she leafs through it with her dry fingers as she sits by the window and rocks. Then she puts it down on the little desk.

Ada regularly brings *Il Giornale della Radio Leonardo Bottinelli* home from the stationery shop, because this newspaper publishes the Italian radio schedule and listings for another ten European countries. Aside from that, the paper registers cultural events of note, and since nothing of note ever happens on Gorizia's cultural scene, Ada at least *reads* of the notable events. Once the race laws are introduced, Jewish names no longer appear in the listings, particularly those of musicians and singers. This, however, happens later, after the Tedeschi family move south and when they are no longer so small. The Tedeschis are an entirely respectable and appealing family with four children, when Ada tells Florian, *Perhaps we should be baptized*, and when Florian tells Ada, *I went to the* fascio *and signed up*. There, in the south, they mainly read *Il Mattino Illustrato*, because it is published in Naples. It comes out on Sundays and has engaging fashion articles, cartoons (Haya remembers them) and beautiful pictures of both ordinary and high life. There are political articles, too, but the Tedeschi family skip over them.

In the late 1920s Trieste is already ailing. Its breath rattles, as if on its deathbed. It is crippled. German schools are closed, street names are changed or Italianized. Trieste is becoming a little world inside a little world. Its centripetal forces are dwindling, it is sucked in by forces separating it from its very self, its organs are near collapse, it is dispersing into microparticles of its history that do not know where to settle or what to latch on to. At the beginning of the twentieth century people abandon it as it lies motionless abed with sores: Conrad, who writes about its dockers, Joyce and Trakl and Rilke and Freud and Mahler and Mann and Slataper; Thomas Mann tinkers with the Buddenbrooks at Hôtel de Ville, Egon Schiele paints a red fisherman's scuttle moored in the harbour, Rainer Maria Rilke composes his *Duineser Elegien*. Back then, and still today, with an occasional twitch, as if nodding to its late great friends and summoning them, *come*, as if pleading with the few friends it has left, *stay*, Trieste is becoming an exit point, a city opening its gates so people can flee, leaving the elderly and small house dogs to count out their days in peace and quiet.

Then, during and after the Great War, some leave Trieste to be killed, some leave to kill themselves, some leave in search of a better life. Others arrive because they have nothing better in mind. Because that is how it is with cities, they flow on eternally, this way or that, so books say.

Francesco Illy, an accountant of Hungarian extraction and a soldier for Austro-Hungary, spent the first part of his war service along the Soča, then in and around Trieste. The war ended, Illy looked around and said, *This is a wonderful city. I will learn Italian,* so he went about selling first cocoa, then coffee. *People just sit there, downing the black stuff,* he said, *as if they were Turks.* Francesco invented an espresso machine so he could achieve it all: to serve all those leisurely customers. *We'll call the little machine the "illetta",* he said, after which the empire of fragrances and tastes opened its doors to him. Today one of his descendants, Riccardo, otherwise known as Sonnenschein, waves his red flag from time to time at raving right-wing Trieste, *olè!* Time for a revolution.

Il Caffè San Marco on Via Battisti serves its first guests in January 1914. During the war it is completely demolished and only in 1920 do the coffee drinkers come back. Saba stops in, so does Giotti, and Svevo the merchant, also known as Ettore Schmitz, comes by. Joyce no longer sits at the Caffè Pasticceria Pirona, but the cakes and wine are still Viennese, and the coffee is Illy. After having made the rounds of several such spots, which seem to be peaceful innocent gathering places to Florian, the proprietor of Caffè degli Specchi at the Piazza Unità tells him, *Come tomorrow at seven.* The Tedeschi family are living in a flat at Via Daniele, a short and dark street, and the church of Santa Maria Maggiore is close by, which is handy for family attendance at Mass.

Haya is six years old and recalls little of Trieste from this time. She remembers her father Florian as he inches, legs rigid, between the tables, holding his tray high above his head, as if collecting the rain. She remembers how she waits for Florian to finish his shift at Caffè degli Specchi in Piazza Unità on Sundays, so they can go for ice cream at an ice-cream stand, because the ice cream there is cheaper. She remembers a family, dressed in finery, dignified somehow, and she remembers how she wants to live in a family like that. Haya observes the woman in her dark striped suit with a cloche hat perched on her head, taking a little mirror from her purse that catches the rays of the sun, and how the lady smiles at her sons in a way that Ada has never smiled at her. Haya watches the boys in their little blue suits and wants to ask them *What language are you speaking?* She wants to say to them, *I am Haya and I can sing to you in Slovenian if you like:*

The gentleman doesn't smile at his sons, because he is reading the paper. He has white hands. He has a moustache and an elegant grey suit with a sheen. The boys drink hot chocolate and Haya suddenly wants some, too. She'd like to sip hot chocolate at the

Caffè degli Specchi in Piazza Unità, and swing her feet and admire the brand-new patent leather shoes she doesn't have. Haya remembers her surprise and her curiosity, *Who are they?* Then, just as when a mirror slips from the fingers, the image shatters. A man from a neighbouring table rises to his feet, the chair tips over, he takes two marching steps, stands behind the man who is reading the newspaper and shouts, he shouts terribly loudly, and he is scowling and his eyebrows are tangling into writhing leeches, and his mouth opens into a small tomb that flashes and all the while he is holding a large cup of coffee in the air as if he were at the Olympics preparing to heave a hammer that looks like a bomb but isn't, it is a white porcelain coffee cup from the Caffè degli Specchi on Piazza Unità full to the brim with aromatic Illy coffee, then he swings and the cup smacks the gentleman below the shoulder and the black liquid starts to steam and soak into the grey suit – to get warm? to hide? – leaving a large, dark, wet splotch.

Schiavo! howls the person who flung the cup. *Schiavo, qui si parla solo italiano!* The boys jump to their feet, pull out handkerchiefs, dip them in the water from their father's glass and mop his back. The coffee flees, sheds its aroma, spreads around the man's belt, trickles down his right trouser leg and wriggles to the ground like a small dead snake. On the light grey suit an image is left resembling a squished cow pat.

One damp Trieste evening, as Florian Tedeschi strolls along the deserted sluices, staring with horror at the empty belly of the port, nearly touching the sundering of the city which joins with his own sense of fragmentation, which, this rift of his, this schism, sinks perilously into rigidity like the calcified spine of an elderly stroller, he catches himself repeating, to the beat of his footsteps: *vorrei dirvi, vorrei dirvi,*

> *one, two,*
> vorrei dirvi,
> *I am a businessman,*
> *not a waiter,*

I am a soldier,
in every businessman,
in every soldier
hides an ache from which the soul cracks like frozen glass.

Florian Tedeschi turns into Via San Nicolò and stops at Number 30, where the sign *Libreria Antiquaria Umberto Saba* still stands today, but Umberto Saba is no longer in Trieste and there is a ribbed iron curtain drawn over the display window of the bookshop.

Tell me about a life and everything
that happens in it
in murky madness
of vainly discordant voices

says Florian Tedeschi staring at the tips of his waiter's shoes.

Words exhaust themselves

he says

I remember everything, but understand nothing.
Time has shrunk like a jumper rinsed in hot water.
It is getting tight.

The next day, on 15 November, 1932, Florian Tedeschi goes to a branch office of the Banca di Napoli and to a friend from his army days, Luciano Grauer, says: *Get me out of here.*

In the 1930s there are about five thousand Jews living in Trieste who quickly leave the city, particularly after 1938. One of the four centres in Italy for the study of the Jewish Question is in Trieste, hard at work "profiling" the Italian nation, so Jews start scattering in every direction. Those who stay are captured efficiently by the Nazis and transported to camps all over Europe. Of the more than seven hundred Trieste Jews who are herded on to the freight cars of the

trains that pull regularly into Trieste train station, fewer than twenty
return after the war. The Tedeschis get out in time without even
realizing it.

In late November, the Tedeschi family sail on the ship *Ganga,* or it
may have been the *Marco Polo,* arranged through an association
known as the Società Adriatica, from which a sticker remains, from
this Adriatic association, the Adriatic ocean liner, whatever, and the
sticker is remarkably preserved, torn from an item of family luggage,
no doubt, which was later lost
without trace, travelling on its
own to a world Haya never knew.
The Tedeschis arrive in Naples.
For Haya, Naples is an image of
blurred colours that mean peace
of mind. There are no outlines,
here and there a spark.

Paula and Orestes are born. Florian works at the Banca di Napoli.
Ada follows Enrico Caruso as he sings *"O, sole mio",* and she cooks
and washes and cooks and washes, and feeds fish and pasta to her
children. After dinner Haya listens to Leoncavallo with her father
Florian, *Pagliacci* is always in fashion, now especially when Gigli is
singing, one of Mussolini's favourites. Every 12 December the family
go out to the square where the Giornata della Madre e del Fanciullo
is celebrated, when the names are announced of the twenty-three
most reproductively active mothers in Italy, each with at least fourteen
sons, and the mothers are received at a ceremony and given a
modest award by Mussolini and the Pope. One year their neighbour
Amalia wins with her eighteen sons, but little red-haired Rita is not
part of the competition, as if she were not even there. Life is beautiful.
The house is roomy. There are oranges in the garden. The children
are given a donkey called Kroo. There are many joyful photographs.
Their mother Ada is wearing a white hat, tipped to the right in all
the pictures. They ride bicycles. Papa Florian goes to work in a suit.
One evening Ada cries as she takes off her wedding ring. Florian
removes his wedding ring, too, but doesn't cry. *We've been ordered to,*

he says. Haya wraps in a yellow flannel cloth the silver coat of arms of Gorizia that had hung in her grandfather Bruno Baar's winery, so Ada says, and which they had brought with them on the long trek to the camp where it had served them, flipped over, as a bread board. *I will not give them Marisa's earrings*, Ada says. Florian shouts, *You must*. With a red-hot needle Ada pierces Haya's ears, though her hands are trembling. *This is all I have of Mother's. There isn't even a grave*, she says, and so it is that the earrings with their wreath of tiny, poorly burnished, grimy diamonds do not go to Mussolini. Haya has been wearing them for seventy-two years. *There, as if they've shrunk*, she says and touches her ear lobes. Then she says *Enough for today* and goes to bed.

She dreams – *the corpse opens like a book. it flips open by itself, like a magic box, and in it are tiny diamonds, a multitude of tiny diamonds like flakes of dead skin – light. then, like a river, they flow. in the corpse which refuses to die, in that now genderless dead person, everything is still except the light which flees. the lack of smell. an embalmed erasure. the skin on the face of the corpse is taut, the eye sockets dry and empty. the skull shows through the dried parchment envelope, in the open mouth the teeth are growing, they get whiter and longer. haya looks into the belly and sees her face in the thousands of miniature surfaces of colourless precious stones, distorted and multiplied*

That year, 1935, a quarter of a million Italians donate their gold and silver for a better future, for the happy days to come. In Rome 250,000 wedding rings are collected; 180,000 in Milan. Benedetto Croce gives up his senator's medal; the Cardinal of Bologna, Nassali Rocca, donates his bishop's chain; and Pirandello, his Nobel Prize medal. A total of 33,622 kilograms of gold is amassed. That same year Mussolini gives three million gold francs to Albania with a promise of additional economic support to follow.

That year, 1935, the slogan "Buy Italian!" is pushed; an autarky is born; imported goods and foreign businesses disappear. Italy cleanses its digestive tract, feeds on purgatives, gloats with self-satisfaction, blossoms in its little corral.

Two years later the demographic campaign reaches its peak.

Mussolini writes a cheque for 700 lire, a good month's wages at the time, to every young man who decides to marry. The administration creates new jobs and welcomes in its embrace child-bearing Italians, pint-sized studs. Fecund mothers, those with at least seven sons, receive a cheque for 5,000 lire and a life-insurance policy. This is a time of wholesale fornication.

MINCULPOP is born, the Ministry of Popular Culture, and with it new dictionaries, orthographies, patriotism; the use of foreign phrases is banned, and they are replaced by Italian surrogates. Maxim Gorky is dubbed Massimo Amaro, but he is swiftly removed from the libraries and bookshops; Louis Armstrong becomes Luigi Fortebraccio, and Benny Goodman is Beniamino Buonuomo; shortly thereafter MINCULPOP bans all jazz performance and broadcasts.

Life in the Tedeschi family goes on. For Haya it is altogether ordinary, completely forgettable, as ordinary life is, until the day when, at the beginning of the school year in September 1938, her teachers Nella Negri, Amato di Veroli, Samuel Tagliacozzo, Massimo Pavoncello and Viola Sass do not show up to teach Geography, Mathematics, History, Italian and Physical Education. Until the day when Florian, after dinner, whispering in a conspiratorial hush, as if about to say something obscene, declares, *We are Jews,* and she asks, *What does that mean?*

So many shocks, so many tragedies, for centuries, with this meaningless fact that people hide even from themselves, or, conversely, of which they boast, as if it determines who they are and what they are, as if faith and blood are in and of themselves a blessing or a curse. She, Haya, has always felt nothing along those lines, or maybe just a little about being someone's daughter or sister, someone's mistress, someone's friend, which does not imply unconditional devotion to those closest to her. She has always been somehow weightless, free of the heavy burden of mother tongues, national histories, native soils, homelands, fatherlands, myths, that many of the people around her tote on their backs like a sack of red-hot stones. Like little Sisyphuses they lug this wretched and perilous load through life, these clusters of tuberculosis and syphilis germs, these elusive, invisible, and oh so infectious containers of putrescence, they even leap into the containers voluntarily, choke on the sewage sludge in their own fermented excrement, imagining, perhaps, that they are duty-bound to do so, thereby expressing their gratitude that they are still here, as if they have been spared. Haya thinks back to a dwarf tree by the road, a diminutive tree with a round crown of violet-hued blossoms, much like a bright child's cap as it stands there alone and smiles. *That little tree is like a kiss*, she whispers. Borders and identities, our executors. Married couples who sow wars, vast upheaval and death.

Instead of her lost faith, Haya, like Kosovel, believes in darkness.

If you had at least been killed for reasons of honour; if you had fought for love or to forage food for your little ones. But no. First they hoodwinked you, then they slew you in war. What do you want me to do with this France which you, like I, it seems, helped survive? What do we do with it, we who lost all our friends? Ah! If it had been to defend the rivers, the hills, the mountains, the sky, the winds, the rain, I would have said: "Gladly, I concur, this is our job. Let's fight! All our life's joy is in the fact that we live here." But we defended a false name for it all. When I see a river, I say "river"; when I see a tree, I say "tree"; I never say "France". There is no such thing, Jean Giono says, although he has been dead for thirty years.

A few months before the school principal fires him, in 1938, Amato di Veroli, Haya's favourite school teacher, brings to class his friend, the mathematician Renato Caccioppoli.* It is May. Naples smells of "Santa Lucia", freshly washed bed linen and lemons. Haya is fifteen. Professor Caccioppoli has a handsome face. Professor Caccioppoli's fingers are stained with tobacco and he is thirty-five. He hops around as he talks. He grins. *If you are afraid of something, measure what you are afraid of and you'll see it is but a trifle*, Professor Caccioppoli says. *You will see, your fear is nearly nothing, almost too small to measure.*

This is when Hitler starts out on his journey; the newspapers are

---

* Born in Naples on 20 January, 1904; dies in Naples on 8 May, 1959.

full of Hitler. They speak of Hitler in history classes, in maths they talk of Hitler, in gym class they talk of Hitler. Hitler arrives in Rome, then comes to Naples; excitement runs high. Four trains follow Hitler's train carrying five hundred foreign diplomats, generals, agents, party leaders and journalists, all in uniform, one uniform or another, an entire little army. Hitler is in a foul mood. He often scowls. He suffers from stomach pain, mostly gas, so he is forever gulping Mutaflor, prescribed by his faithful companion Dr Morell, but he takes scant joy in his encounter with "the little man", King Vittorio Emmanuele. And so, as he is depressed, on his trip to Rome Hitler pens a will. He leaves the Party his personal effects, Berghof, his furniture and paintings, and to Eva Braun, his sisters, his other relatives, secretaries and servants, he leaves tidy sums from the sales of *Mein Kampf*.

At the border crossing by the little town of Brenner, the inhabitants greet Hitler's five trains with enthusiasm; they wave banners, fling flowers on to the train carriages and smile, though it is difficult to say why (they smile). There are Italian soldiers here too, many Italian soldiers, and Fascist troops. A specially rehearsed orchestra plays both anthems, and the Duke of Pistoia, in the name of the king, holds a brief speech in which he tells the Germans how glad the Italians are to see them, and how very welcome they are in their beautiful country. The houses along the railway line are decked with banners sporting slogans that tout German-Italian friendship. The landscape is quaint, the many colours blinding.

Hitler does not enjoy himself in Rome. He is driven to the royal palace in a coach instead of a car, to a dinner with the queen, who sits next to him and to whom he says not one word; and, furthermore, he is irritated by the huge crucifix she wears around her neck, so he stares at her bosom. The king spreads all sorts of stories about Hitler's odd habits, and reveals that during his first night there Hitler asks for a woman to be sent to his room, so that she can tuck him into bed as if he were a child.

A great military and naval review is prepared in Naples – that should brighten Hitler's spirits. It is 5 May, 1938. The bay is full of submarines and torpedo boats. School has been cancelled. The pupils are ordered to join in the welcoming throng, to wave and shout. Haya says, *I am not going.* Ada and Florian say, *That is imprudent. All of us will go.*

Naples is tricked out gaily. There are flowers everywhere in classical style and colourful banners flap in the wind as if readying for Carnival. The façade of San Francesca da Paola at Piazza del Plebiscito is disfigured by dozens of drapes of red and black bunting; as they ripple in the spring breeze, the church beneath them looks maniacal, keening at one moment in deep grief, and at the next, laughing hysterically.

The Italian navy is doing its level best to wow the Führer, performing mock naval battles. The audience is enthralled: gasps of delight and wonder rise to the skies, *aaahhs* and *ooohhs* float in the air like little puffs of breeze. The submarines, like immense black cormorants, dive and surface, seeking imaginary prey; children shriek and cavort; older men and women sit on deckchairs brought from home, as if out to enjoy the sun. After every exercise hats fly into the air, men's and women's hats. Thrill reigns, a sense of community, a vast delight at belonging. To one country, one people, to two leaders. The city has donned its uniform. Secret agents, Fascist spies, the police, military guards, come pouring out of everywhere. The Neapolitan songs slip down under the cobblestones and quiver, crouching, silent, trampled by the newly born *passo romano*.

In the evening Hitler is taken to a performance of *Aida*, to relax. The next day they bring him back to Rome where on 7 May, at a banquet at the Palazzo Venezia, he grants South Tyrol to Italy in a generous gesture. In return, Hitler receives the Discobolus of Myron. Everyone is pleased. The visit is a success.

Late in the school year the students ask their teacher Amato di Veroli, *When will you bring Caccioppoli back?* Professor di Veroli says, *That won't be possible. They've locked him up in a madhouse.*

Many years later, in the 1990s, Haya sees the movie *Morte di un matematico napoletano* with the excellent Carlo Cecchi, and from that, from the film, she learns part of the story of Renato Caccioppoli.

The rest she uncovers on her own. But by then the war is long over. What happened is being forgotten.

All the same, unpaid bills keep arriving. The story of the famous mathematician comes too late for Haya. Only now, as she takes out a picture of that charming and impulsive genius, does she understand what he had said about fear. And something else he said long ago in 1938 at a mathematics class at the state Neapolitan Gymnasium: *I do not know certainty, at best I discover possibilities.*

Just before the Neapolitan parade, Renato Caccioppoli is embroiled in all sorts of antics around town, and there is talk of them which Haya remembers. Having returned to Naples in 1934 from Padua, where he had been head of the Department of Algebraic Analysis since 1931, Caccioppoli teaches group theory and mathematical analysis, works on linear and non-linear differential equations, elliptical equations, and so on and so forth, plays the violin and the piano both in private and in public, speaks of literature and painting, at times sports a beard, dresses in tatters and travels with empty pockets by train from one city to the next in third-class cars, is arrested for loitering and then released, then he goes back to his mathematics, his students adore him, he adores his students, after class they drink together and think.

At the time he looks like this:

Fascism attaches itself to life in the city like the tentacles of an octopus squirting jets of black ink. The police work with dedication; the prisons are crowded; (some) people flee. Caccioppoli measures his fear with mathematical precision and realizes he cannot find it. He protests against the dull, mind-numbing, caricature-like rhetoric of the regime, always the same, the same for centuries, he rebels against the deceptive toys made of nothing but empty sheen and simple melodies for the hungry and ignorant masses, but these are things Haya cannot see (she is only eight in 1931), her father Florian does not see, nor does her mother Ada. They believe that now that they are Catholics they are absolutely safe. They believe in a better tomorrow wrapping their lives in thick black fabric and they become huge silk caterpillars, trapped bugs with squashed lungs, convinced they are already butterflies. They believe in universal obedience. If they are ever bold enough to rebel, they deserve serious punishment, as serious as God's. Caccioppoli shouts, *Italy is a wretched cur on a leash!* Then he goes down Via Chiaia, just when it is teeming with pedestrians, he passes under the old bridge raised in the early seventeenth century, as if he were passing through a small *arc de triomphe* and behind him on a rope he drags a fattened capon. When he is not pulling off stunts, Caccioppoli meets with his friend, the Communist Trotskyite Mario Palermo and at secret meetings held in the taverns of Naples, in private flats or the warehouses of denounced bookshops, he debates, and whenever he gets his hands on a piano or a violin, he plays. In 1937 he meets André Gide, who says of him, *More than a man, he was a soul.*

Just before the parade, two days after Haya's entire school class, entranced by Renato Caccioppoli, decide to dedicate their life to mathematics (as Haya does later), Renato Caccioppoli and Sara Mancuso walk on to the terrace of a small restaurant in the centre of town on 4 May, 1938. The night is luminous, the orchestra plays first waltzes, then marches, then a few Neapolitan songs – for appearance's sake. People are eating pasta, mostly *frutti di mare*, pizzas, *melanzane parmigiana*, little candles flicker on red and white checked tablecloths. It is Wednesday, an ordinary evening. Caccioppoli gulps down the house red wine, rises, approaches the orchestra, and says, *Play the Marseillaise. It goes like this,* he says and whistles a few bars. The orchestra strikes up. The forks held by the plainclothesmen and assorted guests stop halfway to their open mouths. *You heard,* Caccioppoli says, *the hymn to liberty; to liberty that is being suppressed in this country; to liberty which Benito Mussolini does not acknowledge, who with his German ally* . . . Sara and Renato are arrested immediately. The Special Court rubs its hands in gleeful anticipation. But the Caccioppoli family are well placed. Renato Caccioppoli's aunt Maria Bakunin is a chemistry professor at the University of Naples; Mikhail Aleksandrovich Bakunin is his grandfather. The family obtain "medical evidence" showing that Renato Caccioppoli is deranged. They place him first in a prison clinic for the mentally ill run by psychiatrist and university professor Cesare Colucci, then he is put in a private hospital established by Colucci's late friend, also a psychiatrist, Leonardo Bianchi. The Bakunin family have plenty of experience with handling the threatened and those who threaten; their history teems with biographies of the "disobedient" who must be spirited away; Russian history and other histories; this is a story that flows on like a muddy river. Sara Mancuso, whom Caccioppoli later marries, is released. The world of the downtrodden and abandoned literally becomes Caccioppoli's world. Renato has his room and a piano on which he plays the Marseillaise whenever he feels the urge, when he is not working with numbers or coming up with formulae which later (with his blessing) others publish under their own names, as Hermann Weyl does in 1940. The patients adore Caccioppoli. They sing in his chorus, which they dub the "nutcase choir". The whole hospital sings. People from the unreal world sing songs different from the songs sung in the real world, which are not, in fact, for singing, because one can only march to them, not dance. Out there song is drying up; it is no longer song. It is being squeezed out, reduced to pomace. Caccioppoli works at the asylum. He is visited by friends, colleagues, students (though not all of them). Renato goes for brief walks in the mild sun and comes up with new calculations. Haya and her friends are too young, they do not visit

Renato Caccioppoli, they are told, *You cannot understand.* And so Haya's life passes by with her not getting it, or getting it wrong, or getting it late, so she now tries to dismantle this misunderstanding as if it were a magic cube, the pieces of which stay stubbornly clamped shut. She opens, dissects her not-getting-it way of getting the gist into tiny, tiny segments, delving into each and every cell of the vast honeycomb her life has become. She thrusts the slender needle of reason into each of these already empty little chambers, gradually, into one after another, but out of them creep maggots, pure rot.

Renato is visited by Carlo Miranda* and Gianfranco Cimmino.†

> *I go to see him every day. He accepts life among the patients calmly. He understands his incarceration as a special brand of human experience. But we are all concerned. Occasionally, when he is allowed to, we drive my car out into the country, have lunch at a little restaurant and speak of mathematics, war and women.*

In 1938 Guccio Gucci (1881–1953) opens his first shop in Rome; his woman's bag with bamboo handle is a hit.

In 1938 Italy wins the World Cup in football.

In September 1938 Mussolini abrogates the civil rights of Italian Jews.

In November 1938 a domestic version of the Nuremberg Laws comes into effect in Italy.

In 1938 King Vittorio Emmanuele III publicly supports Benito Mussolini in signing the Race Laws, according to which all Jews may be cleansed from the Government, the university, the army and other public services, and their rights to schooling and property ownership strictly limited.

---

* Mathematician, born in Naples on 15 August, 1912; dies on 28 May, 1982.
† Mathematician, born in Naples on 12 March, 1908; dies in Bologna, 30 May, 1989.

In November 1938 Florian Tedeschi loses his job.

They know I am a Jew, he says. The night is balmy. The windows are open. The sea is murmuring. There is no moon.

At university they tell the professors *Wear your black shirts,* which does not appeal to most of them. Italian mathematics loses its finest people. Tullio Levi-Civita* is fired from the University of Padua, other universities fire Vito Voltera,† Guido Fubini‡ and Beniamino Segre.‖ Enrico Fermi⁵ goes to Stockholm in 1938 (with special permission from the Fascist government) to receive the Nobel Prize and does not return. Renato Caccioppoli is released from the asylum in 1943, organizes a railway strike and is nearly killed when strike-breakers disrupt the gathering. He takes part in meetings of the Italian Communist Party, sits often on the editorial board of *Unità*, and with *Unità's* editors, his friends Mario Palermo and Renzo Lapiccerello, he makes the rounds of the bistros, most often Gambrinus and out-of-the-way taverns where, until late into the night, with beer, grappa, cognac or Strega, he tries (with his friends) to work out what to do about the Nazis.

After the war, with many honours, as a member of scholarly academies and institutions, Caccioppoli returns to mathematics. He works on film. He plays music. He publishes. Sara Mancuso leaves him. He drinks. He drinks more. He often prefers to be alone. Occasionally, he goes to the opera with an old priest, to concerts of classical music, and then retreats again into his ravaged universes.

---

* Anti-fascist. Born on 29 March, 1873, in Padua; dies on 29 December, 1941, in Rome.

† Anti-fascist. Born in Ancona on 3 May, 1860; dies in Rome on 11 October, 1940.

‡ Born in Venice on 19 January, 1879, leaves Italy in 1938, teaches at Princeton, dies in New York on 6 May, 1943.

‖ Born on 16 February, 1903, in Turin. Flees in 1938 to Great Britain, and returns in 1946 to Bologna. Dies on 2 October, 1977, in Frascati.

⁵ Born in Rome on 20 October, 1901; dies in Chicago on 28 November, 1954.

Into Euclidian realms and realms of his own. This is what he looks like:

On Friday, 8 May, 1959, around noon, he strolls along his favourite Via Chiaia, he has a short cappuccino and two grappas. He goes home. He waits for his best friend Giuseppe Scorzo Dragoni to arrive from Rome. Giuseppe is one day late.

That evening he shoots himself in the head.

The asteroid 9934 1985 UC is given the name Caccioppoli. Mario Martone makes a film about him. The Mathematics Department at the University of Naples is named *Renato Caccioppoli*.

Behind every name there is a story.

Frantic, on 14 December, 1938, Florian Tedeschi humbly requests to be received by the banker Pasquale Simonelli.*

---

* *Pasquale Isidoro Simonelli* (1878–1960), Commendatore of the Order of the Italian Royal Crown, a Catholic, born in Naples, where he is educated and works as a bank clerk. Goes to the United States in 1897. He first gives Italian language lessons in New York, and in 1898 he gets a job as a librarian in a secondary school. With the help of a certain Joseph Francolini, Simonelli starts his banking career at the Italian Savings Bank of New York City, first as a clerk, then a secretary, and then as a member of the board. He becomes an American citizen in 1902 and joins the Republican Party. Simonelli is Enrico Caruso's personal banker and handles all his business related to the New York Metropolitan Opera. He spends his whole life bringing Italian opera singers to New York and does much to fuel their popularity. Among these are Riccardo Stracciari, Titta Ruffo and Beniamino Gigli. In 1936 he returns to Naples, to Villa Simonelli, to his palace, where he lives until his death. He is buried there in 1960 in his family mausoleum at the Sant' Erasmo cemetery.

Four days later Florian Tedeschi sits in a salon at Villa Simonelli and with a trembling hand he brings a cup of fine, nearly transparent Chinese porcelain to his lips. He quietly sips the black tea. Inanely, though maybe not, he says: *My wife adores Gigli. And I, too, adore Gigli.* Simonelli says not a word.

Simonelli is a large man, and what's more, he's portly. Next to him Florian is tiny. Florian is wearing a beige trench coat, rumpled and tattered, which he doesn't take off while he sips Simonelli's tea. Seven days later, Florian Tedeschi goes to Tirana where a job as an accountant awaits him at a large construction consortium. Everything is as it should be. Florian is not plagued by doubts. In 1938, of the 47,000 Jews then living in Italy, 10,000 are card-carrying members of the Fascist Party.

In early April 1939 Italy attacks Albania. The Albanian Parliament votes to be annexed to Italy. King Zog flees to Greece. In Naples Ada sells her furniture, bedding and rugs; she gives away their clothes. In May the family are reunited. Florian makes headway at his job. He is proud. He buys a new suit, Italian, a new trench coat, black, that he tightens with a belt. In Tirana they tell him *You are being transferred to the Banca di Napoli. You are going to Vlorë. The climate is mild there and you can swim in summer.* So, the Tedeschi family swim that summer.

Vlorë has many names which are differently spelt and pronounced, more names than Gorizia, and all of these names pour into the town on an inlet covered by a blue cloak of air, over which, at night, the mountains whistle. Aulon, Avlon, Avlona, Avlonya, Vallona, Valona, Vlona, Vljora, Vlonë, Vlorë. Olives, black and oiled like the eyes that open Haya's first kiss with Ludovik, whose yellow shirt has a hole on the right shoulder. Ada's vegetable pastries, lambs from Karaburun, cold yoghurt before leaving for school, where, as in Naples, there hang portraits of Vittorio Emmanuele and Mussolini, *harapash*, toasts with *Falanghina*. A new waystation on the journey, the route of which Haya cannot discern. Vlorë, like a pocket-sized Naples. An Italian school, Italian neighbours, Italian chocolate. A romantic trip to the island of Saseno where the troops are stationed (*our troops*, Florian says), the drip that jiggles on the tip of Ludovik's nose, misted by Haya's breath. Valona, fortified just like Gorizia. Her first visit to the theatre. Yet another language for the same departures, the same flights. Sea: *det*; touch: *prekje*; fear: *frikë*; flag: *flamur*; Jew: *çifut*: war: *luftë*; journey: *udhëtim*. Sadik Zotaj street, a bench beneath the window on which Haya kneels and waits, waits? Aron, a mohel from Corfu, arrives and circumcises Orestes, while Florian is off touring Banca di Napoli branch offices in the interior. Oh, yes, life is beautiful. It flows by the Tedeschi family, who find palms, sandy beaches and abundant fresh seafood in Valona to eat with Barilla-brand tortiglione. Many years hence, as so often happens in Haya's old age, the past elbows into her wait like a blow, like a surfacing diver, breaking, transparent and wet, through an elusive wall (of memories), and Valona shimmers before her eyes, completely changed. The bygone decades have formed clusters of insights dwelling in the meanders, the warehouses, the hiding places of her consciousness, wrapped up in the ironed rags of logic, and now they start tumbling out of warped compartments, piling up, like rubbish, around her feet. She tries to bring order to this vast disarray, because after she retires from her job as a maths teacher at the Dante Alighieri Classical Secondary School in Gorizia, she has the time, yes, while she waits, she has the time to wonder *How could I not have known? How could I not have seen?*

The first banner of Albanian independence is raised in Valona back in 1912. When the Tedeschi family move to Valona in 1939, there are about 600 Jews living there, but she, Haya, remembers only Fanny Malli, because Fanny led a rabbit on a leash, and Ruben Ketz, because he had pockets full of black pebbles and spoke Albanian better than she did. In retrospect, she knows there was once a synagogue in Valona, which the Italians turned into a weapons armoury during the Great War, and there had been a Jewish cemetery, because before the bombs began to fall, while walking with Ludovik across a ploughed building site, she noticed a little tablet with a Star of David on it and oddly carved letters. *Those are our enemies*, Florian and Ada say, *the Greeks and the Albanians, the partisan bandits.* Haya believes there are enemies everywhere around them, although she is no longer a child. Italian boats sink in the Albanian port. The Italian confectioners shut down.

We are losing the war, Florian says.

The Germans don't like us, Ada says.

In Tirana, Enver Hoxha closes his shop, called Flora, where he sells alcoholic and non-alcoholic beverages, sandwiches and tobacco, for the opening of which he had submitted the necessary paperwork to the (Italian) municipal administration, signed Envero Hoxha. In a rash of demonstrations, Albanian anti-fascists clash with the *carabinieri* and the local police. The newly sworn-in Albanian prime minister, Mussolini's favourite Mustafa Merlika-Kruja, persecutes, arrests, tortures and kills all those who are against the regime. The Italians capture Koçi Xoxe and condemn him to death by hanging. The youth leader Qemal Stafa is killed. In Korçë, anti-fascists set fire to the barracks of the Italian Army, and on 24 July, 1942, they blow up an armoury with the weapons inside; the Tedeschi family run into the textile shop on the ground floor of their building and hide among the bolts of floral cotton; they themselves becoming a decoration, a pattern, in the growing maelstrom. At Tirana airport the spotlights are smashed; the Communists sabotage the central telephone switchboard and cut all telephone lines, and the organized uprising begins. Florian Tedeschi continues making the rounds of the interior branch offices of the bank where he is a loyal employee. Ada packs the basics. Orestes declares, *I want to go for a swim.* Paula skips rope in the living room. Nora says, *I got my period.* Down in the cellar Haya presses Ludovik's icy fingers between her legs, then twists like the stem of a yellow gerbera and says *ah.* Her whisper and Ludovik's whisper light up the woodshed, from which cats scamper, prowling for rats

> syçkë pëllumb
>
>   lamtumirë
>
> im verdhë ëndërr
>
>   të dua
>
> të dashuroj

Ada's breath smells of cheap perfume. The bus is full of women, children, farm animals. They rumble through the Albanian wilderness and remote mountains. The roads are ghastly. It takes them a week to reach Tirana. Florian locks up his desk as if he will soon be back to his bills, extracts, copies, calculations, interest rates, but he will not. He jumps into a car in Valona, sits next to an Italian general, who is also on the run, and before his family arrive he reaches the Dajti Hotel, only recently opened, orders sausages, *un rocchio di salsiccia*, a mixed salad of all sorts of vegetables, and blackberry and vanilla ice cream: *Genuine Italian, nothing finer*, winks the waiter. At dusk he strolls along Viale Savoia, *A beautiful avenue*, he says, and is breathless at the sight of the elegant villas nestled in Mediterranean vegetation. A new old chapter is being written, one of political intrigue, murders on demand, *secret* services, of people disappeared, families disappeared, stories never to be untangled, whose rotten threads like ratty street brooms poke along the ground and do nothing but smear the shit. Enver Hoxha is photographed more often, his two gold teeth flashing. Ada and the children abruptly forget their pidgin Albanian, and all they repeat is *faleminderit shumë, faleminderit shumë*, after which they fall suddenly silent. The Tedeschi family spend several nights on straw mattresses in the foyer of the Dajti Hotel, while around their heads stomp polished Italian boots. Later, in 1944, in chorus with Ada and Florian, Haya will tell their relatives in Gorizia, *Those were terrible times for us Italians there.*

It is already 1943. How time flies. In early September, when Italy is no longer any factor in Albania, when the director of the Banca di Napoli informs Florian, while they are still in Valona, that he is absolutely free to travel immediately to wherever he would like to go, the Tedeschi family *secretly* accept the help of a small *Jewish* anti-fascist group, which finds them accommodation near the airport, where, since the war is raging, planes keep landing and taking off and bombs drop like falling stars. *Ah, our happy days are forever gone*, hums Ada, swinging her hips and taking a long swig from a flask of brandy. *Terrible*, Ada says to her sister Letizia and brother Carlo after they return to Gorizia in late 1943.

There is not enough food or bread to go around. They use coupons to purchase coffee and sugar. The Albanians are speaking less Italian and more Albanian; some are even speaking German. *These are a wild people*, Ada and Florian say after they return to Gorizia, *but a brave people, yes, indeed.* The German troops attack. German bombs destroy. The Nazis count, catalogue, purify the population, filter it. Every day there are people hanging on the squares, swaying to the rhythm of the palm fronds. Ada believes all this to be a brief and cruel diversion, the work of unruly young men, so one day, after she has had a good swig from the flask that she now hides in the linen cupboard, under the bedding, she goes off to the German Military Command with Haya, convinced she can help free Florian's colleague Sandro Koffler, the banker. *Listen*, Ada says, *Sandro is an honest man. I am telling you. My last name is Tedeschi.* The S.S. officer only glances up at Hitler hanging there on the wall, and waits. *Tedesco in Italian means German*, Ada says, *I am someone you can trust.*

Ja, Tedeschi, the officer says, *ein jüdischer Name.*

On their way home, Ada says to Haya, *Let's get some ice cream, while there still is ice cream to be had, while it is still Italian.* And she also says, *You can't run from your name. Behind every name there is a story.*

The Italian troops in Albania are now entirely out of favour. Former friends who are called Allies in wartime are arresting and killing soldiers. Some soldiers surrender, others flee, many die. The Tedeschi family move again, this time to the centre of Tirana, and prepare for departure, which is called repatriation. It is September 1943. Life dribbles by. Paula and Orestes go off to the abandoned palace of the fascist ministry in their neighbourhood, where they roller skate on the spacious marble floors, shrieking. For Paula and Orestes life is a thrill. The Nazis are stepping up their raids and searching flats. From a window on the third floor Haya watches a scene, as if from a movie. Later she faints. A young man in a yellow shirt with a hole on the right shoulder sprints towards her building, while across the street a Nazi lounging in an open-topped car lines him up in his sights. The barrage of bullets from the machine gun catches the young man two metres short of the front door. In an instant the yellow shirt grins red.

> *In un momento*
> *Sono sfiorite le rose*
> *I petali caduti*
> *Perché io non potevo dimenticare le rose*
> *Le cercavamo insieme*
> *Abbiamo trovato delle rose*
> *Erano le sue rose erano le mie rose*
> *Questo viaggio chiamavamo amore*
> *Col nostro sangue e colle nostre lagrime facevamo le rose*
> *Che brillavano un momento al sole del mattino*
> *Le abbiamo sfiorite sotto il sole tra i rovi*
> *Le rose che non erano le nostre rose*
> *Le mie rose le sue rose*
> > *P.S. E così dimenticammo le rose,**

whispers Ludoviko from Valona, while he watches Haya search for a lost earring in the sand by the sea, imagining himself to be Dino Campana and her to be Sibilla Aleramo, with their last dusk running

---

> * In one moment
> The roses have faded
> The petals fallen
> Because I could not forget the roses
> We searched for them together
> We found roses
> That were her roses, my roses
> This journey we called love
> Out of our blood and tears we made roses
> That shone but a moment in the morning sun
> Under the sun among the briars we withered the roses
> That were not our roses
> Roses that were not ours, not mine, not hers.
> > P.S. And thus we forgot the roses.

out; and Haya (at the time), the goose, has no idea what he is mumbling.

The boy vanishes into Haya's entranceway; she thinks she can touch him. The Nazis go from door to door, banging and shouting. As if the boy has been swallowed whole. The next day Haya ventures out to buy cornbread mixed with chaff, and on the square she sees more than a hundred neatly stacked bodies, some in civilian clothing, some in partisan uniforms. The passers-by do not look; they move quickly past with rubber tread. The men lie there as if sleeping, as if tired of war, as if they were tree trunks for a building project. There is no smell. There are no flies. The shops are open, banners snapping, the shutters on the windows are shut.

Ludoviko is not among those who were killed.

Koffler the banker is not released from prison. They take his wife Angela to the madhouse, because she yanks her hair out and bangs her head on the windowpane. For practically nothing, the Tedeschi family sell what little property they have acquired. Florian's colleagues sail out of Valona, but do not reach Naples: the ship is bombed by British aircraft and sinks. The only survivor is a clerk named Leone Romanelli, who swims for three days to reach the shore, then arrives in Tirana to tell Florian all about it. He, too, loses his mind. His wife and three children are back there, on board, or rather in the sea, on the bottom of the sea. It is not wise to have many children. Then Leone Romanelli is placed in a madhouse. To keep Angela Koffler company. For ever, Haya believes.

Escorted by German soldiers, the Tedeschi family leave Albania and travel for three weeks to Italy. Behind them they leave their physical stench and dead armies, whose generals, Italian and German, lugging maps, registers, medical and army records, dental records and data on medical histories, dragging along with them a priest or two, wandering through the remote mountains and sandy coves of the land of eagles, come back twenty years later, through the mud and rain, the summer heat, regardless, looking for mouldering bones over which crops or skyscrapers have grown.

At the border between Albania and Yugoslavia columns of Italian

Wehrmacht prisoners of war peer frantically about and beg for a crust of bread, while digging in sub-zero temperatures, seeking their way under mounds of snow, looking for a path, an exit. In thin voices that crack with the cold, they call to their loved ones and send them messages. Here, at the border whose encirclement ruptures, making it a passage, an exit, the Tedeschi family, with hundreds of civilians and soldiers on their way to Budapest, clamber into a railway car, never dreaming, not even wanting to know, what is happening just a little further north, what journeys there are, and to what end. Traversing Montenegro, Hungary and Austria, Florian and Ada and their four children arrive in Italy just before Christmas 1943.

The train stands in Budapest for several hours. Off it leap neatly pressed German soldiers, well fed and freshly shaven. The Hungarians toss portions of goulash, bread, milk and little bottles of rum in through the windows to the other passengers. Not three months later, from this same platform at Keleti station and several other smaller train stations in and around Budapest, other train carriages, locked freight cars, cattle wagons, with a hundred people in each, with a bucket for piss and a bucket for drinking water, will depart for a walled-in station, a blind track leading to a cosmic twilight. From early spring to early summer 1944 the crematorium at Auschwitz will work at full capacity, and daily it will vomit up the remains of 6,000 people, murdered, who will float away like gray eiderdown into the sky. And so it is that in two and a half months 400,000 Hungarian Jews will leap on board the "messianic timetable placed on the Index by the new order", in a "wretched reworking of the antediluvian evacuation, this landlocked, earthbound reprise of Noah's ark", which was written for them by an unknown man in long black tails, in a shirt with a "stiff celluloid collar, yellowed like an old domino, the headwaiter's tie with a bohemian knot, swinging his cane high in the air, swaying on his feet like a ship's mast, staring into space", a gentleman by the name of Eduard Sam, a gentleman who, with a glance at his watch "with a dial and Roman numerals showing the *exact time*", steps out of the "frame of the drama and farce of which he is writer".

The way lives interweave yet never touch, only to collide in mutual destruction, inconceivably distant in their simultaneity. In 1944 the former senior inspector of the state railways, by then a "retired senior railway inspector", author of a timetable, Eduard Sam, steps along in a "column of the miserable and the ill, among horrified women and terrified children, going with them and alongside them, tall and bent over, without his spectacles, without his cane, which they had taken from him, staggering along with uncertain steps in the queue of the sacrificed, as a shepherd among his herd, a rabbi with his flock, a school teacher at the head of a group of school children . . . " So Eduard Sam moves towards the trains, towards the train carriages, whose departures and arrivals he has so often calibrated, checked, supplemented, coordinated, *perfected*, and now, as he walks, the times of train departures and arrivals, of *routine departures and arrivals*, run in his head like a refrain, like a ditty, much like the clacking of wheels, in close harmony with his broken step, like a song that will determine his fate, and to himself he repeats those arrivals and departures of trains, those *routine departures*. And, while Eduard Sam strides to his *finality*, high-level Nazi officials in Berlin, Cracow, Warsaw, everywhere, the perfect bureaucrats Dr Albert Ganzenmüller, State Secretary of the Reich Transport Ministry, and his superior, S.S. General Karl Wolff, Himmler's personal adjutant, obediently apply the *special, newly composed* timetable to the new order. S.S. official Dr Albert Ganzenmüller, without a trace of malice, earnestly, with devotion and meticulous attention, crosses out, *annuls* Eduard Sam's *timetable of trains*, of *special trains*, which had been honed for years, and in the serenity of an airy office composes his own *Fahrplanordnung 587, Fahrplanordnung 290*, and so on, *special timetables of trains*, of *special trains,* on which he stamps the official seal of annihilation.

Mr Ganzenmüller, you like trains?

> *Yes, Your Honour, trains are my passion, my obsession.*

From 1928 you've worked for the German Railways,
and as early as 1931, as a member of the Nazi
party, you were involved in anti-Jewish activities.

> I wouldn't put it that way. Things were much more
> complex.

You scheduled civilian trains for deporting Jews to
the camps. From 1942 to 1945 you supervised the
German State Railway.

> I was following orders from above.

You secured the unobstructed running of trains to
the death camps. Thanks to you Operation
Reinhard ran smoothly.

> Operation Reinhard? I only heard of Operation
> Reinhard after capitulation.

You personally drew up many and varied timetables. Such as a timetable for transporting elderly
German Jews to Theresienstadt.

> That was my duty, to see to the unobstructed move-
> ment of trains. Besides, composing timetables was a
> hobby of mine. Like solving challenging crossword
> puzzles.

In 1942 a vast "purge" of the ghettoes begins
throughout the General Government.

> About that I know nothing.

In June and July there are construction works on
the railway line leading to Sobibor – a mass

extermination camp. There is an unplanned halt in the transports, and on 16 July S.S. General Karl Wolff seeks your help.

I don't remember.

Instead of sending 300,000 Warsaw Jews to Sobibor you redirect them to Treblinka. After 22 July a train runs daily with 5,000 Jews from Warsaw to Treblinka, while another train runs twice weekly from Przemysl to Belzec. Further, on 28 July, 1942, you, Albert Ganzenmüller, Secretary of the Ministry of Transport – Reichsverkehrsministerium, and Deputy General Director of the German Reichsbahn, report to S.S.-Gruppenführer Wolff on the measures you have taken.

Have you proof?

We have your correspondence with Wolff. On 13 August, 1942, Wolff writes:
Warm thanks, both in my own and the S.S. Reichsführer's name, for your letter of 28 July, 1942. I was especially delighted to hear from you that already for a fortnight there has been a daily train, taking 5,000 of the Chosen People to Treblinka, thus enabling us to carry out this movement of population at an accelerated pace. I have personally contacted all the agencies involved in the process so that the job can proceed without impediment. I thank you again for your efforts regarding this question and also request that you continue to bring your personal attention to every detail, for which I will be particularly grateful. Sincerely yours and Heil Hitler! W.

I do not recall this correspondence.

So you claim you received Wolff's letter, stamped as Top Secret, a letter from the second highest official in the Third Reich, and you did not read it? Three million Jews were taken to their deaths in that operation.

> *I know nothing of Treblinka. I did not realize that Treblinka was a mass extermination camp. I thought it was a Jewish reservation, so Himmler explained it to me. I knew nothing of the fate of the Jews. I saw nothing. I worked in my office. I was not out strolling around.*

> This is drivel, Ganzenmüller. In May 1942, before the camp was set up, we knew something was going on at Treblinka, and the information was given to us by German railway workers. Some S.S. officials arrived at Treblinka in May 1942 and arrested a hundred men, Jews from both Treblinka and its neighbourhood, and ordered them to clear the land. The Ukrainian guards arrived right after the prisoners. The S.S. claimed that the inmates would work on damming the River Bug to build a new military installation, but the German railway workers stubbornly insisted it was going to be an extermination camp for the Jews.

> Yes? And who are you?

> Franciszek Zabecki, head of the civilian train station at Treblinka. A member of the Polish resistance movement. I followed the arrivals and departures of trains. I noted them down. On 22 July,

1942, I received an official telegram stating a short, regular and very frequent line would run on the Warsaw–Treblinka route. This line was supposed to transport new "settlers", the telegram said. The trains would be made up of sixty covered cattle wagons, or rather closed goods wagons, it said. After unloading, the trains were to be sent back to Warsaw, it said. Why "settlers" in goods wagons, I ask you? Behind bolted doors and narrow slits covered in barbed wire instead of windows; crammed in like livestock, so packed together they couldn't even crouch. That telegram was signed by you.

I don't remember.

You are the person who drew up the train timetable, Mr Ganzenmüller. This was your timetable, Mr Ganzenmüller. There were between eight and ten thousand men, women, the elderly and a lot of children in the first train which arrived on 23 July, 1942. A lot of small children, infants. When it spewed out its freight, the train returned to Warsaw. Empty. To pick up new "settlers". When the horrors became unbearable, and I could tell you about them, the horrors, day and night, you halted all regular passenger traffic to Treblinka, Mr Ganzenmüller. Surely you remember that, Mr Ganzenmüller, you drew up that schedule. After September 1942 the only trains that reached Treblinka were military and deportation trains, there were no picnickers, no excursions; civilians did not come out on nature tours, Mr Ganzenmüller. The trains were met at the station by S.S. men with sleeves rolled up and pistols drawn. Tempo! Schnell! they shouted. *The number of passengers was marked on each wagon with chalk. I wrote it down. For two years I wrote this down, from one day to the next, and I added it up. I know, while others guess. I am the only living witness who was at Treblinka from the day when the extermination of the Jews began to the day the camp was closed on 16 August, 1944. All the German documents were burned, but I copied them. One million two hundred thousand people were killed at Treblinka. There is no doubt about it.*

Even after the rebellion, the transports did not cease. You don't remember Mr Ganzenmüller. You don't remember how you again changed the timetable of trains. How after the rebellion you re-directed the trains to other camps, and you turned Treblinka into a transit station. I remember.
Transport PJ 201: 32 wagons, Bialystok–Lublin via Treblinka, 18 August, 1943.
Transport PJ 203: 40 wagons, Bialystok–Lublin via Treblinka, 19 August, 1943.
Lublin via Treblinka, 19 August, 1943. That same day, transport PJ 204: 39 wagons from Bialystok to Lublin, stopping at Treblinka.
Transport PJ 209: 9 wagons, for Lublin via Treblinka, 24 August, 1943.
Transport PJ 211: 31 wagons left for Lublin on 8 September.
Transport PJ 1025: 50 wagons of Jews from Minsk Litewski were sent to Chelm, in fact to Sobibor, 17 September, 1943.

I don't remember.

On 22 August, and on 2, 9, 13 and 21 September wagons departed from Treblinka loaded with the clothing of the murdered Jews. The liquidation of the camp begins. They cart away the boards, construction material and quicklime. They take away the dredger. Five bolted wagons take away the remaining "workers", meaning prisoners, to Sobibor on 20 October and 4 September, 1943. On 31 October, the metal structures and liquidation equipment were taken away. Everything is recorded here, Mr Ganzenmüller. More than one hundred wagons of goods and material left Treblinka.

Mr Wolff, they call you Karel?

> Yes, Your Honour. Karel is somehow softer than Karl.

Like Ganzenmüller, you too claim that you knew nothing, yet recently in a B.B.C. documentary, The World at War, *you talked about how you were present in 1941 at the execution of Jewish prisoners in Minsk and described the splatter of brains on Himmler's coat.*

> I remembered that later. They reminded me.

When did you first hear of Operation Reinhard? From Himmler?

> I had no idea there was an Operation Reinhard. This is the first time I hear of it. Here in Nuremberg.

And the camps in Lublin and Auschwitz, did you know of them?

> I heard for the first time of those appalling places on 19 March, 1945, when I came to Switzerland. With

horror my Swiss friends gave me newspapers that reported on the atrocities perpetrated in those camps.

When were you transferred to Trieste?

On 9 September, 1943.

Did you belong to the circle of Himmler's close friends?

Yes.

Did you hear Himmler's speech in Poznan in October 1943?

No, Your Honour. At that time I was already in Trieste.

And in Trieste that speech was never talked about?

No, it was distributed to officers who were at the front.

Did you ever hear about Russians and Poles, who were not Jews, being killed and exterminated, did you ever hear about that?

No, I have never heard anything about extermination. Your Honour is probably referring to systematic, planned extermination.

Exactly.

I know nothing about that.

So this is the first you have ever heard of it?

        Please? I don't hear well.

*Is this is the first time you've heard about the mass
extermination of people?*

        *They asked me about it after capitulation. That was
the first time.*

Have you any idea of the extent of the exterminations?

        Not precisely.

All the evidence points to several million victims.

        *I am very grateful, Your Honour, for the informa-
tion you have just given me.*

Did you ever visit the Warsaw Ghetto?

        No.

*Czerniakow in his diary provides the day and
hour of your arrival in Reichsführer S.S. Heinrich
Himmler's company.*

        *Ich bin ein alter Mann, Your Honour. I cannot
remember everything.*

*Herr Wolff, I consider you responsible for the
deportation of 300,000 Jews to the Treblinka
concentration camp during the summer of 1942 and
I sentence you to fifteen years in prison and ten
years' loss of civil liberties.*

Too late, Your Honour. I was released for good behaviour.

The Tedeschi family go on living in the illusion of ignorance. Those who know what is happening do not speak. Those who don't know ask no questions. Whoever asks gets no answers. Then, as now. Hence, since they don't know, the Tedeschi family don't ask, so there is nothing for them to find out, so there is no reason for their getting unduly upset.

In the 1970s Haya, for the second time in her life, enters the belly of Budapest by train, at that same station, at Keleti. The space is now completely changed yet it is the same; it pulses to the rhythm of the walkers lugging a burden different from that wartime cargo. The light in the station sways, trembles, grabs for the little bits of glass embedded on the ceiling, which gleam like a honeycomb, and then glides speedily off, as if saying, *I'll be back.* The faces of the travellers are serene, nearly motionless, but their bodies sway mischievously, almost cheerfully. Not like back then, when a terrible paralysis reigned, with fear swaying in its lap. For, in the 1970s, Haya finally learns of (some) events she knew nothing about in the 1940s, although like cataclysmic floods and earthquakes, with a horrible noise, they were rumbling here, right beneath her window.

Ah, train stations, both a convergence point for and bisector of the clusters of cocooned little worlds that tumble headlong, smashing, nervous and angry at times, jovial at others, bursting apart like the volvox, spewing their contents over the rails, sliding off all over the world. Train stations, tombstones, borders between the living and the dead, between infinitude and the hermetic world of the city, city gates, cities unto themselves. When identities vanish, train stations sprout. If every border had a train station of its own, what marvellous confusion would ensue, what a crush, what mockery.

The Tedeschi family arrive in Venice as the city is coming under attack. Haya expects hands in the air, welcoming formations of waving hands; she expects flowers and hugs, tearful eyes, sad smiles and sighs of consolation, *our poor ones, what terrible times you've been through, benvenuti a casa.* Nothing of the sort. The train pulls into a vast empty station along whose tracks rolls only the huffing of time, as if an owl were sitting on the moon, glowering. *The world has forgotten us,* Haya says and stands in line with her family at the station for food and a free ticket to return to Gorizia, to return home.

Haya's grandfather Bruno Baar is gone. He dies at the age of seventy-two in 1939, when the Tedeschi family are embarking on the ship for Valona from Naples, so Ada does not attend her father's funeral. Haya's grandfather Paolo Tedeschi is in the Republic of Salò with a fascist membership card in his pocket, which is becoming less adequate as a camouflage for his Jewish origins. Gorizia, along with Rijeka, Trieste, Udine, Pula and Ljubljana is part of the new German province Adriatisches Küstenland, Litorale Adriatico, and this is a part of the Reich that eagerly revisits the dream of *Mitteleuropa*. Haya gets to know her relatives. In a whisper Ada describes her life in Naples and Valona to her sister Letizia, and at night switches her plum brandy for grappa. Florian sells umbrellas retail and wholesale at the Delle Tre Venezie shop at Piazza della Vittoria 7 (telephone no. 8–17), and on Sundays, with his boss Francesco Poletti, he goes to the stadium on Via Baiamonti to cheer for the local second leaguers of Gorizia (Busani, Blason, Cumar, Auletta II, Sessa, Ciuffarin, Gimona, Beorchia, Bonansea, Auletta and Zanolla). Who else could he cheer for? Later, when he leaves for Milan in the autumn of 1944, he supports Milan.

Trieste becomes the centre of the O.Z.A.K. (Operationszone Adriatisches Küstenland). At about the same time as the Tedeschi family arrive in Gorizia, Christmas 1943, a whole crowd of old acquaintances is gathering in Trieste. They need to be sent somewhere after Operation Reinhard is shut down in Poland, so Himmler dispatches them urgently to Italy. There are about a hundred men and women from Einsatzkommando Reinhard in Trieste, as well as a number of S.S. troops from Ukraine. Einsatzkommando Reinhard opens offices designated by the abbreviation "R". The Trieste group is R1, the Udine group R2, and the Rijeka group is R3.

Elegant old villas are refurbished, furniture is renovated, servants hired, banquets and balls are held, singers and dancers rehearse a repertoire of entertainments, new films arrive, operas and philharmonic orchestras tour, celebrated chefs prepare delicacies at the newly opened clubs. Trieste lives its schizophrenic moment again, in war, its parallel lives, real and unreal, contradictory.

The Nazi police and soldiers of the Nazi Army stroll around Trieste. On 1 October, 1943, the political and administrative authority of the Adriatisches Küstenland is in the hands of Gauleiter Friedrich Rainer.* Trieste is ailing and, much like a person, it does not want to die without a fight. It struggles to survive as best it can. Abandoned by Italy in 1943, it flails and succumbs, distraught. The restaurants in the harbour gleam, they serve fish such as dentex and gilt-head bream; in return for coupons from the 209–201 series one can get a kilo of potatoes for three lire, or 500 grams per person; the theatres are packed: Wagner's *Lohengrin* and Lehár's *Merry Widow* are the hits of the 1943–44 season; the Istituto Enenkel at Via Battisti 22 (telephone no. 8800) offers accelerated courses in the German language for children and adults, courses in typing and stenography for young ladies, and, after strict security checks, the young ladies

---

* *Friedrich Rainer*, born on 28 July, 1903, in Carinthia (St Veit an der Glan). Attends law school. As of 1930 a member of the German National Socialist Workers Party; from 1936 works in the Party administration in Austria; 1938–41 made Gauleiter, district governor and governor of the Reich in Salzburg; 1941–5 he is in Carinthia and the neighbouring parts of Styria; in 1943 he is appointed defence commissar of the Adriatic Littoral. On 8 May, 1945, hands over his administration to the representatives of the democratic parties, and the British Army extradites him to Yugoslavia. He is tried at Nuremberg. He is put to death as a war criminal on 13 March, 1947, in Ljubljana.

translate *secret* and public documents for the Nazi police; third-rate painter, "agreeable" Angelo Brombo at the Trieste gallery exhibits his picturesque oils with motifs of a joyous Venice, while his colleague Zoran Mušić, born in Gorizia, is off to Dachau shortly thereafter; the "new staff" at the Salone Villa on the Piazza Ponterosso styles and dyes hair in the latest fashion (blonde); football is played with euphoric zeal: Ponziana–Triestina (2:11); Giacomo Cipci, conductor of the full orchestra of Trieste Radio, goes off for a friendly visit to his Viennese counterpart Max Schönherr, after which Max Schönherr

visits Trieste, a city in touch with the world; at the Fenice theatre they stage matinees for children, especially *Snow White and the Seven Dwarfs*; the movie *Venus vor Gericht* (*The Trial of Venus*) shows at the Nazionale cinema, produced by Bavaria Filmkunst of Munich, with Hansi Knoteck in the role of Venus, followed by the documentary *Die Bauten Adolf Hitler* (*The Buildings of Adolf Hitler*), all in German, of course; and Trieste again loses its mind, its compass, looks into itself, horrified, and asks, *Who am I now? To whom do I go? Who is coming to me?* The morass inside it is deep and dark and sick, so sick that no-one and nothing dares go there, so all-embracing that Trieste itself is engulfed.

The old companions from the administration of Belzec, Sobibor and Treblinka kick back in Trieste and the surroundings, have their last good times, their *happy days*, under the watchful eyes of Christian Wirth, the first man of the Trieste Einsatzkommandos, who is laying the foundations for their efficient work as early as September 1943. Christian Wirth comes to Trieste with a team of experts who were working with him on the operation known as Aktion Tiergarten 4, which means that since 1939 he has been exterminating the "terminally ill", first in Germany, then at the camps.

Christian Wirth, S.S.-Sturmbannführer (major), was born on 24 November, 1885, in Oberbalzheim. He is a carpenter and construction worker and, after 1910, a policeman. During World War One he fights on the Western Front. In 1930 he becomes a member of the most vicious unit of the Stuttgart police, already known, even then, for their brutality towards prisoners. A member of the National Socialist Workers' Party, 1931, and part of the S.S. by 1939, when he is given the rank of Kriminalkommissar in the Stuttgart Kriminalpolizei, a section of the Gestapo. Soon thereafter, as Kriminaloberkommissar and S.S.-Obersturmführer, he is transferred to the Grafeneck psychiatric clinic to head their euthanasia programme, which is already up and running. At Grafeneck, Wirth makes the acquaintance of *Josef Oberhauser*, who is in charge of supervising the work of the crematorium, and he becomes Wirth's right-hand man in the death camps throughout Poland. At Grafeneck, Wirth also gets to know the head of the kitchen, *Kurt Franz*, later commander of the Treblinka concentration camp; then he meets *Lorenz Hackenholt* and *Willi Mentz*, with whom he will enjoy the Mediterranean climate of Trieste and its environs, along with *Franz Stangl*, the brutal commander of Sobibor and Treblinka, revelling in brothels and nightclubs.

Wirth is transferred in late 1939 to Brandenburg an der Havel to be chief administrator, where, in a former prison adapted to become a euthanasia centre, the first gassing experiments take place: a group of mentally ill patients is gassed to death using carbon monoxide. Philipp Bouhler, a member of Hitler's Chancellery, comes up with a revolutionary suggestion: gas chambers camouflaged as showers. Shortly thereafter Wirth returns to Grafeneck to be promoted to supervisor of all euthanasia centres in Germany and Austria.

Before Christmas 1941, Wirth arrives in Belzec, a little place in the far south-east of occupied Poland, and is made its first camp commander, with the task and ambition of exterminating all the Jews there. They call him Christian the Terrible. Horrible stories circulate about his savagery.

There is not much information available about Belzec. The atrocities committed in Belzec are slipping into oblivion. Belzec is a forgotten camp today. One of the two men who survived Belzec, Rudolf Reder, testifies at a trial of war criminals in May 1945:

Wirth was a tall, broad-shouldered man
in his middle forties with a vulgar face.
Wirth was a beast.

Kurt Gerstein, an S.S.-Lieutenant, then head of the Technical
Disinfection Services of the S.S.-Waffen, testifies:

> *I arrived in Belzec in late summer 1942. I was supposed to*
> *improve gassing methods and implement a way to disinfect*
> *clothing. A transport of Jews had just arrived from Lvov and*
> *all of them were immediately sent to the gas chamber. Wirth*
> *stood on a small platform and hurried the prisoners along*
> *with a whip, slashing them across the face.*

Chaim Hirszmann also testifies:

Once, when a transport of children arrived in
Belzec, Wirth ordered all the children thrown into a
huge pit and buried alive.

> *I am* Werner Dubois. *At Belzec I drove a truck as*
> *an S.S. officer from April 1942 to April 1943 and*
> *supervised the work of the gas chambers. Wirth was*
> *brutal. He bellowed and threatened all the members*
> *of the German garrison and often struck them on*
> *the face. Only Oberhauser was not afraid of him.*

In August 1942 *Odilo Globočnik*, leader of Aktion Reinhard, names
Wirth as inspector of the S.S.-Sonderkommandos of Aktion
Reinhard. Wirth's first task is to reorganize the Treblinka camp,
which, as a result of poor management, is not functioning well. Wirth
brings his colleague Franz Stangl from Sobibor and puts him in
charge of Treblinka. Globočnik orders a temporary hold on the
transports from Warsaw. Treblinka is expanded, the killing methods
are perfected, larger gas chambers are built. Lorenz Hackenholt

comes over from Sobibor and brings his sketches, drawings and blueprints. Erwin Lambert of the S.S., an expert at building gas chambers, oversees the construction.

In late 1942 Wirth manages the work camps in the Lublin district and moves into a two-storey villa near Lublin military airfield, which was not working at the time. At the airfield Wirth sets up three hangars where all the confiscated property of the victims of Aktion Reinhard is sorted. It is then taken by train to Berlin.

In the summer of 1943 Wirth is promoted to S.S.-Sturmbannführer and, after the Treblinka Revolt of 2 August, 1943, he is transferred to Trieste.

Near Kozina, on 26 May, 1944, on his way from Trieste to Rijeka by car, Wirth is killed by partisans of the 1st Battalion of the Istrian Division, led by Maks Zadnik. Another eleven S.S.-Sonderkommandos, members of Aktion Reinhard and Einsatz R, are killed in combat in northern Italy. All are buried first at the German military cemetery near Villa Opicina, but then between 1957 and 1961 they are exhumed and, with another 21,000 German soldiers, re-interred at the new German military cemetery near Costermano, on the eastern shore of Lake Garda. Although their names have been expunged from the list of war victims and from their headstones, once a year unknown visitors place flowers on their enumerated graves (Wirth's is 716) and salute them with the Nazi salute. To this very day.

Continually obsessed by the "Jewish Question", Wirth installs the infrastructure for proceeding with mass killings. He builds an efficient little crematorium. In and around Trieste he puts to use the methods developed in Poland, and sets up a new concentration camp at the San Sabba rice mill, an abandoned complex of buildings, a former rice-husking plant in the Trieste suburbs. An expert at building crematoria, Erwin Lambert, arrives in Trieste and successfully applies the experience he has gained in Poland to the rice mill. The ovens are inaugurated on 4 April, 1944, with a celebratory test run incinerating seventy bodies of hostages killed at the Villa Opicina shooting range the day before. Wirth's staff is experienced not only in burning prisoners, but in torturing them to death, beating them brutally, while children are ordered to collect firewood for the ovens in which they, too, will burn.

The German occupation makes Trieste a gift of fourteen legally registered brothels under the medical supervision of Italian doctors, and 200 registered streetwalkers. The registered brothels allow in only members of the military (and their previously screened guests), while the unregistered brothels are left to civilians. In the registered houses of passion, the passions are efficiently controlled. Upon entering the brothel the "consumer" would receive a form (in duplicate) in which a "secretary" would officially enter his name and unit, his rank, the date of the visit, the name of the "institution" and the name of the prostitute, after which the customer would be medically examined to make sure he had no pubic pests or gonorrhea or, heaven forbid, syphilis; then he'd undergo prophylactic treatment consisting of a wash with soap and water and mercury bichloride, followed by an intraurethral injection of 2 per cent protargol and an application of calomel powder. Finally, he would be handed a condom, after which, with an intrepid *Heil!*, off he would go to satisfy his sex drive. But managed prostitution is an activity the S.S.-command does not succeed in implementing successfully across the board, not in Trieste or Ljubljana or Rijeka or Gorizia or Pula or Udine. Pretty girls from decent families are strolling around, well dressed, spirited and free; and hunting for prey is what soldiers are trained to do. So syphilis and gonorrhoea flourish, children are born out of wedlock, and little psychiatric clinics sprout *secretly* in the suburbs of the cities and towns of the Adriatisches Küstenland, where S.S. men could be treated for their hysteria, and their war and sex traumas.

The Nazi plan for conquering the world is built on *secrecy*, founded on institutions, confidential documents, dark experiments, obscure war plans, mystical phantasms, occult dreams, hidden factories, camouflaged camps, fake hospitals and cryptic conferences, on dubious industry and esoteric production, vague warfare and ambiguous military campaigns. And at the centre, the axis around which this rotten cosmic vision spreads, ever more like the gigantic cocoon of some freak insect, are sexual organs, the cunt and the cock, their utilitarian and market value, their messianic mission, their battle cry, in other words – fucking, *coitus vulgaris*, which is designed to create a new man and a new age. *The cunt makes a difference, the cock defines the difference.* Castration, sterilization, controlled procreation, fornication and prostitution are the most powerful weapons of the Reich, the greatest *obsession* of the Reich, and, further-more, of the Church.

Whether this took the form of an inflatable doll or a Salon Kitty or a *Lebensborn* farm is immaterial. The brothels in 1943 function smoothly for Himmler's unmarried and married warriors along all fronts, including the Adriatisches Küstenland. To the more than one hundred official houses of ill repute, faced with a shortage of local floozies, vamps and easy women, they bring in *puellae publicae*, dedicated to the "great cause of mankind": women from Paris, Poland, Bohemia, Moravia, even Berlin, some under coercion, some lured by promises, six hundred of them or more to service at least fifty clients a day, while those from the bordello on Klosterstrasse in Stuttgart, for example (and not only they), are put to work for science, using diaphragms in which they collect the semen of their studs for future (*secret*, of course) experiments.

The Trieste courts under German jurisdiction work at full throttle. There are no verdicts of not guilty. People play the lottery. The newspapers are full of classified ads: all sorts of things are being sold, clothing, jewellery, artworks, houses, as if a huge general migration were under way, although many have already been moved.

Life is stronger than war. For most people, for the obedient and the silent, for those on the sidelines, for the bystanders, life becomes a small, packed suitcase that is never opened, an overnight bag slipped under the bed, baggage going nowhere, in which everything is neatly folded – days, tears, deaths, little pleasures, spreading the stench of mould. For those on the sidelines there is no telling what they are thinking, whose side they are on, because they do nothing but stand and watch what is going on around them as if they don't see a thing, as if nothing is happening, as if there is nothing going on.

They live according to the dictates of everyone's laws, and when the wars end this serves them well. There are many bystanders. They are the majority.

Blind observers are "ordinary" people who play for low stakes. They play it safe. They live their lives unimpeded. In war and skirting war, these blind observers look away with indifference and actively refuse to feel compassion; their self-deception is a hard shield, a shell in which, larvae-like, they wallow cheerfully.

They are everywhere: in the neutral governments of neutral countries, among Allies, in occupied countries, in the majority, in the minority, among us. Bystanders. That is who we are.

For sixty years now these blind observers have been pounding their chests and shouting, *We are innocent because we didn't know!*, and with the onset of new wars and new troubles, new observers crop up, armies of young and powerful bystanders are born, blindfolded, feeding on their innocence, on their indestructible compatibility, these yes-men, these enablers of evil.

Little stories are forever surfacing.

When Herbert von Karajan dies in 1989 at the age of eighty, Haya learns of his membership of the Nazi Party, which made it possible for him to conduct whatever orchestra he wanted. Although Karajan is banned from working after the war, the ban lasts only until 1948, after which the audiences flock to his performances again and applaud him with rapture. Ten years later, in 1958, Karajan is named lifelong conductor of the Berlin Philharmonic. His popularity soars and the soil soaks up the past like rain sinking into its belly.

Haya learns of Tom Stoppard, too. She hears that Stoppard was born Tomás Straussler in the town of Zlin, Moravia, where Bata sets up his famous shoe factory. She learns that until 1999 Tom Stoppard has no clue he is Jewish; then (by chance) he finds out that he is. Tomás' father Eugene Straussler works at the factory hospital as a physician. Immediately after the German occupation of Czechoslovakia, in 1939, Mr Bata decides to save his employees, including the physicians, by sending them off to the branch offices he owns all over the world. The Straussler family relocate to Singapore, but before the Japanese occupation, Marta Beck (Straussler by marriage) leaves with her two sons and goes first to Australia, then to India, while Eugene Straussler boards a ship full of refugees somewhat later. The Japanese shell his ship and with it sinks Eugene. In India, Marta Straussler meets a British officer by the name of Stoppard who asks her to marry him. He gives her boys his last name and together they return to his homeland, England, where they live happily ever after, as if their earlier life had never happened, as if there had never been a family, a war, camps, another language, memories, not even a little Czech love. In 1996 Marta Beck (Straussler by marriage, Stoppard by marriage) dies, and at that moment Tomás, no longer a boy, born Straussler, re-born Stoppard, starts digging through his past now that he is tired of writing plays or now that his inspiration has dried up – who knows? – and time unfolds before him. In the Czech Republic Tomás learns that his grandfathers and grandmothers, uncles and aunts, cousins, all of them disappeared as if they had never lived, which, as far as he is concerned, they had not, and he goes back to his lovely English language and his one and only royal homeland, to sort through his impressions of this excursion into his own life.

Or Madeleine Albright, born in 1937 as Madlenka Jana Korbel, who also learns, with a sixty-year delay, that she is Jewish and that her grandfathers and grandmothers, her uncles and aunts, cousins, have disappeared as if they had never lived. Madeleine learns this only when she is contacted by the descendents of a Mr Nebrich, who, though never himself a member of the Nazi Party, lives comfortably throughout the war as a citizen of the Reich (a bystander) in a spacious and luxurious flat in the heart of Prague, at Hradčanski Náměstí 11. Madeleine doesn't learn she is Jewish even when her father Josef Korbel returns to Prague in 1945, after having fled to London in 1939. The new government gives Josef Korbel Mr Nebrich's expropriated flat with all the furniture, Persian carpets and paintings. Today Karl Nebrich, a citizen of Austria and a powerful industrialist, son of the bystander Nebrich, is accusing the late Josef Korbel of absconding with art worth millions of dollars, art that belonged to his by now late father, including a Tintoretto and an Andrea del Sarto, and then seeking political asylum in the United States for himself and his family.

Then there's the Red Cross, which helps the Nazis launder the money of their deported victims, and the Ford Motor Company, which spreads the infectious poison of anti-Semitism, and Singer, and Bayer, and Krupp, and Jena, and Agfa, I. G. Farben, Siemens, Bayer AG, B.M.W., Daimler-Benz, Volkswagen, there is no end to the list of firms and their owners who exploit starving camp internees for material gain, for the love of their homeland, before the Nazis say *This way to heaven, ladies and gentleman. This way to the showers.*

The Tedeschi family are a civilian family, bystanders who keep their mouths shut, but when they do speak, they sign up to fascism.

In Trieste, in September 1943, the new head of the S.S. police for the Adriatic Littoral, Gauleiter Odilo Globočnik,* lives at Via Nizza

---

* *Odilo Lotario Globočnik*, born in 1904 in Trieste to a Slovenian father (a Habsburg cavalry lieutenant who goes on to work as a postal clerk after the war) and a Hungarian mother. In 1923 his family moves from Trieste to Klagenfurt. In Austria in 1931, Odilo Globočnik becomes a member of the Nazi Party and in 1934 he joins the S.S. He takes an active part in forming Nazi cells throughout Austria before its annexation to Germany in 1938, and in 1936 becomes head of the Party for Carinthia. Before he comes to Trieste, he is one of the key people in an operation of vast proportions in which about two and a half million Polish Jews are murdered (Aktion Reinhard). Globočnik arrives in Trieste with a large team of "professionals", with a death squad that has already proved itself in exterminating the populations of Russia, Poland and Germany, as well as in the death camps – Belzec, Sobibor and Treblinka. In 1943, ninety-two members of the Einsatzkommando Reinhard are stationed in Trieste, including a large number of Ukrainian

21. Reichsführer-S.S. Heinrich Himmler, head, at the time, of the Gestapo and Minister of Internal Affairs, orders his friend Globočnik to push political, racial and anti-partisan repression throughout the district. Three doors away is Casa Germanica at Via Nizza 15, and there Globočnik, while waiting for the arrival of his new fianceé Lora Peterschinegg, who is president of the Carinthian League of German Girls (Bund Deutscher Mädel), enjoys the occasional black risotto, goulash with bread dumplings, or rabbit stew, takes in a nice film from time to time, and jokes with the servants, because Globočnik is an unusual policeman, a mischievous policeman, fond of social life. Haya meets Globočnik in May 1944 when she comes to the Casa Germanica with Mr Kurt to watch the Austrian movie *Eine Frau wie Du*, and when Mr Kurt holds her hand in the dark, in secret.

S.S.-troops, both men and women. The Einsatzgruppen or Einsatzkommandos were special squads with the task of "fighting the enemies of the Reich and aiding the troops in combat", in other words, of occupying the territories that had been conquered, to squelch all rebellion and exterminate the non-Aryan population.

The Einsatzgruppen came under the administration of R.u.S.H.A., the Central Department for Security of the Reich (the Reichssicherheitshauptamt), which came, in turn, under the supervision of the Ministry of Internal Affairs, with the Reichsführer of the S.S. and Ministry, Heinrich Himmler, at its head. While in Lublin, in Poland, Globočnik lives in a luxurious villa quite lavishly. He is remembered not only for his monstrous murders of unfathomable proportions but also for his campaign to amass astonishing quantities of stolen and confiscated property from the "undesirable" population living in the occupied territories. Their property is then catalogued and listed in detail, ranging from items such as fountain pens, rings and women's opera glasses, to apartment buildings and factories, the value of which reaches 178 million Reichsmarks. All the stolen goods on the road to Berlin pass through Lublin, and some are warehoused at Trieste harbour. In late 1943, 667 containers, each holding between five and eight cubic metres, wait in Trieste for detailed cataloguing and listing at precisely the time Globočnik is staying at Via Nizza. On 31 May, 1945, near Weisensee in Carinthia, Globočnik is arrested by the British Army. Two hours later he commits suicide by swallowing a cyanide capsule.

Haya cannot remember the house in which she lives at the time. Some details she has no recollection of, while others she recalls clearly. The winter of '43 and '44 is cold and snowy, a harsh winter, that much Haya remembers. In February 150 grams of cooking salt is distributed per person, and one Wednesday she goes to get cheese with her coupons from the 243 series, and buys a piece of Gorgonzola for 18 lire, Provolone for 19 lire and Montenara for 20 lire. This she remembers. In fact, Haya remembers that February clearly. Ada's friend Lucia de Martin receives 8,000 lire from Mussollini in gratitude for bearing and raising fourteen sons, of whom four are fighting at the front, one is a prisoner of war with the British, one is unfit for work because he suffers from war-induced trauma, and the other sons are in the Fascist Night Guard (the Isonzo Istituto de Sorveglianza Notturna, Corso Verdi 28). Haya remembers how a shipment of cooking oil comes in, with a decilitre allotted per person, per month, and tomato paste, 50 grams each. She recalls that the theatre season is lyrical. At the Teatro Verdi they give *Aida*, *La Traviata*, *Rigoletto*, *The Barber of Seville* and *Carmen*, sung by Favero, Malipiero, Casteliani and Filipeschi; she goes to *La Traviata*, after which she cries in her cold bed until dawn for altogether different reasons, not the least operatic. She remembers the curfew from 10 p.m. to 5.30 a.m. and how she hurries home . . . She remembers how the whole family fear thieves and Tito's partisan bandits, bandits most of all. Haya doesn't know how the Germans occupied Gorizia, because at the time, in September 1943, she was not living in Gorizia, so this is not her concern. The cinemas are working: Cinema Teatro Vittoria, Cinema Savoia, Cinema Moderno and Cinema Italia. All of them are owned by Gaier and Gnot, and they show the latest hits, Italian and German, whichever. Gale-force winds howl, the snows pile up, and when she closes her shop, the tobacco shop, the stationery shop, whatever, there at the intersection of Seminario and Ascoli, the shop where her mother worked twenty years before, though the owner is no longer Zora Hochberger, who got lost along the way, but Caterina Cecotti, when Haya shuts up shop, she plunges, bundled like a Russian countess, through the dreamy white silence, into worlds which, she already knows, will elude her grasp. Oh, yes, she remembers, she remembers, and even when she doesn't, here at her feet in the red basket are all manner of old programmes and tickets, two for some shows, one for others, big and little colour posters and black-and-white posters, photographs of movie stars, a coaster or two from the La Perugina sweet shop, all of it arranged for old age, for memories, which now that Haya rummages through them, seem to be porous memories, hollow and spent.

Ah, Kristina Söderbaum, so golden-haired, blue-eyed and virtuous, the perfect incarnation of Aryan femininity in *La Città d'Oro* (*Die Goldene Stadt*), so cruelly punished for a small digression from the "natural" female environment, like Haya, isolated, rejected, abandoned, broken, because of dreams of another life. Oh God.

Haya knows nothing of Kristina Söderbaum, born in Stockholm in 1912, except that Kristina Söderbaum is beautiful the way she, Haya, would like to be beautiful and that Kristina is most certainly as happy and famous as she, Haya, would like to be happy and famous, or maybe only happy, that year, 1943, in her little Gorizian existence, built on the most ordinary of lives. Why should Haya back then, in 1943, have known that Kristina  Söderbaum was starring in bad Nazi films, some of them shorts, others feature-length, all of them moralizing Nazi films of the Third Reich? Haya did not go to see the anti-Semitic historical melodrama *Jud Süss*, because when it was released she was in Valona, and the movie *Jud Süss* did not come to Valona; no, definitely not, because had the anti-Semitic historical melodrama been on the repertoire of the Valona cinema she, Haya, would definitely have gone to see it. And Haya doesn't read the autobiography, Kristina Söderbaum's autobiography, *Nichts bleibt immer so*, in which she counsels people to change, to move forward in life, especially after they have done their patriotic duty, made their patriotic efforts, no matter what these efforts might be, no matter how little, innocent and artistic, such as, for example, acting in the movies. Haya does not read this autobiography written much later, in 1983; in fact, after 1943, Haya no longer keeps track of Kristina Söderbaum's life story, because after 1943 she gets her own life, a life altogether different from the life she had dreamed of. And when Haya learns, in 2001, already moored in her Gorizia outward calm, paralysed by her wait, which has been eating at her just as rust or salt eat little holes, soundlessly, in base metals, so, when from a German newspaper (she still reads the German papers) Haya learns that Kristina Söderbaum has died as an accomplished fashion photographer, that the post-war trial of her husband and director Veit Harlan has been completely forgotten, she merely rocks a bit harder, a little nervously in her rocking chair, *One more yellowed page of history*, she says, and that's that.

But when, sitting under a hood dryer having her hair done at Marisa's styling salon in 1973, Haya reads in a magazine that Hungarian-German-American diva Käthe von Nagy, born in Subotica in 1904, had died of cancer at the age of 69 in California, she lets out a brief glassy cry *Oh Käthe!* In her memory, there at the base of her skull, a long-preserved image, all fashioned of dreams – shatters.

Kristina Söderbaum

Kristina Söderbaum was going to be the model for the famous "disinfected rubber doll in natural size" to be manufactured by Franz Tschakert and Company, the birth of which is the brainchild of Reichsführer-S.S. Heinrich Himmler, fanatic Catholic and poultry farmer, in order to preserve the health of his potent soldiers, so that they do not mate with the "infectious female herds" while dreaming far from home of their stolid and fertile spouses, who never unbraid the braids coiled around their ears, even when their legs are spread, so they won't mess up their *Schneckenfrisure*. *The doll could just as well be a brunette,* suggests the Dane, S.S. physician Olen Hannussen, and psychiatrist Dr Rudolf Chargeheimer exclaims, *Of course! What matters is that the doll offers our soldiers relief, because struggle and only struggle is their goal!* So playful Käthe von Nagy enters the competition with Kristina Söderbaum, except that Käthe von Nagy says *Out of the question. I am not giving my face away to anyone.* So it is that athletics stars, Olympic medallists Wilhelmina von

Bremen and Annette Walter, are ultimately selected. S.S. physician Joachim Mrugowsky is withdrawn from the Geheime Reichssache, the project cloaked in the highest level of *secrecy,* because he is off voluntarily to do the most important task of all – running medical experiments on prisoners from various concentration camps. Later, in 1947, he goes, though not voluntarily, to Nuremberg, where he is condemned (nevertheless) to die. When Mrugowsky leaves the project, the Dane Hannussen exclaims, *But, no! Certainly not beauties! The doll must in no way supplant the honourable mother and the wife, the protectress of family sanctity, the family hearth, the angel of our tomorrows! When a soldier makes love to Borghild* (is the doll called Borghild because she is female cyborg Hilda?), *when a soldier copulates with Borghild, this has nothing to do with love! Borghild will have a boyish haircut – she is part and parcel of our armed forces. She is a field whore, not the Mother of our Homeland.* Borghild is to be produced in three types: Type A (5'6"), Type B (5'9") and Type C (5'11"). They decide to start serial production with Borghild B first, but the members of the project are of two minds as to Borghild's breasts. The S.S. favours them round and full, while Dr Hannussen says, *I want little tits in a rosehip shape; tits that fit snugly in the hand.* Hannussen prevails. In September 1941 Borghild B is born, a Nordic type *par excellence.* The première of Borghild in Berlin is greeted with enthusiasm by S.S. officials, and Himmler immediately orders fifty.

Terrible things happen, however, on the Eastern front, and the Borghilds never reach the soldiers. The only Borghild throughout the war is the prototype, left to languish in the office of her father Franz Tschakert, without satisfying a single lusty soldier. Then, in February 1945, Borghild disappears in the rubble of Dresden.

Going back to the 1930s in Berlin, at Giesebrechtstrasse 11, a fabled (and swanky) brothel run by Madame Kitty Schmidt, known as Salon Kitty, is working flat out. Foreign diplomats and the cream of German public, quasi-social life stop in at Salon Kitty: bankers, industrialists and politicians. Discretion is guaranteed, the services are first class, and the prices are out of this world. But Hitler grows ever more powerful and Kitty Schmidt gets nervous. By 1939 Salon Kitty is no longer frequented by refined Jewish businessmen, because the Brownshirts are beating up the refined Jewish businessmen, shutting down their companies, destroying their property, and then, rough and ready, sweaty and drunk, they come barging into Kitty's to "get relief". The police are running raids more often. Kitty is no fool. Kitty is, in fact, alarmed, and her business losses mount. Through Jews who are leaving Germany, and whom Kitty Schmidt is secretly helping to escape, she transfers her considerable takings to British banks and on 28 June, 1939, she leaves Berlin, meaning to join the riches that await her in London. But the Gestapo functions without a hitch. Kitty Schmidt arrives at the German-Dutch border, where she is immediately arrested by members of the *secret* police and taken straight to Walther Schellenberg, cunning and powerful head of the Sicherheitsdienst, the State counterespionage service, later a major general of the Waffen-S.S. and one of the organizers of the hunt for the Red Orchestra Soviet spy group. They introduce the 57-year-old madam Kitty Schmidt to the darkness of the infamous Prinz Albrechtstrasse, where Walther Schellenberg shoves a fat file under her nose that bulges with her subversive and illegal activities. *Now take a look, dear Kitty*, Walther says. *These accusations guarantee you an unlimited amount of time at some cosy concentration camp. But*, Walther Schellenberg continues, *if you do something for us, perhaps there is something we can do for you.*

Come on, forget those dolls, forget the Borghilds, chuckles S.S.-Gruppenführer Reinhard Heydrich, organizer of the "Night of the Long Knives" and the brain behind the Einsatzgruppen, chairman of the conference at Wannsee, later known as the Butcher of Prague, who at this juncture is head of the S.S. Rasse- und Siedlungshauptamt (R.u.S.H.A.), the race and settlement office, transformed as it was from an unprepossessing institution into a powerful organization wielding authority over a broad network of informants with thousands of dossiers on Communists, unionists, social democrats, on rich industrialists, Jews, even members of their own Nazi Party and S.A. (Sturmabteilung) henchmen. Reinhard Heydrich, the reclusive sadist, accomplished gymnast, skilled fencer, fearless pilot, is raised in high society in a family of musicians and artists. *Forget the dolls!* exclaims Heydrich. *We have genuine, first-class ladies ready to give their all for their homeland!* After the war, while in prison, Walther Schellenberg pens his memoirs, which he calls *Labyrinth*, and in which he asserts that "their" women, who worked at Kitty's, were qualified and cultivated ladies from the Berlin *demi-monde*, but that there were others, too, from the cream of German society, women prepared to serve their homeland without reservation. On account of his liver cancer, Schellenberg is released from prison after serving two years of a six-year sentence, and in 1952 he dies in Turin, convinced that he has been one of the most successful spies of all time.

The war is fast approaching. Information leaks now and then, with wine and beautiful women, in the throes of coital passion, all sorts of things slip out. So Reinhard orders Walther: *Put pressure on Kitty Schmidt*. Kitty Schmidt hands over her famous house of ill repute to the Reichssicherheitshauptamt and signs a *secret* statement, according to which she will ask no questions and do whatever she is told. She also signs that she understands, should she fail to obey, that they will execute her immediately. And so, although prostitution is expressly banned, or rather strictly forbidden, workmen move into the house at Giesebrechtstrasse 11, following Walther Schellenberg's orders. A complete refurbishment ensues; a new, more beautiful, luxurious, perfect brothel is built; a high-class whorehouse for V.I.P.s and spies. All the rooms, from the corridors to the boudoirs on the third floor of the building at Giesebrechtstrasse 11 have double walls into which surveillance equipment is installed, and from it hidden cables run down to a bricked-off portion of the cellar where there are five monitoring desks, each with two record turntables and wax discs spinning on them, which means that conversations from ten rooms can be recorded on those wax discs simultaneously.

Then S.D.-Untersturmführer Karl Schwartz sets out to snare personnel. These unprecedented raids on whorehouses, nightclubs and streets corners multiply. Young women are pulled aside and grilled in a rigorous selection process. Doctors, psychiatrists, linguists and university professors all help Schwartz whittle his shortlist of ninety breathtakingly beautiful potential "activists" down to twenty first-class women. Under lock and key for seven weeks in a sealed-off wing of the Sonthofen Officers' Academy, amid thick forests, small lakes and natural wonders, which they have no chance to appreciate because of the snow, surrounded by fresh air they have no time to enjoy, the beauties spend their nights engaged in a fundamental re-education. After gruelling training in foreign languages, marksmanship and unarmed combat; after instruction in politics and ideology, and courses in international and domestic economics; after the study of *secret* codes and cyphers, and memorizing countless charts of military insignia, uniforms and decorations, twenty peerless Nikitas of Nazism and counter-intelligence are born, *o tempora! o mores!* R.u.S.H.A. finally inserts them into the redecorated Salon Kitty in March 1940, and they write reports after every instance of sexual intercourse, unaware that they, too, are being recorded.

Madame Schmidt receives her final instructions. *Carry on as before*, Schwartz tells her, or was it Schellenberg, either way. *Welcome all your old customers. Keep on your existing girls. But every so often we will send along special guests*, might this be Schwartz speaking? *On no account are you to introduce them to one of your regular girls. Show them this album of twenty girls,* Schwartz, apparently, says.

When they choose their lady friend, phone for her. She will arrive in ten minutes. You will not discuss their clients with these girls, and they will leave immediately after the special guest of yours, of ours, has left the building.

How will I know this is a special guest? asks Madame Kitty, because she can barely wait for work to begin again.

Our guests will use the codeword "I come from Rothenburg", Schwartz says, or was it Schellenberg?

Where is Rothenburg? asks Kitty Schmidt.

Schellenberg immediately reminds Kitty Schmidt of the *secret* agreement she signed, and Kitty Schmidt no longer asks questions, she just coordinates the work and feigns naïveté. A soldier who is genuinely from Rothenburg shows up once at Salon Kitty. He is no special guest, but this soldier receives first-class sexual services with the lady listed in the album as Number 7, and though the soldier from Rothenburg does climax, he gives away no information to anyone, he merely climaxes as he never has; and even after the magnificent orgasm, while he sips champagne, nibbles caviar and whispers foolish promises in the ear of beauty Number 7, he betrays no secrets, because he has none to betray, but the wax discs in the cellar spin, around they spin, recording only moans. Until late 1942 Kitty is visited by various prominent people, domestic and foreign powermongers: Count Galeazzo Ciano, Joachim von Ribbentrop, and their Spanish colleague, Minister of Foreign Affairs Ramón Serrano Súñer, then S.S.-Major-General Sepp Dietrich, a particularly demanding guest who asks for all twenty girls at once for a party, a huge orgy; the cables on the "bugs" are red hot from his sexual potency and physical stamina. The confidential staff in the cellar are astonished and agitated. The only time the recording and listening equipment is turned off is during Reinhard Heydrich's regular, in fact, frequent "tours of inspection". Spies stop in at Salon Kitty, such as Roger Wilson, a British spy who gives his name as Ljubo Kolčev, a staff member at the Bulgarian Embassy. He happens to trip over a surveillance cable while workmen for the secret service are running it from the cellar of Giesebrechtstrasse 11 to the offices of the main staff of the Sicherheitsdienst (S.D.) on Meinekestrasse, in the close vicinity of the building where Nobel Prize winner Imre Kertész happens to live today, a man whose fate was probably tailored by Eichmann in the mid-1940s right there at Meinekestrasse. Upon seeing other things besides sex going on at Salon Kitty, Wilson, the British spy, *secretly* introduces his own secret British service of counter-espionage. Forget poor Borghild. *Those were the days, my friend.* In 1940 alone, more than 10,000 men take the stairs up to the third floor of Number 11 on Giesebrechtstrasse in Berlin. In just one month there are more than 3,000 orgasmic sessions recorded. But as time passes there are more and more special guests; they outnumber the ordinary clients, and the "special ladies" work full steam, spending more time at Madame Kitty's parlour. They drink more, report less, discipline dwindles in the sexual headquarters of counter-intelligence, the Gestapo send in additional quantities of food and drink. This all costs a pretty penny – there's a war on – and Heydrich's dissatisfaction grows. In July 1942 a bomb falls on the building on Giesebrecht-strasse, and the Gestapo wash their hands of the operation. The bugging apparatus is hastily removed. Kitty and all the girls, the special girls whose golden carriages have overnight turned to pumpkins, and the ordinary Cinderellas who have been with her for years, set up shop on the ground floor of the building and go on working. Until her death in 1954 Kitty never breathes a word about the entire operation. Twenty-five thousand recorded discs in the Gestapo archive mysteriously disappear after the Russians enter Berlin, and word has it that they end up at Stasi headquarters, and the war waged via cunts proves yet again to be without effect.

Ah, yes, Haya also remembers Marika Rökk, the Hungarian, who conquers the great compact heart of Nazi Germany in *Die Frau meiner Träume*, *Leichte Kavallerie* and *Der Bettelstudent*; who dances and sings and acts in the movies until the 1960s, when she does the same in theatres here and there, everywhere, but the troupes with which Marika Rökk performs do not tour Gorizia, and all Haya is left with is a poster from 1944 and a tinge of melancholy when she

hears over the local Gorizia news of
Marika Rökk's fatal heart attack
at some point in 2004, by which
time Marika Rökk is well into her
nineties. She takes with her to
eternity the jubilee Bambi Award
1948 and the jubilee Bambi Award
1998, named after the much-loved
book by Felix Salten, born Jewish as

Sigmund Salzman, who begins his career as a writer by sending
poems, letters, stories and essays to several Viennese newspapers,
using an array of pseudonyms. *Bambi*, the book of Haya's and Nora's
childhood, is a big hit when it comes out in Vienna in 1923, and for a
decade and more children are crazy about *Bambi*, but it is suddenly
banned in 1936, because the Nazis decide it sends the younger
generation all sorts of terrible messages, and no filthy Jew is going
to stir up their fount of life. So *Bambi* was not a childhood favourite
for Haya's sister Paula and her brother Orestes, who listen instead
to the tales of Snow White, Cinderella and Little Red Riding Hood,
because these are enduring stories, written by brothers whose last
name is Grimm (not someone whose surname is Salzman), boys of
fine, pure blood. This Salten is a prickly fellow. In 1902 he riles the
public with his *in memoriam* to Emile Zola, and in 1910 he ruffles the
feathers of the townspeople of Vienna when he criticizes the city's
recently deceased, beloved mayor of many years Dr Karl Lueger,
a member of the Christian Social Party and a flagrant anti-Semite, a
favourite of Hitler's, whose bronze statue stares straight into Café
Prückel, where celebrated cabaret artists – Jews – performed in the
cellar before they were sent off to the camps, and whose ring road,
the Dr-Karl-Lueger-Ring, still encircles the heart of old Vienna.

So it is that Marika Rökk goes off into oblivion with an award
for life's work; for her contribution to the German film industry. It is
not important, concludes Haya. Chaos rules everywhere, regardless.

Then there is María Mercader in the film *Finalemente soli*, and
Doris Duranti as Contessa Castiglione, and Ernst von Klipstein,

whom Haya doesn't like much because of the long face, and the celebrated Margit Dayka in that movie, what was it called? in which she plays an orphan who learns when she grows up that she is probably Jewish, so she cannot marry her boyfriend, who, like all those actors, is tall and fair-skinned and healthy and strong and has gleaming white teeth, and she loves him so much, and he is forbidden from loving any Jewish woman, no matter what she looks like, even though there are blonde Jews who are tall and healthy, with teeth every bit as white, but there is no chance, absolutely out of the question, and then the girl, Haya thinks the name was Rozsi, yes, this Rozsi played by Margit Dayka plans to kill herself, but everything turns out fine in the end, because it transpires that Roszi is *actually not Jewish after all*, so she can freely marry her beloved. Such a tender film gives Haya hope for a more beautiful life on those bleak nights in Gorizia. In 1944 Haya is dreaming about the future, sometimes while under the covers, sometimes in the darkness of half-empty cinemas; while up there, on the silver screen, which grows and spreads in the dark, stare countless penetrating blue eyes, men's and women's eyes, and she looks back at them, and observes all those mother-of-pearl complexions, the wavy hair, and follows the valiant destinies, Lord, what a world of enchantment in the middle of little occupied Gorizia, in mid-winter, oh Lord, with all of them here it is impossible to be alone.

Meanwhile, neighbours are disappearing.

Francesco Bevk (who lived for a time at Via Montesanto 26) *is no longer around,* says Amalia Valich, new owner of the building, and Ada cannot find his children's book, the one in Slovenian, and she would really like to find a copy, because now that she is drinking grappa and Strega more often and hiding it less, so much so that even spraying her mouth with cheap perfume doesn't mask it, now, when things are as they are, in war and poverty, the voices of her ancestors, the poems her mother Marisa used to read to her, flit through her thoughts, and it happens that Ada lies there for hours, overcome and whimpering, and then, dishevelled and snivelling, she natters on about things no-one understands . . .

Nemiren sem, ko voda, ki šumi,
razbit ko slap, ki v brezdno moč prši
in sam si šteje kaplje bolečine,
ki padajo vse dni, vse dni . . .*

Today in Nova Gorica, something Haya knows, the central square is named after France Bevk, and there is a statue to France Bevk there, and the library there is also called France Bevk Knjižnica.

Costatino Costatini, the architect who used to live at Via P. Diacono 51, has apparently moved away somewhere, Florian Tedeschi says one morning, sweetening his coffee with condensed milk, which he gets through a contact, though in limited quantities, fifty grams per person every month. *I was thinking about building a partition to divide the children's rooms.*

Carlo Hakim de Medici, a sculptor who lives at Via Petrarca 3, does not mange to finish work on the tombstone for Ada's father, Bruno Baar; at the clinic of Ada's and Letizia's family doctors, Luigi Bader and Glauco Bassi, the patients are received by some new doctors. Giovanni and Luigi Fuchs, the goldsmiths at Via Rastello 28, do not seem to be opening their shop.

Enough! says Florian Tedeschi and turns up the radio, because it is 2 p.m. and they are broadcasting the *giornale radio in lingua tedesca* on 263.2 megaherz.

Life knits circular pathways. It submerges in a repetitiveness without which it would die. Like her mother Marisa twenty years ago and more, Ada bakes crescent rolls and macaroons, and takes them to the club at the Aosta barracks on Via Trieste, although the image is a little blurred, because Ada's hair doesn't ripple; Ada has

---

* I am restless like murmuring water,
Shattered like a waterfall spraying chasmward its force,
And numbers to itself droplets of pain,
That drip every day, every day.

limp hair with no shine and Ada does not sway her hips provocatively, and her shoes are old and all of it, all the palaver that for twenty years has stretched like thin, sticky dough, the smiles drawing out the lips, the wait for life to begin, all this is beating Ada down, she doesn't feel like doing much any more, there is no music in the house, no-one sings, not even Gigli. Colonel Scharenberg, commander of the German forces in Gorizia, awaits Ada with a smile, slips his hand into the napkin-covered basket, as if preparing for seduction, stuffs two *rošćići* cookies into his mouth, and says *Danke* as he chews. The sweet crumbs dance mischievously on his whiskers. Ada points to them and says, *Staubzucker*. The same way each time.

Transports have been running for a long time now.

Quietly, almost conspiratorially, the freight trains run through Gorizia at night, when the moon draws a black veil over its face. Gorizia is blocked. One can enter or exit only with special permission from Gauleiter Globočnik, which means almost never. The names of the residents are put on lists. There must be order. Colonel Wellhausen, commander of the operative zone, issues a directive on 23 September, 1943, according to which all who have moved to Gorizia since 8 September must leave.

The station slumbers by day and by night it dies in the phantasmal light of the lanterns of the train dispatchers, which sway, so everything on the platform looks as if it is dancing, the tracks, the train cars, the hanging baskets with flowers, as if in a wild, musicless *Tanz* in which outlines twist and fracture, sliding along the entire fenced-in area, which turns into a gigantic human face contorted with pain, shedding no tears.

Transport 3

The train leaves Cairo Montenotte camp (Savona-Liguria) on 8 October. It arrives in Gusen on 12 October, 1943, and in Mauthausen on 23 January, 1944, whence it departs the next day for Auschwitz. On that train there are 999 people of Italian nationality from Gorizia, Trieste and Kopar.

Transport 48

The train leaves Trieste on 31 May, 1944 – destination Dachau. It stops along the way in Gorizia and Udine, where new internees are boarded: civilians, anti-fascists who have been arrested, partisans and Italian soldiers. The train arrives in Dachau on 2 June, 1944, and there are between 342 and 352 "travellers" on board. Ten wagons leave Trieste, and the German authorities add another eight in Udine.

Transport 58

The convoy leaves Gorizia on 27 June, 1944, and arrives in Dachau three days later. There are 194 people on board; 190 of them reach the destination.

Transport 79

The convoy leaves Trieste on 29 August, 1944. It stops in Gorizia, where new internees and prisoners are loaded on board. Number of deportees: 289.

Transport 87

The convoy leaves Trieste on 2 October, 1944 – and arrives in Dachau three days later. It stops in Udine and Gorizia to take on more people. Number of deportees: 289.

Transport 101

The convoy leaves Trieste on 15 November, 1944, and arrives in Dachau on 17 November. It stops in Udine and Gorizia to take on more people. Number of deportees: 42.

Transport 109

The convoy leaves Trieste on 8 December, 1944. It arrives in Dachau on 11 December, 1944. The train stops in Gorizia and Udine, where additional deportees are boarded. Four hundred and fifty people arrive in Dachau. There are 200 prisoners in the convoy from the Trieste Coroneo, as well as a group of Slovenes and Croats under

S.S. guard. The convoy leaves Gorizia at about four o'clock in the morning.

Transport 120

The train leaves Trieste on 2 February. It arrives in Mauthausen on 7 February, 1944. New internees and prisoners are loaded on board in Udine and Gorizia. Number of deportees: 365. In this convoy is the youngest deported resident of Gorizia, three-month-old Bruno Faber. He is killed at Auschwitz on 26 February, 1944.

Of the 123 convoys that leave from Italy for the Nazi camps, 69 of them depart from Trieste, right here, next to Gorizia, practically in its immediate vicinity, not counting the 30 convoys that travel to the forced labour camps. More than 23,000 former soldiers are distributed throughout the camp factories in which they are bringing to life the light and heavy industry of the Reich. By mid-1944 half a million Italians are working for the German war machine.

The transports continue to run until the end of February 1945. The army and police of the Republic of Salò puppet state and the Third Reich transport to the concentration camps about 40,000 Italians, of whom 10,000 are Jews and 30,000 are partisans, anti-fascists and workers arrested after the massive strikes in March 1944. Of the 40,000 deported, 36,000 men, women and children are murdered or die.

So, this is the winter of 1944. Battles flare around Gorizia. A civilian is killed now and then by a German bullet. From time to time Nazis march small columns of dangerous partisan bandits through town, probably to a firing squad, or prison, or the former rice mill, but these are isolated incidents, or so Haya believes since she reads no newspapers. Had she read them, she would have learned that these are "great war victories for the Nazi Army in Gorizia", because the Trieste paper *Il Piccolo* has a special page entitled "Cronaca di Gorizia", and aside from that *Il Piccolo* has a local editorial board in Gorizia on the 1st floor at Via Crispi 9, where one can go to hear the latest news, or even to *bring in* an interesting news item, which the police are constantly urging citizens to do, to bring news in, to rat on each other. Haya, therefore, has no idea what is going on around her. While it snows outside, and while she waits for customers to turn up, she works on maths problems and keeps track of changes in the cinematic repertoire.

The high commissar of the Adriatisches Küstenland, Gauleiter Friedrich Rainer, has big plans for "his" district. After the war all of Friuli province is to flourish. Trieste, this "little Berlin" at the heart of Rainer's future provincial paradise, is to spring to life, it will awaken and take flight (within limits). The artists and writers will come flocking back, except the Jews or decadents. The port within the structure of the new German empire will be a pure and virtuous port of a new age. The new man will work there in earnest. He will be supernatural, strong, robust. Rainer will not be able to separate all the ethnic chaff from the golden grain of his imperial periphery. The Slavonic, Slovenian and Croatian corncockle will linger; the Italian Friulians will linger; the rather crude Ćići and Morlaks, with their unfortunate allies; the belligerent Cossacks, whom Gauleiter Rainer has compelled to come from the East, promising them the *Heimat* they never had, their own little Cossackland at the foot of the Carinthian alps in the rugged and impoverished area around Tolmezzo and the River Tagliamento, to which they drag their horses and their tents, their women and their children, until 1945 when nearly all 50,000 of them are repatriated to the Soviet Union and killed, without succeeding, as Gauleiter Rainer had hoped, in defending the Friuli-Venezia Giulia province from the incursions of crude partisan bands, unbridled bandits and infidels. But in 1944 Rainer is hard at work building a compact Furlanentum, carving out a Furlani nation in which Trieste is to become part of German territory, even though the entire province, this special sunny oasis on the edge of the empire of *Mitteleuropa*, is tainted by the inferior Slavonic race, which, thank God, is in the minority. The workers need better living conditions, Rainer insists, so he is particularly attentive to them. Even Florian, who is selling umbrellas, is not so badly off. Perhaps that is why he doesn't complain. Rainer sees to it that

Italian and Slovenian workers have new (workers') clothing and new (workers') footwear, since they are soon to become German workers. The clothing and footwear the workers have been wearing make them look like tramps, and the workers are the heart and soul of his (Rainer's) project. Rainer has an almost communistic vision of how to set up his provincial realm. He establishes canteens and kitchens, *Werkküchen*, in which workers are to be given more generous and tasty portions than the rest of the non-working population, so they can bring verve and efficiency to their labours, with a song on their lips. Florian is satisfied. *These shoes are excellent,* he says, *though I am not fond of brown,* and he wears Rainer's workboots when he has to and when he doesn't, at home, for instance, while listening to Rainer's radio broadcasts, while leafing through Rainer's propaganda newspaper, and while smoking Rainer's cheap cigarettes. *We're not so badly off,* Florian says then, *at least everyone has an umbrella.* The office for labour, at an order from Friedrich Rainer, introduces a special supply of cigarettes for Rainer's workers, because although some may claim that tobacco is not essential for life, as Rainer declares in his new newspaper, *Deutsche Adria-Zeitung*, cigarettes are certainly one of those little things that make our everyday life, especially this wartime travail of ours, more bearable, and bring it a touch of brightness, as Rainer says in *Deutsche Adria-Zeitung*. And aside from that, as a student of the Law, Rainer had undoubtedly come across the notion of *mens sana in corpore sano*, so he introduces numerous cultural and recreational activities, in factory halls as well as at stadiums, such as those *Werkskonzerte* of his that are held during lunch break, which all workers, the local managerial staff and representatives of the Nazi administration, are obliged to attend, charged with noting down who comes and who does not. Health matters. Gauleiter Friedrich Rainer knows that health is key: an ailing population becomes depressed and sluggish, productivity diminishes, and with it, patriotic fervour. That is why everywhere in "his" district Rainer has built playgrounds and parks. He organizes competitions and little local festivities, which are advertised along with the broadcast of marches and sentimental hits that alternate on the new hour-long local programme *Die Stunde der Friulaner*, so that the listeners can dream out their Austrian dreams and navigate the healing waters of saccharine nostalgia. Meeting the cultural needs of the working class is just as important as providing adequate compensation for human labour, Friedrich Rainer says in his *Deutsche Adria-Zeitung*, because man does not live by bread alone, Rainer says. Rainer's paper, the *Deutsche Adria-Zeitung*, is delivered regularly after 14 January, 1944, to Haya's tobacco shop and Haya takes the *Zeitung* home and Florian reads it, often aloud, so that everyone in the house can hear, so they will take note of what Rainer recommends and not forget their, his, Rainer's, German language. In order to secure peace among the civilians, for he has enough headaches with the partisans (Italian, Slovenian and Croatian), Rainer starts a local, separatist weekly called *La Voce di Furlania*, co-opts Slovenian and Croatian collaborationists, and re-opens the Slovenian schools, so the Tedeschi family get a free set of fourth grade textbooks for Orestes, over which Ada then pores, searching for (and not finding) the lost, distorted time of her mother Marisa (*neé* Brašić) and her grandmother Marija (*neé* Krapez). The final issue of *Deutsche Adria-Zeitung* comes out on Saturday, 28 April, 1945, but Haya doesn't open up her little shop that Saturday, because she is already touched by a fate from which, as Saba says, one does not die but loses one's mind instead.

If he were alive, Haya's grandfather Bruno Baar would probably have told her which of the Gorizia newspapers he read, what papers piled up in the house, which ones Marisa used to wash the windows or to wrap what was left of her set of drinking glasses as they got ready to evacuate the city, back in 1917. And Ada would be able to tell her, tell Haya, which magazines and newspapers she had sold at her tobacco shop before they left Trieste, before fascism dropped the curtain behind which it tapped out the first steps of its diabolic dance, still tentative at that point and with no musical accompaniment, the audience mostly sitting in the theatre and waiting (and finally watching) the beginning of the dramatic second act. But Haya did not ask, Haya does not ask, and Ada soon forgets not only her own life, but life in general.

Before the Great War they read Gaberšček's *Soča* and *Primorec* in Gorizia and Trieste. There is a political paper called *Gorica*, and *Primorski Gospodar*, and weeklies such as *Novi Čas* and *Goriški List*, and were she to poke around her grandfather Bruno's now abandoned wine cellar, Haya would find old issues of the monthly *Cvetje* among the dry barrels, with essays by Škrabec, the Franciscan monk, on the Slovenian language. She would find dusty bottles draped with sheets of paper from *Naši Zapiski* and *Veda*, crumpled vestiges, traces of a time that was only just birthing, as if that time were a premature infant which the war was compelling to rest, swaddled, waiting. And now here is another war, the campaigns follow one upon another like the seasons; the commands from invisible powers spurt in brief, sluggish sprays and well-worn history flows like lava down the streets and squares, seeping into rooms and turning people to stone. Like Trieste, Gorizia lives its maddened parallel lives again, careening along railway lines from which the rails have been stripped. In it, in that accursed blot on the three-way border, at the intersection of four languages and invisible pasts, carelessly buried, dispersed or swept aside like squandered alluvia, only occasionally does ordinary life gleam forth, like a flash from the sky that sticks to the windowpane and on it, dies.

The underground press printed illegally by the partisans is not, of course, delivered to Haya's tobacco shop, so as far as Haya is concerned that sort of press, anti-fascist, focused on national liberation, in Slovenian, Croatian and Italian, does not exist. Had she by chance stumbled upon papers such as those, she would have learned that the German Army was suffering losses, that the German generals were gradually losing their patience, and becoming more strict and brutal. She would have learned all sorts of things. She would have read about horrors, and her civilian life might have stepped out of the ordinary, or maybe not. In any case, for Haya the only newspapers are the official press, the papers read by the German soldiers and the Italian soldiers, and the other honest folk who don't ask about things that aren't their business. Nevertheless, throughout the Adriatisches Küstenland, all through the war, newspapers circulate, song books, dictionaries, children's picture books, poetry and prose, cranked out on Cyclostyle machines in *secret*, in homes, warehouses, bakeries, carpentry workshops, are distributed despite the life-threatening danger to all those who know of them and want to know. *Slovenski Poročevalec, Zakaj je Propadala Jugoslavija, Morje, Snežnik, Ljudska Pravica, Mladi Puntar, Mladina, Mladi Rod, Il Nostro Avvenire, Bollettino, Naša Žena, Il Lavoratore, Otroške Pesmi*, a whole library of another reality that always exists, everywhere, at every age and time.

Sometimes there is no running water in town, and sometimes the electricity goes out, but good Lord, things like that happen in peacetime, too. Haya's Aunt Letizia says that in October the previous year (in 1943, right?) she happened to be near the Casa di Cura Villa San Giusto and she saw the Germans firing at the train station, *for no particular reason, as if they were having a bit of a lark*, and she saw the large clock topple off the front of the building, and *time simply stood still*, and *time dies anyway during a war*, she says. *The heart of time beats in secret*, she says. *Time isn't going anywhere*, she says, so they don't need that clock up on the railway station building anyway. She says that she kept walking along the Corso and happened upon two Italian armoured vehicles that were shooting left and right, *like crazy*, Letizia says, *though there was practically no-one out on the street, only me with my five fresh eggs*, she says, and she saw another woman, *over there by the Parco della Rimembranza*, and how the woman did not have time to run into the nearest entranceway, because they shot her. Letizia's husband Parigi Puhaz says that on 22 September (he remembers exactly when) a shell hit the Braunizer house on Piazza Vittoria, and the next day one hit the Vittoria cinema. Four people were wounded, he remembers that precisely. Four. Then he says, *You, Haya, you don't have to see every single show*. After that short conversation Haya's uncle Parigi Puhaz goes to Vienna, where he dies in a flower shop in 1945, no-one ever finds out how. Florian listens to these and many of the other little stories that find their way into the dining room of the Baar family home, where the Puhaz family and the Tedeschi family are now living. He listens to these stories, these tales, fabrications which take a seat, uninvited, at their table, while they eat their rationed meals, more often than not in silence.

Haya's brother Orestes, who turns ten in 1944, goes out with his pals and collects bits of shrapnel on the streets and in the parks, and already has an enviable collection of metal fragments, the exemplars of which he trades and hoards on a shelf in the kitchen in the large apothecary jar, the same jar in which Marisa used to keep her flour, but this shrapnel has nothing to do with what is real, these are just children's games, reason the members of the household.

In February 1944 Haya goes to see Mrs Donati, who sells "exclusive" caps and hats, *cappelli di lusso*, at *Grosso Valtz & Co.*, her fashion salon at Via Garibaldi 5, because Haya would like to replace her black knitted cap with a little blue hat, or maybe even a red one. There she runs into two ladies who are whispering while she tries on the hats in front of a mirror, and she overhears what they are saying, she can't help it. The older woman says that Rina Luzzatto, a teacher, has been forced, meaning prematurely, into retirement, which immediately reminds Haya of her school in Naples, but heavens, after all the times are grim, and she hears how *maestra Luzzatto* is in *un' stato deplorevolissimo*, because nearly all the Jews of Gorizia, or so says *maestra* Luzzatto, including her brother and some others from nearby towns, are arrested at first, because there are suspicions they are in league with the partisans, and then, on that terrible night of 23 November, 1943, they are thrown into cattle wagons headed for Auschwitz.

In February 1944 Haya has no idea about the terrible night of 23 November, 1943, because at that point she was not in Gorizia. Afterwards, while the war goes on, Gorizia shrinks, because of nights like that, turns into a tiny ball wrapped in a membrane of silence, and then oblivion settles over it like sodden snow.

But Haya remembers 18 March, 1944.

What does she remember?

It is a Saturday. The snow is melting. Spring is on its way. She goes to the Ospedale Civile for a check-up with Dr Boschetti, who says, *Everything is fine. Come back in a month.* Airplanes buzz over Gorizia at about eleven o'clock. At 11.30 the bombs begin to fall. Haya huddles under the counter in her tobacco shop.

At dinner Florian says, *At least one hundred and fifty people were killed.*

Orestes says, *Enzo blew up into thin air.*

Ada asks, *Enzo who?*

Enzo, my eight-year-old pal, says Orestes.

Enzo Vida. The son of that Gigette, daughter of Luigi Spanghero, Letizia says.

He is in the partisans, Florian says.

Then Orestes shouts, *Today I collected a whole pile of nifty shrapnel!*

Haya says nothing.

This is the day.

Yes, Gorizia lives a parallel life, parallel lives, fractured, schizoid, from the inside.

In 1991 Haya finds a book, *Un Altro Mare* by Claudio Magris, in her postbox, sent to her by Roberto Piazza, a former student of hers. Roberto Piazza writes that he wouldn't be surprised if she, Professor Tedeschi, has no memory of him, because he was an average student, in fact a poor mathematician, but that doesn't worry him at all. He, on the other hand, remembers his teacher, whom he hasn't thought of for years, probably because he was busy with other things that had nothing to do with mathematics. All the same, Roberto Piazza says, when he read the book he is sending her, his former maths teacher Haya Tedeschi, when he read the slender but powerful volume he is giving her, his former teacher, as a gift, through the mail, like this, it hit him that in all the five years she taught them (from 1971 to 1976, right?), she, their teacher Haya Tedeschi, never once spoke of the war, or of the people who disappeared in town during the war, World War Two, you know? writes Roberto Piazza. Also, he writes, he is surprised that she, their maths teacher, never spoke to them, her students, the class of 1971–76, of Renato Caccioppoli, the famous mathematician, especially since word got around school that she, Haya Tedeschi, attended the gymnasium in Naples at roughly the same time Caccioppoli was living there, in Naples, and that he was an anti-fascist, isn't that so? And the fascists arrested him and he had to hide out in an insane asylum, writes Roberto Piazza, but since she, their teacher was just an ordinary schoolgirl at the time, who maybe decided to become a mathematician later, you know, because of awkward things going on in her life, perhaps, you know, *maybe* it isn't so strange that she *doesn't seem* to have known anything about Professor Caccioppoli. He, writes Roberto Piazza, lives in Rome now where he works in graphics, in a manner of speaking – he is a graphic designer, and he is now working on the layout of a book about Gorizia's famous people, and so he came across names which none of his teachers at the Dante Alighieri Gymnasium had ever mentioned during his five years there from 1971 to 1976, you know, while he, Roberto Piazza, was going to the Gymnasium more or less every day, and, writes Roberto Piazza, he finds this very surprising. For instance, writes Roberto Piazza, only when he read the book he is sending her, her, his maths teacher, only when he read *A Different Sea*, *Un Altro Mare*, did he understand that there are threads interwoven in Gorizia, the beginnings of which are impossible to divine, threads that can no longer be disentangled, in whose snarl lies an entire cocooned history.

His uncle, Bruno Piazza, writes Roberto Piazza, escaped alive from the San Sabba rice mill, unlike thirty-three members of his, their, immediate and larger family, and they are Alceo Piazza, Antelo Piazza, Angelo Piazza, Anita Piazza, Bruno Piazza, Donato Piazza, Edvige Piazza, Elio Piazza, Elisa Piazza, Elvira Piazza, Emanuele Piazza, Fernanda Piazza, Giacomo Piazza, Gina Piazza, Gino Piazza, Giuseppe Piazza, Maria Luisa Piazza, Rachele Piazza, Regina Piazza, Sed Angelo Piazza, Sed Camilla Piazza, Sed Cesira Piazza, Sed Consola Piazza, Sed Costanza Piazza, Sed Emma Piazza, Sed Ester Piazza, Sed Eugenio Piazza, Sed Leda Piazza, Sed Marco Piazza, Sed Rosa Piazza, Sed Sara Piazza, Umberto Piazza, Virginia Piazza, who ended up at Auschwitz and Dachau, among them his grandfather, also Bruno Piazza, writes Roberto Piazza. I lay on the floor, on boards, as his uncle, Bruno Piazza, tells it, writes Roberto Piazza, and they beat me until I passed out. At night voices reached my cell, telling me what was happening, and horrible things were happening, someone on the other side of the wall whispered: I am buried alive, no air, thirsty, tonight they'll shoot me, Bruno Piazza says, but the next morning the man was *incinerated*, not shot, *incinerated*, Bruno Piazza says, as Roberto Piazza writes. Then a woman spoke up who said that every night they were shooting people in the back of the head, and after every shot the dogs barked something terrible, that was how they killed lots of partisans, but I got out, says his uncle Bruno Piazza, writes Roberto Piazza.

In the envelope are the names of about 9,000 Jews who were deported to Nazi camps between 1943 and 1945 or killed in Italy, writes Roberto Piazza. There are people from Gorizia, maybe his teacher remembers some of them, writes Roberto Piazza. On the list there are forty-four people with the last name Tedeschi: Ada Tedeschi, Ada Tedeschi, Adelaide Tedeschi, Adele Tedeschi, Adolfo Tedeschi, Alberto Sebastiano Tedeschi, Arrigo Tedeschi, Benvenuta-Ines Tedeschi, Bianca Tedeschi, Bice Tedeschi, Emanuele Amedeo Tedeschi, Emma Tedeschi, Emma Bianca Tedeschi, Ermenegilda Tedeschi, Ernesta Irma Tedeschi, Eugenia Tedeschi, Ezio Tedeschi, Francesca Tedeschi, Franco Tedeschi, Giacomo Tedeschi, Giacomo Tedeschi, Giacomo Tedeschi, Giacomo-Mino Tedeschi, Gino Tedeschi, Gino Tedeschi, Giorgio Eugenio Tedeschi, Giuliana Tedeschi, Gualtiero Tedeschi, Irene Tedeschi, Lidia Tedeschi, Lionello Tedeschi, Luciano Tedeschi, Mafalda Ida Tedeschi, Marco Tedeschi, Marisa Tedeschi, Natalia Tedeschi, Sabato Giuseppe Tedeschi, Salomone Tedeschi, Salvatore Tedeschi, Silvio Tedeschi, Umberto Tedeschi, Vittoria Tedeschi, Vittorio Tedeschi, Wanda Tedeschi, had his teacher, Haya Tedeschi, heard of some of these people? Had she known some of them? writes Roberto Piazza. Was his former teacher, Haya Tedeschi, aware of them? he enquires.

Since he is working on designing this book on famous Gorizians, writes Roberto Piazza, he thought of her as well, his teacher Haya Tedeschi, and he wants to take this opportunity to ask what the war years were like for her, his teacher, does she have any memories, and he would also like to ask her, the maths teacher from the Dante Alighieri Gymnasium in Gorizia, why she never took them in 1975 to visit the museum, which opened that year on the site where the San Sabba camp had been.

Roberto Piazza writes in detail to his former maths teacher from the Gorizia Dante Alighieri Gymnasium about the philosophy of Carlo Michelstaedter, though when she perused his little tractate in 1991 Haya Tedeschi hadn't understood what it was all for.

Michelstaedter came from a prominent Gorizia Jewish family, writes Roberto Piazza. He wanted to study mathematics in Vienna, but he went to Florence to study art history. She, his teacher Haya Tedeschi, must surely have heard of him, of Michelstaedter, writes Roberto Piazza. Today Carlo Michelstaedter is very popular, writes Roberto Piazza, he is even mentioned in the little Gorizia tour guides. He doesn't want to tire her with philosophy and Carlo Michelstaedter's biography, writes Roberto Piazza, but if she is interested in the life and philosophy of Carlo Michelstaedter, if she is interested in his paintings and poems, she will find plenty of material even in the modest Gorizia bookstores, he merely wants to remind her of the fate of his (Carlo's) mother Emma Luzzatto, the fate of his (Carlo's) sister Elda, the fate of his close friend Argia Cassini, to whom, in 1908, two years before he shoots himself with a pistol belonging to his friend Enrico Mreule, Carlo pens these verses in Piran

> *Parlarti? e pria che tolta per la vita*
> *mi sii, del tutto prenderti? – che giova?*
> *che giova, se del tutto io t'ho perduta*
> *quando mia tu non fosti il giorno stesso*
> *che c'incontrammo?*

While Argia Cassini, Argia Cassini the pianist, in love with Carlo Michelstaedter, plays, writes Roberto Piazza, Carlo paints her portrait, a portrait of Argia Cassini, and on the piano a crystal glass of Picolit rings, and their lips touch and touch the marzipan and blackberries nestled in a warm Gorizia pastry. Argia has thick dark hair, writes Roberto Piazza, and she is twenty-one, the same age as Carlo. Argia Cassini is in the convoy that takes Elda, Carlo Michelstaedter's sister, first to Mauthausen, then to Auschwitz, Roberto Piazza writes. When the Nazis arrest Argia Cassini and seize all of her property, writes Piazza, she entrusts her daughter forever to the care of her school and wartime friend Elsa Finzi. Roberto Piazza wishes to remind her, Haya Tedeschi, he writes, of her three compatriots, who were taken to Auschwitz that terrible night in November 1943, where Carlo's eighty-year-old mother Emma and his eldest sister Elda die almost as soon as they arrive, while the third, Argia Cassini, the pianist, dies a year later, writes Roberto Piazza, and he wants her, his former maths teacher, to look for Professor Verzegnassi (he believes the man lives at Via Giovanni 1, if he is still alive) to tell him that he can trust his former pupil Roberto Piazza and send him the drawing of Carlo's, which along with more of Carlo's writings Professor Verzegnassi managed to preserve, through the war, from the Nazis, who were bent on destroying what they called degenerate art, because Roberto needs the drawing for the book he is designing, and he will return it to him personally as soon as he comes up to Gorizia, and he will write to him himself, all he needs is his teacher's blessing, Roberto Piazza writes. He understands the fate of his teacher, Haya Tedeschi, and he urges her to comb through Carlo's thoughts on persuasion and rhetoric, because in them she may find respite from her nightmares, but, of course, he is not advising her to kill herself. Small towns always have a contingent of chronically unhappy people, writes Roberto Piazza, and hence the general atmosphere of unhappiness leads to numerous suicides to which the weather conditions also contribute. In small towns people are always inclined to suicide. All of them have the feeling they are suffocating, because they are not able in any way to alter the situation they find themselves in. Bernhard says so, too, writes Roberto Piazza. He, Roberto Piazza, agrees with Carlo Michelstaedter that human life is formed of remorse, a guilty conscience, melancholy, boredom, fear, rage and suffering, and that all man's endeavours show how much he, man, is a *passive* being who throughout his life re-works, revises and appends his own biography and the biographies of those around him, writes Roberto Piazza. Therefore he doesn't blame her, his former teacher, for not knowing who was doing what and who was doing the killing at the San Sabba camp, while she, Haya Tedeschi, was going to the cinema and engaging in lovers' trysts.

An infernal messenger flew just now along the avenue
to a chant of thugs; an orchestra pit,
firelit and arrayed with swastikas,
seized and devoured him, the windows,
shabby and inoffensive, though adorned
with cannon and war toys, are shuttered up,
the butcher who laid berries on the snouts
of his slaughtered goats has closed; the feast
of the mild murderers still innocent of blood
has turned into a foul Virginia reel of shattered wings,
larvae on the sandbars, and the water rushes in
to eat the shore and no-one's blameless any more.

So this is how Roberto Piazza wraps up his letter, with lines from Montale, as if she, Haya Tedeschi, doesn't get it. Long after the war, and until just a few years earlier, Haya Tedeschi had been reading all sorts of texts, even Michelstaedter; she read Heidegger and Wittgenstein; she studied the paintings of Kokoschka, Kirchner and Heckel, looking through those works for confirmation of her own rage at language, for her own revolt against the European logocentric tradition, which had proved to be deeply vacuous, if, indeed, vacuity has depth, seeking from these works endorsement for her campaign to confront language; out of many years of painful reckoning she emerged, faltering and mute, the loser. This much she sees. She is aware that her disdain for language subsides in a schism, much like a gaping wound in the middle of which swirls a terrifying silence, death transformed. Life is a delusion for those who function rhetorically, the scientist and merchant, the teacher, the priest and prophet, Michelstaedter says, and Haya agrees and wonders with him how to find again what has disappeared in the course of living, what has been lost, what perhaps never was, the *nothing* that begins to think, which says to itself *I have my inner being, which I do not know.*

When a spirit no longer finds its identity anywhere, when everything it knows as constant, enduring, all values in their outward form disappear, it searches for the sole surviving identity, for the *source* of all values, the key to all valency. If the experience of historical events is, in essence, the experience of the self, then to possess oneself means to possess everything, Michelstaedter says, and Haya concurs. But self-awareness is an illusion, elusive and impossible to attain. Self-awareness leads to self-destruction.

Haya senses that a little cemetery is sprouting in her breast with a jumble of tilting tombstones like the ones at the old Valdirosa burial ground; she feels as if the already rotten, damp and blackened crosses and faded stars are knocking against her ribs; *they are crowded*, the crosses, the stones, the stars seem to be growing in her breast, reaching her throat and choking her, so she says, *I'm having trouble breathing*. There is a need to look inside, set to rights the proliferating hotchpotch before it breaks through her armour, before she, like a gigantic hedgehog, continues along the paths of her every-day life, before this cemetery of hers in her breast collapses and in its place yawns a chasm at the bottom of which, in the dark, beats a tired heart. She can no longer say whose heart this is.

In 1991 Haya Tedeschi is already retired, but fully *in gamba*. She goes off for walks, because the walks shorten her wait. She listens to symphonic music, because symphonic music has no words and everything that has no words is fine with Haya Tedeschi. She plays with mathematical formulas, turns them around and shifts them, comes up with new ones, remembers old ones, tries to tailor a new language using symbolic language. *Words are quickly exhausted*, Haya Tedeschi says. *I no longer know what to do with them*, she says

> *Je suis né. Je suis né de l'ombre,*
> *je suis né dans l'ombre et mon désir*
> *fut longtemps qu'on ne m'arrache pas*
> *à l'ombre où je suis*

and says out loud the words of Pierre Goldman as if they are hers. *One should speak with the hands, using the language of the deaf and dumb*, Haya says, *there would be fewer misunderstandings, the messages would be short and terse*, she says, and starts moving her twisted fingers, gesticulating with her wrinkled palms as if shooing or summoning shadows. Then she laughs aloud and says *Bah!*

Haya Tedeschi looks at the envelope sent to her by her former student Roberto Piazza, of whom she has no recollection. It is a thick envelope, bulging, and inside are only the dead. Haya Tedeschi shivered back then in 1991 and laid the envelope on the bottom of the red basket, as if lowering it into a grave. Now, in 2006, while she waits, while she sifts through the past as if opening dry beanpods from which the beans fall like sealed, enslaved little stories composed of images flitting by in flashes, while she digs through the red basket at her feet uncovering the crusty layers in the little piles of sealed lives, out slips the envelope, so she puts it on her lap and rocks it as if it is a stillborn child.

It is January 1944, a Wednesday. A darkness is descending all wrapped in snow-white sparks, resembling the crystals flying into the La Gioia tobacco shop when the door opens, and like magic dust it settles on the golden-yellow wooden counter steeped in the fragrance of tobacco, the fragrance of honey and cherries, over which Haya, like Ada before her, with her index finger traces out her future. With a smile of closely held hope, Haya awaits the last customer that evening. A thirty-year-old German in a uniform comes into her tobacco shop. Oh, he is as handsome as a doll. The German already has the Polish nickname Lalka, but at this point, when she first sees the dashing German, Haya knows nothing of that, the dashing German tells her later, I am no Lalka, you are my Lalka. The German is tall and strong and oh, firm and gentle. The German takes out his Voigtländer Bessa, leans over the counter, looks deep into Haya's green eyes and says *Ein 120 Film, bitte. Ein Kodak, bitte*, softly, as if whispering to her breathless by an open hearth – *Strip off your clothes*. So, after twenty-one years, when the love story of Ada Baar and Florian Tedeschi is already spent and falling away in tatters, the little brass bell on the door of the La Gioia tobacco shop announces the beginning of a new life, ding-a-ling, the beginning of a new love story in the Tedeschi family. And so begins the war romance of Haya Tedeschi and Kurt Franz, because the dashing German second lieutenant, S.S.-Untersturmführer, is named Kurt Franz.

Kurt Franz is a passionate amateur photographer. From his Voigtländer Bessa jump all sorts of little black-and-white scenes, 45 x 60 millimetres; like, for instance, one shot from the Gorizia fortress in the spring of 1944, when Kurt takes a picture of his colleague Willi, after which the three of them, Kurt, Willi and Haya, go out for *Kaiserfleisch* at the Trattoria Leon d'Oro on Via Codelli. Kurt and Haya meet *secretly*, of course, in the private rooms of out-of-the-way inns, in the Gorizia suburbs, but they also go for a day's excursion to Trieste when an engaging opera or operetta is playing, because Kurt likes music and after outings like that with Haya he is awash with a special tenderness. They go to see Lehár's *The Merry Widow*, but also Wagner's *Lohengrin* at the Verdi theatre. They take in a new film at the Casa Germanica and enjoy a good *Apfelstrudel*, because Kurt adores *Apfelstrudel*, because *Apfelstrudel* reminds him of his mother, whom he also reveres and loves, and Haya has nothing against sweets, but she does prefer *panna cotta* to *Apfelstrudel* and they did not offer *panna cotta* at the Casa Germanica at Via Nizza 15. They, Haya and Kurt, almost always go to matinees so that Haya can be back in Gorizia in time; so that no-one will suspect her passionate love, which, Haya knows, she needs to keep secret. Sundays, Kurt visits Franca Gulli, a violin teacher in Trieste, at Viale Sonnino, where he spends at most two hours playing simple, brief compositions by famous masters, such as a Bach minuet or the Brahms "Lullaby" ("*Wiegenlied*"), Op. 49, No. 4, or Gershwin's "Summertime" (with Professor Gulli accompanying on the piano), or Shostakovich's "Little March" from his pieces for children, because Kurt genuinely loves music. Haya, meanwhile, goes to church, each time to a different one. At church she makes a full confession, is given absolution, and then everything is fine. Kurt tells Haya all sorts of pretty tales. He talks the most to her about his dog Barry; his big beautiful mutt who looks like a St Bernard, but he had to leave it back in Poland, where he used to work at a park on the edge of a beautiful forest near a charming little railway station where there was a zoo with pheasants and rabbits, which he, Kurt, knew how to serve up like a master chef, because he was trained, among other things, as a cook, and where he took so many great photographs, which he keeps in a special photo album called "*Schöne Zeiten*", meaning "The Good Times", and under the title he writes "*Die schönsten Jahre meines Lebens*", meaning "The most wonderful years of my life", although now, while he is with Haya, he says he's no longer so sure they were.

From Kurt Franz's album, photographs given to Haya Tedeschi in Gorizia in 1944

Kurt Franz on an outing with Haya near Gorizia in May 1944

Kurt Franz, October 1937

Kurt Franz with his mother in Düsseldorf, 1937

Kurt's beloved Barry, 1943

In late March 1944 the Tedeschi family move to Milan. Florian gets a job through his contacts there. Being a *capo ufficio* in a firm engaged in the distillation of molasses seems like dignified work to Florian, compared to selling umbrellas at the Della Tre Venezie in Gorizia. Haya says *I am not going. I need to look after the shop*, and she stays with Aunt Letizia; in good hands, her mother believes. From Milan Haya's sister Nora writes and calls. Roses are not blooming, it seems, for them there. The family arrive in Milan by train on a cold and rainy night just as the city is under air attack, the same way the Tedeschi family arrived in Venice after leaving Albania back then – ah, these repetitions, these wartime coincidences, Nora complains to Haya, and there they all perch on their suitcases, she, Nora, Paula, Orestes and Ada, they are drenched for hours at night in the pouring rain at the corner of Via Broletto and Via Bossi, waiting for Florian to bring the keys to a flat, and the bombs are falling, *incendiary bombs*, Mama Ada says, who is drunk as soon as night falls, *people die from bombs like these*, she says. The office, the distillery – whatever it is, where Papa works – is on the outskirts of town, all the way out of Milan, Nora writes, and they live in a house that has been allotted to them as refugees, which she, Nora, cannot understand, because the people around them are Italians, although there are plenty of Germans, too – so how can they be refugees? But Ada says things are like that in wartime: civilians are forever on the run, mostly going to where they have family, where they think they'll be safe, and she, Nora, no longer knows who is "them" and who is "us", she writes, because in Albania at first they weren't refugees, then overnight they were, writes Nora. It's not very nice – the house where they are living – writes Nora. They are on the second floor, and on the first floor are some crude people who speak no Italian and greet them in German with *Heil!* Maybe these people are refugees, too, writes Nora, there is always shooting going on, so none of them – she or Paula or Orestes – attend school, *too dangerous*, Papa Florian says, and she is already old for school anyway, she writes, soon she'll be turning eighteen. Papa, Nora writes, has found her a place in "his" company, and she is already working there as a translator from the

German and as a typist, so now every morning she goes with Papa on the local train to work. The Underwood typewriter is so big and cumbersome to type on, writes Nora. There are no dictionaries and she often asks the German soldiers for help. They seem to be everywhere, writes Nora, and they aren't the least bit unpleasant, in fact, they are courteous, there are even good-looking men among them, just as Haya told her about how decent Kurt is. The trains are packed, the electricity often goes out, and they travel an hour or more to work every day, and the bombs are always dropping, writes Nora, and besides they do not have enough to eat, life was better in Gorizia, she writes. One day Paula took Florian's bicycle, Florian bought a new bike, really light, aluminium, writes Nora, and she went into a field to steal a few potatoes, but they saw her so she ran off and now they do not have the bike any more, writes Nora, and they are all turning yellow from the carrots. In early May Nora writes that on 21 April she and Florian barely survived when they were on their way home from work, they had heard shooting all day, which was pretty normal, but there was something terrible going on at the train station, total chaos, people were saying that Milan had fallen into the hands of the partisans, in any case, writes Nora, the Germans seem to know they are losing the war, some are even deserting, and she and Papa Florian walked for five kilometres, and, sure enough, the partisans showed up and shoved people around, they were really rough, they had the people line up and walk towards Milan; and they, Nora and Florian, did not walk along in the middle of the road, they walked along the edge, by the ditch; and she saw dozens of dead bodies, writes Nora, mutilated bodies, actually, in the ditch, the handiwork of the partisans for sure; and she writes that she was amazingly lucky to be alive, because she had on her a membership card for the Fascist Republic of Salò, and if the partisans had found it they definitely would have killed her, but luckily they did not touch her, writes Nora, and she writes how the partisans during those days did many bad things, and then, thank God, the Allies got there. She almost started crying, writes Nora, when she saw how in the courtyard of a school they were shooting a fascist whom they'd caught. They stood him up against a wall, writes Nora, and gave this ten-year-old boy a gun – the boy was no older than ten, not a day over ten, like our Orestes, writes Nora – and ordered the boy to shoot, because he, the fascist, had killed the boy's father. *Shoot!* they shouted, and the little boy did not know how, writes Nora, and all that, the shooting, ended badly: the boy shot and shot and the fascist kept not falling, he just bled more, then they killed a few Germans who wouldn't surrender, right there in front of us. This is what Nora writes.

Milan is mainly "cleansed" by March 1944, and the Tedeschi family are not under suspicion, because had they been suspicious they wouldn't have been living in the house where they were living, in a flat whose previous tenants had gone off for a "long trip abroad", as Florian's contact had put it.

At San Vittore prison there are empty beds. At platform twenty-one of the main train station there are fewer freight cars waiting to be loaded. The trains are loaded at night, quickly, and in *secret*. The Tedeschi family know nothing about the morning of 30 January when six hundred people are pushed into a long train, including some forty children, big and small, and older people of whom the eldest is Smeralda Dina, 88, like Emma Luzzatto from Gorizia. Seven days later, on 6 February, the train arrives at Auschwitz-Birkenau and the *Meister aus Deutschland* calls out

... thrust deeper into the earth some of you the rest of you sing and play
... thrust deeper with your spades some of you the rest of you play on
    for the dance
... play your violins more darkly then you'll rise like smoke into the air
then you'll have a grave in the clouds where there is plenty of room

and in only a few hours five hundred travellers fly off to their heavenly cemetery.

At a 1969 meeting in Zurich of secondary school mathematicians from Italy, Switzerland and Austria, Haya Tedeschi meets Elvira Weiner from Zurich. At the meeting there is talk not only of mathematics, but also of the past. There is always talk of the past, so that people can get to know each other better. That is how it goes. Conversations about the past are like little confessions, like unburdenings, after which the soul returns to the present on angel wings, fluttery and luminous.

This street is nice, but I don't like train stations; there have been terrible train stations, Haya Tedeschi says to Elvira Weiner during a free afternoon when they go for a walk, window-shopping along Bahnhofstrasse.

Yes there have, says Elvira Weiner, *let's go and have a snack of something sweet*, she adds. *I was sixteen*, says Elvira Weiner, *and at home there was a lot of talk about trains, about coal coming from Germany through Switzerland, through the St Gotthard tunnel to Italy, and this was discussed in our family. There was a lot of talk, though more of it was a whisper, it was like an open secret – everybody knew. One day my mother said, There was a request made of the Swiss government to allow trains through Gotthard with people on them, but towards Germany, my mother told me*, says Elvira Weiner, *and my mother also said, They asked me, this committee, if I wanted to help, because they say there are people coming. We don't know who those people are or where they are going, my mother said*, says Elvira Weiner, *but actually, that wasn't the way it was*, says Elvira Weiner. *She knew. She knew who those people were. Come on, join us, this is a humanitarian effort, the trains will stop in Zurich and then we will distribute*

*blankets and coffee and soup, they told me in this committee, my mother
said*, says Elvira Weiner. *We thought, this is just a made-up story, we
didn't believe it, in 1944 I was sixteen, but there was more talk. And
then finally my mother at one point came home and said to my father,
I have volunteered, and I'm going to go and help, she said*, says Elvira
Weiner, *and my father was against it, why get involved? he asked my
mother, but she said, I feel I have to do this, I must*, says Elvira Weiner,
*then later we heard that this was a deal, that the German and Swiss
governments had made a deal, and the Swiss Red Cross got involved,
their deal was that the trains could pass through Gotthard and not
through the Brenner, since otherwise trains went through the Brenner,
but the Brenner Pass was closed because of the snow and they couldn't
ship anybody through the Pass. Italians and Gypsies – yes, Gypsies too,
who they were transporting through Germany and beyond, somewhere
beyond, so the Germans had suggested using these empty coal carriages
to ship them back with people, so they wouldn't return empty and the
Swiss Red Cross at that point intervened, and they negotiated a deal
whereby these railway carriages would stop at night in Zurich, and they
said, Fine, we agree, at night, the Swiss Red Cross said, and our people
will give the travellers blankets and warm coffee and warm soup, so
they can travel in greater comfort, the Swiss Red Cross said*, says Elvira
Weiner. *Mama went around town and asked people to contribute their
coffee, because coffee was rationed, and also she asked everybody if
they could donate some beans. Beans were not rationed, but still, you
couldn't get them so freely*, says Elvira Weiner. *And these beans were
used to make soup with a few carrots and potatoes, I suppose – yes, and
potatoes. So we went around doing this, and then, another night, my
mother said we were going to a meeting and I went along. It was
somewhere in, I believe, a school building, I no longer remember which
school, and at the meeting we got instructions about what to do when
the trains arrived. And there was a Red Cross official, a lady, who told
us the trains would come in at night, and we were supposed to bring
torches, we were definitely supposed to bring torches, she said. We would
be in teams of four, she said, and we would be stationed at certain
marked spots along the platform, the lady from the Swiss Red Cross*

said, says Elvira Weiner, *and we would have to bring all the goods – the blankets and the coffee and the beans the day before to the spot where they would be collected, the lady from the Swiss Red Cross said*, says Elvira Weiner. *I don't remember where the collection point was*, says Elvira Weiner, *and we were also supposed to bring our gas masks, which I didn't at all understand at that time, why we had to take our gas masks*, says Elvira Weiner. *Now everybody had a gas mask at that time. Every building had so many gas masks, but we never used them. Switzerland was neutral. So my mother did everything as the lady from the Swiss Red Cross said: she took all the coffee and all the blankets and all the soup in, and then the day came. We had no car and at that time there were constant blackouts so we took the tram and we had our gas masks, and we had also been told we would have to make a chain. Then we will bring you cauldrons of soup and big pots of coffee and you will ladle out the soup into smaller containers and you will hand them down from one person to the other, they said from the Swiss Red Cross, and there would be one person who would be stationed right next to the railway carriages, they said*, says Elvira Weiner. *So we arrived. It was about, I think, nine o'clock at night and we were four in our team – my aunt, my mother, the housekeeper and myself – and my mother was the one who stood next to the railway carriage. And I think there were maybe ten teams like ours and we were placed at intervals along the platform, and we waited. And when everything was done and when everybody was waiting, they brought out the huge containers of hot soup – I don't know where they made it. Yes, I do know, at the Jewish community house. I am not certain, but I think my aunt told me the soup was made there. And then they brought vats of coffee. And my job was the soup. I had to ladle the soup into smaller containers – not plates*, gamellas *they called them. Metal ones. And so we waited*, says Elvira Weiner, *and then we saw them, the train carriages coming into the station, very slowly, and then they stopped. And somebody from the outside opened the door, because they were sealed shut somehow, the carriages, someone took off the bar and then unlocked the door and then the door slid open and we all were standing there, waiting, and a man came out and he stood and stood* there; then he nodded that we could start and then I began ladling the soup. I remember it was very difficult, because I had put the torch on the ground, and the soup was hot, pretty hot. I had to ladle it and then I gave it to the housekeeper, her name was Ida, Ida Ban, and Ida would hand the soup to my aunt and my aunt to my mother and she to this man and the man turned around, and handed the gamella to someone in the carriage, because the gamella disappeared, that means that there were people in the train. And this went on for about half an hour, and the atmosphere was very tense, and we were told not to talk, absolutely not to whistle, not to do anything, it was a very tense situation, very, and I also remember I thought, What would happen if now all these people came tumbling out of the railway carriages? And I was trying to imagine, what it was like in these railway carriages? Did they have beds? Or chairs? Was there a stove in these railway carriages? It was very cold, very raw weather. And I was wondering, If they do come out, what are we supposed to do? Are we supposed to push them back in? Or would we keep them here in Zurich and maybe bring them home and I would share my bed with one of them, with a little girl or a young woman my age? Because my mother had brought home Jews, refugees who were living in camps, she often invited them at weekends. And I always had to share my room with them, so I thought maybe I'd have to share my room again, only now for a longer time. But nothing happened. When we had emptied the containers, says Elvira Weiner, when the soup was finished and the coffee was done, and the blankets were distributed, we went home, the same way we'd come, by tram. We had to keep to a certain time to catch the last night tram.

When everything was done, the train didn't pull out, says Elvira Weiner, they bolted the door again and the carriages stood there. And then there was an article in the newspaper . . . the citizens with houses near the train station, near platform one, had complained about the noise, says Elvira Weiner, because those in the railway carriages shouted, Let us out! Let us get out! and inside the people were banging so loudly that the people living around the train station could not sleep, so they protested, and then it was suggested these transports should *be left on the side of the Landesmuseum, all the way beyond the Hauptbahnhof, on Museumstrasse, because there were no people living there and the transports wouldn't be disturbing anyone, that is what they suggested,* says Elvira Weiner, *because I don't think we wanted to know what was happening. We knew these people were going to Germany, we knew there were Jews inside, we knew about the concentration camps, and we had helped them, so why were they hollering now at night? That is what we were thinking,* says Elvira Weiner. *We gave them blankets and coffee and soup, why are they protesting? That is not polite, we thought, they are making a racket and we can't sleep. That is how our citizens wrote, you know, this was wartime,* says Elvira Weiner, *and we all had our worries and that troubles me today,* says Elvira Weiner, *because if we hadn't left the people like that, if the Government had gone back on its word, if we had said, We are not letting these people go on to Germany, then I guess the other transports wouldn't have followed – and they did come, there were many transports, I think they had about eight, maybe twelve, and I went once more with my mother and, sure enough, the carriages were far away, near the Schweizerisches Landesmuseum, on the last platform, and the same thing happened, the blankets, the coffee, the soup, the banging and shouting, and then my mother said, You can't go to the train station any more. You have to think about school. You can't be coming home so late. You have to get your sleep. I don't know which people went there to help. We didn't dare talk. It was* verboten *to talk,* says Elvira Weiner. *It was pretty dark anyway. We had only our torches, it was very dark, but I remember when the door opened on one of the carriages I saw a man with a white face at the door, with a terribly white face in the darkness. At that meeting I saw people I knew, people my age. I had gone skiing with some of them. The adults I didn't know. My aunt knew them. I think there were Jews there, I knew one man, a lawyer, he said, Hello, kid, but there at that platform he pretended not to know me. The Swiss Red Cross contacted Jews, I think that the Swiss Red Cross contacted Jews in* secret, *I think the other people knew nothing about those transports, I think they had no clue, and the Swiss Red Cross felt they were making a grand gesture, a great humane gesture,*

128

besides the Swiss Red Cross behaved that way, as if it were the saviour, as if the Swiss Red Cross saved all those people with those blankets, that coffee and that soup. I don't know if the Swiss Red Cross ever considered stopping these trains, freeing the people. I don't know, says Elvira Weiner. We knew nothing, we knew only that there were Jews and Gypsies going to Germany and beyond – we didn't know where beyond – and that they had to go through Switzerland, because the Brenner Pass was closed. That's what my mother told me, but at the meeting somebody also asked, Why do they have to go through Switzerland? I mean, nobody was happy about the trains going through Switzerland, that Switzerland was involved, because Switzerland claimed to be a neutral country, and it turned out not to be so neutral after all, especially as far as the banks were concerned, that still remains to be proved, says Elvira Weiner. At the meeting someone said, Maybe they are political prisoners, but I knew, in my family we knew, we knew, we assumed that they were taking those people to concentration camps, we knew there were different camps: Dachau, Bergen Belsen, Theresienstadt. Theresienstadt was a good camp. They didn't kill there, we could have done something, at the time I didn't think that way, everyone was thinking that the blankets, and the coffee, and the soup, that this was enough. I was sixteen – I was going to school – when we were waiting as those trains came slowly in to the station. We waited for the doors to open, and I thought, What will happen now? What if all those people come pouring out? What if they push away that man in uniform standing at the door and they start jumping off the train? What will we do then? Will someone put them back into those carriages? I wanted the people to get free, but I didn't want them to get out here, with us, like when you look at animals at the zoo, you feel sorry for them for being in the cages, but you don't want them to get out right where you are, they should be set free in some wild place, you think, says Elvira Weiner. Later I wondered – not then, later – why I had been saved, and some others were not, now I know: no-one was saved. When the war ended, my mother didn't want to talk about it, she wanted to forget. I would ask her, What do you think happened to those people from the train? and she would say, Oh, Elvira, those were bizarre times. All that happened in late 1943 and early 1944. It was very cold. Later I heard it was no coincidence, there are no coincidences. I looked for information about those people – later, when my mother died – I looked for information. I heard how the partisans tried to sabotage the freight trains and stop them before they entered Switzerland, and how the Nazis rounded up people in the villages and towns and offered them free cigarettes, and then arrested them and loaded them onto trains and shipped them to Germany to the work camps, I heard they were successful, occasionally, in derailing trains, saving some people, says Elvira Weiner. In the archives there is information. I looked for it. In the archives it says that traffic through the Gotthard Pass in 1943 and 1944 was intense, that German trains passed through Switzerland every ten minutes on their way to Italy, and then I searched the archives of the Red Cross, but there is not a line in the archives of the Red Cross about the trains that passed through Zurich, not a line about the organized support, about those blankets and the coffee and the soup, nothing about the little help to the Italian prisoners, which was really nothing to speak of. Perhaps that is why there is no information about it anywhere, as if it never happened . . . says Elvira Weiner. But some-where I found a little document, says Elvira Weiner, a slip of paper on which it says that the representative of the Swiss Red Cross in January 1944 contacted the German command, some S.S. officials, someone named Globočnik and someone named Rainer in northern Italy, related to "coordination of effort to offer aid to Italian citizens", and then I went through the archives of the Swiss railways, says Elvira Weiner. I didn't find anything. At the archives of the Swiss railways they said that in 1960 they moved their offices and at that time all their information about the train schedules and the movement of trains during the war was destroyed. Destroyed, says Elvira Weiner. The worst is that the freight carriages were sealed. They could only be opened from the outside, says Elvira Weiner. Maybe that was the worst.

I, too, have train-station nightmares, train-station nightmares, nightmares, frightening dreams, repeats Haya, while she digs around in the red basket, then finds a little photograph that, back in 1944, slid in – she doesn't know how, she doesn't know how, how did it slide in? – among the pictures that S.S.-Untersturmführer Kurt Franz gave her. *Here it is*, she says.

On 31 October, 1944, at about 6 p.m., Ada's sister, Haya's aunt, Letizia Puhaz, shouts: *Fanny, run and fetch Teresa from Via Caporetto!* At 8.17 p.m. Teresa Cavalieri, a midwife from Via Caporetto 51, delivers Haya Tedeschi's baby. Antonio "Toni" Tedeschi comes into the world.

Kurt Franz sees his son twice. In late December, leaning over the counter at La Gioia, Kurt Franz twiddles a lock of Haya's light-brown hair between his index finger and his ring finger, leans in to her face and whispers: *My little Jewess, we can't go on like this. Oh, yes, I know, Tedeschi ist ein jüdischer Name. Besides, my fiancée is waiting for me at home. Heinrich Himmler, Minister of the S.S. Rasse- und Siedlungshauptamt has finally granted me permission to wed. I am leaving for Düsseldorf at Christmastime, and when I come back, I will not be in touch. Please do not ask for me.*

This is when Haya seeks out Don Baubela. Antonio Toni is baptized as every good Catholic should be, in the presence of Letizia and Laura Puhaz and Teresa the midwife, he is entered into the church books with his father's name, yes, Kurt Franz, and is given the mother's surname, Tedeschi. *All of this should remain a secret*, Haya says to Don Baubela. *The times are risky*, she says. Don Carlo Baubela probably says not a word, because that is the way of priests. Don Baubela dies in 1946, having lived to more than eighty. Gorizia believes that Antonio's father has died in combat, but in whose army? On whose side? This doesn't interest many. The times are murky.

Gorizia is a small town. Nevertheless.

On Friday, 13 April, 1945, Haya takes Antonio Toni, as usual, to the Duchessa Anna d'Aosta Asilo Nido in Via Veneto, in other words to a nursery where he is cared for by Iolanda Visintin, a friend of her mother Ada's from elementary school days. At the front door the postman says, *You have a letter. Your parents are sending you money from Milan. Sign here.* When Haya turns around, Toni's pram is empty. There is no-one walking along Via Veneto. Not a single passer-by. The morning is brisk, sunny, and the air is clear after several days of driving rain; the trees are shyly blooming in white and pink. The postman and Haya stare, appalled, at how this magic trick has happened. And so it is that, five months after his birth, Antonio Toni Tedeschi disappears, suddenly and quietly, as if he had never lived.

Oh yes, Haya searches for Antonio high and low, high and low. Gorizia is on its feet. The police investigate, dispatches fly, phones jangle, tears well, chaos reigns in her mind. The nights do not pass. The days do not pass. Time grows like yeast, time swells, then one day it overflows, pours out of Haya's breast, clambers up on to a merry-go-round and off it flies. Nothing could be done.

History decides to hide, to go underground for a spell. *I need a break*, says History, turns its back on the here and now, sweeps up all its rattles, leaving a huge mess behind, a hill of rubbish, vomit everywhere, and with a satanic cackle, witch-like, it soars heavenward. On Saturday, 28 April the partisans kill Mussolini and Clara Petacci at Mezzegra and on Sunday they hang them head down on a gas pump at an Esso petrol station at Piazzale Loreto in Milan, somehow gauging this at precisely the same moment that Hitler swears his fidelity to Eva Braun "until death do us part". On Monday, 30 April, 1945, Adolf and Eva kill themselves; Dachau is liberated by the Americans; and on Tuesday, 1 May the Yugoslav 4th Army and the Slovenian 9th Corps march into Trieste. Who has the time to look for one stolen child?

In 1946 Ada comes back to Gorizia with Paula and Orestes from Milan, and Florian and Nora go off to Salò, where old Tedeschi and his second wife Rosa have come through the war essentially unscathed. They burn their Fascist Party membership booklets, although they needn't have; no-one asks them for anything.

After the war there are no heroes, the dead are forgotten

immediately, pipes up Jean Giono. *The widows of heroes marry living men, because these men are alive and because being alive is a greater virtue than being a dead hero. After a war*, says Giono, *there are no heroes, there are only the maimed, the crippled, the disfigured, from whom women avert their eyes*, he says. *When a war ends, everyone forgets the war, even those who fought in it. And so it should be*, says Giono. *Because war is pointless, and there should be no devotion for those who have dedicated themselves to the pointless*, he says.

Listen, Romain Rolland says, *war is not over, nothing is over; humankind is in fetters.*

Old Paolo Tedeschi lives in a neo-Baroque villa on the shore of Lake Garda, but he is not at peace. The words *Tedeschi ist ein jüdischer Name* pound in his head throughout the war; they press against his chest. When events reach fever pitch, when Paolo Tedeschi *feels* they may reach fever pitch, he slips into hospital where his friend Dr Armando Bosi sets him up in the intensive-care unit. There, in intensive care, Paolo Tedeschi gets vitamins intravenously, a lovely view of the hospital garden and a sense of the seasons passing. When the birds chirp Paolo Tedeschi listens to the birdsong. When rain falls he listens to the patter and it lulls him to sleep. Then he is given a laxative and says, *Ah, this, too, will end.* Paolo's stays in the hospital are brief and well rehearsed. After them, he goes home heartened and stronger. Paolo's sons Sergio and Walter take their mother's surname, Brana (after the war they take back their father's, Tedeschi). In 1944 they report to the Italian branch of the German Army and manage mini-submarines, which attack the Allied forces. Paolo's youngest son Ugo, otherwise a flautist, crosses over into neutral Switzerland before September 1943 to the little town of Untersiggenthal in the Aargau canton, and entertains the beer drinkers on a second-hand accordion in a local tavern. In the mid-1950s he sends his parents a postcard from the *Gripsholm* translatlantic Swedish-American ocean liner, writing that he is sailing on the Gothenburg–New York line, playing in the ship's orchestra. In 1954 the *Gripsholm* is rechristened the *Berlin*, but Ugo no longer writes. Catholicized Jew Paolo Tedeschi dies in 1948, and his second wife, Rosa Brana, a Catholic born and bred, dies a year later. Paolo's eldest son Florian remarries in 1963. Walter and Sergio find work in a nearby liqueur factory. Nora starts her own family.

As if there had never been a war.

Years follow in which deaths are what is remembered, some gentle and quiet, anticipated, peacetime deaths, some violent and maybe unjust. Haya attends the funerals of her closest family as if going off to shallow confessions from which she lugs back to Gorizia her bundles of deaf nausea and second-hand incredulity. Paula dies of cancer in Trieste in 1963; Florian, on the shore of Lake Garda in 1972. After Orestes graduates from secondary school in 1952 he abandons Gorizia. *All of you are full of shit!* he shouts, and as a member of the Red Brigades he dies in a Roman prison on 17 March, 1978, of a heart attack a day after he takes part in the assassination of Aldo Moro; while Nora, as a happy housewife, closes her eyes with God's blessing in Brescia in 1990.

Ada is the first to go.

Ada drinks more in Gorizia. She drinks so much, especially in the afternoons, that she can no longer manoeuvre herself downstairs. She falls. She has cuts all over, especially on her face. Later they treat her at the hospital, stitch her up. And so the years pass. Ada's face is scribbled with scars and the visible traces of surgical sutures, the knots tied to close her open wounds. Ada looks more and more like a patch, a rag, totally unusable. She often cries for no reason. Her words jumble into long, snotty, garbled sequences, which she swipes at with the back of her hand, but fails. She finds it hard to bring the fork to her mouth. Her food dribbles on to her bosom. Her clothing is covered in greasy stains. She is soiled and unkempt, the situation, in general, is serious.

So they commit Ada to the psychiatric ward of Gorizia hospital, where she decants absinthe, grappa, vodka or any alcoholic beverage she can lay her hands on, into perfume flasks, which, with great effort and cunning, she tucks into toilet cisterns, pillow cases, other people's bags, through which she rummages frantically at night, barefoot and urine-soaked.

At this point, in 1953, Haya begins to study mathematics in Trieste.

Ada gets to know Umberto Saba at the hospital and they have long conversations, all sorts of conversations, while both of them stand, elbows on the sill, at a tall window with iron bars and sniff the fresh Gorizia air. Later, in 1961, when prominent psychiatrist Franco Basaglia comes to Gorizia, the iron bars are removed, the front door is left unlocked, the patients stroll around the gardens, some slowly as if dreaming, some spry, on their way home. Ada wears two sprigs of white oleander behind her ear and sings, then, when Basaglia comes to the hospital, as he indulges her little alcoholic binges. But by the time Basaglia gets there, Saba is gone. Saba dies in 1957, Ada dies five years later.

It's nice here, Ada tells Haya when she comes to visit. *Sad people live here. Jews, too. Umberto speaks of Trieste, where there is also plenty of sorrow, and*

> *next to the hill there's a graveyard*
> *in ruins, which funerals pass*
> *and where no-one's been buried for as long*
> *as I can remember*
> *says Umberto,*
> *my ancestors lie here,*
> *he says, and he is a Jew, too*, Ada tells her.

Umberto says, Trieste is a pungent and melancholy city, the strangest city, Umberto says, a city of boyish adolescence and rude charm, so he says, says Ada, *then he takes me for a stroll, and we amble around Trieste, this isn't the Trieste we lived in when Florian was serving coffee at the Piazza Unità, this Trieste is serenely innocent, so Umberto says*, says Ada, *it is a lovely world, Umberto says, and he paints that world for me, he paints me suppressed longing and aching love, so he says, I'll paint you unspoken longing and aching love and exhausted words* fiore-amore *in that murky madness, Umberto says, in that madness in which vainly discordant voices reverberate, he says, this is a lovely Trieste, not the Trieste we fled*, Ada says.

Where I dreamed of patent-leather shoes, and never got them, Haya jumps in, but Ada doesn't hear, Ada is ambling around Trieste with Umberto, and Haya is skipping after her.

There, Ada says, we go off to the Ponterosso, Umberto and I, and we look at the birds, because Umberto likes birds, Ada says, and now I like birds too, though the stuffed birds Grandfather Angelo had were frightening, their dead glassy eyes, Ada says, and he takes me, Umberto, to Via Riborgo or Via Pondares, I forget, to the house where he was born, in what was the Jewish ghetto then, but those houses are gone now, the house I was born in is gone, Ada says, today that's an altogether different house – houses are disappearing, Haya, people, too, now I see – and we make the rounds of the trattorias Umberto remembers, and we have a grappa at the Alla Bella Isoletta, I am a little island, too, Haya, a barren little island, left behind, but it wasn't always like that, no. Then we go to where Carolina was born, she was Umberto's wife, and Umberto talks about her a lot, and he talks a lot about Lina – Linuccia – he uses pet names for her, I never used pet names for you, Haya. We were always in a hurry. We had no time for tenderness. I don't know how that happened, that we were left without time. What would I have called you? Haya, Hayuccia, Hayichen? asks Ada and starts to sob, then through the tears, she says, *You could have brought me another couple of bottles. These bottles are so small. They are very little, these bottles you bring me. And Umberto ran away, you know, just like we did, he ran away from fascism, so he tells me,*

We ran into *fascism,* Haya interrupts, but Ada doesn't hear.

and he hid in attics. I hid everywhere, Umberto says, in attics in Paris, in Florence, in Rome, says Umberto, says Ada, and she also says, *The next time you come, bring some ampoules of morphine for Umberto and little bottles of rum for me, and when I die, bury me at Valdirosa, over there, in Slovenian soil. And he, Umberto, talks to me, you know, says* Ada, *he tells me about train stations we didn't know about, and he asks me,*

Stations, do you remember? At night, full
of final farewells, unchecked weeping,
crammed with people the transport takes.
The order "move" given by the
sob of a trumpet;
and ice, ice around your heart.

but I don't remember, Haya, I don't, says Ada, *maybe it's the drink. And,
you know, says* Ada, *Umberto's last name isn't Saba anyway, though
that is exactly what he is called, Umberto Saba, because his name is
actually Umberto Poli. Did you know that? Though he might have
been Umberto Coen. He could have, says* Ada. *He could have been
Coen, because his mother was Jewish and her last name was Coen, not
his father's, his father's was Poli, says* Ada, *and he left them, Umberto
and his Mama Rahela, a nice name, Rahela, says* Ada, *Jewish,* she
says, *and then Umberto declared, I will take the name Saba, because
none of this matters anyway, you know, what your last name is, he
said, though I'm not so sure it doesn't matter, I am not so sure, and
that is how Umberto takes the last name Saba, because he had a nanny
whose name was Pepa and he loved her a lot and she was Slovenian,
like my Mama Marisa, my Mama Marisa from Gorizia, your grandmother, Haya, who also disappeared. Oh Haya, how people vanish.
It's so painful, and Umberto says there are no unborn or dead, there is
only the living life for eternity; pain that passes, happiness that stays,
Umberto says, whose last name is Saba, though really his last names
are Poli and Coen. There is pain that passes, Umberto says, and so it
is that your pain will pass, Haya, and so it is that Rahela sent Pepa
packing, and Pepa's last name was Sabaz, and then Umberto declared,
That will be my last name, after my Pepa from Gorizia, because it
doesn't matter anyway what your name is, says Umberto, says* Ada.
Sometimes he doesn't feel like talking, Umberto, Ada says, *so he,
Umberto, recites poems about birds for me, and we look at the trees
and I listen to his poems about birds, and he recites for me his poems
about birds, and I long to be a bird, and Umberto says,*

the leaving, this year, of the swallows
because of a thought my heart will squeeze,
and he says,
my loneliness will be bereft of swallows,
and love at my advanced age will freeze,

says Umberto, and then we go on looking into the garden, which is shadowy, and we observe those trees, and then I say to Umberto, Look at how shadowy this garden is. We could hide out there, if they allowed us to walk around it sometimes, around the shadowy garden, and he says, There is no shadow where my tiredness could find shelter. But I am tired, too, Ada says, and she says, Haya, don't forget to bring me rum. They think they'll cure me. They will not cure me. I don't want to be cured, because I'm not ill, but Umberto says, If you feel like drinking, drink, they won't cure you here. Though it isn't bad here, though I would like to go for a walk, maybe even sing. For the time being I sing softly, more to myself, then I ask Umberto, Am I crazy? because sometimes it seems to me that all this, this life, my life, your life, that all this is a serious madness, but Umberto says, says Ada, Umberto says that Dr Weiss says (and I trust Dr Weiss, Umberto says), Dr Weiss says, Craziness is a dream from which a person doesn't awake. That is what Dr Weiss says, Umberto says. Haya, bring some rum for sure. If there's no rum, buy gin, in a little bottle, a mini-bottle, in several little bottles, and bring Umberto morphine. He sometimes sits and whispers a poem that isn't his. He whispers a poem that is called "Solitudine"; then I see that everything is different from what it seems, because he sits and whispers:

But my shouts
strike
like lightning
the heaven's
muted bell

they plunge back
down in fright

That is what he whispers. I think this is a poem by Ungaretti. Yes, it's Ungaretti's. It is called "Loneliness", solitudine, solitude. Yes, then I worry about Umberto, because you see, I told you,

BEHIND EVERY NAME
THERE IS A STORY

The names of about 9,000 Jews who were deported from Italy, or killed in Italy or in the countries Italy occupied between 1943 and 1945.

Abeasis Clemente
Abeasis Ester
Abeasis Giorgio
Abeasis Rebecca
Abeasis Renato
Abel Otto
Abeles Francesca
Abenaim Elia
   Giuseppe
Abenaim Ettore
Abenaim Mario
Abenaim Mario
Abenaim Oreste
Abenaim Ottorino
Abenaim Renzo
Abenaim Teofilo
Abenaim Wanda
Abenimol O.
Abishous Caden
Aboaf Abramo
   Marco
Aboaf Achille
Aboaf Gino
Aboaf Giuditta Rita
Aboaf Guido
Aboaf Ida
Aboaf Regina
Aboaf Salomone
   Girolamo
Aboaf Umberto
Abolaffia Rebecca
Abolaffio Adolfo
Abolaffio Camelia
Abolaffio Guido
Abolaffio Regina
Abolaffio Simeone
   Edgardo
Abolaffio Vanda
Abouaf Allegra
Abouaf Clara
Abraham Arminio
Abraham Carlotta

Abraham Hilde
   Fanny
Abraham Yvonne
Abrahamson Betti
Acco Allegra
Acco David Dario
Acco Giacomo
Acco Marco
Acco Rachele
Acco Sabino
Acco Vittorio
Acco Vittorio
   Zaccaria
Ackerman Feige
Adato Amata
Ades Elio
Adler
Adler Albert
Adler Anita
Adler Giuseppe
Adler Marion
Adler Oscar Zeliko
Adler Oswald
Adler Stefan
Adler Zora
Adut Rosa
Afnaim Leone
Afnaim Matilde
Afnaim Regina
Afnaim Salomone
Afnaim Vittoria
Afnaim Vittorio
Agatstein Perl
Ajo' Abramo
Ajo' Adele
Ajo' Angelo
Ajo' Celeste
Ajo' Elisabetta
Ajo' Giacobbe
Ajo' Grazia
Ajo' Pacifico
Alalouf Caden

Alalouf Mosè
Alati Concetta
Alati Gianantonio
Alati Liliana
Alatri Lionello
Alatri Vittoria
Albertini Ida
Alcanà Bianca
Alcanà Celebi
Alcanà Celebi
Alcanà Elia
Alcanà Esther
Alcanà Estrella
Alcanà Giacobbe
Alcanà Giovanna
Alcanà Giuseppe
Alcanà Isacco
Alcanà Isacco
Alcanà Maria
Alcanà Matilde
Alcanà Rachele
Alcanà Rachele
Alcanà Rachele
Alcanà Rachele
Alcanà Rebecca
Alcanà Rebecca
Alcanà Salva
Alcanà Sara
Alcanà Sara
Alcanà Stella
Alcanà Viola
Alcanà Vittoria
Alcanà Vittoria
Alexander Gertrude
   Sara
Algranti Giacomo
Algranti Rebecca
Alhadeff Abramo
Alhadeff Abramo
Alhadeff Alberto
Alhadeff Alberto
Alhadeff Alberto

Alhadeff Alessandro
Alhadeff Allegra
Alhadeff Allegra
Alhadeff Allegra
Alhadeff Amelia
Alhadeff Aronne
Alhadeff Aslan
Alhadeff Baruch
Alhadeff Bellina
Alhadeff Bellina
Alhadeff Bezalel
Alhadeff Bohor
Alhadeff Bulissa
Alhadeff Bulissa
Alhadeff Caden
Alhadeff Caden
Alhadeff Celebi
Alhadeff Chety
Alhadeff Davide
Alhadeff Davide
Alhadeff Diana
Alhadeff Diana
Alhadeff Donna
Alhadeff Elia
Alhadeff Ester
Alhadeff Ester
Alhadeff Ester
Alhadeff Ester
Alhadeff Ester
Alhadeff Ester
Alhadeff Ester
Alhadeff Estrella
Alhadeff Estrella
Alhadeff Giacobbe
Alhadeff Giacobbe
Alhadeff Giacobbe
Alhadeff Giacobbe
Alhadeff Giacobbe
Alhadeff Giacomo
Alhadeff Giacomo
   Giacobbe
Alhadeff Giamila

Alhadeff Giamila
Alhadeff Giovanna
Alhadeff Giovanna
Alhadeff Giuseppe
Alhadeff Giuseppe
Alhadeff Giuseppe
Alhadeff Giuseppe
Alhadeff Giuseppe
Alhadeff Giuseppe
Alhadeff Haim
Alhadeff Haim
Alhadeff Hanula
Alhadeff Herzel
Alhadeff Isacco
Alhadeff Isacco
Alhadeff Isacco
Alhadeff Israele
Alhadeff Jachir
Alhadeff Jahiel
Alhadeff Jahiel
Alhadeff Ketty
Alhadeff Lea
Alhadeff Lea
Alhadeff Lea
Alhadeff Maria
Alhadeff Maria
Alhadeff Maria
Alhadeff Maria
Alhadeff Maria
Alhadeff Maria
Alhadeff Matilde
Alhadeff Matilde
Alhadeff Matilde
Alhadeff Matilde
Alhadeff Matilde
Alhadeff Mazaltov
Alhadeff Mazaltov
Alhadeff Mazaltov
Alhadeff Miriam
Alhadeff Mirù
Alhadeff Mirù
Alhadeff Moisè
Alhadeff Mosè
Alhadeff Mosè
Alhadeff Mosè
Alhadeff Mosè
Alhadeff Mosè
Alhadeff Mosè
Alhadeff Ner
Alhadeff Ner
Alhadeff Nissim
Alhadeff Nissim
Alhadeff Nissim
Alhadeff Perahia

Alhadeff Perahia
Alhadeff Perahia
Alhadeff Perla
Alhadeff Rachele
Alhadeff Rachele
Alhadeff Rachele
Alhadeff Rachele
Alhadeff Rachele
Alhadeff Rachele
detta Lina
Alhadeff Rebecca
Alhadeff Rebecca
Alhadeff Rebecca
Alhadeff Rebecca
Alhadeff Regina
Alhadeff Renata
Reina
Alhadeff Rica
Alhadeff Rica
Alhadeff Rica
Alhadeff Rosa
Alhadeff Rosa
Alhadeff Rosa
Alhadeff Rosa
Alhadeff Rosa
Alhadeff Rosetta
Alhadeff Rosina
Alhadeff Ruben
Alhadeff Ruben
Alhadeff Ruben
Alhadeff Ruben
Alhadeff Sadok
Alhadeff Salomone
Alhadeff Salomone
Alhadeff Salvatore
Alhadeff Samuele
Alhadeff Samuele
Alhadeff Samuele
Alhadeff Samuele
Alhadeff Samuele
Alhadeff Santo
Alhadeff Sara
Alhadeff Sara
Alhadeff Sara
Alhadeff Sara
Alhadeff Saul
Alhadeff Scemaria
Alhadeff Silvia
Alhadeff Sofia
Alhadeff Stella
Alhadeff Stella
Alhadeff Stella
Alhadeff Stella
Alhadeff Vida
Alhadeff Vidal

Alhadeff Viola
Alhadeff Virginia
Alhadeff Vittorio
Alhadeff Zimbul
Alhadeff Zimbul
Alhaique Emilio
Alhalel Brazo
Alhalel Moisè
Alhanà Abramo
Alhanà Allegra
Alhanà Estrea
Alhanà Estrea
Alhanà Giuseppe
Alhanà Jochevet
Alhanà Matilde
Alhanà Miriam
Alhanà Mirù
Alhanà Mosè
Alhanà Nissim
Alhanà Rebecca
Alhanà Reina
Alhanà Rosa
Alkalay Hermann
Alkalay Josif
Alkalay Miscia
Almagià Arnaldo
Almagià Delia
Almagià Emma
Almagià Enrico
Almagià Erminia
Almagià Ortensia
Almansi Adele
Almasy Vera
Almeda Guglielmo
Almeleh Abramo
Almeleh Alfredo
Almeleh Bella
Almeleh Bulissa
Almeleh Caden
Almeleh Fassana
Almeleh Giacobbe
Giacomo
Almeleh Hahamaci
Almeleh Haim
Almeleh Luna
Almeleh Mari
Almeleh Matilde
Almeleh Mercada
Almeleh Miriam
Almeleh Rachele
Almeleh Raffaele
Almeleh Rebecca
Almeleh Samuele
Almeleh Sara
Almeleh Sara

Almoslino Olga
Alphandary Bianca
Alpron Enrichetta
Alpron Ernesto
Alt
Alt Giovanni
Altaras
Altaras
Altaras Donna Ester
Altaras Jilian
Altarass Cesare
Altaraz Sara
Altberger Ester
Alter Leopold
Altmann Ferdinando
Altmann Giuditta
Altmann Giuliano
Altmann Guglielmo
Altmann Hinde
Altschueler Samuel
Amati Alberto
Amati Giulio
Amati Letizia
Amati Michele
Amati Rosa
Amati Rosa
Amato Alessandro
Amato Aslan
Amato Caden
Amato Davide
Amato Ester
Amato Giacobbe
Amato Giacomo
Amato Giuseppe
Amato Giuseppe
Bochor
Amato Lea
Amato Mardocheo
Amato Matilde
Amato Michele
Amato Mosè Behor
Amato Nissim
Amato Rachele
Amato Rahamin
Amato Regina
Amato Ruben
Amato Sadik
Amato Samuele
Amato Sol
Amato Stella
Amato Stella Esther
Amato Violetta
Ambonetti Olga
Ambrosini
Guglielmo

144

Americano Carolina
Amgyfel Riwka Sara
Amiel Abramo
Amiel Davide
Amiel Isacco
Amiel Isacco
Amiel Leone
Amiel Maurizio
Amiel Rachele
Amiel Rachele
Amiel Vidal
Amster Rebecca
Amsterdam Arthur
Amsterdam Israel
 Isidoro
Amsterdam Selma
 Sara
Anau Eloisa
Anav Adalgisa
Anav Anita
Anav Eleonora
Anavi Rebecca
Ancona Achille
Ancona Ada
Ancona Ada
Ancona Bruno
Ancona Edoardo
Ancona Elisa
Ancona Gastone
Ancona Giulio
Ancona Guglielmo
Ancona Ida
Ancona Ines
Ancona Irma
Ancona Margherita
Ancona Marisa
Ancona Olga
Ancona Roberto
Ancona Vittoria
Andrzenczek Eva
Angel Alessandro
Angel Bella
Angel Bulissa
Angel Giacobbe
Angel Gioia
Angel Giuseppe
Angel Haim
Angel Leone
Angel Maria
Angel Samuele
Angel Sara
Angel Signora
Anscherlik Augusta
Anscherlik Franca
Anscherlik Paola

Anteras Salomon
Anticoli
Anticoli Abramo
Anticoli Adelaide
Anticoli Adolfo
Anticoli Alberto
Anticoli Alberto
Anticoli Alfredo
Anticoli Angelo
Anticoli Angelo
Anticoli Angelo
Anticoli Angelo
Anticoli Angelo
Anticoli Anna
Anticoli Aron
Anticoli Attilio
Anticoli Attilio
Anticoli Celeste
Anticoli Celeste
Anticoli Cesare
Anticoli Emanuele
 Vittorio
Anticoli Emma
Anticoli Emma
Anticoli Enrica
Anticoli Enrichetta
Anticoli Ester
Anticoli Ester
Anticoli Esterina
Anticoli Fiorella
Anticoli Fiorella
Anticoli Fiorella
Anticoli Fiorella
Anticoli Fiorella
Anticoli Flaminia
Anticoli Fortuna
Anticoli Franca
Anticoli Gemma
Anticoli Gemma
Anticoli Geremia
 Attilio
Anticoli Giacomo
Anticoli Giancarlo
Anticoli Giuditta
Anticoli Glauco
Anticoli Grazia
Anticoli Italia
Anticoli Lazzaro
Anticoli Lazzaro
Anticoli Lazzaro
Anticoli Lazzaro
Anticoli Lello
 Samuele
Anticoli Leone
Anticoli Letizia

Anticoli Letizia
Anticoli Luciana
Anticoli Luciano
Anticoli Manrico
Anticoli Marco
Anticoli Marco
 Mosè
Anticoli Mario
Anticoli Mario
Anticoli Mario
Anticoli Marisa
Anticoli Pacifico
Anticoli Rosa
Anticoli Rosa
Anticoli Rosella
Anticoli Rosina
Anticoli Sabatino
Anticoli Salvatore
Anticoli Sergio
Anticoli Vanda
Anticoli Vitale
Antmann Adele
Antmann Gelb
 Charlotte
Antmann Josef
Anzer Sofia
Anzubel Jakob
Apelbaum Pinchas
 Paul
Apfel Davide
Appel Bojla
Appelbaum Armand
 Moise Herz
Ara Coen Anna
Araf
Araf
Araf Lazar
Araf Marco
Araf Matilde
Arany Giorgio
Arbib Alice
Arbib Enrico
Arbib Rachele
Arbib Simon
Arbib Wassi
Arbisse Raimondo
Archivolti Liliana
Arditi Alberto
 Abramo
Arditi Clara
Arditi Davide
Arditi Esther
Arditi Gioia
Arditti Giuseppe
Arditti Masaltov

Armani Heischmann
 Adolf Umberto
Armani Heischmann
 Gino
Armut Edita
Armut Enika
Armut Gustav
Armut Iva
Arnoldi Guido
Arnstein Ernest
Aron Vita
Aronson Angiolina
 Cecilia
Arouch Renata
Artom Faustina
Artom Margherita
Artom Riccardo
Artom Vittorina
Arughetti Caden
Arughetti Giacobbe
Ascarelli Adele
Ascer Rachele
Ascer Salvo
Ascer Sara
Ascher Rosa
Aschnowitz Otto
Ascoli Adalgisa
Ascoli Alessandro
Ascoli Alfredo
Ascoli Angelo
Ascoli Elisa
Ascoli Emma
Ascoli Enrico
Ascoli Ernesta
Ascoli Ferruccio
Ascoli Gabriella
 Fernanda
Ascoli Giacomo
Ascoli Irma
Ascoli Lidia
Ascoli Lidia
Ascoli Margherita
Ascoli Marta
Ascoli Michele
Ascoli Olga Luigia
Ascoli Vito
Ashabett Silvia
Ass Ester
Assa André Jacques
Assa Isaac
Assael Rachele
Assael Regina
Asseo Linda
Asseo Rachele
Astegiano Margherita

Astrologo Aldo
Astrologo Anita
Astrologo Attilio
Astrologo Cesare
Astrologo Costanza
Astrologo Diamante
Astrologo Donato
Astrologo Emanuele
Astrologo Ennio
Astrologo Enrichetta
Astrologo Ester
Astrologo Fortunata
Astrologo Giacomo
Astrologo Giuditta
Astrologo Giuseppe
Astrologo Isacco
Astrologo Italia
Astrologo Lamberto
Astrologo Lello
 Samuele
Astrologo Leone
Astrologo Leone
Astrologo Letizia
Astrologo Letizia
Astrologo Maurizio
Astrologo Milena
Astrologo Pellegrino
Astrologo Riccardo
Astrologo Rinaldo
 Leone
Astrologo Rosa
Astrologo Sara
Astrologo Silvia
Astrologo Vitale
Astrologo Vittorio
Atias Neta
Atias Nora
Atlas Margherita
Attal Ada
Attal Benito
Attal Davide
Attal Dina Bona
Attal Fortuna
Attal Mario
Attias Giacobbe
 Giacomo
Attias Giacomo
Attias Nella
Attias Sara
Attias Vitale
Auerhahn Israel
Auerhahn Mosè
Aufrecht Anna
Augapfel Jacob
Aussenberg Chaskel

Aussenberg Sara
Austerlitz Laura
Avigdor Enrico
Avigdor Federico
Avigdor Giacomo
Avigdor Isacco
Avigdor Miranda
Avigdor Rachele
Avigdor Rachele
Avigdor Stella
Avramovic Mika
Avramovic Sarika
Avzaradel Allegra
Avzaradel Baruch
Avzaradel Clara
Avzaradel Esther
Avzaradel Gioia
Avzaradel Graziella
Avzaradel Irma
Avzaradel Laura
Avzaradel Lea
Avzaradel Regina
Avzaradel Renata
 Regina
Avzaradel Rosa
Avzaradel Selma
Azicrì Rosina
Azra Misa
Azria Luigi
Azzarelli Lina
Baar Giulia
Bacharach Elisabetta
Bachi Aldo
Bachi Aldo
Bachi Annibale
Bachi Armando
Bachi Arturo
Bachi Arturo Enrico
Bachi Avito
Bachi Luigi
Bachi Michele
Bachi Pia
Bachi Roberto
Bachi Vittoria
Bachmann Fritz
Bader Elena
Bahir Moshè
Bakker Joseph
Balassa Elena
Balbi Nerina
Ballatti Lina
Balog Adalberto
Balog Anna Maura
Balog Lodovico
Ban Eleonora Irene

Bangen Mirella
Bank Hersz
Baquis Giorgio
Baquis Giuliana
Barabas Silvio
Baraffael Fiorina
Baranes Ida
Barbout Fortunata
Barda Barkana
Barda Giacomina
Barda Oliviero
 Ruggero
Barda Salomone
Barda Simeone
 Lionello
Bardavid Alessandro
 Behor
Bardavid Caden
Bardavid Elia
Bardavid Ester
Bardavid Mary
Barnstein
 Diamantina
Baroccio Clara
Baroccio Virginia
Baron Emma
Baruch Abramo
Baruch Ada Sara
Baruch Avram
Baruch Baruch
Baruch Behor
 Michele
Baruch Clara
Baruch Elia
Baruch Eliezer
Baruch Enrichetta
Baruch Ezdra
Baruch Flora
Baruch Franca
Baruch Giacomo
Baruch Giorgio Elia
Baruch Giosuè
 Alessandro
Baruch Giuditta
Baruch Isacco
Baruch Isacco
Baruch Isacco
Baruch Isacco
 Mario
Baruch Liliana
Baruch Marco
Baruch Mosè
Baruch Natan
Baruch Perla Allegra
Baruch Raffaele

Baruch Raffaello
Baruch Rita
Baruch Sabetai
Baruch Salom
Baruch Salomon
 Silvio
Baruch Salvatore
Baruch Susanna
Baruch Violetta
Baruch Zimbul
Baruk Clara
Basevi Adele
Basevi Attilio
Basevi Elena
Basevi Emma
Basevi Ida
Basevi Lazzaro
Basevi Pasqua
Basevi Tullio
Basevi Vittorio
Bass Isamor
Bass Stefania
Bassani Albertina
Bassani Anna
 Enrichetta
Bassani Bruno
Bassani Carlo
Bassani Clelia
Bassani Edgardo
Bassani Edoardo
Bassani Franco
Bassani Gemma
Bassani Giulietta
Bassani Giuseppe
Bassani Giuseppe
 Benedetto
Bassani Lydia
Bassani Marcella
Bassani Tina
Bassano Bianca
Bassano Rita
Bassi Alberto
Bassi Ettore
Bassi Fanny
Bassi Marco
Bassi Vittorio
Basso Bruno
Batschis Helene
Batschis Olga
Battich Luciano
Battino Giuseppe
Bauer Isacco
Baum Lodovico
Baum Olga
Baumann Margarethe

Baumwollspinner Wolf
Bayona Carlo
Bayona Davide
Bayona Dora
Bayona Isacco
Bayona Lucia
Bayona Rita
Bear Rachele
Beck Irma
Bedussa Regina
Bedussa Rosa
Beer Karl
Beer Lazar
Begaz Rosa
Behar Allegra
Behar Berta
Behar Davide
Behar Donna
Behar Elisa Tovà
Behar Giuseppe
Behar Lea Rebecca
Behar Rachele
Behar Rachele Rosy
Bein Anton
Bein Salomon
Beiner Stefania
Belgrado Mario
Belgrado Ubaldo
Belinkis Cecilia
Bella
Bellak Evelyn
Bellak Giorgetta
Belleli Aldo
Belleli Allegra
Belleli Anna
Belleli Anna
Belleli Armando
Belleli Armando
Belleli Armando
Belleli Bruno
Belleli Davide
Belleli Dorina
Belleli Elio
Belleli Enrichetta
Belleli Enrichetta Matilde
Belleli Enrichetta Rachele
Belleli Fortunata
Belleli Fortunata
Belleli Giulia
Belleli Isacco
Belleli Isacco Samuele

Belleli Jossua Salvatore
Belleli Lazzaro
Belleli Lazzaro
Belleli Lazzaro
Belleli Marco
Belleli Moisè
Belleli Nissim
Belleli Pace
Belleli Pietro
Belleli Pietro
Belleli Rebecca
Belleli Roberto
Belleli Salvatore
Belleli Stameta
Belleli Vittorina
Bembassat Giacomo
Bembassat Vittorio
Bemporad Ada
Bemporad Ada
Bemporad Adolfo
Bemporad Aldo
Bemporad Amedeo
Bemporad Anna
Bemporad Annita
Bemporad Arnoldo
Bemporad Bianca
Bemporad David Giuseppe
Bemporad Elvira
Bemporad Gemma
Bemporad Gina
Bemporad Giorgio
Bemporad Jole
Bemporad Lelia
Bemporad Lidia
Bemporad Liliana
Bemporad Marcella
Bemporad Mirella
Bemporad Silvio
Bemporad Ugo
Bemporat Lazzaro
Ben Aron Jenni
Benaroyo Fortunata
Benatar Baruh
Benatar Giuseppe
Benatar Lea
Benatar Mazaltov
Benatar Nissim
Benatar Nissim
Benatar Rachele
Benatar Regina
Benatar Sara
Benatar Sara
Benathan Giuseppe

Benbassà Rachele
Bendaud Jole
Benedetti Elena
Benedetti Jole
Benedetti Luciano
Benedetti Valentina
Benezra Matilde
Benghiat Maurizio
Beniacar Bulissa Luisa
Beniacar Giacobbe Giacomo
Beniacar Matilde
Beniacar Moise
Beniacar Perla
Benigno Alberto
Benigno Emma
Benigno Eugenio
Benigno Giulia
Benigno Letizia
Benjamin Abramo
Benjamin Anna
Benjamin Clemente
Benjamin Daisy
Benjamin Elisa
Benjamin Ester
Benjamin Eugenio
Benjamin Geltrude
Benjamin Giacomo
Benjamin Hlafo
Benjamin Lidia
Benjamin Messauda
Benjamin Meta
Benjamin Mosè
Benjamin Rachele
Benjamin Regina Nella
Benjamin Renato
Benjamin Samuel
Benjamin Silvana Maria
Benjamin Smeralda
Benjamin Vittorio
Benjamin William Abramo
Benonsisso Nisso
Benosiglio
Benosiglio Levi
Benosiglio Morris Mosè
Benosiglio Moses
Benrey
Benrey Moise
Benscioan Ascer

Bensussan Berthe
Bensussan Eleonora
Benun Abramo
Benun Abramo
Benun Alberto
Benun Alfredo
Benun Bianca
Benun Bulissa
Benun Caden
Benun Clara
Benun Comprada
Benun Davide
Benun Davide
Benun Elia
Benun Elia
Benun Elia
Benun Esther
Benun Giacomo
Benun Giamila
Benun Haim
Benun Haim
Benun Isacco
Benun Isacco
Benun Luciana
Benun Marco
Benun Maria
Benun Maria
Benun Maria
Benun Matilde
Benun Mazaltov
Benun Mordechai
Benun Mosè
Benun Nissim
Benun Nissim
Benun Nissim
Benun Nissim
Benun Rachele
Benun Rahamin
Benun Rahamin
Benun Regina
Benun Regina
Benun Rosa
Benun Sadok
Benun Salomone
Benun Samuel
Benun Samuele
Benun Sara
Benun Sara
Benun Stella
Benun Vittoria
Benveniste Abramo
Benveniste Alberto
Benveniste Davide
Benveniste Davide
Benveniste Estrella

Benveniste Estrella
Benveniste Isacco
Benveniste Isacco
Benveniste Linda
Benveniste Mosè
Benveniste Nissim
Benveniste Nissim
Benveniste Nissim
Benveniste Palomba
Benveniste Paolo
  Raul
Benveniste Roberto
Benveniste Sarota
Benveniste Stella
  Esther
Benvenisti Giannina
Bercu Anne Marie
Berger Adolf
Berger Alberto
Berger Arnold
Berger Carlo
Berger Elisabetta
Berger Erna
Berger Eugenio
Berger Geza
Berger Giuseppe
Berger Giuseppe
Berger Hedwig
Berger Margarete
Berger Maurice
Berger Max
Berger Nora
Berger Rosina
Bergmann Gino
Bergmann Theodor
Berl Silvio
Bermann Abramo
Bermann Alfred
Bermann Enrico
Bermann Ermanno
Bermann Friedrich
Bermann Ida
Bermann Melania
Bermann Moritz
Bernau Ida
Berndt Elisabetta
Bernheim Luisa
Bero Boaz
Bero Davide
Bero Fani
Bero Rebecca
Bero Ruben
Bero Stella
Bero Uriel
Berolsheimer Aldo

Berro Amelia
Berro Bulissa
Berro Elisa
Berro Giacobbe
Berro Lea
Berro Matilde
Berro Nissim
Berro Oriel
Berro Rosa
Berro Ruben
Berro Salvatore
Bersciadski Semil
Bertiner Berta
Bertram Rifka
Beru Mazaltov
Berussi Elisa
Besso Elsa Jolanda
Besso Lina
Besso Marco
Besso Menachem
Bettmann Henriette
Bianchi Emerico
Bianchini Giulia
Bianchini Livia
Bick Max Herbert
Bick Sigismondo
Bick Sofia
Bidussa Elsa
Bielenkzy Evelina
Bigiavi Edoardo
Bilis Caden
Bilschowski Hans
Bilschowski Werner
Bincer Giovanni
Bindefeld Clara
Bindefeld Mayer
Bindefeld
  Sigismondo
Birkenfeld Ignaz
Birkenwald Gabriel
Birkenwald Pinkus
Birkenwald Rachele
Birkenwald Sara
Birnbaum Max
Birnbaum Rosa
Birò Alberto
Birò Andrea Mario
Biscardo Luigi
Bises Abramo
  Alberto
Bisson Giulia
Bisson Vittorio
  Zadock
Biton Lea
Biton Rebecca

Bivash David
Blanes Raffaello
Blank Debora
Blatteis Emilio
Blatteis Massimo
Blauer Massimiliano
Blaustein Giorgio
Blinder Etta Caterina
Bloch Alessandra
Bloch Katherina
Bloch Margarethe
Blody Rosa
Bloede Gerson
Blonder Sara
Blueh Ernestina
Bluehweiss Federica
Blum Enrichetta
Blum Gelweiler
  Carolina
Blumenfeld Elena
Blumenthal Jacob
Blumenthal Olga
Boccara Sciaula Dori
Bodner Magda
Bodner Mayer
Boehm Malka
Boehm Michelangelo
Bogner Anna
Bolaffi Annita
Bolaffio Amadio
Bolaffio Giacomo
Bolaffio Giulio
Bolaffio Moisè Ettore
Bonacar Giacomo
  Giacobbe
Bonacar Giuditta
Bonacar Luna Malkà
Bonacar Sara
Bondì Alfredo
Bondì Anna
Bondì Benedetto
Bondì Elena
Bondì Fiorella
Bondì Giuseppe
Bondì Leone
Bondì Margherita
Bondì Pace
Bondì Umberto
Bondy Ella
Boniel Stella
Boraks Gustav
Boralevi Giuseppe
Borchert Carlo
Bordignon Giannina
Borg Irma

Borger Riccardo
Borgetti Ernestina
Borghi Giorgia
Borsetti Luigi
Boton Malcunna
Botton Ester
Bottoni Maria
Brainin Giulia
Brandes Ernesta
Brandes Regina
Brandes Riccardo
Brandi Mario
Brasch Elsa
Brasch Heinrich
Brauer Jolanda
Braun Berta
Braun Bianca
Braun Carola
Braun Clara
Braun Erminia
Braun Francesco
Braun Giulia
Braun Roberto
Brauner Jolanda
Brender Hermann
Brennitzer Franz
Bretschneider
  Magdalena
Breuer Edmondo
Breuer Guglielmo
Breuer Rosalia
Brezel Giuseppina
Briegler Maria
Brill Attilio
Brill Davide
Brill Fortunata Argia
Brill Sofia
Bringer Paul
Broeder Elisabetta
Broeder Ernesto
Broeder Eva
Brogi Giuseppe
Brosan Berta
Brucker Samuele Noè
Bruckner Olga
Brull Giulia
Brunell Raymond
Brunell Robert
Bruner Bernhard
Brunner Egone
Bryl Rosa
Buaron Ester
Buaron Esterina
Buaron Giacobbe
Buaron Hamus

Buaron Hlafo
Buaron Hlafo
Buaron Leone Felice
Buaron Margherita
Buaron Messauda
Buaron Salma
Bublil Zariffa
Bucabsa Sarina
Bucci Alessandra
Bucci Tatiana Liliana
Buchalter Aron
Buchaster Haim
Buchaster Jakob
Buchaster Manfred
  Bernhard
Buchbinder Rosina
Buchsbaum Clara
Buchsbaum Kurt
Buechler Ida
Bueno Dino
Bueno Silla
Bueno Sirio Renzo
Buetow Wally
Burbea Abramo
Burbea Beniamino
Burbea Daniele
Burbea Gabriel
Burbea Gazala
Burbea Giacobbe
Burbea Giora
Burbea Giorgio
Burbea Giuseppe
Burbea Hammus
Burbea Hammus
Burbea Hammus
  detto Nennes
Burbea Huato
Burbea Isacco
Burbea Jacob
Burbea Jacob
Burbea Jusef
Burbea Jusef
Burbea Mordechai
Burbea Musci
Burbea Rachele
Burbea Selma
Burbea Silvana
Burbea Silvina
Burbea Simeone
Burbea Simone
Burbea Sion
Burbea Smeralda
Burbea Vittorio
Burbea Vittorio
Burbea Zaccaria

Burlan Lella
Bursztyn Sara
Cabibbe Pia
Cabilio Masalta
Cadranel Comprada
Cadranel Lea
Cadranel Maria
Cadranel Miru
Cadranel Rachele
Caffaz Cesare
Caffaz Cipriano
Caffaz Ida
Cagli Bruno
Cagli Guido
Cagli Laura
Caimi Enrichetta
Caimi Leone
Caivano Angelina
Calabi Adele Maria
Calabi Benedetto
Calabi Pia
Calabresi Enrica
Calef Emilia
Calef Joseph
Calef Maurice
Calef Raoul Raffaele
Calimani Emma
  Geltrude
Calimani Ida
Calimani Lea Rita
Calimani Moisè
Calimani Susanna
Calò Alberta detta
  Albertina
Calò Alberto
Calò Alberto
Calò Alberto
Calò Alberto detto
  Cuccio
Calò Angelo
Calò Angelo detto
  Lupetto
Calò Anselmo
Calò Armanda
Calò Armanda
Calò Aureliano
Calò Bellina
Calò Bendetto
Calò Benvenuta
Calò Cesare
Calò Cesira
Calò Dante
Calò David
Calò David
Calò David

Calò Elena
Calò Elena
Calò Elena
Calò Elena
Calò Elena
Calò Eleonora
Calò Emilio
Calò Enrica
Calò Ernesto
Calò Ester
Calò Ester
Calò Ester
Calò Eugenio
Calò Fatina
Calò Fernando
Calò Fiorella
Calò Fiorina
Calò Flora
Calò Giovanni
Calò Giovanni
Calò Giuseppe
Calò Giuseppe
Calò Giuseppe Felice
Calò Grazia
Calò Grazia
Calò Graziadio
Calò Graziella
Calò Graziella
Calò Ines
Calò Jak Emanuele
Calò Lello Samuele
Calò Marco
Calò Marco detto
  Chicco
Calò Margherita
Calò Mario
Calò Matilde
Calò Mosè
Calò Mosè Marco
  detto Moro
Calò Nella
Calò Pacifico
Calò Prospero
Calò Quintilio
Calò Raffaele Paul
Calò Raimondo
Calò Raimondo
Calò Renata
Calò Renzo
Calò Ricca
Calò Roberta Rina
Calò Romolo
Calò Romolo
Calò Rosa detta
  Rosina

Calò Rosanna
Calò Rosina Rosa
Calò Sara
Calò Sergio
Calò Virginia
Calò Vittorio
Calò Zaira
Cambi Gisella
Camerini Corinna
Camerini Elda
Camerini Emilia
  Lea
Camerini Letizia
Camerini Natalie
Camerini Olga
Camerini Raffaele
Camerini Ulda
Camerino Adele
Camerino Aurelia
Camerino Benvenuta
Camerino Elena
Camerino Emilia
Camerino Enzo
Camerino Ettore
  Felice
Camerino Eugenia
Camerino Gilberto
Camerino Italo
Camerino Jole
Camerino Leone
Camerino Luciano
Camerino Vanda
Camhi Simha
Caminada Arturo
Camis Ulda
Cammeo Lorenzo
Cammeo Maria
Cammeo Mario
Campagnano Aldo
Campagnano Donato
Campagnano Saul
Campagnano Teresa
Campagnano Vito
Campi Anna Lia
Campi Massimiliano
Camponore Elio
Campos Gisella
Canarutto Anna
Canarutto Bechor
  Viktor
Canarutto Emilio
Canarutto Emma
Canarutto Giorgina
Canarutto Giuseppe
Canarutto Leone

Canarutto Marcella
Nina
Canarutto Moisè
Mario
Canarutto Ofelia
Canarutto Oscar
Canarutto Regina
Cantoni Alessandra
Cantoni Amelia
Cantoni Carlotta
Cantoni Ida Eugenia
Cantoni Luciano
Cantoni Mamiani
della Rovere
Vittorio Angelo
Cantoni Margherita
Cantor Charles
Cantor Chela
Capelluto Adele
Capelluto Alberto
Capelluto Bulissa
Capelluto Bulissa
Capelluto Daniele
Capelluto Davide
Capelluto Davide
Capelluto Davide
Capelluto Diamante
Capelluto Dora
Capelluto Eleonora
Capelluto Elia
Capelluto Esther
Capelluto Esther
Capelluto Estherina
Capelluto Estrella
Capelluto Fortunata
Capelluto Giacobbe
Capelluto Giacobbe
Capelluto Giacobbe
Giacomo
Capelluto Giamila
Capelluto Giannetta
Capelluto Giulia
Capelluto Giuseppe
Capelluto Giuseppe
Capelluto Giuseppe
Capelluto Guidalia
Capelluto Guidalia
Capelluto Haim
Capelluto Herzel
Ascer
Capelluto Ida
Capelluto Isacco
Capelluto Isacco
Capelluto Isacco
Capelluto Lea

Capelluto Lea
Capelluto Lea Lucia
Capelluto Leone
Capelluto Maria
Capelluto Maria
Capelluto Maria
Capelluto Maria
Bohora
Capelluto Matilde
Capelluto Matilde
Capelluto Matilde
Capelluto Matilde
Capelluto Matilde
Capelluto Matilde
Capelluto Matilde
Capelluto Mazaltov
Capelluto Moise
Capelluto Mussani
Capelluto Nissim
Capelluto Nissim
Capelluto Nissim
Capelluto Nissim
detto Nisso
Capelluto Rabeno
Capelluto Rachele
Capelluto Rachele
Capelluto Rachele
Capelluto Rachele
Capelluto Rachele
Capelluto Raffaele
Capelluto Raimondo
Capelluto Rebecca
Capelluto Rebecca
Capelluto Rebecca
Capelluto Rebecca
Capelluto Rebecca
Capelluto Rebecca
Capelluto Regina
Capelluto Renata
Capelluto Renata
Capelluto Roberto
Capelluto Rosa
Capelluto Rosa
Capelluto Rosa
Capelluto Rosa
Capelluto Ruben
Capelluto Salvatore
Capelluto Salvatore
Capelluto Salvo
Capelluto Samuele
Capelluto Samuele
Capelluto Sara
Capelluto Sol
Capelluto Sol
Capelluto Susanna
Capelluto Tamar

Capelluto Violetta
Capelluto Violetta
Capelluto Vittoria
Capelluto Vittoria
Vida
Capelluto Vittorio
Capon Augusto
Capua Paolina
Capuia Dora
Capuia Jeuda Leon
Capuia Nissim
Capuia Roberto
Capuia Signorù
Carcassoni Eugenia
Carcassoni Tullio
Cardoso Rosa
Cardoso Ugo
Carmi Adele
Carmi Cesare
Carmi Ermelinda
Colombina
Carmi Ermene Ester
Carmi Ida Gina
Carmi Isaia
Caro Alberto
Caro Claudio
Caro Giuseppe
Caro Violetta
Caroglio Carla
Carpi Alberto
Carpi Germana
Carpi Olimpia
Carpi Renzo
Carusi Maurizio
Cases Ida
Cases Moisè Giulio
Cassin Alberto
Cassin Arturo
Salomone
Cassin Eugenia
Cassin Ezechiele
Cassin Sergio
Cassuto Albertina
Cassuto Anna
Cassuto Nathan
Cassuto Ugo
Castelbolognesi
Bellina
Castelbolognesi
Federico
Castelbolognesi
Luciano
Castelbolognesi
Silvana
Castelfranchi Renato

Castelfranco Elena
detta Nella
Castelfranco Emma
Castelfranco Olga
Castelletti Aldo
Castelletti Beniamino
Castelletti Eugenio
Castelletti Isacco
Castelletti Stella
Castelletti Viktor
Castelli Adriana
Castelli Elena
Castelli Enrico
Castelli Giulio Cesare
Castelli Guido
Aronne
Castelli Laura
Castelli Olga Renata
Castiglioni Nella
Cava Aldo
Cava Enzo
Cava Franca
Cava Perla
Cavaglione Emanuele
Cavaglione Emma
Cavalieri Alina detta
Lina
Cavalieri Argia
Cavalieri Gianna
Cavalieri Giuseppina
Cavalieri Gustavo
Cavaliero Alessandra
Cave Bondì Gina
Caviglia Adamo
Caviglia Adolfo
Caviglia Beniamino
Caviglia Elia
Caviglia Enrica
Caviglia Ester
Caviglia Giacomo
Caviglia Grazia
Caviglia Guglielmo
detto Bibbidone
Caviglia Letizia
Caviglia Orabona
detta Eleonora
Caviglia Perla Emma
Caviglia Renato
Caviglia Rita
Caviglia Santoro
Caviglia Settimio
Caviglia Sole
Caviglia Umberto
Ceres Enrico
Ceres Vittoria

Cervi Maurizio
Cesana Carlotta
Cesana Davide
Cesana Davide
Cesana Emilio
Cesana Giacomo
Cesana Isaia
Cesana Matilde
Cesana Menahem
Armando
Cesana Pia
Cesana Rachele
Cesana Sara
Cesana Vittorio
Cesar Antonia
Chami Simha
Charin Markus
Chimichi Alberto
Chimichi Eugenio
Elia
Chimichi Evelina
Chimichi Piero
Cienhanosiska Sella
Ciggian Anna
Cingoli Noemi
Cinmanas Abramo
Ciprut Vittoria
Citoni Angelo
Citoni Arrigo
Citoni Carlo
Citoni Colomba
Citoni Costanza
Citoni Ettore
Citoni Giacomo
Guido
Citoni Giuseppina
Anita
Citoni Prospero
Citroën Renée Marie
Henriette
Cittone Abramo
Bechor
Cittone Elia
Cittone Gioia
Giulietta
Cittone Leone
Cittone Mordechai
Max
Cittone Nissim
Cittone Nissim
Cittone Raffaele
Cittone Sol
Cittone Vitale
Cittone Vittoria
Civere Donna

Civiak Moshek
Cividali Aldo
Cividali Angelo
Cividali Sergio
Clerle Alba
Clerle Cesira Amelia
Clerle Emilia
Codron Alessandro
Codron Elsa
Codron Esther
Codron Hitzkia
Codron Laura
Codron Leone
Codron Lina
Codron Maria
Codron Maria
Codron Maurizio
Codron Nissim
Codron Rachele
Codron Rachele
Codron Ruben
Codron Sara
Codron Sipura
Codron Sipurà
Coen Adele
Coen Aharon
Coen Alberto
Coen Alberto
Coen Alberto
Coen Alberto
Girolamo
Coen Alice
Coen Alvaro
Coen Amelia
Coen Amelia
Coen Armando
Coen Aronne
Coen Arrigo
Coen Arturo
Coen Asher
Coen Avraham
Coen Baruh
Coen Bella detta
Bellina
Coen Beninfante
Franco
Coen Beninfante
Lucio
Coen Beninfante
Renzo
Coen Bianca
Coen Bulissa
Coen Clara
Coen Daniele
Coen Dante

Coen Diamante
Coen Diana
Coen Edi
Coen Elena
Coen Elena
Coen Eliakim
Coen Eliakim
Coen Elisa
Coen Emilia
Coen Enrica
Coen Enzo
Coen Esther
Coen Ettore
Coen Flora
Coen Fortunata
Coen Fortunata
Coen Fortunato
Coen Franca
Coen Giacobbe
Coen Giacobbe
Coen Giacobbe
Giacomo
Coen Giacomo
Coen Gilda
Coen Giorgina
Guglielma
Coen Giorgio
Coen Giuseppe
Coen Giuseppe
Coen Giuseppe
Coen Giuseppe detto
Beppino
Coen Giuseppina
Coen Graziella
Coen Guglielmo
Coen Guido
Coen Haim
Coen Haim
Coen Hanula
Coen Hanula
Coen Hizkià
Coen Ione
Coen Irene
Coen Isacco
Coen Isacco
Coen Isacco
Coen Ivonne
Coen Lea
Coen Lea
Coen Lea
Coen Leone
Coen Lucia
Coen Luzzato
Giacomo
Coen Mahir

Coen Marcello
Coen Margherita
Coen Marta
Coen Matilde
Coen Matilde
Coen Matilde
Coen Mosè
Coen Mosè
Coen Mosè
Coen Mosè
Coen Mosè
Coen Mosè
Coen Natan
Coen Nella Corinna
Coen Nissim
Coen Norina
Coen Olga
Coen Oscar
Coen Pacina
Coen Pirani
Corrado
Gustavo
Coen Pirani Liana
Coen Porto Amelia
Coen Porto
Augusto
Coen Porto Vittorio
Coen Porzia
Coen Rachele
Coen Rachele
Coen Rachele
Coen Raffaele
Coen Rahamin
Coen Rebecca
Coen Regina
Coen Regina
Coen Regina
Fortunata
Coen Renato detto
Monchino
Coen Renée
Coen Rica
Coen Rica
Coen Romilda
Coen Sacerdoti
Eugenio
Coen Sadok
Coen Salomone Saul
Coen Salva
Coen Sara
Coen Sara
Coen Sara Rosa
Coen Saverio
Coen Stella
Coen Susanna

Coen Umberto
Coen Virginia
Coen Vittoria
Coen Vittoria
Coen Vittorio Angelo
  detto Uccio
Coen Zaira
Cogo Guglielmo
  Enrico
Cohen Adolfo
Cohen Alberto
Cohen Allegra
Cohen Amelia
Cohen Anna
Cohen Azzar
Cohen Caden
Cohen Clarissa
Cohen da Silva
  Giacomo
Cohen da Silva
  Guido
Cohen da Silva
  Renato
Cohen David
Cohen Eliakim Behor
Cohen Ester Stella
Cohen Estrea
Cohen Flora
Cohen Giulia
Cohen Giuseppe
Cohen Isacco
Cohen Isacco
Cohen Isidoro
Cohen Ivonne
Cohen Leone
Cohen Lidia
Cohen Manlio
  Emanuele
Cohen Marcello
  Leone Mosè
Cohen Marco Nissim
Cohen Maria
Cohen Mazaltov
Cohen Menahem
Cohen Mosè
Cohen Nissim
Cohen Noemi
Cohen Perla
Cohen Rachele
Cohen Rachele
Cohen Raffaele
Cohen Rahamin
Cohen Rebecca
Cohen Rebecca
Cohen Regina

Cohen Regina
Cohen Rica
Cohen Roberto
  Samanto
Cohen Ruben
Cohen Salomon
Cohen Sara
Cohen Stella
Cohen Tullio
Cohen Venezian
  Carlo
Cohen Venezian
  Luisa Itala
Cohen Venezian Olga
Cohen Vittoria
Cohn
Cohn Erich
Cohn Hella
Collin Kaethe
Colombo Ada
Colombo Alberto
Colombo Aldo
Colombo Alessandro
Colombo Alessandro
  detto Sandro
Colombo Amerigo
Colombo Angelo
Colombo Angelo
Colombo Benvenuto
  Gabriele
Colombo Claudio
Colombo Decima
Colombo Donato
Colombo Elda
Colombo Elena
Colombo Elena
Colombo Elia Enea
Colombo Elsa
Colombo Enrico
Colombo Ester
  Giovanna
Colombo Eugenio
Colombo Federico
  Giacomo
Colombo Gemma
Colombo Giulia
  Giuditta
Colombo Israele
  Ferdinando
Colombo Mario
Colombo Mario
Colombo Norma
Colombo Pacifico
Colombo Prima
Colombo Rita

Colombo Sara
Colombo Tullio
Colonna Leo
Colonna Palmira
Colorni Bellina Lina
  Augusta
Colorni Claudina
Conè Alberto
Conè Giacobbe
  Giacomo
Conè Giuseppe
Conè Lucia
Conè Matteo
Conè Mosè
Conè Mussani
Conè Nissim
Conè Rachele
Conè Samuele
Conè Sara
Conegliano Bruno
Conegliano Giulio
Conegliano Giuseppe
Conegliano Italo
Consarelli Ida
Consigli Clelia
Consolo Giulia
Corcos Felice
Cordoval Abramo
Cordoval Alberto
  Abramo
Cordoval Asher
Cordoval Beniamino
Cordoval David
Cordoval Eliakim
Cordoval Giacobbe
Cordoval Giuseppe
Cordoval Giuseppe
Cordoval Grazia
Cordoval Isacco
Cordoval Isacco
Cordoval Isacco
Cordoval Isacco
Cordoval Matilde
Cordoval Nahama
Cordoval Natan
Cordoval Natan
Cordoval Nissim
Cordoval Oro
Cordoval Rachele
Cordoval Rica
Cordoval Rosa
Cordoval Ruben
Cordoval Salvo
Cordoval Sipurà
Core Rebecca

Cori Esther
Cori Vitale
Corinaldi Ada
Corinaldi Bice
Corinaldi Cesare
Corinaldi Corinna
  Anna
Corinaldi Emilio
Corinaldi Gino
Corinaldi Gustavo
Corinaldi Olga
Corinaldi Rosita
Corkidis Luisa Lenca
Cornicer Jean
Cossmann Ida
Costantini Cesare
  Augusto Benedetto
Costantini Giovanna
  Ester
Costantini Giulia
Costantini Giulio
Costantini Mario
Costantini Roberto
Cottignoli Bruno
Covo Mario Abramo
Cramer Natalia
Cremisi Elia Arduino
Cremisi Giulio
Cremisi Moisè
  Adolfo
Cremisi Vittorio
Crespin Abramo
Crespin Judith detta
  Juddi
Crespin Vittoria
Cszopp Bernardo
Cugno Alberto
Cugno Ascer
Cugno Dora
Cugno Ester
Cugno Giacobbe
Cugno Giacobbe
Cugno Giuseppe
Cugno Isacco
Cugno Lazzaro
Cugno Lucia
Cugno Lucia
Cugno Maria
Cugno Rachele
Cugno Rebecca
Cugno Samuele
Cugno Vittorio Haim
Cugnu Rachele
Curiel Achille
  Samuele

Curiel Alberto
Curiel Aldo
Curiel Amelia
Curiel Attilio
Curiel Bruno
Curiel Carlo
Curiel Giacomo
Curiel Giorgio
Curiel Ariel Livia
Cutiszra Dea
Cuzzeri Amalia
Cuzzeri Elisa
Cuzzeri Ennio
Cuzzeri Eugenia
Cuzzeri Giacomo
Cuzzeri Irma
Cuzzeri Olga
Cuzzeri Pia
Cuzzi Corinna
Curilla
Czackes Nathan
Czackes Nedda
Vittoria
Czerkl Alberto
Czerkl Elvira
Czerkl Emerico
Czerkl Margherita
Czolosinska Sofia
D'Angeli Carlo
D'Angeli Mario
D'Angeli Massimo
D'Italia Adele
Corinna
D'Italia Gerolamo
D'Italia Giovanna
Da Costa Kurt
Da Fano Isabella
Dag Margherita
Dag Vittorio
Dalla Torre Aronne
Dalla Torre Bruno
Dalla Torre Giacomo
Dalla Torre
Giuseppe
Dalla Torre Laura
Dalla Torre Roma
Dalla Torre Vittorio
Dalla Volta Alberto
Dalla Volta Alfredo
Ariel
Dalla Volta Anna
Viola
Dalla Volta Enrico
Dalla Volta Guido
detto Volta

Dalla Volta
Margherita
Dalla Volta Paolo
Dalla Volta Riccardo
Dames Samuel
Damidt Erna
Dan Anna
Dana Ester
Dana Isacco
Dana Lea
Dana Maria
Dana Mosè
Dana Salomone
Dana Salvatore
Dana Samuele
Dana Sara
Dana Stella
Dana Stella
Danelon Ottavio
Dann Ester
Dann Giuseppe
Dann Regina
Dann Sara
Dann Schulem
Danon Abramo
Danon Alessandro
Danon Beatrice
Danon Davide
Danon Davide
Danon Ester
Danon Joel
Danon Miriam
Danon Moreno
Danon Rachele
Danon Rachele
Danon Salomone
Danon Salomone
Danon Sarina
Danziger Mortka
Darmon Massimo
Daskovic Julka
David Isaak
David Lotar
David Matilde
David Sandor
Davidoff Dora
De Angeli Aldo
De Angeli Enrichetta
De Angeli Riccardo
De Angeli Umberto
De Angelis Bona
De Angelis Ercole
De Benedetti
Achille
De Benedetti Alice

De Benedetti Amalia
Perla
De Benedetti
Benvenuta Perla
De Benedetti Bruno
De Benedetti Claudio
De Benedetti Elisa
De Benedetti Emilia
Eva Gentile
De Benedetti Enrica
De Benedetti Ernesta
De Benedetti
Esterina
De Benedetti
Eugenio
De Benedetti
Giacomo
De Benedetti Giorgia
De Benedetti Giorgio
De Benedetti Ida
De Benedetti Jolanda
De Benedetti
Leonardo
De Benedetti Lucia
De Benedetti Mario
De Benedetti
Massimo
De Benedetti Matilde
De Benedetti Piero
De Benedetti Ugo
De Benedetti Vittorio
De Castro Hans
De Cori Gabriella
De Cori Ida
De Cori Vera
De Kaiser Bruno
De Kaiser Trude
De Leon Davide
De Leon Michele
Attilio
De Leon Rosa
De Nola Riccardo
De Nola Sergio
De Nola Settimio
Carlo
De Nola Settimio
Carlo
De Nola Sergio
De Nola Riccardo
De Salvo Elena
De Semo Vittorino
De Simone Sergio
Debasch Beniamino
Debasch Ester
Debasch Fortunata

Debasch Fortunato
Debasch Giuditta
Debasch Jolanda
Debasch Jolanda
Debasch Leone
Debasch Rina
Debasch Ruth
Deiler Rosa
Del Mare Ada
Del Mare Germana
Del Monte Amedeo
Del Monte Anita
Del Monte Anna
detta Annita
Del Monte Costanza
Del Monte Franca
Del Monte Giulia
Del Monte Giuseppe
Del Monte Grazia
Del Monte Italia
Del Monte Leonello
Del Monte Luigi
detto Gigi
Del Monte
Margherita
Del Monte Rina
Del Monte Velia
Del Monte Vittorio
Del Monte Vittorio
Emanuele
Del Vecchio Emma
Del Vecchio Maria
Ada
Del Vecchio Paolina
Del Vecchio Raffaele
Delfiner Chana
Deligtisch Ray
Dell'Ariccia Alba
Bella
Dell'Ariccia
Benedetto
Dell'Ariccia
Benedetto
Dell'Ariccia Emma
Dell'Ariccia Ernesto
Dell'Ariccia Giovanni
Dell'Ariccia Italia
Dell'Ariccia Lello
Dell'Ariccia Manlio
Dell'Ariccia Samuele
Dell'Ariccia Stefo
Della Pergola Cesare
Davide
Della Pergola Donato
detto Tato

Della Pergola Ester
Della Pergola Giulio
Della Pergola
 Giuseppe
Della Pergola Mario
Della Pergola Steno
Della Riccia Aldo
Della Riccia Berta
Della Riccia Erasmo
Della Riccia
 Fortunato
Della Riccia Franco
Della Riccia Luciana
Della Riccia Mirella
Della Rocca Alberto
Della Rocca Angelo
Della Rocca Angelo
Della Rocca Chiara
Della Rocca Costanza
Della Rocca Costanza
Della Rocca David
Della Rocca
 Elisabetta
Della Rocca Emma
Della Rocca Enrica
Della Rocca Gina
Della Rocca Lazzaro
Della Rocca Lello
Della Rocca Nella
Della Rocca Rubino
Della Rocca Settimio
Della Rocca Silvio
Della Rocca Virginia
Della Rocca Viviana
Della Seta Adriana
Della Seta Alberto
Della Seta Dino
Della Seta Eva
Della Seta Franca
Della Seta Gina
Della Seta Giovanni
Della Seta Giovanni
 Carlo detto
 Giancarlo
Della Seta Leonello
Della Seta Livia
Della Seta Samuele
 Leone
Della Seta Valentina
Della Torre Ada
Della Torre Attilio
 Salomone
Della Torre Cesira
Della Torre Elena
 Gina

Della Torre Ester
Della Torre Giacomo
Della Torre Manlio
Della Torre Massimo
Della Torre Mosè
Della Torre Odoardo
Della Torre Ofelia
Della Torre Oliviero
Della Torre Pia
Della Torre Vanda
Demeter Netty
Dente Anna
Dente Matilde
Dente Matilde
Dente Moise Morris
Denti Giulia Gioia
Denti Sara
Denti Susanna
Derczanski Maurice
 Mosè
Dereschowitz
 Samuel
Deutsch Adolfo
Deutsch Erminia
 Emma
Deutsch Etel
Deutsch Frida
Deutsch
 Massimiliano
Deutsch Nada
Deutsch Nicola
Deutsch Vittoria
Deutsch Zeliko
Deutscher Eliana
Deutscher Hertz
Devaux Raimonda
Di Capua Amadio
Di Capua Angelo
Di Capua Annita
Di Capua Chighino
Di Capua Clotilde
Di Capua Clotilde
Di Capua Elisabetta
 Margherita
Di Capua Elvira
Di Capua Enrica
Di Capua Ernesta
Di Capua Gilda
Di Capua Mosè
Di Capua Mosè
Di Capua Pacifico
Di Capua Pia
Di Capua Rina
Di Capua Rosa
Di Capua Rosina

Di Capua Sabatino
 detto Settimio
Di Capua Serafina
Di Capua Zaccaria
Di Castro Adolfo
Di Castro Adolfo
Di Castro Adolfo
Di Castro Angelica
Di Castro Angelo
Di Castro Angelo
Di Castro Angelo
Di Castro Angelo
Di Castro Angelo
Di Castro Anselmo
Di Castro Attilio
Di Castro Attilio
Di Castro Cesare
Di Castro Cesare
Di Castro Crescenzio
Di Castro Crescenzio
Di Castro Crescenzio
 detto Pizzanella
Di Castro David
Di Castro Emma
Di Castro Emma
Di Castro Ermelinda
Di Castro Giorgio
Di Castro Giovanni
Di Castro Giuliana
 Colomba
Di Castro Giuseppe
Di Castro Graziano
Di Castro Leonello
Di Castro Letizia
Di Castro Lidia
Di Castro Marietta
Di Castro Mario
Di Castro Mario
Di Castro Michele
Di Castro Pace
Di Castro Pacifico
Di Castro Perna
Di Castro Samuele
Di Castro Settimio
Di Castro Teresa
Di Cave Angelo
Di Cave Betta
Di Cave Cesare
Di Cave Edmondo
Di Cave Elena
Di Cave Elisa
Di Cave Emanuele
 Vittorio
Di Cave Eugenio
 Simone
Di Cave Eva

Di Cave Fernanda
Di Cave Franca
Di Cave Franco
Di Cave Guglielmo
Di Cave Luigia
Di Cave Pia
Di Cave Rosina
Di Cave Sandro
Di Cave Settimia
Di Consiglio Ada
Di Consiglio Cesare
Di Consiglio Cesare
Di Consiglio Cesare
 detto Nicolino
Di Consiglio Cesare
 Elvezio
Di Consiglio Clara
Di Consiglio David
Di Consiglio Enrica
Di Consiglio Ester
Di Consiglio Franco
Di Consiglio
 Graziano
Di Consiglio Leone
Di Consiglio
 Leonello
Di Consiglio Lina
Di Consiglio Marco
Di Consiglio Marco
Di Consiglio Mario
 Marco
Di Consiglio Marisa
Di Consiglio Mirella
Di Consiglio Mosè
Di Consiglio Pacifico
Di Consiglio Pacifico
Di Consiglio Pacifico
Di Consiglio Regina
Di Consiglio Rina
 Ester
Di Consiglio
 Salomone
Di Consiglio Santoro
Di Consiglio
 Tranquillo
Di Consiglio Virginia
Di Cori Amedeo
Di Cori Amedeo
Di Cori Angelo
Di Cori Beniamino
Di Cori Dario
Di Cori Giovanni
Di Cori Giulia
Di Cori Sara
Di Cori Settimio

Di Cori Settimio
Di Cori Settimio
Renato
Di Fano Achille
Di Fano Annetta
Di Fano Elsa
Di Fano Giuseppina
detta Pineta
Di Fano Maria
Di Gioacchino Anna
Di Gioacchino Cesira
Di Laudadio Angelo
Di Laudadio Gemma
Di Nepi Adriana
Di Nepi Alberto
Di Nepi Amedeo
Di Nepi Angelo
Di Nepi Celeste
Di Nepi Cesare
Di Nepi Cesare
Di Nepi Cesare
Di Nepi Cesare
Di Nepi Elisabetta
Di Nepi Elvira
Di Nepi Elvira
Di Nepi Emma
Di Nepi Eugenio
Di Nepi Giacomo
Giacobbe
Di Nepi Giorgio
Di Nepi Giovanni
Di Nepi Giuseppe
Di Nepi Giuseppe
Di Nepi Laudadio
Di Nepi Laudadio
Lello
Di Nepi Leone
Di Nepi Mosè
Di Nepi Rina
Di Nepi Samuele
Di Nepi Samuele
detto Lello
Di Nepi Ugo
Di Neris Esterina
Di Neris Isacco
Di Neris Raimondo
detto Zanella
Di Neris Samuele
Di Neris Settimio
Di Nola Alfredo
Donato
Di Nola Delia
Di Nola Elda
Di Nola Ugo
Di Porto Ada

Di Porto Adelaide
Di Porto Alberta
Di Porto Albertina
Di Porto Alberto
Di Porto Alberto
Di Porto Amedeo
Di Porto Angelo
Di Porto Angelo
Di Porto Angelo
Di Porto Angelo
Di Porto Angelo
Di Porto Angelo
Di Porto Angelo
Di Porto Angelo
Di Porto Angiola
Di Porto Annita
Di Porto Bellina
Di Porto Celeste
Di Porto Celeste
Di Porto Cesare
Di Porto Cesare
Di Porto Cesare detto
Sganzese
Di Porto Cesira
Di Porto Costanza
Di Porto Costanza
Di Porto Costanza
Di Porto Crescenzio
Di Porto Crescenzio
Di Porto Elena
Di Porto Elvira
Di Porto Elvira
Di Porto Emanuele
Di Porto Emma
Di Porto Ester
Di Porto Ester
Di Porto Ester
Di Porto Esterina
Di Porto Fanny
Di Porto Finizia
Di Porto Fortunata
Di Porto Fortunata
Di Porto Fulvio
Di Porto Gabriele
Di Porto Giacomo
Di Porto Giacomo
Di Porto Giacomo
Di Porto Giuditta
Di Porto Giuditta
Di Porto Giuditta
Di Porto Giuseppe
Di Porto Giuseppe
Di Porto Giuseppe
Di Porto Grazia
Di Porto Graziella

Di Porto Graziella
Di Porto Graziella
Di Porto Italia
Di Porto Lazzaro
Di Porto Letizia
Di Porto Lilia
Di Porto Mario
Di Porto Mario
Di Porto Mario
Di Porto Mario
Di Porto Marisa
Di Porto Maurizio
Di Porto Pacifico
Di Porto Pacifico
Di Porto Perla
Di Porto Renata
Di Porto Romolo
Di Porto Rosa
Di Porto Rosa
Di Porto Rosina
Di Porto Rubino
Di Porto Sabatino
Di Porto Sergio
Di Porto Settimio
Di Porto Settimio
Di Porto Settimio
Di Porto Settimio
Di Porto Settimio
Di Porto Vitale
Di Porto Vitale detto
Fastidio
Di Porto Wilma
Di Segni Adelaide
Di Segni Adelaide
Di Segni Alba
Di Segni Alberto
Di Segni Alberto Elia
Di Segni Angelo
Di Segni Angelo
Di Segni Angelo
Di Segni Angelo
Di Segni Anita
Di Segni Anna detta
Annetta
Di Segni Armando
Di Segni Benedetto
Di Segni Benedetto
Di Segni Bruno
Di Segni Cesare
Di Segni Clara
Di Segni Clotilde
Di Segni Colomba
Di Segni Colomba
Di Segni David

Di Segni David
Di Segni David
Di Segni Diodato
Di Segni Elia
Di Segni Emanuele
Di Segni Emanuele
Vittorio
Di Segni Emma
Di Segni Enrica
Di Segni Enrica
Di Segni Ester
Di Segni Franco
Di Segni Giacomo
Di Segni Gianna
Di Segni Giovanni
Di Segni Giulia
Di Segni Giuseppe
Di Segni Grazia
Di Segni Grazia
Di Segni Grazia
Di Segni Graziella
Di Segni Graziella
Di Segni Irene
Di Segni Italia
Di Segni Lello
Di Segni Lello
Di Segni Lello
Samuele
Di Segni Leo
Di Segni Leone
Di Segni Liliana
Di Segni Luciana
Di Segni Marco
Di Segni Marco
Di Segni Margherita
Di Segni Maria
Di Segni Mario
Di Segni Pace
Di Segni Pacifico
Di Segni Pacifico
Di Segni Pacifico
Di Segni Pacifico
Di Segni Pacifico
Di Segni Prospero
Adolfo
Di Segni Renato
Di Segni Renato
Di Segni Riccardo
detto Peppone
Brusolinaro
Di Segni Rina
Di Segni Rina
Di Segni Roberto
Di Segni Roberto
Di Segni Rosa

Di Segni Rosa
Di Segni Rosa
Di Segni Rossana
Di Segni Salvatore
Di Segni Settimio
Di Segni Silvia
Di Segni Tosca
Di Segni Umberto
Di Segni Virginia
Di Tivoli Adelaide
Di Tivoli Albertina
Di Tivoli Angelo
Di Tivoli Fatina
Di Tivoli Fatina
Di Tivoli Gemma
Di Tivoli Giuseppe
   detto Nasosfranto
Di Tivoli Lazzaro
Di Tivoli Leonardo
Di Tivoli Leone
Di Tivoli Marco
Di Tivoli Mirella
Di Tivoli Pacifico
Di Tivoli Rina
Di Tivoli Rossana
Di Tivoli Salomone
Di Tivoli Settimio
Di Tivoli Speranza
Di Tivoli Virginia
Di Tivoli Vittorio
Di Veroli
Di Veroli Abramo
Di Veroli Adolfo
Di Veroli Alberto
Di Veroli Angelo
Di Veroli Asdriele
Di Veroli Attilio
Di Veroli Bellina
Di Veroli Bruno
Di Veroli Celeste
Di Veroli Celestina
Di Veroli Colomba
Di Veroli David
Di Veroli David
Di Veroli Donato
Di Veroli Donato
Di Veroli Donato
Di Veroli Donato
Di Veroli Elisabetta
Di Veroli Emma
Di Veroli Emma
Di Veroli Enrica
Di Veroli Enrico
   David
Di Veroli Ernesta

Di Veroli Ester detta
   Rina
Di Veroli Esterina
Di Veroli Eugenio
Di Veroli Fernando
Di Veroli Giacomina
   detta Mimì
Di Veroli Giacomo
Di Veroli Giacomo
Di Veroli Giacomo
Di Veroli Giovanni
Di Veroli Giuditta
Di Veroli Giuditta
Di Veroli Giuditta
Di Veroli Giuditta
Di Veroli Giuseppe
Di Veroli Gualtiero
Di Veroli Italia
Di Veroli Lalla
Di Veroli Lazzaro
Di Veroli Leonardo
Di Veroli Leone detto
   Leo
Di Veroli Letizia
Di Veroli Lidia
Di Veroli Liliana
Di Veroli Marco
Di Veroli Marco
Di Veroli Mario
Di Veroli Mario
Di Veroli Michele
Di Veroli Michele
Di Veroli Michele
Di Veroli Michele
Di Veroli Mosè
Di Veroli Mosè
Di Veroli Pacifico
Di Veroli Pacifico
   detto Mario
Di Veroli Prospero
Di Veroli Renato
Di Veroli Rina
Di Veroli Rina
Di Veroli Rosa
Di Veroli Samuele
   detto Lello
Di Veroli Sara
Di Veroli Settimia
Di Veroli Settimio
Di Veroli Settimio
Di Veroli Silvia
Di Veroli Silvia
Di Veroli Tranquillo
Di Veroli Ugo
   Giorgio

Di Veroli Umberto
Di Veroli Valeria
Di Veroli Virginia
Di Veroli Virginia
Diamante Ermanno
Diamante Guglielmo
Dias Bruno
Dias Davide
Diaz Dario
Diaz Emma Edma
Diaz Giuseppe
Dickstein Berta
Dickstein Stella detta
   Scheindel
Diena Augusta
Diena Davide
   Giuseppe
Diena Ester Wanda
Diena Giacomo
Diena Giorgio
Diena Giuseppina
Diena Ida
Diena Lea
Diena Remigio
Diena Rodolfo
Dienstfertig Jenni
Dihi Diamantina
Dihi Simeone
Dina Adele
Dina Amalia
Dina Anna
Dina Anna
Dina Benedetta
Dina Dino Davide
Dina Emilia Ida
Dina Giorgia detta
   Giorgina
Dina Guido
Dina Guido
Dina Leone
Dina Mario
Dina Salomone
   Moisè Davide
Dina Smeralda
Dinkelsbuehler
   Marianne
Dlugacz Giuseppe
Doczi Alfredo
   Aladar
Doenias Astrid
Doenias Baruch
   Alfredo
Domaic Maria
Donati Clelia
Donati Vittorio

Donetti Amalia
Donner Celeste
Dorfmann Fania
Drechsler Lina Sali
Dresner Lisa
Dreyfuss Eugen
Driller Siegfried
Drucker Salomone
Dubinski Gina
Dubinski Saul
Dubinsky Giacomo
Dubois Jules
Ducci Eva
Ducci Rodolfo
Ducci Teodoro
Duegnas Vittorio
Duri Fiammetta
Dym Desiderio
Dymscitz Maria
Echl Barbara
Eckert Sidonia
Edelheit Gertrud
   Jerica
Edelmann Ester Sara
   detta Sali
Edelmann Salomon
Efrati Abramo
   Umberto
Efrati Adelaide
Efrati Alberto
Efrati Angelo
Efrati Aronne
Efrati Augusto
Efrati Cesare
Efrati Costanza
Efrati Dora
Efrati Egle
Efrati Elia
Efrati Enrica
Efrati Fortunata
Efrati Grazia
Efrati Graziano
Efrati Lazzaro detto
   Burrasca
Efrati Leone
Efrati Leone
Efrati Leone detto
   Lello
Efrati Marco
Efrati Marco
Efrati Marco
Efrati Marco
Efrati Marco
   Giacomo Giuseppe
Efrati Marco Mosè

Efrati Mirella
Efrati Olga
Efrati Pacifica
Efrati Rina
Efrati Settimio
Efrati Speranza
Efrati Umberto
Egert Rosa
Ehrenwert Antonia
Ehrmann Alexander
Eibuschitz Friederike
  Sarah
Eibuschitz Israel
  Heinrich
Eifermann Isaak
Eifermann Maurizio
Eilaender Rosalie
Einhorn Adolfo
Einhorn Bernardo
Einhorn Isacco
Einhorn Renata detta
  Renée
Einstein Anna Maria
Einstein Luce
Einstein Roberto
Eipschitzer
  Alessandro
Eiseck Hans
Eisenscher Chana
Eisenstaedter Greta
Eisenstaedter
  Guglielmo
Eisig Sara Rosa detta
  Sali
Eisinger Massimo
Elia Emanuele
Elia Rosa
Elias Mazaltov
Eliezer Abramo
Eliezer Giuseppe
Eliezer Lucia
Elkan Salomè
Eminente Aida
Engel Fanny Jette
Engel Marco
Engelsman Sophia
  Maria
Enriquez Isacco
Epstein Edvige detta
  Hedy
Epstein Heinrich
Epstein Pinchas
Epstein Simon
Ercoli Ladislao
Erdreich Michele

Erdreich Xenia
Ergas Perla
Ergas Solo
Erlbaum Margarethe
Errera Gino
  Emanuele
Errera Paolo
Eschenazi Mosè
Eschenazi Rachele
Eschenazi Vida
Esdra Giuseppe
Esdra Leo
Esdra Rosina
Eskenasi Bora
Eskenasi Marina
Eskenazi Giuseppe
Esquenazi Ester
Esquenazi Leone
Esquenazi Rebecca
Esquenazi Salomone
Fahn
Fahn Regina
Fahn Rudolf
Fahn Sidney
Falck Paula
Fano Alba Fausta
Fano Alessandro
Fano Augusto
Fano Bice
Fano Cesare
Fano Clementina
  detta Clemy
Fano Elena
Fano Elio
Fano Emilio Felice
Fano Enrico
Fano Ermanno
Fano Fausta
Fano Giorgio
Fano Giulia
Fano Giuseppe
Fano Giuseppina
Fano Guglielmo
Fano Liliana
Fano Lina Ester
Fano Luciano
Fano Marco
Fano Renato
Fano Roberto
Fano Ugo
Fano Vittoria
Farber Bruno
Farber Davide
Farberow Rosa
Farchi Giacomo

Farchi Sarina detta
  Olga
Farchy Michele
Fargion Elisa
Fargion Regina
Farina Teodolinda
  detta Linda
Farkas Desiderio
Farkas Giorgio
Farkas Paolo
Fassel Adele
Fatucci Amadio
  Sabato
Fatucci Amedeo
Fatucci Angelo
Fatucci Angelo
Fatucci Attilio
Fatucci David
Fatucci Emma
Fatucci Olga
Fechter Ferdinand
Fedrigoni Rachele
Feigenbaum Szmerl
Feintuch Anna
Feintuch Henia
Feintuch Jakob
Feintuch Manfredo
Feintuch Mayer
Feintuch Rosa
Feith Maurizio
Feiwel Leib Wolf
  Leone
Felberbaum Giovanni
Feld Romana
Feldhammer Jacob
Feldhorn Hanna
Feldmann Berta
Feldmann Etla
Feliks Maurizio
Fellah Buba
Fels Guglielmo
Felsner Adele
Fernandez Diaz
  Blanchette
Fernandez Diaz Dino
Fernandez Diaz Jean
Fernandez Diaz
  Pierre
Fernandez Diaz
  Robert
Ferrari Angela
Ferrera Ester
Ferrera Lea
Ferrera Mercada
Ferrera Mosè

Ferrera Mosè
Ferrera Reina
Ferrera Rosa
Ferrera Samuele
Ferri Luigi
Ferro Adalgisa
Ferro Anna
Ferro Ferruccio
Ferro Giuseppe
Ferro Mario
Ferro Ugo
Feuermann
  Sonnenschein Ester
  Elsa
Feuerstein Kurt
Fiano Amedeo
Fiano Angelo
Fiano Anna Lina
Fiano Chiara
Fiano Emilia Olga
Fiano Enzo
Fiano Fortunata
Fiano Giuseppe
Fiano Giuseppe
  Benedetto
Fiano Nedo
Fiano Olderigo
Fiano Salomone
Fiano Sergio
Fiedler Joseph
Fieiner David
Finder Breinde
Fink Benzion
Fink Ester
Fink Isacco
Fink Lina
Finz Alfredo
Finz Marcello
Finzi Adriana
Finzi Amelia
Finzi Anna Maria
Finzi Beatrice
Finzi Carlo
Finzi Cesare
Finzi Clara Jolanda
Finzi Clotilde
Finzi Contini Dora
Finzi Davide
Finzi Edgardo
Finzi Edgardo
Finzi Edgardo
Finzi Elena
Finzi Elvira
Finzi Emma Laura
Finzi Enrico

Finzi Fanny
Finzi Fausta
Finzi Gigliola
Finzi Gina
Finzi Gina
Finzi Gino
Finzi Giuseppe
Finzi Giuseppe
Finzi Giuseppina
Finzi Greca Nella
Finzi Guglielmo
  detto William
Finzi Ida
Finzi Ines
Finzi Irma
Finzi Isidoro
Finzi Jolanda
Finzi Lucia
Finzi Luciana
Finzi Marcello
Finzi Mario
Finzi Marta
Finzi Moisè Roberto
Finzi Natale detto
  Natalino
Finzi Nora
Finzi Regina
Finzi Renzo
Finzi Sabatino
Finzi Silvio
Finzi Tito
Finzi Vilma
Finzi Vittorio detto
  Samuele
Finzi Wanda
Fiorentini Ernesta
Fiorentini Piera
Fiorentini Pierina
Fiorentini Renata
Fiorentini Salvatore
Fiorentino Ada
Fiorentino Alberto
Fiorentino Alda
Fiorentino Carlo
Fiorentino Cesare
Fiorentino Ester
Fiorentino Fortunata
Fiorentino Giacomo
Fiorentino Giuliana
Fiorentino Iginia
Fiorentino Lello
Fiorentino Leone
Fiorentino Leone
Fiorentino
  Margherita

Fiorentino Salvatore
Fiorentino Samuel
  Emilio
Fis
Fis Allegra
Fis Ascer
Fis Giacobbe
Fis Giosuè
Fis Isacco
Fis Rachele
Fis Rebecca
Fischbein Davide
Fischel Kurt
Fischer Alessandro
Fischer Isidoro
Fischl Caterina
Fischof Feiga
  Francesca
Fiser Jelka
Fiser Mira
Fiser Regina
Fiser Vera
Fitzer Feige Adele
Fiz Giulia
Fiz Mario
Fiz Riccardo
Fiz Roberto
Flank Jeruchem
Fleischer Amalia
Fleischer Davide
Fleischer Olga
Fleischmann Carlo
Flesch Julius
Flisser Rosa
Florenthal Rosalia
Foà Alberto
Foà Aldo
Foà Alessandro
Foà Anita
Foà Anna detta Nina
Foà Annina
Foà Anselmo
Foà Armando
Foà Arnoldo detto
  Dino
Foà Arturo
Foà Augusto
Foà Bianca
Foà Davide
Foà Descio detto
  Dezio
Foà Donato
Foà Emilio
Foà Emma
Foà Enrica

Foà Estella
Foà Fortunata
Foà Giacobbe
Foà Giacomo
Foà Giacomo
Foà Giancarlo
Foà Giorgio
Foà Giorgio
Foà Giorgio Amos
Foà Giorgio Nullo
Foà Giuseppe
Foà Giuseppe
Foà Giuseppina
Foà Guido
Foà Guido
Foà Ida
Foà Italo
Foà Jole
Foà Marietta
Foà Mario
Foà Mario
Foà Matilde
Foà Noemi
Foà Olga
Foà Pacifico
Foà Perla
Foà Pio
Foà Raffaele Filippo
Foà Samuele Leone
Foà Sansone
Foà Sergio
Foà Ugo Abramo
  Sansone
Foà Vittoria
Foà Vittorio Enzo
Foà Wanda Debora
Fodor Alfredo
Fodor Lilly
Fodor Magda
Foerder Elfriede
Fogel Giulia
Fogel Martin
Fogel Nathan
Foh Adolfo
Foh Alex
Foh Sidney
Fontanella Dante
Fontanella Ermanno
Forconi Palmira
Forlì Gaggia
Formiggini Giulia
Formiggini Marcella
Fornari Alberto
  Giuliano
Fornari Angelo

Fornari Carlo
Fornari Emilia
Fornari Ermelinda
  detta Linda
Fornari Guglielmo
Fornari Mario
Fornari Perla Emma
Fornari Raffaele
Fornari Renato
  Alberto
Fornari Rossana
Fornari Umberto
Fornaro Erina
Fornaro Giacomo
Fornaro Leone
Forti Alberto
Forti Anna
Forti Anna
Forti Anselmo
  Giuseppe
Forti Berta
Forti Bruno
Forti Carmela
Forti Elda
Forti Emilia
Forti Emma
Forti Gilberto
Forti Gilda
Forti Giuditta
Forti Giulia
  Enrichetta
Forti Giuliio
Forti Giulio Cesare
Forti Ida
Forti Lina
Forti Lionello
Forti Livia
Forti Lucia
Forti Marianna detta
  Elvira
Fraenkel Ada
Fraenkel Arturo
Fraenkel Markus
  David
Fraenkel Martino
Fraenkel Walter
Franchetti Argia
Franchetti Augusta
Franchetti Elvira
Franchetti Ida
Franchetti Olga
Franchetti Ugo
Franco Abramo
Franco Allegra
Franco Aronne

Franco Aronne
Franco Aronne
Franco Baruh
Franco Behor Hizkià
Franco Beniamino
Franco Bianca
Franco Bona
Franco Bruno
Franco Caden
Franco Carlo
Franco Celebi Nissim
Franco Cesare
Franco Davide
Franco Elisa
Franco Emilio
Franco Enrica Gisella
Franco Enzo
Franco Ester Signuru
Franco Eugenia
Franco Giacobbe
Franco Giacomo
Franco Giacomo
   Giacobbe
Franco Girolamo
Franco Giulia
Franco Giuseppe
Franco Giuseppe
Franco Giuseppe
Franco Giuseppe
Franco Graziella
Franco Hanula
Franco Isacco
Franco Isacco
Franco Jannette
   Hanula
Franco Lea
Franco Lea
Franco Lea
Franco Lea
Franco Lea
Franco Leone
Franco Lucia
Franco Luisa
Franco Luna
Franco Maria
Franco Maria
Franco Masliah
Franco Mordehai
Franco Mosè
Franco Perahia
Franco Rabina
Franco Rachele
Franco Rachele
Franco Rachele
Franco Rachele

Franco Raffaele
Franco Raffaele
Franco Rebecca
Franco Rosa
Franco Rosa
Franco Rosa
Franco Rosula
Franco Salomon
Franco Salomone
Franco Samuele
Franco Sara
Franco Selma
Franco Stella
Franco Vittoria
Frandze Regina
Frangi Leon
Frank Edmondo
Frank Eduard
Frank Francesco
Frank Rodolfo
Frankel Margherita
Frankl Miroslav
Frascati Angelo
Frascati Clelia
Frascati Emma
Frascati Ester
Frascati Fausta
Frascati Fiorella
Frascati Giorgio
Frascati Ida
Frascati Irma
Frascati Lello detto
   Il Beccamorto
Frascati Marisa
Frascati Samuele
Frascati Settimia
Frascati Settimio
Frascati Silvana
Frascati Vittorio
Frassineti Rodolfo
Frassinetti Alfredo
Freiberg Nachman
   detto Nachme
Freiberg Sara
Freiberger Ada
Freiberger Alice
   Caterina
Freiberger Enrichetta
   Olga
Freiberger Leviah
   Gilda
Fremont Max
Frenkel Malka
Frenkel Naftali
Fresco Dora

Fresco Fernando
Fresco Marco
Fresco Nailè
Fresia Ebe
Freud Giuseppina
Freund Alberto
Freund Anna Elena
Freund Augusta
Freund Ella
Freund Frieda
Freund Sigfrido
Fried Margherita
Frieder Frieda
Friedmann Carlo
Friedmann Ernst
Friedmann Francesco
Friedmann Oscar
   Gianpietro
Friedmann Rosalia
Friedrich Andrea
Frisch Azriel
Frisch Fritz Efraim
Frisch Leni
Frisch Max
Frischauer Olga
Frischman Giulia
Froehlich Lotte
Frost Robert
Frotzlovsky Rachmil
Fubini Aldo
Fubini Mario
Fubini Renzo
Fubini Rosetta
Fuchs Irene
Fuchs Oscar Moritz
Fuchs Rosa
Fuerst
Fuerst Arturo
Fuerst Kurt
Fuerst Margarethe
Funaro Abramo
   Lamberto
Funaro Ada
Funaro Adolfo
Funaro Alberto
Funaro Alberto
Funaro Alberto
Funaro Alfredo
Funaro Angela
Funaro Angelo
Funaro Angelo
Funaro Angelo
Funaro Anita
Funaro Aron
Funaro Cesare

Funaro Cesare
Funaro Dario
Funaro Davide
Funaro Ettore
Funaro Ettore
Funaro Gabriella
Funaro Giacomo
Funaro Giuditta
Funaro Giuseppe
Funaro Giuseppe
Funaro Leo
Funaro Lina
Funaro Marco
Funaro Marco
Funaro Maria
Funaro Mattia
   Ernesto
Funaro Milena
Funaro Mosè Marco
Funaro Nella
Funaro Pacifico
Funaro Pacifico
Funaro Rosa
Funaro Rosetta
Funaro Samuele
Funaro Samuele
Funaro Settimio
Funaro Vittorio
Funaro Wanda
Funas
Funkenstein Haim
Futtermann Bernard
Futtermann Hersel
Futtermann Marcel
Gabay Kadem
Gabay Rebecca
Gabbai Carlo
Gabbai Giovanni
   Yomtov
Gabbai Luisa
Gabbai Salomone
Gabbai Salomone
Gabriel Clara
Gabriel Eleonora
Gabriel Giacobbe
   Giacomo
Gabrile Mosè
Gai Ettore
Galandauer Bella
Galant Abraham
Galant Betty
Galant David
Galant Jehuda
Galant Menachem
Galant Regina Anna

Galant Renata
Galante Abramo
Galante Abramo
Galante Aronne
Galante Baruch
Galante David
Galante Davide
Galante Davide
Galante Diana
Galante Esther
Galante Felicina
Galante Giannetta
Galante Giovanna
Galante Isacco
Galante Johevet
Galante Lea
Galante Matilde
Galante Mazaltov
Galante Mosè
Galante Mosè
Galante Nissim
Galante Nissim
Galante Rachele
Galante Rachele
Galante Rahamin
Galante Ricca
Galante Rosa
Galante Rosa
Galante Salomon
Galante Sara
Galante Stella
Galante Violetta
Galante Vittoria
Galante Yomtov
Galapo Rosa
Galletti Clara
Galletti Olga
Galletti Piera
Galletti Valentina
Gallichi Cesare
  Davide
Gallichi Dario
Gallichi Teofilo
Gallico Amelia
Gallico Augusto
Gallico Giulietta
Gallico Lucia Luna
Gallico Lucio
Gallico Sergio
Gallico Tina
Gani Alberto
Gani Ester
Gani Giuseppe
Gani Regina
Ganon Bohora

Ganz Frieda
Gaon Aronne
Gaon Clara
Gaon Davide
Gaon Diamante
Gaon Gilda
Gaon Grazia detta
  Graziella
Gaon Rachele
Gaon Rosa detta
  Rosetta
Gaon Silvia
Gaon Susanna
Garda Donato
Garda Germana
Garfinkel Hulda
Gartner Hermann
Garzoli Crescenzio
  Salvatore
Garzoli Debora
Garzoli Mario
Gaspard Vilma
  Maria
Gassenheimer
  Hedwige
Gasser Maria
Gattegna Armando
Gattegna Gabriele
  Enrico
Gattegna Gino
Gattegna Israele
Gattegna Perla
Gattegno Alberto
Gattegno Amelia
Gattegno Armando
Gattegno Caterina
Gattegno Elia
Gattegno Elia
Gattegno Elisa
Gattegno Haim
Gattegno Lea
Gattegno Lea
Gattegno Leone Juda
Gattegno Luna
Gattegno Michele
Gattegno Regina
Gattegno Roberto
Gattegno Salvatore
Gattegno Virginia
Gavijon Davide
Gavijon Elia
Gavijon Isacco
Gavijon Leone
Gavijon Marcello
  Conorte

Gavijon Marco
  Mordo
Gavijon Sabino
Gavijon Salvatore
Gavijon Sultana
Gavijon Susanna
Gebel Naftali
Gehan Norina
Gehan Samina
Gehermann Doroteo
Gehermann Ernesto
Geiringer Claudio
Geiringer Laura
Geiringer Pietro
Gelbart Alberto
Gelbart Mendel
Geller Ernestina
Gelles Alice detta
  Litzi
Gellisch Matilde
Gellman Giuditta
Geltner Minka Sara
Geltner Renée
Geltner Salomone
Gemelli Giulia
Gemunder Sali
Genazzani Abramo
Genazzani Davide
Genazzani Elena
Genazzani Gilda
Genazzani Lia
Gentili Maria
Gentili Teresa Elsa
Gentilli Arrigo
Gentilli Davide
Gentilli Edvige
Gentilli Enrichetta
Gentilli Giuditta
Gentilli Margherita
Gentilli Regina
Gentilli Umberto
  Alberto
Gentilli Vittorio
Gentilli Vittorio
  Moisè
Gentilomo Adele
Gentilomo Arturo
Gentilomo Gisella
Gentilomo Jolanda
Gentilomo Nina
  Benvenuta
Gepesz Carlotta
Gepesz Daniele
Gepesz Dora
Gepesz Elisabetta

Gepesz Frida
Gepesz Giovanni
Gerbi Abramo
Gerbi Azra
Gerbi Elia
Gerbi Haim
Gerbi Miriam
Gerbi Rachele
Gerbi Sarina
Gerschenzon
  François
Gerschenzon Simon
Gerstenfeld Elena
  Amalia
Gerstenfeld Giacomo
Gerstl Matilde
Gertner Haim
Gertner Maddalena
Geschlieder Elena
Gesess Elia
Gesess Sara
Ghernis Zula
Ghiron Dolce
  Eugenia
Ghiron Enrichetta
Ghiron Ettore
Ghiron Gemma
Ghiron Lea
Ghiron Regina
Ghissin Serafina
Gimpel Evelina
Gimpel Peter
Ginesi Bice
Ginesi Olga
Gittermann Enrico
  detto Giovannin
Giuili Elisa
Giuili Giora
Giuli Besso
  Abramo
Giuli Enrica
Giuli Sergio
Givrè Gina
Givrè Jacob
Givrè Raffaele
Givrè Raffaele
Gizelt Rosalia
Glaeser Ferdinando
Glaeser Gertrud
Glam Giulia
Glanzerberg Laja
Gleichmann Elena
Glueck Ilona
Gluecksmann
  Eugenio

Glueksmann Ferdinand
Gochbaum Jankiel
Godelli Martino
Goetz Leopoldo
Goetz Maurizio
Goetzl Alberto
Golberti Ada
Golberti Irene
Gold Angela
Gold Elena
Goldbacher Alberto
Goldberg
Goldberg Dora
Goldberg Elisabetta
Goldberg Israel
Goldberg Jetta
Goldberg Josef
Goldberger Caterina
Goldberger Rosa
Goldenberg Leon
Goldfarb Avraham
Goldfarb Gisella
Goldfarb Rosa
Goldfrucht Lea
Goldmann Albert
Goldschmied Giuseppe
Goldschmied Livio
Goldschmied Samuele
Goldschmied Stefania
Goldschmiedt Giorgio
Goldschmiedt Ida
Goldstaub Bianca
Goldstaub Clotilde
Goldstaub Ernesta Vittorina
Goldstaub Vittorio
Goldstaub Zevulun detto Gino
Goldstein Amalia
Goldstein Bluma
Goldstein Bronia Beatrice
Goldstein Daneo detto Dan
Goldstein Ester
Goldstein Hirsch Zwi
Goldstein Jacob
Goldstein Oscar
Goldstein Rachele detta Lala

Gollenstepper Olga
Golombek Elena
Golombek Perla Anna
Golombek Rifka
Gomel Sara Giamila
Gomez de Silva Ubaldo detto Baldo
Gonda Ladislaus
Gordon Elisabetta Ruth
Gormezzano Stella
Gorniki Mosè
Goslino Giuseppe
Gottesmann Georg
Gottesmann Marcello
Gottesmann Maria
Gottesmann Mendel
Gottlieb Anna Maria
Gottlieb Enrica
Gottlieb Nicola
Gottlieb Ruth
Gottsegen Enrico
Grabar Dominice
Grabowski Enrico Ernesto
Grad Amalia
Grandi Teodora Anita
Grassini Angelo
Grassini Attilio
Grassini Bruna
Grassini Mirna
Grassini Nella
Grassini Raffaele
Grauer Marco
Grauer Samuel
Grauer Tito
Graziani Adalgisa
Graziani Elvira
Graziani Ettore
Graziani Haim Vitale
Graziani Maria
Graziani Raffaello
Graziani Sara
Greco Vladimiro
Grego Gisella
Gregori Giovanna
Gremboni Alessandro
Gremboni Simeone
Grinbaum M.J.
Grini Mauro
Grob Leib
Gronich Dorotea

Grosman Maja
Gross Chaim
Gross Ella
Gross Etel
Gross Gisella
Gross Ignatz
Grossberger Francesca
Grossmann Max
Grozze Riguetta
Gruber Isacco
Gruber Michele Salomone
Gruber Simone Giuseppe
Gruen Alfred
Gruen Carlo
Gruen Friedrich
Gruen Leone
Gruenbaum Dora
Gruenbaum Israel
Gruenbaum Margit
Gruenberg Davide Erberto
Gruenberger Enrico
Gruener Adolfo
Gruenfeld Enrico
Gruenfeld Moritz
Gruenfeld Tobia
Gruenspan Rosa Maria
Gruenwald Anna
Gruenwald Francesco Oliviero
Gruenwald Margherita
Gruenwald Miroslav
Gruner Bronia
Gruzdas Smarja
Guastalla Celestina
Guastalla Eugenio
Guastalla Irene
Guastalla Luciano
Guastalla Vittorio
Guetta Albertina
Guetta Alberto
Guetta Margherita
Guetta Pier Luigi
Guetta Vivienne
Guggenheim Bona
Guglielmi Achille
Guglielmi Gino
Gurewicz Ada
Gurewicz Anczel
Gurfein Leo

Gutenberger Elda
Gutmann Magda
Gutmann Malvina
Guttentag Cara
Gyarmatj Elemer
Haar Pavel
Haar Rosa
Haas Moritz
Haas Robert
Haas Sabine
Habib Allegra
Habib Antonietta
Habib Bochor
Habib Bohora
Habib Donna
Habib Ester
Habib Gemma
Habib Isacco
Habib Jacob detto Kino
Habib Leone
Habib Mosè
Habib Mussani
Habib Nathan
Habib Nissim
Habib Nissim
Habib Nissim
Habib Nissim
Habib Rita
Habib Rosa
Habib Salva
Habib Shalom
Habib Shalom Haim
Habib Silvana
Habib Simone
Habib Sol
Habib Sultana
Habib Virginia
Habib Vittoria
Habib Zelda
Habib Zimbul
Hacker Margarete
Haddad Mantina
Haendler Feigel
Haendler Margarete
Haendler Michele
Haffner Gisella
Hafter Elisabetta
Haggiag Giora
Hahn Edith
Hahn Paolo
Haim Abramo
Haim Diamante
Haim Esther
Haim Gabriele

Haim Gioia
Haim Giuseppe
Haim Giza
Haim Yomtov
Hain Ignaz
Hakim Caden
Hakim Matilde
Halber Samuele
Halberstam Chaim
Halfon Clara
Halfon Esther
Halfon Estrella
Halfon Giacobbe
Halfon Giacobbe
  Giacomo
Halfon Isacco
Halfon Israele
Halfon Rica
Halfon Signorù
Halfon Zula
Haller Ottone
Halperin Ludovico
Halpern Armida
  Aurelia
Halpern Enrico
Halpern Giorgio
  Gershon
Halpern Maurizio
Halpert Lenke
Halpert Malvine
Halua Allegra
Halua Rachele
Hammer Abramo
Hammer Ester
Hammer Lazzaro
Hammerschmidt
  Jenny Eugenia
Hanan Abner
Hanan Abramo
  Alberto
Hanan Alberto
Hanan Allegra
Hanan Amalia
Hanan Ascer
Hanan Ascer
Hanan Asher
Hanan Behor
Hanan Behor
Hanan Bella
Hanan Bellina
Hanan Bension
Hanan Boaz
Hanan Bulissa
Hanan Caden
Hanan Daisy

Hanan Davide
Hanan Enrico
Hanan Ezra
Hanan Gella
Hanan Giacobbe
Hanan Giacobbe
Hanan Giuseppe
Hanan Giuseppe
Hanan Giuseppe
Hanan Haim
Hanan Herzel
Hanan Ida
Hanan Isacco
Hanan Isacco
Hanan Lea
Hanan Lora Laura
Hanan Maria
Hanan Matilde
Hanan Matilde
Hanan Matilde
Hanan Mercada
Hanan Moris
Hanan Mosè
Hanan Myriam
Hanan Nissim
Hanan Nissim
Hanan Rachele
Hanan Rebecca
Hanan Rosa
Hanan Rosa
Hanan Salomon
Hanan Salomon
Hanan Salva
Hanan Salvatore
Hanan Samuele
Hanan Samuele
Hanan Sara
Hanan Sarina
Hanan Sol
Hanan Susanna
Hanan Ventura
Hanan Violetta
Hanau Giorgio
  Max
Hanau Margherita
Hanau Mario
Hanau Vittore
Hannuna Renata
Harmik Isak
Harpfen Arturo
Hartmeier Sigfried
Hartstein Wilmosch
Hartwig Umberto
Haschi Giulia
Haschlaus Feighe

Hasdà Giacomo
  Augusto
Haselnuess Anna
Haselnuess Lea
Hasenlauf Israel
Hassan Buba
Hassan Gerda
  Yvonne
Hassan Maria
Hassan Nathan Carlo
Hassan Rachele
Hassid Behor
  Samuele
Hassid Giuseppe
Hasson Abner
Hasson Abramo
Hasson Alberto
Hasson Alfredo
Hasson Allegra
Hasson Amelia
Hasson Amelia
Hasson Amelia
Hasson Aronne
Hasson Aronne
Hasson Baruh
Hasson Behora Stella
Hasson Bella
Hasson Bellina
Hasson Bellina
Hasson Bochor
Hasson Bohor
Hasson Bohor
Hasson Bulissa
Hasson Bulissa
Hasson Caden
Hasson Caden
Hasson Caden
Hasson Caden
Hasson Caterina
Hasson Caterina
Hasson Celebi
Hasson Clara
Hasson Davide
Hasson Davide
Hasson Davide
Hasson Diana
Hasson Dona
Hasson Donna
Hasson Donna
Hasson Dorina
Hasson Edith Nelly
Hasson Elia
Hasson Elieto
Hasson Elieto Elia
Hasson Elisa

Hasson Elsa
Hasson Elsa
Hasson Esther
Hasson Esther
Hasson Fany
Hasson Felicina
Hasson Flora
Hasson Fortunata
Hasson Fortunata
Hasson Fortunata
Hasson Fortunata
Hasson Fortunata
Hasson Gabriele
Hasson Giacobbe
Hasson Giacobbe
Hasson Giacobbe
Hasson Giacobbe
Hasson Giacobbe
Hasson Giacobbe
Hasson Giacobbe
Hasson Giacobbe
Hasson Giacobbe
Hasson Giacobbe
  detto Giaco
Hasson Giacobbe
  Giuseppe
Hasson Giacomo
Hasson Giamila
  Rosula
Hasson Giannetta
Hasson Gilberto
Hasson Gioia
Hasson Gioia
Hasson Gioia
Hasson Giovanna
Hasson Giovanna
Hasson Giovanna
Hasson Giovanna
  Giannetta
Hasson Giuseppe
Hasson Giuseppe
Hasson Giuseppe
Hasson Giuseppe
Hasson Giuseppe
Hasson Giuseppe
Hasson Giuseppe
Hasson Haim
Hasson Haim
Hasson Hanula
Hasson Hasday
Hasson Isacco
Hasson Isacco
Hasson Isacco
Hasson Isacco
Hasson Jacques

Hasson Jean Pierre
Hasson Jeuda
Hasson Jeuda
Hasson Jeuda
Hasson Johevet
Hasson Juda
Hasson Laura
Hasson Laura
Hasson Lea
Hasson Lea
Hasson Lea
Hasson Lea
Hasson Lea
Hasson Lea
Hasson Lora
Hasson Luna
Hasson Luna
Hasson Matilde
Hasson Matilde
Hasson Matilde
Hasson Mazaltov
Hasson Mazaltov
Hasson Mazaltov
Hasson Mazaltov
Hasson Meir
Hasson Michele
Hasson Mosè
Hasson Mosè
Hasson Mosè
Hasson Mosè
Hasson Mosè
Hasson Mosè
Hasson Mosè
Hasson Mosè
Hasson Natan
Hasson Natan
Hasson Natan
Hasson Nissim
Hasson Nissim
Hasson Nissim
Hasson Nisso
Hasson Rachele
Hasson Rachele
Hasson Rachele
Hasson Rachele
Hasson Rachele
Hasson Rachele
Hasson Rachele
Hasson Rachele
Hasson Rachele
Hasson Rebecca
Hasson Rebecca
Hasson Rebecca
Hasson Rebecca
Hasson Rebecca

Hasson Regina
Hasson Regina
Hasson Regina
Hasson Regina
Hasson Regina
Hasson Rosa
Hasson Rosa
Hasson Rosa
Hasson Rosa
Hasson Rosa
Hasson Ruben
Hasson Sadis
Hasson Sadok
Hasson Salomon
Hasson Salomone
Hasson Salomone
Hasson Salomone
Hasson Salvatore
Hasson Salvo
Hasson Samuele
Hasson Samuele
Hasson Samuele
Hasson Sara
Hasson Sara
Hasson Sara
Hasson Sara
Hasson Signoru
Hasson Silvia
Hasson Silvia
Hasson Simha
Hasson Simone
Hasson Sol
Hasson Stella
Hasson Sultana
Hasson Uriel
Hasson Vida
Hasson Vida
Hasson Violetta
Hasson Violetta
Hasson Violetta
Hasson Vittoria
Hasson Vittoria
Hasson Vittoria
Hasson Vittorio
Hasson Vittorio
Hasson Vittorio
Hasson Vittorio
Haim
Hasson Zaffira
Haus Leo
Hauser Arnaldo
Hauser Bela
Hauser Eugen
Hauser Lania Laura
Hauser Moritz

Hauser Pessla
Hauser Susanna
Hauser Umberto
Hausmann Rosa
Hayat Giacomo
Hazan Alberto detto
  Lekarz
Hazan Clara
Hazan Colette
Hazan Estrea
Hazan Giacobbe
  Giacomo
Hazan Giacomo
Hazan Ginetta
Hazan Giuseppe
Hazan Isacco
Hazan Matilde
Hazan Maurizio
Hazan Maurizio
Hazan Michele
Hazan Nissim
Hazan Rebecca detta
  Becky
Hazan Regina
Hecht Otto
Heier Fanny
Heim Anna
Heim Enrica
Heim Leopoldo
Heiman Felice
Heimann Wanda
  Piera
Heinrich Bernardo
Heinrich Marcello
Heliczer Jacob
Heller Samuele
Hendrix Gertrude
Hening Beer
Hering Elisa
Hering Isabella Iginia
Hering Samuele
  Umberto
Hering Sofia
Hering Vittorio
Herlinger Adele
Herlinger Hermann
Hermann Julius
  Hersch
Herschtal Ester
Herscovici Abraham
Herskovits Agata
  detta Goti
Herskovits Luigi
Herskovits
  Margherita

Herskovits Maurizio
  Zoltan
Herskovits Tiberio
Herskovitz Rella
Herz Theresia
Herzberg Maddalena
Herzberg Siegbert
  Israel
Herzer Ida detta Ada
Herzer Joseph
Heschenthal Bruno
Hess Richard
Heymann Clara
Heymann Elena
Hinin Barkov
  Michael
Hirsch Bianca
Hirsch David
Hirsch Gerolamo
Hirsch Gino
Hirsch Philippe
Hirsch Regina
Hirsch Susanna
Hirschen Haendel
Hirschhaut Eugenia
Hirschhorn Israel
  Hersz
Hirschhorn Lea
Hirschl Erich
Hirschl Hinko
Hirschl Slava
Hirschl Vera
Hirschler Bozjena
Hirschler Zora
Hochberger Bela
Hochberger Evelina
Hochberger Lilly
Hochberger Wilhelm
  detto Willy
Hochberger
  Wolfgang
Hochwald Carolina
Hodara Clara
Hodorowitz Giusto
Hodorowitz Michael
Hoenig Israel
  Giuseppe
Hoenig Regina
Hofbauer Giovanna
Hoffmann Johanna
Hoffmann Luisa
Hoffmann Olga
Hoffmann Stella
Hohn Zora
Hoitsch Hugo

Horitzki Adele
Horitzki Regina
Hornstein Andrea
Hornstein Fanny
Hornstein Irene
Horowitz David
Horowitz Fanny
Horowitz Gisella
Horowitz Marcello
Horowitz Markus
Horschtorn Fanny
Horvatic Ivana
Horzel Oscar
Hugnu Abramo
Hugnu Abramo
Hugnu Abramo
Hugnu Alberto
Hugnu Alfredo
Hugnu Aronne
Hugnu Aronne
Hugnu Bianca
Hugnu Diamante
Hugnu Elia
Hugnu Flora
Hugnu Fortunata
Hugnu Giacobbe
Hugnu Giuseppe
Hugnu Giuseppe
Hugnu Haim
Hugnu Haim
Hugnu Isacco
Hugnu Jakob
Hugnu Laura
Hugnu Lora
Hugnu Lucia
Hugnu Luna
Hugnu Mardocheo
Hugnu Maria
Hugnu Maria
Hugnu Matilde
Hugnu Matilde
Hugnu Moreno
Hugnu Mosè
Hugnu Nathan
Hugnu Nissim
Hugnu Rachele
Hugnu Rachele
Hugnu Rahamin
Hugnu Regina
Hugnu Rica
Hugnu Rica
Hugnu Rosa
Hugnu Rosa
Hugnu Salomon
Hugnu Salomon

Hugnu Sara
Hugnu Sara
Hugnu Sara
Hugnu Sipura
Hugnu Stella
Hugnu Violetta
Hugnu Vittoria
Hugnu Vittoria
Hugnu Vittoria
Hugnu Vittorio
Hulli Sarina
Iacoboni Giacomo
Iacoboni Gisella
Iacoboni Sofia
Ickowics Monica
Iesi Carolina
Igel Regina
Iohana Anna
  Adalgisa detta
  Mima
Isaac Johanna
Isakovic Jacob
Isakovic Josif
Israel Alberto
Israel Allegra
Israel Anna
Israel Aronne
Israel Aslan
Israel Bension
Israel Boaz
Israel Bulissa
Israel Bulissa
Israel Caterina
Israel Celebi
Israel Daniele
Israel Davide
Israel Davide
Israel Davide Dario
Israel Diana
Israel Elia
Israel Elia
Israel Eliezer
Israel Elio
Israel Ester
Israel Flora
Israel Flora
Israel Flora
Israel Giacobbe
Israel Giacobbe
Israel Giacobbe
Israel Giacomo
Israel Giovanna
Israel Giovanna
Israel Giuseppe
Israel Haim

Israel Hanula
Israel Ida
Israel Isacco
Israel Isacco
Israel Isacco
Israel Isacco
Israel Isacco
Israel Isacco Gino
Israel Jesua
Israel Leone
Israel Liko Moshe
Israel Lucia
Israel Luna
Israel Mahir
Israel Mardocheo
Israel Maria
Israel Matilde
Israel Matilde
Israel Matilde
Israel Matilde
Israel Mazaltov
Israel Mazaltov
Israel Mazaltov
  Matilde
Israel Mosè
Israel Mosè
Israel Mosè
Israel Nissim
Israel Nissim
Israel Nissim
Israel Nissim
  Salvatore
Israel Pacina
Israel Pacina
Israel Rachele
Israel Rachele
Israel Rachele
Israel Rachele
Israel Rachele
Israel Rachele
Israel Rahamin
Israel Rebecca
Israel Rebecca
Israel Rebecca
Israel Regina
Israel Regina
Israel Regina
Israel Regina
Israel Rica
Israel Rina
  Allegra
Israel Rosa
Israel Ruben
Israel Ruben
Israel Ruben

Israel Ruben
  Avraham
Israel Sabetai
Israel Sabino
Israel Samuele
Israel Samuele
Israel Samuele
Israel Samuele
Israel Samuele
Israel Sara
Israel Sara
Israel Sara
Israel Sara
Israel Scemarià
Israel Semah
Israel Sol
Israel Stametta detta
  Stanni
Israel Susanna
Israel Vittoria
Israel Yomtov
Issel Arturo
Italia Emma Elena
Italia Raffaele
Italia Raffaele
Itzkowitz Simon
Jabes Giuseppe
  Enrico
Jablonka Jankel
Jacchia Beatrice
Jacchia Diana
Jacchia Dina
Jacchia Edoardo
Jacchia Ermanno
Jacchia Ezia detta
  Lilly
Jacchia Giorgio
Jacchia Lidia
Jacchia Lina
Jacchia Mario
Jacchia Riccardo
Jachia Alberto
Jachia Anselmo
Jachia Armando
Jachia Ercole
Jachia Ida
Jachia Nino
Jachia Pasqua
Jacob Diamante
Jacoby Paolo
Jacubowski Isidor
Jaffè Isaac Elia
Jaffe Raffaele
Jaffe Silvio
Jaffe Ugo

Jakobsohn Paul
Jakobstamm
  Rosabella
Jalowiec Janina
Jani Emilio Gustavo
Jankowsky Kalman
Janovitz Edoardo
Janovitz Silvio
Janovitz Tullio
Janovitz Vittoria
Jansen Francis
Jarach Angelina
Jarach Anna
Jarach Anna
Jarach Augusta
Jarach Giulia
Jarach Giuseppe
Jarach Marco
Jarach Mario
  Giacobbe
Jelcich Maria
Jenna Lina Arianna
Jenna Moise detto
  Cesare
Jenna Ruggero
Jerchan Rivka
Jeret Marie
Jerusalmi Gioia
Jesi Carlo
Jesi Rosina
Jessoula Clara
Jesurum Arrigo
  Giuseppe
Jesurum Berta Anna
Jesurum Gilda
Jesurum Giuseppina
Jesurum Jole
Jesurum Marisa
Jewell Phoebe
Joachinsthal Ruth
Joffe Isidoro
Joffe Olga
Joffe Paola
Joheli Jehuda
John Matilde
Jolles Salomon
Jona Amadio
Jona Anna
Jona Annetta
Jona Bellinzona
  Leonella
Jona Benvenuta
  Regina
Jona Elda
Jona Enrica

Jona Enrichetta
Jona Ezechia
  Leopoldo
Jona Felice
Jona Fortunato
  Aristide
Jona Gabriele
Jona Gino
Jona Giora
Jona Giorgio
Jona Giuseppe
Jona Giuseppe
Jona Giuseppe
Jona Leone
Jona Luigi detto Gigi
Jona Mariana Bona
  Esmeralda
Jona Massimo
Jona Olga
Jona Raimondo Luigi
  Eugenio
Jona Remo
Jona Rinaldo
Jona Roberto
Jona Roberto
Jona Rosa Bianca
Jona Ruggero Achille
  Rodolfo
Jona Smil
Jona Ugo
Jonas Elsa
Jonas Geltrude
Jordan Rosa
Josefowicz Bella
Josefowicz Stefania
Josefowicz Zelig
Josefowitz Jolan
Josefowitz Schmil
Joseph Georges
Josephson Enrichetta
Josz Aurelia
Juchwid Hirsch
Judkowsky Israel
Judkowsky Samuele
Jung Bertha
Junger Frieda
Jungerman Alberto
Jungermann Marcel
Jungermann Meilech
Jungerwuerth
  Theofila
Jupfer Michele
Jupiter Marco
Kabilio Josef
Kabiljo Hana

Kabiljo Hanika
Kabiljo Josefu
Kabiljo Levi
Kaesz Margarete
Kahlberg Hans
Kahn Michele
Kajon Erna Herdonia
Kaldegg Erwin
Kalik Teresa
Kalisch Yvonne
Kalker Alessandro
Kalker Erminia
Kalker Sigismondo
Kalmann Ulrich
Kammer Karl
Kamras Elisabetta
Kanni Giacomo
Kapitz Teresa
Kaplan
Kaplan Paolo
Kaposi Elena
Kaposi Oscar
Kapper Eva
Kapper Gustavo
Kapper Pietro
Karafiol Feiga
Karafiol Ida
Kardos Zlata
Karma Elle
Karpeles Anna
Karpeles Arturo
Kass Jacob
Kass Jacob
Kasterstein Aron
Katz Ermanno detto
  Hero
Katz Ernestina
Katz Ethel detta Etja
Katz Giuseppe
Katz Israele
Katz Juda
Katz Sofia
Katz Susanna
Katzenstein Ester
Kauber Josef
Kaufer Alfred
Kaufmann Sofia Sara
Kazar Gabriella
Keil
Kell Irma
Kepinscki Davide
Kerbes Lemel
Kern Carlo
Kirschbaum Sara
Klein Dora

Klein Eva
Klein Margherita
Klein Maurizio
Klein Norberto
Klein Oscar
Klein Roberto
Klein Teresa
Klein Cominotti
  Carlo
Klein Cominotti
  Edoardo
Kleinberger Clara
Klempmann
  Abraham
Knapp Wally
Knoll Oscar
Koen Milo
Koen Nina
Koen Oscar
Koenig Ana
Koenig Anna
Koenig Giuseppe
Koenig Koelmann
Koffler Leopoldo
Koffler Michael
Kohl Salomone
Kohn Alessandro
Kohn Bruno
Kohn Cesare
Kohn Geltrude
Kohn Gerhard
Kohn Giulia
Kohn Jolanda
Kohn Margherita
Kohn Rosa
Kohn Shalom
Kohner Alfredo
Kolb Clara
Koppl Hilde
Korbel Hugo
Koretz Amalia
Korn Victor
Kornblum Giacomo
Kornitzer Milon
Kornweitz Karin
Kosicek Leopolda
Kovacs Bela
Kovacs Gabriella
Kovacs Giuseppina
Kovacs Rosa
Krachmalnikoff
  Isacco
Kramm Carlo
Kramm Emil
Kramm Ernesto

Kraus Giorgio
Kraus Ivan
Kraus Marcello
Krauss Gisella
Krausz Rosalia
Krawietz Abraham
Krawietz Beniamino
Krawietz Ryna
Krebs Giuseppe
Krebs Martino
Kreiner Edith
Kresic Anna detta
  Anika
Krohn Martin Israele
Kroo Alessandro
Kroo Giuseppe
Kroo Luigi
Krumer Ghena detta
  Genia
Krupenic Irene
Krys Betty
Krys Marco
Krzentowsky Sali
Krzentowsky
  Salomone detto
  Salo
Krzentowsky
  Simeone
Krzesny Gianna
Krzesny Herbert
Kudlik Ariè
Kuenstler Abramo
  detto Romolo
Kugler Elena Anna
Kugler Gisella
Kugler Maddalena
Kuh Ermanno
Kuh Meta Marie
Kuhn Ada
Kuhn Beatrice detta
  Bice
Kupfer Elena
Kupfer Jankel
Kupferberg Abraham
Kurtz Carlotta
Kurtz Samuele
Kurz Taube
Kurzrock Anna detta
  Netty
Kurzrock Erminio
Kurzrock Giuseppe
Kuster Paul
Kwadratstein Debora
Labi Abner
Labi Abramo

Labi Abramo
Labi Alfredo
Labi Anna
Labi Aron
Labi Aronne
Labi Aronne
Labi Buba
Labi Davide
Labi Diamantina
Labi Diamantina
Labi Diamantina
Labi Diana
Labi Elia
Labi Elia
Labi Elia
Labi Elisa
Labi Ersel
Labi Ester
Labi Fortuna
Labi Fortunata
Labi Giacomo
  Giacobbe
Labi Gino
Labi Giulia
Labi Giulia
Labi Giulia
Labi Giulia
Labi Giulia
Labi Giuseppe
Labi Giuseppe
Labi Grazia
Labi Hammus
Labi Ida
Labi Isaak
Labi Isacco
Labi Isacco
Labi Isacco
Labi Isacco
Labi Jolanda
Labi Josef
Labi Juda
Labi Lidia
Labi Lizzi
Labi Loris
Labi Lulli Alba
Labi Marcello
Labi Maria
Labi Messala
Labi Messauda
Labi Messauda
Labi Messauda
Labi Mosè detto
  Musci
Labi Mosè detto
  Musci
Labi Musci

Labi Nissim
Labi Quintina
Labi Rachele
Labi Raclin
Labi Regina
Labi Rosa
Labi Rosa
Labi Rubina
Labi Rubina
Labi Salomone
Labi Sanin
Labi Sara
Labi Scialom
Labi Scialom
Labi Scialom
Labi Sion
Labi Sion
Labi Sion
Labi Sion
Labi Susanna
Labi Tita
Labi Vittorio
Labi Vittorio
Labi Wanda
Labi Wanda
Labi Zatuba
Lacher Brucha
Laemmle Minna
Lager Luisa Elena
  detta Lenke
Lager Marco
Lagny Elisabetta
Lakatos Zoltan
Lallum Ninetta
Lamm Lea
Lamm Salomone
Lampronti Carlo
Lampronti Irma
Lampronti Marco
Lampronti Rina
Lampronti Umberto
Landau Bernardo
Landau Erich
Landau Felicitas
Landau Isacco
Landau Lea
Landau Malvina
Landesberger Edith
Landesman Boris
Landmann Mendel
Landmann Moses
Landmann Rita
Landmann Simon
Landmann Walter
  Heinz

Landmans Giulio
Landsberg Ernesto
Langfelder Cecilia
  detta Lilly
Langstein Johann
Laniado Bahia
Lapajowker
  Francesca
Laparini Ermanno
Lascar Bruno
Lascar Flora
Lascar Italia
Lascar Luciana
Lascar Mario
Lascar Renzo Leone
Lascar Umberto
Lascar Wanda
Latis Leone
Latis Liliana
Lattes Angela
Lattes Anna
Lattes Decima
Lattes Edvige
Lattes Franca
Lattes Irma
Lattes Itala Rachele
Lattes Laura Regina
Lattes Leone Davide
Latzer Margherita
Laufer Bianca
Laufer Ladislav
Laurent Renata
Lausch Guglielmo
Lausch Olga
Lauterstein Hanna
Leblis Giuseppe
Leckner Giuseppe
Leder Eugenia
Lederer Ernst
Leghziel Misa
Leghziel Raffaele
Lehmann Frieda
  Emilia Alisa
Lehr Aurelia
Leichtmann Hanni
Leim Sofia
Leinberg Marco
Leipen Lucia
Lemberger Marcella
Lemberger Wolf
Lenger Aronne
  Meilach
Lenghi Walter
Lenk Felice
Leon Alessandro

Leon Allegra
Leon Amelia
Leon Elly Sara
Leon Estrea
Leon Giacobbe
Leon Isacco
Leon Jeudà
Leon Maria
Leon Maria
Leon Maria
Leon Matilde
Leon Matilde
Leon Nissim
Leon Rachele
Leon Sara
Leon Sol
Leon Sol
Leoni Arturo
Leoni Attilio
Leoni Augusto
Leoni Elsa
Leoni Ferruccio
Leoni Gabriella
Leoni Giulia
Leoni Gustavo
Leoni Lauretta
Leonzini Lina Perla
Lerer Samuel
Levi Abramo
Levi Abramo
Levi Abramo
Levi Abramo
Levi Abramo
Levi Abramo
Levi Abramo
  Giuseppe
Levi Ada
Levi Ada
Levi Alberto
Levi Alberto
Levi Alberto
Levi Alberto
Levi Alberto
Levi Alda
Levi Alda Silvana
Levi Aldo
Levi Aldo
Levi Aldo
Levi Aldo
Levi Aldo
Levi Aldo
Levi Alessandra
Levi Alessandro
Levi Alessandro
Levi Alfredo

Levi Alfredo
Levi Alighiero
Levi Allegra
Levi Alvise
Levi Amalia
Levi Amelia
Levi Amelia
Levi Amelia
Levi Amelia
Levi Amelia
Levi Angela Sara
Levi Angelo
Levi Angelo Giacomo
Levi Angelo Isaia
  Ferruccio
Levi Anita
Levi Anna
  Margherita detta
  Anita
Levi Annetta
Levi Argia
Levi Armando
Levi Aronne Nino
Levi Arrigo
Levi Arrigo
Levi Arturo
Levi Attilio Raffaele
Levi Augusto
Levi Aurelia Allegra
Levi Bea
Levi Beniamina
Levi Beniamino Ugo
Levi Bianca
Levi Bianka Nora
Levi Bochor
Levi Bochor
Levi Bochura
Levi Bruno
Levi Bulì
Levi Caden
Levi Carlo
Levi Carlo
Levi Carlo
Levi Celebi
Levi Celestina
Levi Cesare
Levi Cesarina
Levi Clara
Levi Clara
Levi Clotilde
Levi Clotilde
Levi Davide
Levi Davide
Levi Diamantina
Levi Diana

Levi Dina
Levi Dina
Levi Dino Italo Pace
Levi Donatella
Levi Donato Giorgio
Levi Donna
Levi Edgardo
Levi Elda
Levi Elda
Levi Elena
Levi Eleonora
Levi Eleonora detta
  Norina
Levi Elia
Levi Elia
Levi Elia
Levi Elia Aurelio
Levi Elia Eliakim
Levi Elia Lelio
Levi Elide
Levi Elide
Levi Elio Nissim
Levi Elios Natale
Levi Eloisa
Levi Elsa
Levi Emilia
Levi Emilia
Levi Emilia
Levi Emilia
Levi Emilio
Levi Emma
Levi Emma
Levi Emma
Levi Enrichetta
Levi Enrico
Levi Ercolina
Levi Ernesto
Levi Ernesto
Levi Ester Elvira
Levi Ester Vittoria
Levi Esther
Levi Esther
Levi Esther
Levi Estrea
Levi Estrea
Levi Estrea
Levi Estrella
Levi Estrella
Levi Ettore
Levi Fausto
Levi Federico Simone
Levi Felice
Levi Felicia
Levi Fortunata
Levi Fortunata

Levi Fortunata
Levi Fortunata
Levi Fortunata
Levi Franco
Levi Gastone
Levi Giacobbe
Levi Giacobbe
Levi Giacobbe
Levi Giacobbe
Levi Giacobbe
Levi Giacobbe
Levi Giacobbe
  Giacomo
Levi Giacobbe
  Giacomo
Levi Giacomo
Levi Giacomo
Levi Giamila
Levi Giannetta
Levi Gino
Levi Gioia detta
  Giuna
Levi Giorgio
Levi Giorgio
Levi Giorgio
Levi Giorgio
Levi Giosuè
Levi Giovanna
Levi Giovanni
Levi Giuditta Gioia
Levi Giulia
Levi Giulio
Levi Giulio
Levi Giusepina
Levi Giuseppe
Levi Giuseppe
Levi Giuseppe
Levi Giuseppe
Levi Giuseppe
Levi Guglielmo
  detto Bibi
Levi Guido
Levi Guido
Levi Haim
Levi Haim
Levi Heschielle
  Nissim
Levi Ines
Levi Isacco
Levi Isacco
Levi Isacco
Levi Isacco
Levi Isacco Bochor
Levi Israele
Levi Italo

Levi Italo Gustavo Davide
Levi Jehuschvo
Levi Jeudà
Levi Josef
Levi Laura
Levi Lazzaro
Levi Lea
Levi Lea
Levi Leon
Levi Leone
Levi Leonella
Levi Lia Marta
Levi Libera
Levi Lida
Levi Lino
Levi Lisan
Levi Lucia
Levi Luciana
Levi Luigia
Levi Luisa
Levi Luisa
Levi Marcello
Levi Marco
Levi Marco
Levi Marco
Levi Marco
Levi Mardocheo
Levi Margherita
Levi Maria
Levi Maria
Levi Maria
Levi Maria
Levi Maria Ester Anna
Levi Marietta
Levi Mario
Levi Mario
Levi Mario
Levi Mario
Levi Mario
Levi Mario
Levi Mario
Levi Mario Moisè
Levi Masaltov
Levi Matilde
Levi Matilde
Levi Matilde
Levi Matilde
Levi Maurizio
Levi Menachem
Levi Michele
Levi Minzi Augusto
Levi Minzi Marcello

Levi Misha Naftali
Levi Moise
Levi Mordechai
Levi Moritz
Levi Mosè
Levi Mosè
Levi Mosè
Levi Mosè
Levi Mosè
Levi Mosè Renzo
Levi Moshè
Levi Myriam
Levi Nailè
Levi Nerina
Levi Nissim
Levi Nissim
Levi Nissim
Levi Nissim
Levi Noemi
Levi Noemi
Levi Nora
Levi Noris
Levi Olga
Levi Oreste Ezechiele
Levi Oscar
Levi Ottavio
Levi Pacifico
Levi Paolo Shaul
Levi Perla
Levi Pia
Levi Pia Clelia
Levi Primo
Levi Rachele
Levi Rachele
Levi Rachele
Levi Rachele
Levi Raffaele
Levi Raffaele
Levi Raffaele
Levi Raffaele Carlo
Levi Rahamin
Levi Rebecca
Levi Rebecca
Levi Rebecca
Levi Regina
Levi Regina
Levi Regina
Levi Regina
Levi Regina
Levi Regina
Levi Renata
Levi Renato
Levi Renato Menachem

Levi Renzo
Levi Riccardo
Levi Rina
Levi Roberto
Levi Rodolfo
Levi Rodolfo
Levi Rosa
Levi Rosa
Levi Rosaldo
Levi Rosetta
Levi Ruggero
Levi Sadik
Levi Salomone
Levi Salomone Bochor
Levi Salva
Levi Salvatore
Levi Salvatore
Levi Salvatore
Levi Salvatore
Levi Salvatore
Levi Samuele
Levi Samuele
Levi Samuele
Levi Samuele Enea
Levi Sara
Levi Sara
Levi Sara
Levi Sara
Levi Sara
Levi Sara Ester
Levi Sarota
Levi Selma
Levi Selma
Levi Sergio
Levi Sergio
Levi Sida
Levi Silvana
Levi Simeone
Levi Simha
Levi Stella
Levi Stella
Levi Stella
Levi Sultana
Levi Susanna
Levi Tullio
Levi Ugo
Levi Valentina
Levi Vida
Levi Vittoria
Levi Vittoria
Levi Vittoria
Levi Vittoria
Levi Vittoria

Levi Vittoria
Levi Vittoria
Levi Vittoria
Levi Vittorina detta Rina
Levi Vittorio
Levi Vittorio
Levi Vittorio
Levi Vittorio
Levi Zelinda
Levi Zoe
Levi delle Trezze Giorgio
Levic Davide
Levic Stella
Levie Buba
Levin Erna
Levin Hugo
Levinas Idalco
Levinsky Felix
Levis Ida
Levitan Alessandro
Levitus Gustavo
Levy Adriana
Levy Alene
Levy Beniamino
Levy Berta
Levy Brunilde
Levy Elia Amedeo
Levy Enzo
Levy Eva Maria detta Cicci
Levy Federico
Levy Matilde
Levy Maurizio
Levy Paul
Levy Rudolf
Levy Silvia
Levy Vittorio
Levy Vittorio
Lewenstain Armin
Lewi Georg
Lewin Alfred
Lewinski Joachim
Lewinsohn Carlotta
Lewis James
Libeck Eduard
Lichtenstadt Rosina
Lichtenstein Serena
Lichtenstern Angela
Lichtmann Ada
Lichtwitz Joachim
Lichtwitz Otto Israel
Lieber Cypra
Liebgold Giovanna

Liebmann Erminia
detta Etta
Liebmann Giacomo
Paolo
Liebmann Pietro
Liebmann Pietro
Lilienthal Reinhold
Limentani Alberto
Limentani Angelo
Limentani Angelo
Limentani Anselmo
Limentani Cesare
Limentani Cesare
Limentani Cesira
Limentani Chiara
Limentani Costanza
Limentani Costanza
Limentani David
Limentani David
detto Baccalà
Limentani Davide
Limentani Giovanni
Limentani Giuseppe
Limentani Israele
Limentani Marco
Limentani Mario
Limentani Mario
Limentani Massimo
Limentani Rosa
Limentani Rosa
Limentani Settimio
Limentani Settimio
Angelo detto
Burione
Limentani Settimio
detto Russo
Lind Kurt
Lind Moses
Linden Giacomo
Lindenberg Ester
Linder Berthold
Linder Frieda
Linder Raimond
Linder Regina Maria
Linder Rolando
Linder Wilhelm
Linsen Tewel
Lipschitz Eugenio
Lipschitz Giuseppina
Lipschitz Michel
Lissauer Hans
Litter Samuele
Littmann Mayer
Littmann Romualdo
Livoli Allegra

Livoli Elvira
Livoli Pacifico
Livoli Pacifico
Livoli Rachele
Livoli Speranza
Livoli Vittoria
Loeb Gertrude
Loeb Hilde
Loeb Ilse
Loeb Moritz
Loebenstein Ugo
Loebl Dorothea
Loebl Gertrude detta
Trude
Loebnitz Enrico
Loebnitz Lidia
Loerber Alice
Loerber Evelina
Loew Abramo
Loew Alessandro
Loew Draga
Loew Ella
Loew Giuseppe
Loew Jacob
Loew Lavoslaw
Loewenstein Gerda
Loewenthal Eugenia
Loewenthal Guido
Loewenthal Helmuth
Loewenthal Paola
Loewenthal Roberto
Loewenthal Ugo
Loewenthal Vittorio
Loewenwirth Elia
Loewinson Ermanno
Loewinson
Sigismondo
Loewsztein Joseph
Loewy Alice
Loewy Anna
Loewy Charlotte
Loewy Ella
Loewy Emilio
Loewy Enrico
Loewy Lidia
Loewy Livio
Loewy Marta
Loewy Massimo
Loewy Olga
Loewy Olga
Loewy Regina
Loewy Riccardo
Loewy Sigfrido
Loewy Vidor
Lolli Corrado

Lolli Enzo
Lombroso Alberto
Lombroso Arturo
Cesare
Lombroso Carolina
Lombroso Prospero
Longo Lidia
Lonzana Formiggini
Cesare
Lopes Pegna
Fernando
Lopes Pegna Lidia
Lopes Pegna
Massimo
Lopez Perera Olga
Lorant Geltrude detta
Trude
Loria Guido
Lossi Alfredo
Lowj Anna
Lublinski Lipa
Lucovich Fabio
Luft Adolfo
Luft Ignazio
Luft Ilse
Luft Massimiliano
Luftschitz Arminio
Luftschitz Roberto
Luisada Arnoldo
Luisada Augusto
Luisada Clara
Luisada Dante
Luisada Franco
David
Luisada Giacomo
Luisada Lina
Luisada Piero
Lumbroso Carlo
Lumbroso Edwin
Lumbroso Isidoro
Luria Cesare
Lusena Alda
Lusena Aldo
Lusena Bianca Maria
Lusena Piero
Lusena Said
Lusena Silvio
Lust Bruno
Lust Edmondo
Lust Fanny
Lust Zoe
Lustig Rudolf
Luzzati Estella
Luzzati Guido
Zaccaria

Luzzato Marcella
Luzzatti Davide detto
Carlo
Luzzatti Enrico
Luzzatti Giuseppe
Luzzatti Ida
Luzzatti Isacco detto
Oscar
Luzzatti Silvio
Luzzatto Alice
Luzzatto Anna detta
Paola
Luzzatto Cesare
Luzzatto Cesare
Salomone
Luzzatto Elodia
Luzzatto Emma
Luzzatto Eugenia
Luzzatto Giacomo
Luzzatto Gina
Luzzatto Iginio
Luzzatto Ines
Luzzatto Margherita
Luzzatto Maria
Grazia detta Beppè
Luzzatto Mario
Luzzatto Mario
Luzzatto Maurizio
Luzzatto Natalia
Luzzatto Olga
Luzzatto Riccardo
Guido
Luzzatto Rina Sara
Luzzatto Rosalia
detta Rosa
Luzzatto Silvia
Luzzatto Vittoria
Lyon Emil
Macerata Carlo
Maestro Alfredo
Maestro Danilo
Maestro Ezio
Maestro Fausto
Maestro Gemma
Maestro Giulio
Maestro Guido
Maestro Ida
Maestro Jacob
Maestro Nina
Maestro Salomone
Akibà detto Carlo
Maestro Sigfrido
Maestro Vanda
Magenta Nissim
Magnel Sara

Magrini Isa
Magrini Silvio
Mahler Alexander
Mailand Gerhart
Maio Giacobbe
Maio Leone
Maio Maria detta
  Meri
Maio Miriam
Maio Mosè
Maio Regina
Maio Sara
Maio Violetta
Maissa Rachele
Maizels Bernardo
Makowski Abraham
Malek Brucha
Mallel Allegra
Mallel Diana
Mallel Giuseppe
Mallel Nissim
Mallel Nissim
Mallel Sara
Mallel Violetta
Maller Szmul
Mallowan Carlo
Malvert Georges
Malvert Jacques
Malvert Lucie
Manasse Delia
Manasse Erminia
  Rosa
Manasse Herbert
Manasse Vittorio
Manasse Wolfgang
Mandel Elvira
Mandel Gisella
Mandel Israele
  Pinkus
Mandel Maria
  Mimmi
Mandel Pinchas
  Philip
Mangel Samuel
Mangel Wilma
Mankevitz Anna
Mankevitz Ernst
Manli Bruno
Manli Luciano
Mann Walter
Mannsovich Ida
Mano Gioia Perla
Mansbach Henriette
Mansberger
  Giuseppina

Maon Rachele
Marbach Herbert
Marcaria Bellina
Marcaria Ernesto
Marcaria Giacomo
Marcaria Ida
Marcaria Raffaele
Marcaria Stella
Marcos Luna
Marcos Rebecca
Marcos Sara
Margules Maurice
Mariani Ada
Mariani Anita
Mariani Bettina
Mariani Elena
Mariani Enrico
Mariani Ernesto
Mariani Francesco
  Isacco
Mariani Ida
Mariani Leo
Mariani Luciano
Mariani Ugo
Mariani Vittorina
Marienberg Isacco
Marienberg Michele
Marienberg Simona
Marino Angelo
Marino Pacifico
Marino Settimio
Markoviski Johanna
Markovits Emilia
Markovits Melita
Markowiez Theodora
Markus Elena
Markus Moses
Marmaros Carlotta
Maroni Dora
Maroni Pace Augusto
Maroni Rita
Maroni Venturina
  Marianna
Marsiglio Gino
Marsiglio Riccardo
Marton Rodolfo
Marzolini Bianca
Masfary Levi Carlo
Masklis Dora
Masliah Rosa
Masriel Cadina
Massa Marietta
Massarani Olga
Massarani Tullo
Matalon Elia

Matatia Camelia
Matatia Nino
Matatia Nissim
Matatia Roberto
Matatia Samuel
Mattersdorfer
  Alfredo
Mattersdorfer Carlo
  Felice
Mattersdorfer Liliana
Mauer Frimeta
Mauri Luigi
Mayer Arnaldo
Mayer Ernest
Mayer Grego Elda
Mayer Grego
  Enrico
Mayer Grego
  Giacomo
Mayer Guido
Mayer Karoline
Mayer Risa
Mazzetti Agar
Mazziotti Proietti
  Clorinda
Mazzus Emilia
Mazzus Rebecca
Mazzus Sofia
Meisel Albert
Melauri Paolo
Melli Abramo
Melli Ada
Melli Amalia
Melli Amelia
Melli Bellina
Melli Benedetto
Melli Carlo
Melli Ebe
Melli Elena
Melli Elio
Melli Enrichetta
  detta Rina
Melli Giuliana
Melli Giulio
Melli Guido
Melli Mario
Melli Medea
Melli Novella
Melli Sergio
Melli Vittoria
Melli Zaira
Meltzeil Gustavo
Menascè Abramo
Menascè Alberto
Menascè Amelia

Menascè Behor
  Aaron
Menascè Bension
Menascè Bernardo
Menascè Bianca
Menascè Boaz
Menascè Boaz
Menascè Boaz
Menascè Caterina
Menascè Catina
Menascè Daniele
Menascè Davide
Menascè Eleonora
Menascè Eliezer
Menascè Esther
Menascè Estrea
Menascè Estrella
Menascè Farida
Menascè Fassana
Menascè Fassana
Menascè Fassana
Menascè Fortunata
Menascè Giacobbe
Menascè Giacobbe
Menascè Gioia
Menascè Giuseppe
Menascè Giuseppe
Menascè Giuseppe
Menascè Haim
Menascè Lea
Menascè Leon
Menascè Lucia
Menascè Mardocheo
Menascè Mardocheo
  Marco
Menascè Maria
Menascè Maria
Menascè Maria
Menascè Matilde
Menascè Mazaltov
Menascè Mazaltov
Menascè Michele
Menascè Michele
Menascè Mordehai
Menascè Morris
  Mosè
Menascè Mosè
Menascè Mosè
  Bochor
Menascè Nissim
Menascè Nissim
  detto Nisso
Menascè Norma
Menascè Rachele
Menascè Rachele

Menascè Rachele
Menascè Raffaele
Menascè Raffaele
Menascè Rahamin
Menascè Rebecca
Menascè Regina
Menascè Regina
Menascè Regina
Menascè Reina
Menascè Rivka
Menascè Salomon
Menascè Stella
Menascè Violetta
Menascè Vittoria
Menascè Yahir
Menasci Alberto
Menasci Camillo
Menasci Cesare
Menasci Enrico
Menasci Enrico
Menasci Ernesta
Menasci Raffaello
Menasci Roberto
  Raffaello
Menasci Umberto
Menasci Vittore
Menassè Davide
  Vittorio
Menassè Rosa
Menassè Vittorio
Mendel Raffaele
Mendelsohn
  Abraham
Mendelsohn Benzion
Mendelsohn Israel
Mendelsohn Jechiel
Mendelsohn Miriam
Mendelsohn Moritz
Mendes Angelina
Mendes Davide
Mendes Ida
Mendes Marcello
Mendes Maurizio
Mendes Stella
Mendes Umberto
Mendler Leopold
Menier Elena
Menkes Leia
Merdjan Elia
Merdjan Marco
Mernau Arrigo
Messiah Arbib
Messiah Isacco
Messica Emilia
Metzenberger Leonia

Metzger Samuel
Meyer Daisy
Meyer Paul
Meyohas Giacomo
Mezei Moritz
Michalup Karoline
Micheletti Elio
Michelstaedter Ada
Michelstaedter Elda
Michelstaedter
  Malvina
Michelstaedter
  Rachele
Mieli Adolfo
Mieli Alba
Mieli Alberto
Mieli Angelo
Mieli Armando
Mieli Cesare
Mieli Claudio
Mieli Corinna
Mieli Crescenzo
Mieli Enrica
Mieli Ernesta
Mieli Ester
Mieli Giacomo
Mieli Gina Giulia
Mieli Giovanni
Mieli Guglielmo
Mieli Ida
Mieli Israele Cesare
Mieli Lazzaro
Mieli Letizia
Mieli Marco Aurelio
Mieli Marina
Mieli Mario
Mieli Michele
Mieli Pacifico
Mieli Pacifico
Mieli Renato
Mieli Rossana
Mieli Sergio
Mieli Settimio Bruno
Mieli Tranquillo
Mieli Ugo
Mieli Umberto
Migliau Giuseppe
Milani Carolina
Milano Angelo
  Salvatore
Milano Elda Camilla
Milano Giorgina
Milano Raffaello
Milano Silvana
Milano Tullio

Milano Ugo
Milch Desiderio
Milch Emilio
Milgrom Carmi
Milgrom Isak
Milgrom Rea
  Jeannette Giovanna
Milhofer Maria
Milla Aldo
Milla Amelia
Milla Amelia
Milla Ferruccio
Milla Laura
Milla Lina
Milla Ninetta
Milla Ugo
Millul Achille
Millul Egisto Mario
Millul Lia Sara
Millul Liana
Milstein Josef
Milul Isacco Gino
Milul Lina Fortunè
Minerbi Aldo
Minerbi Gino
Minerbi Marcello
Minerbi Moisè detto
  Menotti
Minikes Mosè
Miranda Alfredo
Misan Adele
Misan Clara
Misan Diamantina
Misan Elio
Misan Enrica
Misan Ester
Misan Giuseppe
Misan Isacco
Misan Isaia
Misan Sarina
Misano Benedetto
Misano Claudio
Misano Costanza
Misano Fulvio
Misano Lina
Misano Marco
Misano Servadio
  Achille
Misco Giorgio
Misrachi Bulissa
Misrachi Bulissa
Misrachi Davide
Misrachi Eliezer
Misrachi Giacobbe
Misrachi Giacobbe

Misrachi Gioia Perla
Misrachi Haim
Misrachi Lea
Misrachi Linda
Misrachi Mazaltov
Misrachi Rachele
Misrachi Regina
Misrachi Samuele
Misrachi Sara
Misrachi Stella
Misrachi Virginia
Misul Alfredo
Misul Frida
Mittag Anita
Mizrachi Elia
Modena Leone
Modena Luigia detta
  Gina
Modiana Giacomo
  Elia
Modiano Carlo Elia
Modiano Daniele
Modiano Elisa
Modiano Flora
Modiano Giacobbe
Modiano Giacomo
Modiano Giacomo
Modiano Giuseppe
Modiano Grazia
Modiano Grazia
Modiano Isacco
Modiano Laura
Modiano Lucia
Modiano Lucia
Modiano Mosè
Modiano Samuele
Modiano Samuele
Modigliani Clara
  Rosa
Modigliani Elisa
Modigliani Giacomo
Modigliani Milena
Modigliani Umberto
Modigliani Vittorio
Molco Oreste Sergio
Moldauer Leopoldo
Molho Abramo
Molho Aldo
Molho Dario
Molho Giovanni
Molho Leone
Molho Olga
Molho Renata
Molho Vittorina
Molnar Elena

Momigliano Aldo
Momigliano Dante
Momigliano Ester
  Tranquilla
Momigliano Ida
Momigliano Iolanda
Momigliano Italo
Momigliano Pilade
Momigliano Zechia
  Bonaiuto
Monat Ignazio
Mondolfi Maria
Mondovì Linda
Montagnana Aida
  Sara
Montagnana Rosina
Montalcini Virginia
Montanari Alberto
Montecorboli Arturo
Montecorboli
  Giorgio
Montefiori Nella
Montias Leon
Montiglia Giacomo
Montiglia Regina
  Elena
Morais Alberto
Morais Alberto
Morais Amalia
Morais Carlo
Morais Emma
Morais Giorgina
Morais Graziella
Morais Leonello
Morais Umberto
  Mosè
Moravetz Carlo
Mordo Abramo
Mordo Diamantina
Mordo Elio
Mordo Massimo
Mordo Salomone
Morelli Leone Vita
Morello Arturo
  Aronne
Morello Erminia
Moresco Alberto
Moresco Angelo
Moresco Anselmo
Moresco Cesare
Moresco Cesare
Moresco David
Moresco Elisabetta
Moresco Esterina
Moresco Giorgio

Moresco Giuditta
Moresco Grazia
Moresco Grazia
Moresco Ida
Moresco Pacifico
Moresco Romolo
Moresco Zaccaria
Morgenstern Edith
Morgenstern Fanny
Morgenstern Irma
Morpurgo Abram
  Alberto
Morpurgo Alice
  Annetta
Morpurgo Bianca
  Maria
Morpurgo Carlo
Morpurgo Elda
Morpurgo Elena
Morpurgo Elio
Morpurgo Emma
Morpurgo Emma
Morpurgo Enrico
  detto Morpurghetto
Morpurgo Fortunata
Morpurgo Gaddo
Morpurgo Gina
Morpurgo Ida
Morpurgo Marco
Morpurgo Maria
Morpurgo Maura
Morpurgo Olga
Morpurgo Oscar
Morpurgo Pia Elvira
Morpurgo Umberto
Morpurgo Vittoria
Mortara Corrado
Mortara Giuseppe
Mortara Vittorio
  Mario
Mortera Abramo
  Giulio
Mortera Jole
Morterra Elda
Mosbach Egon
  Sigmund
Mosberg Margit Sofia
Moscatel Rosa
Moscati Alba
Moscati Alberto
Moscati Aldo
Moscati Angelo
Moscati Angelo
Moscati Angelo
Moscati Anselmo

Moscati Asriele
  Cesare
Moscati Bruno
Moscati Cesare
Moscati Cesare
Moscati David
Moscati Elda
Moscati Elio
Moscati Emanuele
Moscati Eva
Moscati Giacobbe
Moscati Giacomo
Moscati Giorgio
Moscati Giovanni
Moscati Ida
Moscati Letizia
Moscati Marco
Moscati Maria
Moscati Pace
  Anselmo
Moscati Reale detta
  Tina
Moscati Rosa
Moscati Rosa
Moscati Rosa
Moscati Sarina
Moscati Vanda
Moscati Vito
Moscato Bruno
Moscato Bruno
  Anselmo
Moscato Celestina
Moscato Elia
Moscato Elia
Moscato Emma
Moscato Ester
Moscato Franco
Moscato Giacomo
  detto Bufolone
Moscato Giuseppe
Moscato Giuseppe
Moscato Lazzaro
Moscato Lazzaro
Moscato Orabona
Moscato Pace
Moscato Pacifico
Moscato Renato
Moscato Servadio
Moscato Virginia
Moscato Vito
Moses Clara
Moses Frieda
Moses Hedwig
Moshopola Jacopo
Moskovic Felix

Moskovic Julius
Moskovic Viera
Mosseri Alberto
Mosseri Enrico
Mosseri Giacomo
  Renato
Mosseri Lauretta
Mosseri Marco
Moster Mauro Anton
Mozes Esther
Muehlstein
  Guglielmo
Mueller Maria
Mueller Stefania
Muenz Julius
Muenz Karl
Muggia Aldo
Muggia Amelia
Muggia Attalo
  Sansone
Muggia Celeste
Muggia Doralice
Muggia Franca
Muggia Giuseppe
Muggia Lia
Muggia Lino
Munk Hans
Munk Liselotte
Murgi Gino
Musafia Marcela
Musafja Jakob
Musatti Elia Gino
Mussafia Carla
Mussafia Margherita
Mussafia Valeria
Mussafir Rachele
Mussafir Regina
Mussafir Rica
Mussafir Vittorio
Mustacchi Anna
Mustacchi Daniele
Mustacchi Felice
Mustacchi Giuseppe
Mustacchi Leone
Mustacchi Marco
Mustacchi Marco
  Moisè
Mustacchi Marianna
Mustacchi Matilde
Mustacchi Michele
Mustacchi Michele
Mustacchi Moisè
Mustacchi Rachele
Mustacchi Rosa
Mustacchi Salomone

Mustacchi Samuele
Mustacchi Sofia
Nacamulli Elena
Nacamulli Gina
Nacamulli Guido
Nacamulli Iside
Nacamulli Lina
Nacamulli Mara
Nacamulli Mario
Nacamulli Ruggero
Nacamulli Umberto
Nacamulli Vittorio
Nacamulli Vittorio
  detto Pupo
Nacamully Wally
Nachmann Caroline
Nachmansohn
  Moise
Nacson Anna
Nacson Elia
Nacson Giulia
Nacson Leone
Nacson Leone
Nacson Pacina
Nacson Rebecca
Nacson Rebecca
Nacson Sara
Nacson Stella
Nacson Stella
Nador Margherita
Nagler Giacomo
Nagler Salo
Nahmias Rica
Nahmias Rosa
Nahmias Stella
Nahon Margherita
Nahoum Camelia
Nahoum Rosa
Nahoum Valerie
Nahum Emilio
Nahum Rebecca
  detta Becky
Nahum Zula
Naim Vittorio
Namias Bruna
Namias Enzo
Namias Ferruccio
Namias Guglielmo
Nasch Albert
Nasch Ingeborg
Nasch Karl
Nathan Arthur
  Abramo
Nathan Assalonne
Nathan Fritz

Nathan Fritz
Nathan Jeannette
Nathan Raoul Elia
Nathan Simon
Nathan Rogers
  Romeo
Nathansen Samuel
Nauri Misa
Navarro Achille
Navarro Alessandro
Navarro Amalia
Navarro Lina
Navarro Regina
  Allegrina
Navarro Rosina
Nazimov Ludwig
Nazimov Simon
Negri Guglielmo
Nehama Sam
Neisser Arthur
  Aaron
Nelken Richard
Nemes Ferdinando
Nemes Maria
Nemni Abramino
Nemni Davide
Nemni Giulia
Nemni Hlafo
Nemni Isacco
Nemni Isacco detto
  Kaki
Nemni Josef
Nemni Jusef
Nemni Miriam
Nemni Misa
Nemni Mosè
Nemni Renato
Nemni Scelbia
Nemni Simone
Neppi Gino
  Emanuele
Neppi Olga
Neubauer Hugo
  Israel
Neuberger Ugo
Neufeld Irma
Neufeld Nina
Neufeld Paolina
Neumann Alessandro
Neumann Aranka
Neumann Eugenio
Neumann Federica
Neumann Francesco
Neumann Frieda
Neumann Giovanna

Neumann
  Giuseppina
Neumann Kurt
Neumann Livia
Neumann Marcello
Neumann Maria
Neumann Viktor
Neumann Zoltan
Neuwohner Charlotte
Nichtberger Bobi
Nichtberger Dina
Nichtberger Markus
Nicolone
  Pierfrancesco
Ninos Luisa
Nissim Alberto
Nissim Augusta
Nissim Graziella
Nissim Luciana
Nissim Magenta
Nissim Marcella
Nizza Michele
  Eugenio
Nizza Umberto
Noah José
Nordlinger Elsa
Norsa Diana
Norsa Gaby
Norsa Germana
Norsa Giorgio
Norsa Giulio
Norsa Laura
Norsa Mario
Norsa Sergio
Norza Ida
Norzi Anna Luciana
Norzi Edvige
Norzi Guido
Norzi Marco
Norzi Todros
Notrica
Notrica Allegra
Notrica Giuseppe
Notrica Graziella
Notrica Haim
Notrica Hanula
Notrica Isacco
Notrica Jochevet
Notrica Judà
Notrica Lucia
Notrica Matilde
Notrica Matilde
Notrica Matilde
Notrica Mazliah
Notrica Miryam

Notrica Perahia
Notrica Rachele
Notrica Rachele
Notrica Rachele
Notrica Raffaele
Notrica Rebecca
Notrica Regina
Notrica Renata
Notrica Rosa
Notrica Sadis
Notrica Salomon
Notrica Salvo
Notrica Samuele
Notrica Samuele
Notrica Sara
Notrica Sara
Notrica Sultana
Novelli Ugo
Nuernberg Salomone
Nunes Adua
Nunes Olga
Nunes-Vais Adolfo
  detto Fofi
Nussbaum Ernst
Oberdorfer Ada
Oberdorfer Irene
Oberdorfer Olga
Obernbreit Adele
Oberzanek Emanuele
Oberzanek Samuele
Oberzanek Thea
Oblath Alessandro
Oblath Bianca
  Maria
Oblath Dragica
Oblath Ivan Gelza
Offner Sigismondo
Ojalvo Marco
Ojalvo Sara
Oransz Maurizio
Orefice Clotilde
Orefice Edoardo
Orefice Emma
Orefice Fanny
Orefice Giuseppe
Orefice Guido
Ornstein Tina
Oroster Masia
Ortona Bella
  Marianna
Ortona Bellina detta
  Adele
Ortona Delfina
Ortona Renato
Orvieto Ada

Orvieto Adolfo
Arturo
Orvieto Aldo
Orvieto Alessandro
Orvieto Amelia
Orvieto Angiolo
Orvieto Elisa
Orvieto Guido
Fortunato
Orvieto Leone
Alberto
Orvieto Lodovico
Orvieto Nello
Orvieto Rodolfo
Orvieto Rosina Clelia
Orvieto Ugo
Oser Cecilia
Osillag Elena
Osimo Ada
Osimo Giulio
Osmo Dario Davide
Osmo Ester
Osmo Lucia
Osmo Ninetta
Osmo Rachele
Osmo Roberto
Osmo Rosa
Osmo Sabino
Osmo Sabino
Osmo Vittoria
Ossia Israel
Ostrowka Alfredo
Ottenfeld Max
Ottolenghi Ada
Ottolenghi Adolfo
Ottolenghi Aldo
Ottolenghi
Alessandro
Ottolenghi Beatrice
Ottolenghi Dorina
Ottolenghi Emma
Ottolenghi Enrica
detta Tina
Ottolenghi Felice
detto Felicino
Ottolenghi Giacomo
Ottolenghi Giacomo
Giorgio
Ottolenghi Giano
Olao detto Gianni
Ottolenghi Giorgio
Ottolenghi Giulio
Ottolenghi Giuseppe
Ottolenghi Gustavo
Ottolenghi Lidia

Ottolenghi Lina detta
Ninì
Ottolenghi Linda
Ottolenghi Livia
Ottolenghi Marco
Ottolenghi Mary
Ottolenghi Olga
Maria Teresa
Ottolenghi Salvatore
Ottolenghi Silvio
Salomon
Ottolenghi Tesaura
Ottolenghi Vittorio
Ovadia Corinna
Ovazza Ada
Ovazza Alessandro
Ovazza Elena
Ovazza Ettore
Ovazza Riccardo
Pace Armando
Pace Celeste
Pace Corrado
Pace Giacomo
Giacobbe
Pace Gino
Pace Renato
Pace Salomone
Pace Sergio
Pace Umberto
Pacht Anny
Pacifici Ada
Pacifici Alberto
Pacifici Aldo
Pacifici Clelia
Pacifici Elena
Pacifici Emma
Pacifici Giulia
Pacifici Giulia
Pacifici Goffredo
Pacifici Ines
Pacifici Loris
Pacifici Luciana
Pacifici Riccardo
Pacifici Samuele
Pacifici Sonia
Pacifici Spartaco
Padoa Carlo
Padoa Celina detta
Marcella
Padoa Leone
Maurizio
Padoa Olga
Padova Giorgina
Padovani Grazia
Lidia

Paecht Karl Joseph
Paggi Dante
Paggi Goffredo
Pahrah Elisabetta
Palagi Franca
Palagi Gino Umberto
Palombo Giacobbe
Palombo Leone
Palombo Matilde
Palombo Nahman
Palombo Regina
Palombo Sara
Paneth Emil
Panzer Aron
Panzer Bianca
Panzer Maurizio
Panzer Susanna
Papini Alfredo
Papini Franco
Papo Salomone
Papo Sara
Papo Vittoria
Pardo Bea
Pardo Elvira
Pardo Roques
Giuseppe Abramo
Parenzo Giuseppe
Parenzo Italo
Parigi Giorgio
Parigi Renzo
Parigi Ugo
Parin Gino Federico
Paschir Liana
Passigli Eligio
Alfredo
Passigli Enzo
Passigli Ernesto
Passigli Giuseppe
Passigli Goffredo
Passigli Guido
Passigli Guido
Passigli Jenny
Passigli Leone
Passigli Lidia
Passigli Liliana
Passigli Rodolfo
Passigli Stella
Pavia Amelia
Pavia Egidio
Pavia Roberto
Pavoncello Abramo
Pavoncello Alfredo
Pavoncello Allegra
Pavoncello Allegra
Pavoncello Angelo

Pavoncello Anselmo
Pavoncello Anselmo
Pavoncello Anselmo
Pavoncello Anselmo
detto Chaim
Pavoncello Camilla
Pavoncello Cesare
Pavoncello Cesare
Pavoncello Chiara
Pavoncello Clelia
Pavoncello Dora
Pavoncello Elio
Pavoncello Emanuele
detto Picchio
Pavoncello Emanuele
Vittorio
Pavoncello Emilia
Pavoncello Emilia
Pavoncello Enrico
Pavoncello Giacomo
Pavoncello Giacomo
Gaetano
Pavoncello Giuditta
Pavoncello Graziella
Pavoncello Leone
Pavoncello Leone
detto Cirillo
Pavoncello Lina
Pavoncello Rebecca
Pavoncello Renata
Pavoncello Samuele
Pavoncello Sergio
Pavoncello Umberto
Pawlowsky Hofman
Pea Karl
Pecar Davide
Pecar Leone Remo
detto Leo
Pecar Zina Mirella
Pelech Bernardo
Pelech Dora
Pelletier Alice
Pelosof Edgardo
Pepes Rachele
Percowiez Adolfo
Perera Gabriella
Perera Luciano
Perera Mirella
Peretz Eliana
Rachele
Perez Grazia
Perez Graziella
Perez Haim
Perez Rachele
Perez Vittoria

Pergola Aldo
Pergola Bixio
Pergola Eleonora
Perl Alice
Perl Meier
Perlmutter Achille
Perlmutter Bruno
Perlmutter Gilmo
Perlow Aron Ernesto
Perlow Gisella
Perlow Giuseppe
Perlow Mario
Perlow Mira
Perlow Paula
Perlow Silvio
Perlow Sonia
Pernetz Massimiliano
Perugia Angelo
Perugia Angelo
Perugia Angelo Vito
Perugia Cesare
Perugia Clelia
Perugia Debora
Perugia Debora
Perugia Enrica
Perugia Fortunata
Perugia Gabriella
Perugia Giacomo
Perugia Gilberto
    Giuseppe Alberto
Perugia Giovanni
Perugia Italia
Perugia Laura Elena
Perugia Lello
Perugia Letizia
Perugia Marcella
Perugia Margherita
Perugia Mario
Perugia Rosa
Perugia Sara detta
    Serafina
Perugia Settimio
Perugia Vito
Perugia Vittoria
Perugia Vittoria
Perugia Vittorio
Pesaro Ada
Pesaro Arnaldo
Pesaro Canzio
Pesaro Cesare
Pesaro Costanza
Pesaro Gualtiero
Pesaro Ida Benedetta
    detta Tina
Pesaro Lieta

Pesaro Maurogonato
    Adolfo
Pesaro Oddone
Pescarolo Claudio
Pescarolo Eleonora
Pescarolo Enrico
Pescarolo Tullio
Pfeffer Rosa
Philipson Beniamino
Piacentino Rubino
Piattelli Bruno
    Settimio
Piattelli Cesare
Piattelli Dora
Piattelli Elda
Piattelli Ezechiele
    Luigi
Piattelli Franco
Piattelli Giacomo
Piattelli Giacomo
    Marco
Piattelli Lello
Piattelli Letizia
Piattelli Marco
Piattelli Servadio
Piattelli Settimio
    detto Negus
Piattelli Zaccaria
    Cesare
Piazza Alceo
Piazza Angelo
Piazza Angelo
Piazza Anita
Piazza Bruno
Piazza Donato
Piazza Edvige
Piazza Elio
Piazza Elisa
Piazza Elvira
Piazza Emanuele
Piazza Fernanda
Piazza Giacomo
Piazza Gina
Piazza Gino
Piazza Giuseppe
Piazza Maria Luisa
Piazza Rachele
Piazza Regina
Piazza Umberto
Piazza Virginia
Piazza Sed Angelo
Piazza Sed Camilla
Piazza Sed Cesira
Piazza Sed Consola
Piazza Sed Costanza

Piazza Sed Emma
Piazza Sed Ester
Piazza Sed Eugenio
Piazza Sed Leda
Piazza Sed Marco
Piazza Sed Rosa
Piazza Sed Sara
Picciaccio Emanuele
Piccoli Amalia
Pick Edvino
Pick Gabriella
Pick Giuseppe detto
    Riccardo
Pick Nathan Oscar
Pick Valeria
Pick Vittoria
Pickholz Augusta
Pieri Rosa
Piha Bellina
Piha Caden
Piha Davide
Piha Diana
Piha Isacco
Piha Maurizio
Piha Myriam
Piha Rachele
Piha Rebecca
Piha Rebecca
Piha Regina
Piha Salomon
Piha Sara
Piha Sol
Piha Vida
Pilas Estrella
Pilosoff Aronne
Pilosoff Bulissa
Pilosoff Eliezer
Pilosoff Fassana
Pilosoff Giuseppe
Pilosoff Haim
Pilosoff Isacco
Pilosoff Maria
Pilosoff Matatia
Pilosoff Matilde
Pilosoff Matilde
Pilosoff Mazaltov
Pilosoff Nissim
Pilosoff Rachele
Pilosoff Rachele
Pilosoff Susanna
Pincherle Emilia
Pincherle Emma
Pincherle Ernesto
Pincherle Giulia
Pincherle Giulia

Pincherle Giuseppe
Pincherle Giuseppina
Pincherle Lina Dina
Pincherle Vicini
    Luigi
Pincherle Vittorio
    Samuele
Pincsohn Ernst
Pincus Eric
Pinhas Naftali
Pinkus Giulia
Pinsk Regina
Pinto Vera
Pinto Wanda
Pintora Giamila
Piperno Abramo
    Aronne
Piperno Ada
Piperno Adriana
Piperno Aldo detto
    Chianuglione
Piperno Aldrato
Piperno Amelia
Piperno Angelina
Piperno Angelo
Piperno Angelo
Piperno Angelo
Piperno Anna
Piperno Augusto
Piperno Aurelio
Piperno Benedetto
    Ugo
Piperno Cesare
Piperno Cesare
Piperno Claudio
Piperno Corinna
Piperno Elena
Piperno Enrica
Piperno Ernesto
Piperno Fernanda
Piperno Fernando
Piperno Giacomo
Piperno Giacomo
Piperno Gino
Piperno Giuditta
Piperno Giuseppe
Piperno Letizia
Piperno Mario
Piperno Mosè
Piperno Nino
    Giorgio
Piperno Odorico
Piperno Rambaldo
Piperno Renato
Piperno Renzo

Piperno Roberto
Mosè
Piperno Sarina
Piperno Settimio
detto Peppone
Piperno Sigfrido Ezio
Piperno Tranquillo
Mario
Piperno Vera
Piperno Virginia
Piperno Virginia
Pirani Clara
Pirani Lina
Pisa Ida
Pisante Elvira
Pisante Giuseppe
Pisanti Giamila
Pisarz Josef
Pisetzky Arturo
Pisetzky Dorotea
Pitigliani
Bonaventura
Evelina
Plau Erich
Plesneri Rachele
Plitzka Sarah
Podolski Beatrice
Podolski Siegbert
Poggetto Alberto
Poggetto Clelia
Poggetto Moise
Pokorin Paolo
Polacco Abramo
Polacco Alba
Polacco Albino
Polacco Aldo
Polacco Athos
Polacco Carlo
Polacco Cesare
Polacco Clementina
Giuseppina
Polacco Elda
Polacco Emma
Polacco Enrica
Polacco Ercole
Polacco Estella
Polacco Giacomo
Polacco Giulia
Polacco Giuseppe
Polacco Ines
Polacco Iride Frida
Polacco Leda
Polacco Linda
Polacco Linda
Polacco Marcello

Polacco Maria
Polacco Mario
Polacco Massimiliano
Polacco Moisè
Polacco Mosè
Polacco Olga
Polacco Regina
Polacco Regina
Polacco Roberto
Polacco Ruggero
Polacco Venturina
detta Annina
Polak Ginetta
Polak Jacob
Polak Wolf
Polatschek Elvira
Polgar Emerico
Polgar Mario Claudio
Poliakoff Xenia
Politi Dora
Pollack Carlo
Pollak Alberto
Pollak Anna
Margherita
Pollak Cort
Pollak Edoardo
Pollak Giacomo
Pollak Giulio
Pollak Ida
Pollak Jaques
Pollak Leo
Pollak Ludovico
Pollak Paul
Pollak Susanna
Pollak Valeria
Pollak Volfango
Pollitzer Giulio
Pollitzer Ilona
Pollitzer
Massimiliano
Pompas Vittorio
Haim
Pontecorvo Carlo
Pontecorvo Clelia
Pontecorvo Ester
Pontecorvo
Gianfranco
Pontecorvo Letizia
Pontecorvo Luigia
Pontecorvo Nella
Pontecorvo Olga
Pontecorvo Sara
Pontremoli Amelia
Pontremoli Daniele
Pontremoli Violetta

Popelik Carla
Popelik Erminia
Popper Alice
Popper Elisa
Popper Gertrude
Popper Olga
Poras Catterina
Poras Francesca
Poras Isidoro
Poras Rosa
Porlitz Roberto
Ignazio
Portaleone Armando
Prato Laura
Prausnitzer Caterina
Preiss Edgardo
Preninger Sarah
Pressburger Alfredo
Pressburger Ernst
Pressburger Gertrude
Pressburger Heinrich
Pressburger Joseph
Priester Meta
Printz Lillo
Prister Clementina
Prister Leone Ettore
Prister Margherita
Prister Sara Luigia
Pristiges Regina
Pritsch Jacob
Privitera Giuseppe
Procaccia Ada
Procaccia Aldo
Procaccia Amedeo
Procaccia Amelia
Procaccia Elda
Procaccia Ernesto
Procaccia Giuseppe
Procaccia Paolo
Procaccia Rina
Procaccia Sabatino
Procaccia Umberto
Prosckauer Fanny
Provenzal Federico
Provenzali Ada Rita
Pugliese Anna
Pugliese Emilia
Pugliese Gemma
Pugliese Sandra
Puhaz Chaja
Rabà Edo
Rabà Ivo
Rabà Lanciotto
Rabà Lina
Rabà Vasco

Rabbeno Carla detta
Jolanda
Rabbeno Rodolfo
Rabello Adele
Rabello Armida
Rabinoff Anna
Raccah Aldo
Raccah Giuseppe
Raffael Emilia
Ragendorfer Benno
Ragendorfer Lucia
detta Luzzi
Rahamin Alice
Rahamin Daniele
Rahamin Elia
Rahamin Giacobbe
Rahamin Matilde
Rahmiel Rosa
Rahn Jeanne
Rahn Nicola
Rajner Darko
Rajner Hela
Rajnik Elisabetta
Cornelia
Rakosi Tibrio
Alexander
Ramras Enrico
Randegger Irene
Rapaport Caterina
Raphael Clara
Rappaport Regina
Rataud Henri
Rath Elisabetta
Rath Emanuele
Rath Nelly
Rath Salomon detto
Salo
Ravà Alice
Ravà Beatrice
Ravà Eloisa
Ravà Lazzaro
Ravà Renato
Ravah Elia
Ravah Lucia
Ravenna Alba Sofia
Ravenna Bianca
Ravenna Ciro
Ravenna Enrico
Ravenna Eugenio
Ravenna Eugenio
detto Gegio
Ravenna Franca
Eugenia
Ravenna Germana
Ravenna Gino

Ravenna Giorgio
Ravenna Giulio
Ravenna Guido
 Anselmo
Ravenna Ida
Ravenna Marcello
Ravenna Margherita
Ravenna Mario
Ravenna Rino
 Lazzaro
Ravenna Roberto
Ravenna Rodolfo
Ravenna Ugo
Ravenna Vittorio
Ravicz Alessandro
Ravicz Jean Jacques
Rawicz Evelina
Razdovitz Wilma
Razon Nissim
 Raffaele
Razon Sultana
 Susanna
Razon Vittoria
Recanati Elena
Recanati Flora
Recanati Rebecca
 detta Rita
Rechnitzer Eugenio
Rechnitzer Matilde
Rector Arturo
Redlich Giuseppina
Reggio Gisella
Reggio Iole
Reggio Rina
Reginiano Abramo
Reginiano Abramo
 William
Reginiano Alfonso
Reginiano Amalia
Reginiano Beniamino
Reginiano Buba
Reginiano Camilla
Reginiano Dora
Reginiano Efraim
Reginiano Esmeralda
Reginiano Ester
Reginiano Ester detta
 Rina
Reginiano Fortunata
Reginiano Ghibri
Reginiano Grazia
Reginiano Hamani
Reginiano Hamus
Reginiano Hlafo
Reginiano Hlafo

Reginiano Ida
Reginiano Irma
 Daisy
Reginiano Isacco
Reginiano Julia
Reginiano Lidia
Reginiano Liliana
Reginiano Lina
Reginiano Louis
Reginiano Mario
Reginiano Nissim
Reginiano Quintilio
Reginiano Raffaele
Reginiano Raffaele
Reginiano Rahmin
Reginiano René
Reginiano Rina
Reginiano Rina
Reginiano Saul
Reginiano Scialom
Reginiano Scialom
Reginiano Vana
Reginiano Vera
Reginiano Vilma
Reginiano Vittorio
Reginiano Vittorio
Reginiano Vittorio
Reginiano Vittorio
Reginiano Vittorio
Reginiano Vittorio
 William
Reich Adele
Reich Alessandro
Reich Elisabetta
Reich Lazzaro
Reich Mariska
Reich Rosa
Reich Sandro
Reich Teresa
Reich Willy
Reicher Marian
Reichmann Leopoldo
Reinach Ernesto
Reinach Etta Maria
Reiner Max
Reininger Gustavo
Reiter Eduard
Reitzmann Alexander
Reknitzer Adolfo
Reknitzer Carlo
Reknitzer Mehemed
Remondini Marcella
Rendel Augusta
Resignani Itala
Resignani Silvia
Resinger Etele

Reutlinger Albertina
Reven Adolfo
Revere Adriana
Revere Alessandro
Revere Enrico
Revere Ines
Revere Olga
Rexinger Ernesta
Reznik Michel
Ricchetti Edoardo
Richetti Elisa
Richetti Enrico
Richetti Nora
Richetti Vittorina
Richter Sara Jalka
Richter Sigfried
Riesenfeld Berthold
Riesenfeld Hans
Riesenfeld Hermann
Rietti Alfredo
Rietti Carlo
Rietti Emma
Rietti Gastone
Rietti Giulia
Rietti Ilma
Rietti Jole
Rietti Leonella
Rietti Marco
Rietti Nello
Rignani Armando
Rignani Enrico
Rignani Marco
Rignani Mario
Rimini Daniele
 Ettore
Rimini Eleonora
Rimini Elvira
Rimini Emilia
Rimini Enrichetta
Rimini Lucia
Rimini Margherita
Rimini Pia
Rimini Rosina
Ritter Ester
Riviere Elena
Roberti Guido
Robitschek Caterina
Rocca Cesare
Rocca Gilberto
Rocca Giulio
Rocca Valeria
Roccas Laura
Roccas Mario
Roccas Renzo
Roditi Luciano Israel

Roditi Rosa
Rodriguez Berta
Roger Martin
Roger Oscar
Rogonzinski Johanna
Romanelli Angelo
Romanelli Carla
Romanelli Elsa
Romanelli Elsa
Romanelli Ernesta
Romanelli Giorgio
Romanelli Lamberto
Romanelli Laura
Romanelli Michele
 Marco
Romanelli Raffaella
Romanin Bianca
Romano Abramo
 detto Beniamino
Romano Ester
Romano Ferdinando
 Vittorio
Romano Giacobbe
Romano Hanula
Romano Violetta
Romano Vittorio
Rosati Paola
Rosenbaum Elena
Rosenbaum Elena
Rosenbaum Ernst
Rosenbaum Lea Isa
Rosenbaum Moses
Rosenbaum Rachele
Rosenberg Elena
Rosenberg Eliahu
Rosenberg Esther
 Laja
Rosenberg Friedrich
Rosenberg Lucia
Rosenberg Otto
Rosenberg Sofia
Rosenberg Thea
Rosenblatt Raphael
Rosenblum Fayga
Rosener Sara
Rosenfeld Bertha
Rosenfeld Davide
Rosenfeld Haim
 Enrico
Rosenfeld Ottone
Rosenfelder Heinrich
Rosenholz Emilia
Rosenholz Ester Elsa
Rosenholz Ignazio
 Isacco

Rosenholz Leone
  Lajb
Rosenkranz Feige
Rosenschein Sara
Rosenschein Teresa
Rosenstein Amalia
Rosenthal Baruch
Rosenthal Debora
Rosenthal Hanna
Rosenthal Ilka
Rosenthal Leib
Rosenthal Maria Sara
Rosenthal Nahum
Rosenthal Otto
Rosenthal Paola
Rosenthal Rodolfo
Rosenthal Werner
Rosenwald Anna
  Clementina
Rosenzweig Maria
Rosenzweig Nathan
Rosner Emma
Rosner Libe
Rosner Rosa
Rosselli Lucia
Rosselli Marcella
Rossetti Maria
Rossi Bice
Rossi Corrado
Rossi Gino
Rossi Giulio
Rossi Letizia
Rossi Margherita
Rossi Milena
Rossi Moisè Alberto
Rossi Sergio
  Pellegrino
Rossman Elisa
Roth Alcher
Roth Aron Henri
Roth Emilie
Roth Noel
Roth Sabina
Roth Silvano
Roth Tereza
Rothbarth Guido
Rothschild Elsie
Rothschild Menny
Rothschild Myriam
Rothstein Adele
Rothstein Giorgio
Rothstein Giuseppe
Rothstein Sara
Rothstein Wanda
Rotschild

Rotschild Paula
Rozanes Rosa
Rozanes Sultana
Rozay Teodoro Elia
Rozio Ester
Rozio Esther
Rozio Jacob
Rozio Jacob
Rozio Rachele
Rozio Rahamin
Rozio Sara
Rozio Silvia
Rubin Giulia
Rubin Misa
Rubinfeld Chaim
Rubinfeld Edward
Rubinfeld Enrica
Rubitscheck Fanny
Rubitscheck Laura
Rudnitzky Elena
Rudnitzky Maurizio
Rudnitzky Regina
Rudnitzky Roberto
Rudoi Caterina Gitzel
Ruerst Armando
Rukig Jetti
Rumeld Leib
Rumpler Adele
Russi Ada
Russi Ada
Russi Giacomo
Russi Irma
Russi Pia
Russi Sergio
Russi Zoe
Russo Abramo
Russo Alfredo
Russo Benvenuta
Russo Esther
Russo Esther
Russo Maria
Russo Oro
Russo Rebecca
Rutkowski Maria
Ruzicka Elena
Ruzicka Vera
Sabatelli Perla
Sabatello Abramo
Sabatello Angelo
Sabatello Carlo
Sabatello Carlo
  Salvatore
Sabatello Celeste
  Alba
Sabatello Dattilo

Sabatello Eleonora
Sabatello Emma
Sabatello Emma
Sabatello Enrica
Sabatello Franco
Sabatello Giovanni
Sabatello Graziella
Sabatello Italia
Sabatello Leone
Sabatello Letizia
Sabatello Liana
  Ornella
Sabatello Michele
Sabatello Settimio
Sabatello Tranquillo
Sabatello Umberto
Sabbadini Elio
Sabbadini Salvatore
Sabbadini Sylva
Sabbadini Vittoria
Sabban Sultana
Sabetai Davide
Sabetai Nissim
Sabetai Salomone
Sacerdote Bice
Sacerdote Camillo
Sacerdote Cesare
Sacerdote Claudio
Sacerdote Claudio
Sacerdote
  Clementina
Sacerdote Davide
Sacerdote Debora
  Dorina
Sacerdote Emanuele
Sacerdote Emilio
Sacerdote Emma
Sacerdote Ernesta
Sacerdote Estella
Sacerdote Giacomo
Sacerdote Giorgio
Sacerdote Giuseppe
Sacerdote Laura
Sacerdote Lea Elena
Sacerdote Luciana
Sacerdote Marianna
Sacerdote Matilde
Sacerdote Nella
Sacerdote Rosy
Sacerdote Sabato
Sacerdote Sergio
Sacerdote Teodoro
Sacerdoti Adele
  Elvira
Sacerdoti Alessandro

Sacerdoti Camilla
Sacerdoti Clara
Sacerdoti Emilio
Sacerdoti Evelina
Sacerdoti Franco
Sacerdoti Olimpia
  detta Pia
Sacerdoti Renzo
Sacerdoti Valeria
Sachs Elsa
Sachs Selma
Sadis Esther
Sadis Matilde
Sadis Nissim
Sadis Regina
Sadis Salomone
Sadun Amiel
Sadun Diodato
  Gastone
Sadun Gina
Sadun Gino
Sadun Lelio
Sadun Lya
Sadun Paolo
Sadun Vittorio
  Emanuele
Sagi Luigi
Sagi Nicolò
Saglia Luisa
Salambrassi Vassiliki
  Basilia
Salem Emanuele
Salem Salem
Salem Samaim
Salmona Josef
Salmoni Angelo
Salmoni Bianca
Salmoni Celeste
Salmoni David
Salmoni Dora
Salmoni Gilberto
  Raffaele
Salmoni Gino
Salmoni Renato
Salmonì Riccardo
Salmoni Romeo
Salmoni Rubino
Salmoni Rosa
Salom Aldo
Salom Moise
Salomon Emmy
Salomon Herbert
Salomone Paolina
Salonicchio
  Abramo

Salonicchio
Alessandra detta
Sarina
Salonicchio Ester
Salonicchio Lucia
Salonicchio
Salomone
Saltiel Giacomo
Saltiel Giovanni
Maurizio
Saltiel Joseph
Saltiel Moise
Saltiel Rachele
Saltiel Sanson
Salzberger Edoardo
Salzer Edmondo
Samaia Angelo
Samaia Ida
Samuel Esther
Samuel Sigismondo
Samuel Simeone
Samuelides Sam
Sander Lilli detta
Babette
Sander Ugo
Sandmann Sigfried
Sanguinetti Bruno
Sanguinetti Emilia
Sanguinetti Renato
Sanguinetti Umberto
Sansonovitch Anna
Saphier Henni
Saphir Emma
Saralvo Cesarina
Saralvo Corrado
Saralvo Giorgio
Saralvo Giovanna
Saralvo Lilio
Saralvo Lindo
Saralvo Mario
Saralvo Rino
Saraval Bruno
Saraval Eugenio
Saraval Ida
Saravalle Emma
Sarfatti Lisa
Sas Giulio
Sass Ernst
Sass Peter
Sass Rosa
Sattler Caterina
Saul Estrella
Saul Rebecca
Saveri Oscar
Savic Antonio

Savic Giorgio
Savic Stefano
Saya Giacomo
Sayowici Baruch
Sayowici Dorotea
Sayowici Maurizio
Sbrana Gina
Scandiani Bianca
Scandiani Luisa
Scapa Mazaltov
Scaramella Messulam
Adelaide
Scaramella Messulam
Anna
Scaramella Messulam
Rosetta
Scarar Francesco
Scazzocchio Clotilde
Scazzocchio Riccardo
Scazzocchio Virginia
Scemarià Abramo
Scemarià Bulissa
Scemarià Dora
Scemarià Elia
Scemarià Esther
Scemarià Giacobbe
Scemarià Giacobbe
Giacomo
Scemarià Giuseppe
Scemarià Haim
Vittorio
Scemarià Hanula
Scemarià Lea
Scemarià Leone
Scemarià Lucia
Scemarià Marco
Scemarià Mosè
Scemarià Mosè
Scemarià Saruta
Schacherl Emil
Schanzer Rodolfo
Schapira Leopold
Schapira Paul
Schapiro Elena
Schattner Grete
Schatz Jakob
Schenkel Enrichetta
Schenkel Giuseppe
Scherzenberg Elena
Schfargel
Schickler Elena
Schieber Rosa
Schiff Sigismondo
Schiffeldrin Kurt
Schiffeldrin Mosè

Schiffer Alessandro
Schiller Giulia
Schingazz Anna
Schingazz Giuseppe
Schlaf Israele Isidoro
Schlesinger
Schlesinger Luisa
Schlesinger Ruth
Schlesinger Stella
Schlochoff Erich
Schloss Hans Werner
Schloss Hermann
Schloss Iolanda
Schloss Paolo
Schluesselberg
Salomon
Schmidt Antonia
Schmier Gisella
Schmierer Felice
Schmierer Pinkas
Schmolka Filippa
Schnapp Gerda
Schnapp Littman
Eisig
Schneider Michele
Schneider Theodor
Schoenberger
Giuseppe
Schoenbrunn Joseph
Schoenfeld Bela
Schoenfeld Elvira
Schoenhaut Leopoldo
Schoenheit Carlo
Schoenheit Franco
Schoenstein Rosette
Schott Alberto
Schott Enrico
Schotten Irma
Schrecker Erwin
Schreier Sofia
Schrotter Anna
Schubert Hans
Schuler Augusta
Schulmann Gabriel
Schumann Davide
Schuskind Sabine
Schuster Eva
Schustermann Enrico
Schustermann Jacob
Schustermann
Marcella
Schustermann Moritz
Schwartz Hans Israel
Schwarz Adolf
Schwarz Arthur

Schwarz Benno
Schwarz Giuseppe
Schwarz Gustavo
Schwarz Maria
Schwarz Serena
Schwarz Siegried
Schwarzschild Berta
Schwarzschild Ernst
Schwertfinger Ester
Schwitz Eliana
Schwitz Fanny
Schwolka Hermine
Sciaki Menachem
Sciaki Nathan
Scialom Humbert
Scialom Liliana
Sciami Giacobbe
Sciami Giovanna
Sciami Luna
Sciami Nissim
Sciami Salvatore
Sciarcon Bulissa
Sciarcon Esther
Sciarcon Estrella
Sciarcon Felicia detta
Felicina
Sciarcon Fortunata
Sciarcon Giulia
Sciarcon Giuseppe
Sciarcon Isacco
Sciarcon Lucia
Sciarcon Lucia
Sciarcon Matilde
Sciarcon Morris
Sciarcon Mosè
Sciarcon Mosè
Sciarcon Selma
Scikamovic Rachele
Scioa Camilla
Scitrug Vittorio
Benedetto
Sciunnach Alberto
Sciunnach Dattilo
Giovanni
Sciunnach Fortunata
Sciunnach Giuditta
Sciunnach Leone
Sciunnach Letizia
Sciunnach Marco
Sciunnach Marco
Sciunnach Settimio
Sdraffa Berta
Sed Alberto
Sed Alberto
Sed Angelica

Sed Angelo
Sed Angelo
Sed Cesira
Sed Emma
Sed Ester
Sed Fatina
Sed Gioia
Sed Giulia
Sed Giulia
Sed Giuseppe
Sed Graziano
Sed Lello
Sed Leonardo
Sed Marco
Sed Pacifico
Sed Pacifico detto Il
  Toscanino
Sed Piazza Giuseppe
Sed Piazza Graziadio
Sed Piazza Pacifico
Sed Silvana
Seemann Hermann
Segall Maximilian
Segre Abramo
Segre Adele Regina
Segre Adriana
Segre Alberto
Segre Alberto
Segre Alberto
Segre Alberto
Segre Alberto Carlo
  Maurizio
Segre Alice
Segre Anna
Segre Annetta
Segre Attilio
Segre Beniamino
Segre Carmen
Segre Cesare
Segre Cesare Davide
Segre Clotilde
Segrè Clotilde
Segre Delia
Segre Egle
Segre Elena
Segrè Elena
Segrè Elena
Segre Emanuele Sion
Segre Emma
Segre Ermelinda
  Bella detta Bettina
Segre Ester
Segre Eugenia
Segre Eva Raffaella
Segre Ezechiele

Segrè Fortunata
  Gemma
Segrè Girolamo
  Ettore
Segrè Giulia Rosa
Segrè Giulio
Segre Giuseppe
Segrè Ida
Segre Ines
Segrè Isidoro
Segrè Italia
Segrè Lea
Segre Lelio Leone
  Davide
Segrè Lidia
Segre Liliana
Segre Marco
Segre Marco
Segre Margherita
Segre Maria Bice
Segrè Marianna
  Fanny Nella
Segre Mario
Segre Massimo
  Daniele
Segre Mirella
Segrè Moise
Segre Moise
Segre Moise Mario
Segrè Nedda
Segrè Ottavio
Segre Pia
Segre Regina
Segre Riccardo
Segre Roberto
Segre Rosa
Segrè Rosa Emilia
Segrè Salvatore
Segre Salvatore
Segre Salvatore
  Samuele
Segre Sanson
Segre Silvio
Segre Spartaco
Segre Tullio
Segre Ugo
Segrè Valentina
Segrè Vittoria
Segre Vittorina
Segre Vittorio
Seidenpelz Stella
Seidl Edith
Seif Giacomo
Seifter Adele
Seifter Bernhard

Selinsky Leo
Semele Ester
Semmel Tynya
Semo Anita
Semo Ester
Semo Giuliana detta
  Lilly
Semo Leone
Senigaglia Arrigo
Seppilli Alessandrina
Seppilli Emma
  Mazaltov
Seppilli Lidia
Sereni Aldo
Sereni Angelo
Sereni Eena
Sereni Enzo
Sereni Giacobbe
  Giacomo
Sereni Isacco
Sereni Paolo
Sereni Ugo
Sereno Clara
Serman Emil
Sermoneta Alvaro
Sermoneta Amedeo
Sermoneta Amelia
Sermoneta Angelo
Sermoneta Anita
Sermoneta Benedetto
Sermoneta Benedetto
Sermoneta Benedetto
Sermoneta Benedetto
Sermoneta Celeste
Sermoneta Costanza
Sermoneta Costanza
Sermoneta Emma
Sermoneta Eugenio
Sermoneta Eugenio
Sermoneta Franca
Sermoneta Giuseppe
Sermoneta Giuseppe
  Benedetto
Sermoneta Isacco
Sermoneta Isacco
Sermoneta Isaia
  Sergio
Sermoneta Marco
Sermoneta Mario
Sermoneta Mario
Sermoneta Pacifico
Sermoneta Pacifico
Sermoneta Pellegrino
Sermoneta Prospero
Sermoneta Renata

Sermoneta Rosa
Sermoneta Rosa
Sermoneta Rosa
Sermoneta Salvatore
Sermoneta Salvatore
Sermoneta Salvatore
Sermoneta Silvia
Sermoneta Virginia
Sermoneta Vittorio
Seror Mina
Servadio Letizia
Servadio Nives
Servi Affortunata
Servi Aldo
Servi Arturo
Servi Carlo
Servi Corrado
Servi Elda
Servi Ester
Servi Fernanda
Servi Giovacchino
Servi Ida
Servi Irma
Servi Lucia
Servi Margherita
Sessa Virginia
Sessi Ester
Sestieri Aldo
Sestieri Celeste
Sezzi Augusto
Sezzi Riccardo
Sforni Dosolina
Sforni Elda
Sforni Gianfranco
  detto Franz
Sforni Guido
Shalom Esther
Shalom Rebecca
Shalom Samuele
Shalom Stella
Shoumann Jolanda
Sidi Lisa
Sidi Renee
Sidi Behor
Sidis Clara
Sidis Isacco
Sidis Luna
Sidis Maria detta
  Marietta
Sidis Matilde
Sidis Mordochai
Sidis Rachele
Sidis Stella
Siebzehner Joseph
Sierzantowicz Lili

Sierzantowicz
Maurizio
Sigura Stella
Silber Ferdinando
Silberberg Berta
Silberger Nadia
Silbermann Berta
Silbermann Carlotta
Silbermann Valeria
Silberstein Elena
Silberstein Richard
Silberstein Stella
Silberstein Walter
Silva Umberto
Giorgio
Silvera Lelio
Silvera Violetta
Simberger Heda
Simkovics Ermanno
Simkovics Eva
Simkovics Giorgio
Simkovics Giuditta
Simkovics Giuseppe
Simkovics Guido
Simkovics Mayer
Simkovics Nora
Simkovits Adolfo
Simon Max Guenther
Simon Paula
Simoro Vittoria
Simsolo Clara
Simsolo Zafira
Singer Franziska
Singer Mira
Sinigaglia Alda
Sinigaglia Angelica
Sinigaglia Angelo
Sinigaglia Attilio
Sinigaglia Italo
Sinigaglia Leone
Sinigaglia Livia
Sinigaglia Nino
Sinigaglia Oreste
Sinigaglia Paride
Sinigaglia Teresina
Sinigaglia Vittoria
Sinigallia Luigi
Siptzinger Alberto
Skrzynsky Mottel
Slam Esther
Slatopoloski
Alexander
Sleidinger Arturo
Slovak Margherita
Slukin Anna

Sobalska Rachele
Sojke Bernard
Solal Olga
Soliani Arturo
Soliani Umberto
Som Sauro
Som Silvia
Sommer Taube
Sommerfeld Leo
Sommermann Carlo
Somogy Tiburzio
Sona Giuseppe
Sonino Guido
Sonino Paola
Sonne Feldora
Regina
Sonnenfeld Ella
Sonnino Adele
Sonnino Alberto
Sonnino Aldo
Sonnino Amadio
Sonnino Amedeo
Sonnino Amedeo
Sonnino Angelo
Sonnino Angelo
Sonnino Angelo
Sonnino Angelo
Sonnino Angelo
Sonnino Angelo
Sonnino Angelo
Sonnino Bice
Sonnino Celeste
Sonnino Cesira
Sonnino Costanza
Sonnino David
Sonnino David
Sonnino Davide
Sonnino Edda
Giuditta
Sonnino Elisa
Sonnino Enrico
Sonnino Ester
Sonnino Ettore
Sonnino Eugenio
Sonnino Fabrizio
Sonnino Fortunata
detta Nella
Sonnino Gabriele
Sonnino Gabriele
Sonnino Giacobbe
Sonnino Gina
Sonnino Giorgio
Sonnino Giuliana
Sonnino Giuseppe
Sonnino Grazia
Sonnino Grazia

Sonnino Guglielmo
Sonnino Ida
Sonnino Ilda
Sonnino Isacco
Sonnino Isacco
Sonnino Lalla
Sonnino Leone
Sonnino Lina Maria
Sonnino Marco
Sonnino Margherita
Sonnino Maria Luisa
Sonnino Mario
Sonnino Mario
Sonnino Mario
Sonnino Massimo
Sonnino Michele
Sonnino Michele
Sonnino Moise
Sonnino Mosè Marco
Sonnino Mosè Marco
Sonnino Nella
Sonnino Pacifico
Sonnino Pacifico
Armando
Sonnino Paolo
Sonnino Piera
Sonnino Piero
Sonnino Pilade
Sonnino Rachele
Sonnino Renato
Sonnino Roberto
Sonnino Rosa
Sonnino Rubino
detto Traballa
Sonnino Salomone
Vito
Sonnino Samuele
Sonnino Samuele
Sonnino Samuele
detto Lello
Sonnino Samuele
Sandro
Sonnino Sara
Sonnino Speranza
Sonnino Tina
Sonnino Umberto
Sonnino Virginia
Sonntag
Sonsino Nissim
Sorani Aldo
Soria Davide
Soria Sofia
Soriano Bellina
Soriano Bulissa
Soriano Davide

Soriano Esther
Soriano Fortunata
Soriano Giacobbe
Soriano Giacobbe
Soriano Jenni
Rachele
Soriano Mosè
Soriano Nissim detto
Maurice
Soriano Perlina
Soriano Rachele
Soriano Rachele
Soriano Rachele
Soriano Rachele detta
Lily
Soriano Sara
Soriano Stella
Soriano Sultana
Sorias Giuseppe
Sorias Moisè
Sornaga Anna
Sornaga Elena
Sornaga Enrichetta
Spagnoletto Aurelio
Spagnoletto
Leonardo
Spagnoletto
Leonardo
Spagnoletto Mario
Spagnoletto Noè
detto Peppino
Spagnoletto Perla
Emma
Spagnoletto Rosa
Spagnoletto Samuele
Spagnoletto Settimio
detto Vespillone
Spagnoletto Sofia
Spagnoletto Virtuosa
Spagnoletto Virtuosa
Spiegel Felice
Spiegel Jonas
Spiegel Pia
Spielberg Arturo
Spierer Helene
Spira Gisela
Spira Sigmund
Spiro David
Spitz Alberto
Riccardo
Spitz Alfredo detto
Fredy
Spitz Anna
Spitz Ella
Spitzer Emma

Spitzer Eugen
Spizzichino Ada
Spizzichino Adelaide
Spizzichino Alberto
Spizzichino Alberto
Spizzichino Alberto
Umberto
Spizzichino Alfredo
Spizzichino Allegra
Spizzichino Angelo
detto Cazzodoro
Spizzichino Bruno
Pellegrino
Spizzichino Costanza
Spizzichino Elvira
Spizzichino Enrica
Spizzichino Enrica
Spizzichino Enrica
Spizzichino
Enrichetta
Spizzichino
Enrichetta
Spizzichino Ester
Spizzichino Eugenio
Spizzichino Eugenio
Spizzichino Fiorina
Spizzichino
Fortunata
Spizzichino
Fortunata
Spizzichino Franca
Spizzichino Giacomo
Spizzichino Giacomo
Spizzichino Giacomo
Spizzichino Giuditta
Spizzichino Giuseppe
Spizzichino Grazia
Spizzichino Graziano
Spizzichino Graziella
Spizzichino Ines
Spizzichino Iride
Spizzichino Jader
Spizzichino Lazzaro
Spizzichino Letizia
Spizzichino Letizia
Spizzichino Luciana
Spizzichino Marco
detto L'Americano
Spizzichino Mario
Spizzichino Mario
Spizzichino Michele
Ezio
Spizzichino Mosè
Otello detto
Bracarolo

Spizzichino Norina
Spizzichino Pacifico
Spizzichino Pacifico
Spizzichino Pacifico
Spizzichino Pacifico
Spizzichino Regina
Spizzichino Ricca
Spizzichino Rina
Spizzichino Rosa
Spizzichino Rosa
Spizzichino Rosa
Spizzichino Rubino
Spizzichino Sara
detta Sarina
Spizzichino Settimia
Spizzichino Stella
Spizzichino Umberto
Spizzichino Umberto
Spizzichino Vittorio
Emanuele
Spizzichino Vittorio
Emanuele
Spizzichino Virginia
Springer Elisa detta
Lizzi
Spritzmann Samuele
Stabholz Menasse
Stahl Olga
Staineri Carlo
Staineri Emanuele
Starc Teodora
Stark Paola
Steigman Moses
Stein Hildegarde
detta Hilde
Stein Samuel
Steinbach Arturo
Steiner Abramo
Adolfo
Steiner Aurelia
Steiner Ernst
Steiner Eugenio
Steiner Margherita
Steinitz Regina
Steinlauf Davide
Steinmann Filippo
Steinmann Iris
Steinmann Regina
Stempa Adolf
Stendler Giuseppe
detto Pino
Stendler Lina
Stern Francesca
Stern Gitl
Stern Haskel

Stern Josephine
Stern Katalina
Stern Rachele Lea
Stern Samuele
Stern Simel Chaim
Sternbach Chaim
Sternfeld Paolo
Sternthal Wolf
Stettauer Paola
Stiassny Ludwig
Stilermann Giulia
Stockfisch Armand
Stockfisch Chaia
Isacco
Stockfisch Henri
Stockfisch Kalman
Stockfisch Maria
Matza
Stolowiek Robert
Josef
Stolzberg Czama
Stolzberg Israel
Stolzberg Pinkas
Strauber Gisela
Strauss Julius
Strawczynski
Zigmund
Strehler Sara
Stricks
Stricks Isidor
Strilzov Ljuba
Strykowski Abraham
Stuhl Herman
Sturm Isacco
Sturm Jacob
Sturm Maria
Sturm Nissim
Stutz Hava
Stutz Jenny
Stutz Saya
Stutz Sonia
Stutzel Antonio
Stutzel Arnaldo
Subert Edvige
Suesskind Arthur
Suessmann Giulia
Sulam Amelia
Sulam Rachele
Sulam Ruben
Sullam Gisella
Supino Teresa
Surmani Abramo
Surmani Caden
Surmani Calomira
Surmani Eliezer

Surmani Esther
Surmani Giacobbe
Surmani Haim
Surmani Mirù
Surmani Mosè
Surmani Orietta
Stella
Surmani Rachele
Surmani Rachele
Surmani Samuele
Surmani Sara
Surmani Stella
Suzeman Rachel
Syrkus Paul
Szabo Emerico
Szabo Emerico
Szakacs Peter
Szapiro Ester
Szatkownik Daniele
Szatkownik Henri
Szatkownik Sara
Szcrycky Chaim
Szecso Giuseppe
Szego Paolo
Szekely Adele
Szekely Alice
Szklozer Eva
Szmidt Szlama
Szoelloessy Irene
Szorenyi Adolfo
Szorenyi Alessandro
Szorenyi Arianna
Szorenyi Carlo
Szorenyi Daisy
Dorotea
Szorenyi Lea
Szorenyi Rosalia
Szorenyi Stella
Szuecks Margherita
detta Manzi
Szwarc Simon
Tagger Eliezer
Tagliacozzo Ada
Tagliacozzo Amedeo
Tagliacozzo Angelo
Tagliacozzo Arnaldo
Tagliacozzo Celeste
Tagliacozzo Colomba
Tagliacozzo David
Tagliacozzo Enrica
Tagliacozzo Enrica
Tagliacozzo Ester
Tagliacozzo Ester
Tagliacozzo Gino
Tagliacozzo Italia

Tagliacozzo Michele
Tagliacozzo Pacifico
Taich Federica
Taieb Ester
Taigman Kalman
Talmazschii Ghers
Talmazschii Regina
Talmazschii Valerio
  detto Willy
Tammam Giulia
  Smlei
Tapiero Leone
Tarica Alice
Tarica Amelia
Tarica Bulissa
Tarica Elvira
Tarica Ester
Tarica Esther
Tarica Esther
Tarica Esther
Tarica Esther
Tarica Fassana
Tarica Flora
Tarica Flora
Tarica Fortunata
Tarica Giacobbe
Tarica Ketty
Tarica Loretta
Tarica Marco
Tarica Maria
Tarica Maurizio
Tarica Mazaltov
Tarica Mosè
Tarica Mussani detto
  Il Vegliardo
Tarica Olga
Tarica Rachele
Tarica Rachele
Tarica Rebecca
Tarica Rebecca
Tarica Rosa
Tarica Sarina
Tarica Sarota
Tarica Simha
Tarica Sipura
Tarica Sol
Tarica Violetta
Tarica Yeudà
Tarica Yohevet
  Bohora
Tarnover Julius
Tarnowsky David
Tarnowsky Giuseppe
Tarnowsky Renato
Tauber Edvige

Taussig Walter
Tayar Ester
Tazartes Fatima
Tedeschi Ada
Tedeschi Ada
Tedeschi Adelaide
Tedeschi Adele
Tedeschi Adolfo
Tedeschi Alberto
  Sebastiano
Tedeschi Arrigo
Tedeschi Benvenuta
  detta Ines
Tedeschi Bianca
Tedeschi Bice
Tedeschi Emanuele
  Amedeo
Tedeschi Emma
Tedeschi Emma
  Bianca
Tedeschi
  Ermenegilda
Tedeschi Ernesta
  Irma
Tedeschi Eugenia
Tedeschi Ezio
Tedeschi Francesca
Tedeschi Franco
Tedeschi Giacomo
Tedeschi Giacomo
Tedeschi Giacomo
Tedeschi Giacomo
  detto Mino
Tedeschi Gino
Tedeschi Gino
Tedeschi Giorgio
  Eugenio
Tedeschi Giuliana
Tedeschi Gualtiero
Tedeschi Irene
Tedeschi Lidia
Tedeschi Lionello
Tedeschi Luciano
Tedeschi Mafalda Ida
Tedeschi Marco
Tedeschi Marisa
Tedeschi Natalia
Tedeschi Sabato
  Giuseppe
Tedeschi Salomone
Tedeschi Salvatore
Tedeschi Silvio
Tedeschi Umberto
Tedeschi Vittoria
Tedeschi Vittorio

Tedeschi Wanda
Tedesco Ada
Tedesco Adele
Tedesco Cesare
Tedesco Giulia
Tedesco Rocca Laura
Teglio Carlo
Teglio Ivonne
Teglio Margherita
Teglio Rita Sara
Teglio Teresita
Teglio Ugo
Teitel Adele
Teitel Jacob
Tempel Adele Anna
Tempel Hanna
Templer Jacob
Templer Salomon
Tepper Berta
Termini Vittorio
Terni Vittorio
Terracina Adriana
Terracina Alberto
Terracina Amedeo
Terracina Anna
Terracina Anna
  Maria
Terracina Cesare
Terracina Cesira
Terracina Eleonora
Terracina Emanuele
Terracina Emma
Terracina Enrichetta
Terracina Franca
Terracina Giacomo
  detto Ciccio
Terracina Giovanni
Terracina Giuditta
Terracina Leo
Terracina Leone
Terracina Leone
  David
Terracina Leonello
Terracina Letizia
Terracina Marco
Terracina Marco
  Mosè
Terracina Mirella
Terracina Pellegrino
Terracina Piero
Terracina Raffaele
Terracina Rina
Terracina Rosa
Terracina Sergio
Terracina Virginia

Terracini Nella Sara
Tiano Salomone
Tiefenthal Wilhelm
Tiemann Joseph
Tiersfeld Walter
Timberg Sabina
Tint Herbert
Tint Julius
Tint Ugo
Tisminiezky Aronne
  Walter
Tisminiezky Boris
Tisminiezky Ester
Tisminiezky
  Loredana
Todesco Alberto
  Leone
Todesco Angela
Todesco Bruno
Todesco Emilio
Todesco Emma
Todesco Eugenio
Todesco Fanny
Todesco Giuseppe
Todesco Marco
Todesco Mario
Todesco Sergio
Tolentini Oscar
Tolentino Elena
Tolentino Elio
Tolentino Enrichetta
Tolentino Ersilia
Tolentino Giulia
Tolentino Irma
Tolentino Paolo
Topsch Wilhelmine
  Emma
Toribolo Teresita
Torre Marco
Torre Salvatore
Torre Sansone
Torres Raoul
Toscano Elena Ida
Toscano Eleonora
Toscano Elisa
Toscano Mario Mosè
Toscano Rachele
  Lina
Toscano Rebecca
Toscano Rosa
Totter Matilde
  Erminia
Tramer Alfredo
Tramer Enrichetta
Trautmann Regina

Treistmann Ariel
Leib
Treppner Lina
Treves Adelaide
Treves Alda
Treves Alfredo Moisè
Treves Amelia
Treves Dario
Treves Elia Emanuele
Treves Elisa
Treves Elsa
Treves Eugenia
Allegra
Treves Giulia
Treves Giuseppe
Treves Luciano
Treves Mario
Ezechiele
Treves Renato
Treves Roberto
Treves Rodolfo
Trevez Giuseppe
Trevez Regina
Trevi Aldebrando
Trevi Anna
Trevi Aurelio Angelo
Trevi Enrichetta
Trevi Giacomo
Trevi Ida
Trevi Valerio
Trevi Zoe
Triebfeder Nathan
Trieste Celina
Troestler Wilhelm
Trotzer Zoltan
Tsciuba Rachele
Tsciuba Toma
Tuchmann Heinz
Erich
Tuchmann Hilde
Rosy
Tuerkheimer Max
Turad Renata
Turiel Boaz
Turiel Boaz
Turiel Celebi
Turiel Dolly
Turiel Esther
Turiel Ghedalia
Turiel Giuseppe
Turiel Isidoro Ezrà
Turiel Lea
Turiel Lucia
Turiel Maurizio
Turiel Mazaltov

Turiel Michele
Turiel Rachele
Turiel Raffaele
Turiel Rebecca Rifka
Turiel Salvatore
Turiel Sara
Turiel Violetta
Turmann Giuseppe
Turowski Eugen
Turteltaub Edmondo
Turteltaub Hans
Turteltaub Walter
Tylberg Marcello
Uggeri Bruna Teresa
Ukmar Enrico
Ullman Fanni
Ullman Ruth
Ullmann Amelia
Ungar Nada
Unger Charles
Unterberger Isol
Urbach Kurt
Urbach Leo
Urbach Liliana
Urbino Ciro
Urbino Elda
Usigli Edoardo detto
Sacagnao
Usigli Guido
Usigli Silvia
Usiglio Bondì
Giacomo
Uziel Odette
Vacchi Uberto
Vadana Leone
Vajda Eugenio
Valabrega Ada
Valentina
Valabrega Alberto
Valabrega Aldo
Valabrega Alma
Valabrega Anselmo
Valabrega Arturo
Valabrega Bruno
Valabrega Ernesto
Valabrega Evelina
Valabrega Franco
Valabrega Guglielmo
Valabrega Leone
Italo
Valabrega Luciano
Valabrega Michele
Valabrega Roberto
Valabrega Samuele
Davide

Valabrega Samuele
Emanuele
Valabrega Stella
Valabrega Umberto
Valabrega Vincenza
Valech Alba detta
Albina
Valech Ferruccio
Valech Michele
Valech Morosina
detta Mosi
Valech Mosè Davide
Valentini Herbert
Valentinuzzi Iris
Valenzin Mario
Valenzin Raffaello
Valenzin Vittorio
Valobra Alessandro
Valobra Alfredo
Valobra Bruno
Valobra Elsa
Valobra Enrico
Valobra Guglielmo
Valobra Guido
Valobra Lazzaro
Cesare
Valobra Sergio
Valobra Vincenzo
Valobra Violetta
Vamos Alberto
Vamos Mira
Vamos Nelly
Vamos Sigismondo
Van Clef Giuseppe
Varadi Alessandro
Varadi Elisabeth
Varon Allegrina
Varon Ascer
Varon Bohor
Nahman
Varon Dora
Varon Giuseppe
Varon Hasdai
Varon Hasdai
Varon Ida
Varon Laura
Varon Leone
Varon Moisè
Varon Mosè
Varon Salomon
Varon Signurù
Varon Stella
Velc Ida
Venezia Alberto
Venezia Dora

Venezia Elia
Venezia Renata
Venezia Salomone
Ugo
Venezia Silvia
Veneziani Aida
Veneziani Aldo
Veneziani Dario
Veneziani Dario
Veneziani Donato
Veneziani Edgardo
Veneziani Giacomo
Veneziani Guido
Veneziani Lea
Veneziani Margherita
Veneziani Maria
Veneziani Pellegrino
Veneziani Piero
Veneziani Ubaldo
Veneziani Wanda
Veneziano Evelina
Veneziano Mosè
Marco
Ventense Erna
Ventense Lieselotte
Ventoura Lina
Ventura Esther
Ventura Isacco
Ventura Lucia
Ventura Maria
Ventura Zalma
Venziani Marcella
Verderber Hanna
Verderber Leo
Verlengo Cesare
Verona Adriana
Verona Elda Saretta
Verona Giuseppe
Verona Giuseppina
Verona Lina
Verona Umberto
Verschleisser Adolfo
Vic Margherita
Vidal Matilde
Vidner
Vigevani Aida
Vigevani Eda Anna
Vigevani Lionello
Vilma
Vita Margherita
Vita Finzi Alberto
Vita Finzi Laura
Vita Finzi Rosa
Vital Abramo
Vital Davide

Vital Giuseppe
Vital Rosina
Vital Vittorio
Vitale Achille
Vitale Aldo
Vitale Arturo
Vitale Benedetta
Vitale Cesare
Sanson
Vitale Cesira
Vitale Claudio
Vitale Clelia
Vitale Elvira
Vitale Emilia
Vitale Eugenio
Vitale Gemma
Vitale Giuseppe Vita
Vitale Ilka
Vitale Italo
Vitale Lelio
Vitale Lia
Vitale Marco
Vitale Michele
Vitale Prospera
Vitale Rosa
Vitale Sergio
Vitale Sergio
Vitali Ada
Vitali Alessandro
Vitali Ariodante
Viterbo Elena
Viterbo Margherita
Viterbo Piero
Vitta Benvenuto
Mario
Vitta Carlo
Vitta Cesare
Vitta Emma
Vitta Ernesto
Vitta Irma
Vitta Marco Ettore
Vitta Simone
Vitta Zelman
Ferruccio
Vitta Zelman Trieste
Vivante Alba
Vivante Angelo
Fortunato
Vivante Angiolina
Vivante Anna
Vivante Anna
Vivante Carmen
Allegra
Vivante Costante
Vivante Davide

Vivante Davide
Vivante Diamantina
Vivante Enrichetta
Vivante Enrichetta
Vivante Ester
Vivante Felice
Vivante Felice
Vivante Fortunata
Vivante Francesca
detta Fanny
Vivante Giorgio
Vivante Giulia
Vivante Ida
Vivante Leone
Vivante Moisè
Vivante Rachele
Vivante Sabino
Benzion
Vivante Salvatore
Vivanti Alberto
Vivanti Amerigo
Vivanti Angelo
Vivanti Angelo
Vivanti Angelo detto
Il Bassetto
Vivanti Anna
Vivanti Benedetto
Vivanti Benedetto
Vivanti Beniamino
Vivanti Celeste
Vivanti Celeste
Vivanti Diamantina
Vivanti Elisabetta
detta Betta
Vivanti Emanuele
Vivanti Emma
Vivanti Eugenio
Vivanti Fortunata
Vivanti Fortunata
Vivanti Giacomo
Vivanti Giacomo
Vivanti Isacco
Vivanti Italia
Vivanti Laura
Vivanti Leone
Vivanti Letizia
Vivanti Mosè
Vivanti Pellegrino
Vivanti Rachele
Vivanti Raoul
Vivanti Vitale
Vivanti Vito
Vivanti Vito
Vodicka Angela
Vogel Ernestina

Vogelbaum Selig
Vogelmann Schulim
Vogelmann Sifra
Vogelmann Sissel
Emilia
Voghera Augusta
Voghera Enrico
Voghera Ferruccio
Voghera Gino
Volterra Adrio
Volterra Aldo
Volterra Elena
Volterra Ezio
Volterra Federico
Volterra Gastone
Volterra Mario
Volterra Mario
Volterra Nissim
Volterra Oscar
Volterra Ugo
Volterra Umberto
Angelo
Volterra Valentina
Vorgeitz Augusta
detta Gusti
Wachsberger
Arminio
Wachsberger Clara
Wachsmann Mordko
Wachsmann Vasani
Carlo
Wadatz Josef
Wagner
Waiss Paola
Waktor Elsa Maria
Wald Paul
Wald Schachun
Waldbaum Meta
Waldman Alberto
Waldman Franziska
Waldman Saul Behar
Wallach Lote
Wallach Max
Wallach Rosa
Walter Margherita
Wandel Leone
Warcholski Aronne
Warschauer Fritz
Wasser Ruth
Wax Moise Maurizio
Waychman Maurice
Wazsony Eugenio
Wechsler Ferdinando
Wechsler Leopold
Weidenreich Ruth

Weig Otto
Weil Bertoldo
Weil Eva Doris
Weil Hans
Weil Marianne
Weil Sofia
Weiller Alessandro
Weiller Elena
Weinberg Giuseppe
Weinberg Maria
Weinberg Wilhelm
Weinberger
Giuseppina
Weinberger Haim
Joseph
Weinberger Malvine
Weinberger Maria
Weinberger Sara
Weiner Walter
Weingarten Rudolf
Weinreb Sara
Weinreich Hilda
Weinstein Giuseppe
Weinstein Marta
Weinwurm Ernst
Weinzweig Kurt
Weisenfeld Edgardo
Weiser Golda
Weiss Alfredo
Weiss Amalia
Weiss Arnold
Weiss Blanga
Weiss Carmen
Weiss Desiderio
Weiss Desiderio
Weiss Elena
Weiss Eluda
Weiss Felicita
Weiss Franco
Weiss Gisella
Weiss Hermann
Weiss Hilda
Weiss Johann
Weiss Malvina
Weiss Maria Teresa
detta Thea
Weiss Mira
Weiss Nada
Weiss Otto
Weiss Rudolf
Weiss Sonja
Weiss Stefania
Weiss Teresa
Weissbach Anna
Weissberger Marco

Weissbrod Fanny
Weissenstein
  Margherita detta
  Grete
Weisser Paolo
Weisskopf Alois
  Jacob
Weisskopf Ida
Weissmann Frieda
Weisz Alberto
Weisz Alexander
Weisz Elisabetta
Weisz Eugenio
Weisz Oscar
Welicka Ester
Wenkert Isaac
Werczler Davide
Werczler Ernesta
Werczler Guglielmo
Werczler Lazzaro
Werczler Simeone
  Alessandro
Werndorfer Eugenio
Werndorfer
  Guglielmo
Werner Giulia
Wertheimer Silvio
Wessely Max
Wessler Elvira
Westreich Benjamin
Wetterschneider
  Karl
Wiener Max Israel
Windreich Berta
Windspach Amalia
Windspach Guido
Windspach Noemi
Winter Alfredo
Winterfeld Karhe
Winternitz Wolf
Wiskanik Melitta
Wital Ilse
Witscharbe Giacobbe
Witscharbe Valeria
Wodak Mary
Wofsi Joseph
Wohlgemuth
  Alexander
Wohlgemuth Ella
Wohlgemuth Herta
Wohlgemuth
  Margherita
Wohlgemuth Max

Wohlmuth Siegfrid
Wohrisek Hilda
Wolf Emil
Wolf Felicita
Wolf Henry
Wolf Leia
Wolf Mayer
Wolf Nelly
Wolf Rachele
Wolf Sara
Wolff Martino
Wolff Meilech
Wolfinger Nathan
  Norbert
Wolfstein Margarethe
  detta Gretchen
Wollisch Roberto
Wollner Gustavo
Wollner Miranda
Wormann Susanna
Wortitzky Alois
Wortmann
Wortmann Herta
Wortmann Nella
Xapcisk Ceslav
Yaffe Gioia
Yaffe Mosè
Yanni Sara
Yeni Isak
Yeni Pia
Yerusalmi Aronne
Yeshurun Matilde
Yesua Alessandro
Yesua Carlotta
Yesua Davide
Yohai Rebecca
Zaban Amalia
Zaban Giulio
Zaban Marcella
  Annina
Zaban Massimo
Zaban Wally
Zaccar Allegra
Zaccar Speranza
Zaduk Ivan Alfredo
Zaitschek Hans
Zaitschek Josefine
Zaitschek Leopold
Zalai Federico
Zamatto Guido
Zamojra Joseph
Zamojra Markus
Zamorani Amalia

Zamorani Annamaria
Zamorani Arrigo
Zamorani Daniele
Zamorani Elsa
Zamorani Emilio
Zamorani Ilda
Zamorani Maria
Zamorani Massimo
Zarfati Alberto
Zarfati Alessandro
Zarfati Angelo
Zarfati Angelo
Zarfati Aurelia
Zarfati Bianca
Zarfati Camilla
Zarfati Celeste
Zarfati Cesare
Zarfati Cesare detto
  Soricetto
Zarfati Debora
Zarfati Elvira
Zarfati Emma
Zarfati Enrica
Zarfati Enrica
Zarfati Enrichetta
Zarfati Ester
Zarfati Fausta
Zarfati Giacomino
  detto Lupone
Zarfati Giuseppe
Zarfati Grazia
Zarfati Italia
Zarfati Italia
Zarfati Lamberto
Zarfati Lazzaro
Zarfati Leo
Zarfati Leone
Zarfati Leone
Zarfati Leone detto
  Vespilloni
Zarfati Marco
Zarfati Marco
Zarfati Marco
Zarfati Marco
Zarfati Michele
Zarfati Michele
Zarfati Milena
Zarfati Pacifico
Zarfati Paola
Zarfati Primo
Zarfati Rina
Zarfati Roberto
  Abramo

Zarfati Rosa
Zarfati Salomone
Zarfati Sergio
Zarfati Settimio
Zarfati Silvana
Zarfati Vitale
Zarfati Zaira
Zargani Lina Letizia
Zausner Irene
Zeiger Olga
Zeisler Aleksandar
Zeisler Oscar
Zeisler Regina
Zelebonovitz Grete
Zelebonovitz Moritz
Zelikovics Samuele
Zelikovits Karl
Zelikowski Leo
Zeljezniak Edviga
Zelkowicz Heinrich
Zeller Arturo
Zeller Ermanno
Zeltowski Abraham
Zenger Harry
Zerkowsky Eric
Zevi Anna
Zevi Emma
Zieg Samuel Wolf
Ziegler Jack
Ziegler Joseph
Ziegler Liana
Ziegler Susanna
Ziffer Emilio
Ziffer Oscar
Zigdon Rachele
Zimmermann Guilia
Zimmermann Sidoza
  Roha
Zimmerspitz Josef
  Moses
Zimmerspitz Rosalia
Zinger Margherita
Zippel Herta
Zipper Carlotta
Zipszer Giannetta
Zucker Jacob
Zundler Henriette
  Cecilia
Zwirblawsky Enoc
  Hersch
Zylber Szaya
Zynger Jerachmil

A trial begins in Trieste in 1976 to prosecute those suspected of committing crimes at San Sabba. The media are abuzz; the public is agitated. The news does not pass by Haya. It enters her room, sits in her classes, sneaks into her dreams. The dreams circle around her mind, sometimes heavy and slow like a millstone, other times quick like flashes of fireflies; dreams crazed by a web-like ease which in wakefulness knit their sticky net around her, and she doesn't know how to fend them off

in a nightgown she walks easily out of her childhood room, because the door has been smashed. haya goes to the trattoria leon d'oro and says, ein kaiserfleisch bitte, nein, nein, una costata di maiale affumicato cosparsa de cren fresco e accompagnata con gnocchi di pane, *she says.* e, per contorno? *asks the waiter, buttoned up to his throat in a black soldier's uniform.* per contorno, *haya repeats,* per contorno, ein kipfel. ein kipfel? *asks the waiter.* non capisco, *he says. then haya runs off. in her lace nightgown like a mad ophelia she runs into a toilet of which the door has also been smashed, she washes her hands, and at the window over the washbasin stands her white alarm clock, her old-fashioned big white alarm clock with two round white bells on it, and that great white alarm clock of hers ticks, tick-tock, tick-tock, so terribly, so loudly, so terribly loud . . . before haya's eyes the white nightgown gets darker, and she sees herself standing on the walls of the gorica fortress in a smocked black dress that flutters in the wind and turns into a flock of ravens, and the ravens carry her on their wings to the sky*

Haya is fifty-three and she reads the newspapers differently than she did during the war, when she was twenty. Stories circulate around school about the trial prosecuting suspects for crimes committed at San Sabba. In and out of class, grandchildren comb through the fates of their grandfathers, schoolteachers scour the past of their fathers, some aloud, some at a whisper. People divide into warring camps, plant themselves in cafés, evade each others' eyes, turn away, the air around them thick with heavy breathing. Bundles of the past sprout on all sides. They swing like rotten cherries from which worms inch.

The President of the Republic declares the San Sabba rice mill a national monument in 1965, but at that point, in 1965, few people go to see it, because at the time it is still neglected, abandoned, rats breed there, cats roam through it, mildew wafts from the crumbling façades and a muffled echo circles through its walls. Ten years later the San Sabba rice mill is remodelled. It becomes a museum with mementos in glass cases in which whispers of the dead circle once again.

By car along State Highway 202 (exit Valmaura, Stadium, Cemetery) or, as Haya goes in 1976, taking bus Number 8, 10, 19, 20, 21 or 23 from Trieste, one arrives at the Ratto della Pileria 43. Every day (except 1 January and 25 December) between 9 a.m. and 7 p.m. (admission free) one can step into the well-washed, indescribably quiet past; the barking of dogs does not reverberate; the oven has been demolished; there are no soldiers' boots marching; the cells are empty: there are no groans, no ash; in the late evening hours no music swells; there is no licentious women's laughter; no-one is dancing; it's only shadows that flicker. History is served on a platter in a tidy fashion, sifted, polished, compressed into the grains that roll around noiselessly on the stone floors of San Sabba.

So, in 1976, when the trial begins to prosecute those suspected of committing crimes at San Sabba. Haya says, *It is time, yes,* and with a camera around her neck, in October 1976, she goes for a

In 1943 the Nazis move into a plant for husking rice, which at that point was empty, built in 1913 on the outskirts of Trieste, in the town of San Sabba. Inside the walls of the former factory compound stands a complex of buildings, a little city, architecturally almost entirely preserved. So with minor adaptations the Germans change the buildings into a prison, a camp, a "transit camp" from which people travel a long way by train to Auschwitz and Dachau, then briefly, with speed and efficiency, from their cells to the crematorium ovens, right there, not ten metres away. In San Sabba about a hundred and fifty people, Italians, Slovenes, Croats, Jews, Roma, partisans, children, homosexuals, age makes no difference (the Nazis don't split hairs, everything and everyone gets a pass when the S.S. police and S.S. troops lay their hands on them), about a hundred and fifty people disappear daily in the spanking-new oven, the work of the skilled and proud mason Erwin Lambert, the designer of crematoria. The oven at San Sabba is still there on Saturday, 28 April, 1945, but on Sunday, 29 April, 1945, the Nazis blow up the chimney, demolish the crematorium building and remove all traces that can be hastily removed. On Monday, 30 April the detachments vanish – heading for Carinthia. Between three and five thousand souls are killed, following rules and regulations, in a tidy fashion; the job is done. Perhaps it could have been done better. Perhaps there could have been more incinerations, but, heavens, war is unpredictable. The liberators find three paper sacks for cement under the rubble of San Sabba, and in them human bones and ash which the fugitives have not had time to transport to the San Sabba docks, they are in such a hurry to flee. The little collective grave of the nameless shoved into these paper sacks is therefore saved, because the pelting rain of April 1945, perhaps intending to rinse clean the earth before the advancing summer, to set it to rights for a new age, decides suddenly to stop, as if it has had a change of heart. So, thanks to the heavens, the ashes of the last to be incinerated at the San Sabba rice mill are not turned into grey, squeaky mud from which children would make patty cakes had they passed through there, but instead become a burden few know what to do with, even many years later, some fifty years down the road.

> *I used to work at the rice mill. During the war I'd stop by the landing stage, partly out of nostalgia, partly to pick up an odd job. The Germans brought sacks of human ashes there. I saw. The sacks were bursting, the ash was leaking out. Charred, half-burned human bones floated on the sea. I saw them. I am Luigi Jerman from Kopar. I live in Trieste.*

The Allies manage to catch the occasional fugitive; most elude their grasp. The Allies do, however, find trunks and jute sacks full of stolen goods, which the fugitives have not had a chance to cart off with them, and which they had spent two years eagerly collecting, because the Nazis are racing off to Carinthia. The Allies then send the stolen goods to Rome, where the sacks and trunks languish for fifty years in the cellars of the Ministry of the Treasury and Finance, waiting for someone to discover them again. Oh, there are all sorts of things in these sacks and trunks: watches, spectacles, combs, jewellery – rings, brooches, chains; there are powder compacts, pipes, beautiful pipes;

there is money and bonds, furniture, bank books, insurance policies, silver; there are paintings, carpets, clothing, a lot of clothing, bedding, bicycles, typewriters, cameras; there are large wheels of Parmesan cheese, toothbrushes, tableware, fine porcelain – all of it nothing more than patches, debris, shreds of lives no longer living, of lives of those deported to Auschwitz, Buchenwald, Dachau, Mauthausen, Ravensbrück and San Sabba. There are documents, photographs, camp uniforms, passes; there are drawings, maps and charts with locations where the inmates were buried before the oven started working at San Sabba. Something of this is preserved today at the Ljubljana historical archive. Some of it is at the San Sabba museum along with graphics donated by Zoran Mušić, originally from Gorizia, a Dachau prisoner, a student of Babić's in Zagreb, who died a natural death, thank God, in Venice in 2005.

Rainer is a big honcho in the Adriatisches Küstenland – THE honcho. He controls all the regional heads and mayors, and determines the rules of behaviour for the collaboration armies, Italian, Slovenian and Croatian, and they obey him, these armies, humbly. Entire fascist military units enter into service in the S.S. forces, various police squads, the Special Inspectorate of Public Security under the command of Giuseppe Gueli, who lives well in lively Trieste, in a large villa on Via Bellosguardo and helps Rainer nab Jews and partisans. Rainer visits San Sabba often. Rainer loves going to San Sabba. A visit to San Sabba is like a little holiday for Rainer, a way to relax. Rainer's buddies live at San Sabba, his companions from the camps, closed by then, in which they used to party after their hard labours. The central, six-storey building at San Sabba is a barrack; on the upper floors are the quarters of the German, Austrian, Ukrainian and Italian S.S. men, all of them small fry, and Rainer does  not linger there. The kitchens and mess halls, clean and aired, are on the lower floors; the staff smile and Rainer is pleased. Outside, a small building is visible from the road, housing the sentries who guard everything and everybody, especially Commander Josef Oberhauser, whose flat is on the ground floor. Friedrich Wirth most often escorts Rainer on the rounds. After Wirth is killed by the partisans in May 1944, Rainer is accompanied by August Dietrich Allers.

The camp has a large yard. To the right of the entrance stood a building, no longer there. It housed the offices and flats of the officers and the Ukrainian women. Today there is a green lawn with trees and flowers. From the building that is gone there runs an underground corridor to the death cell. From the death cell captives exit quickly; to torture, then shooting, then the oven.

A bus arrived one Sunday crammed with people from, I think, Trieste. They were pushed quickly into that cellar there with the bricked-up window, the death cell; that same night all of them were shot. I believe they were hostages the Germans had rounded up in Trieste raids; there was an underground in Trieste. From my cell I witnessed an old man being savagely beaten, who, whilst sweeping up the courtyard had failed to put the rubbish in the exact place he had been ordered to by the S.S. officer. During a bombardment two prisoners managed to escape from their cells, while the

Germans took refuge in the bunkers. By way of revenge they shot all the companions of the two prisoners. It was June 1944 when I realized what was happening. They were killing victims in the garage that one entered through a secret door in the kitchen, which led to the crematorium. One evening we saw a lorry arrive loaded with soldiers. We saw only their boots; their bodies were covered with blankets. When the lorry entered the garage they made us carry in all the wood we had previously sawn up. From the courtyard at night we could hear people coming and going, people screaming, crying and begging for mercy, uttering heart-wrenching pleas. The Germans turned up the volume on the music from their entertainment hall. Then the lorries turned on their motors and this incited the dogs to bark and growl, and we knew that the Nazis were killing people, we just couldn't tell how. Only when we found the clothing of the people they'd killed and it wasn't at all bloody, hardly a single drop of blood, did we realize. It was mostly the Ukrainians who did the killing, because by early in the afternoon they were already drinking, so by evening they'd be in good shape for killing. And the Germans took part in these orgies. One night they pulled five men out of our cell who never came back. I am Giovanni Haimi Wachsberger from Rijeka.

To the left of the entrance was a building which still exists. On the ground floor were workshops for tailoring and cobbling in which the prisoners must have done sewing; they were up to something there, repairing the officers' shoes, just to

keep busy, passing the time. The prisoners did not sew much nor did they fix shoes for long, because they hadn't the time; they were soon replaced. In the building where the sewing was done and the shoes

repaired were the halls for the S.S. officers and soldiers. In those halls the S.S. officers and soldiers drank a little, played a few rounds of cards; listened to the radio. There were seventeen small prison cells in that building, with six prisoners in each. In those little cells partisans, Jews and political prisoners had no time to relax. They stayed in the little cells for a few days, several weeks at most, and then they left, they were gone.

I was in cell Number 8, alone in the dark with the rats. There was only a tiny vent in the ceiling where air and light could filter in. Our food was passed through a little window in the cell door, which was otherwise always shut. During the afternoon and evening you could almost always hear people crying out in Slovenian, Italian and Croatian, then a truck would come into the yard and the driver would leave the motor to rumble to cover the wrenching screams. It was then we knew our companions had been dragged off to their deaths in the crematorium. When the sirocco blew, smoke with an unbearable stench seeped into our cells, the smell of burned human flesh. It made all of us vomit. I am Ante Peloza from Velih Muna.

The outlines of the demolished crematorium

The prison building from which camp inmates were taken who were targeted for transfer to Dachau, Auschwitz and Mauthausen

We were afraid of spies. We didn't ask questions, we didn't talk. A certain Kabiglio, a Jewish shopkeeper who was from Mostar, said, Look, that is an oven. They are burning people. *Then I looked and I saw people disappearing beyond the door. Everything was happening at around ten or eleven at night. I heard the footsteps of the prisoners dragging on the stone paving, I heard women's sandals, they made the loudest noise. The S.S. would turn on the engines of their lorries or the music way up, as if they were partying. Sometimes I heard cries for help. Sometimes I didn't. I began to scribble down notes on the goings. There were no comings. One night I counted the footsteps of fifty-six people who went from the courtyard to the entrance of the crematorium; another night, seventy-three. Then I stopped counting, I stopped keeping track. My fourteen-year-old daughter was with me in the cell. They were killing children. I heard children calling out* Mamma! Mamma! *I am from Trieste. My name is Majda Rupena.*

I am Albina Škabar from near Trieste. I was stripped bare, strung up to a beam by my plaits and beaten until I passed out. Then I was shoved into cell Number 7. At night I remember hearing terrible screams, horrible screams, coming mainly from the first few cells. Those people were taken away first. I can remember a woman who screamed, I am from Grabovizza! I am from Grabovizza! *and she screamed,* The S.S. killed my baby in its cradle! *There was also one Olga Fabian from Slovenia there. I remember a 67-year-old woman from Trieste, from Via Milano. She kept saying,* I am innocent! I am innocent! *The smell of burned hair was the worst. After the war, I went back once to the rice mill and immediately fainted.*

The S.S. officers dragged in all sorts of stolen goods along with the prisoners. Through a hole in the wall I saw soldiers pulling people across the yard, clutching them by the shoulders, and the people weren't moving. One day a group of Jews interned on the island of Rab arrived. Most of them were from Zagreb. I remember a beautiful girl, they told me she was Greek. The whole group was transported to a German concentration camp, to Auschwitz, that is what they told me. Before they loaded them onto the train, they took everything from them, all their money and jewellery; we watched through a crack in the door. They knew where they were being taken. They told us, Lucky you who are staying here. *They knew they would never come back.*

Branka Maričić from Rijeka

*I saw a tall, heavy S.S. officer, he told me, holding a
little boy by the hand, barely more than an infant,
he said, and leading him to the prison. The boy had
black, curly hair and waddled. He was so small,
he said, that he could barely walk. Then, suddenly,
the infant, barely more than a infant, he said, the
infant suddenly tripped and fell and the S.S. officer
began kicking him furiously and he kicked the
little boy, he kicked him and kicked him, and all
the while he shouted and cursed and kicked him, he
told me, until the little boy's skull cracked open, then
he stopped, he said. My name is Carlo Schiffer. I am
testifying on behalf of my friend.*

> *I am from Rijeka. My name is Dara Virag. I spent a
> year at the rice mill. They tortured me terribly. Till
> this very day I shiver at every sound. The sound of
> boots on the paving still makes me start and think,
> They're coming!*

In 1976, before and during the trial of those suspected of committing
the crimes at San Sabba, lists of the accused are printed, their biographies are published, or rather *summaries* of their lives, because many
of the people who were milling around the Adriatisches Küstenland
between 1943 and 1945 have fat criminal dossiers, interesting and
dynamic. Some of them have already been tried in Germany and are
doing time for the monstrosities they committed in mental hospitals
which were turned into euthanasia centres throughout the Reich, or
at the camps of Belzec, Sobibor, Treblinka and beyond, the list is
long, there were many concentration camps; some are dead (of old
age, illness, execution, suicide), some have been released (most of the
accused are released), some escape, some change their identity and
vanish without a trace, most of them live here, there, everywhere,
until today, until tomorrow. Christian Wirth, Gottfried Schwarz,
Franz Reichleitner, Karl Gringers, Alfred Löffler, Karl Pötzinger, Kurt

Richter, a crowd of companions, pals, old buddies, rests there in the German war cemetery on the slopes of Monte Baldo in picturesque Costermano, between the eastern shore of Lake Garda and the tourist town of Verona. Surrounded by vineyards and olive groves, the German war cemetery in Costermano lies in the shade of old cypress trees and is described as an attractive site by tourist brochures. There are more than eight hundred German war cemeteries the world over, in which tens of thousands are buried. Costermano is host to 21,972 German graves. So when the trial begins in April 1976 in Trieste against those suspected of being responsible for the crimes committed at the San Sabba rice mill during the German occupation of Italy, the bench for the accused is empty – *the bench for the accused is empty* – and the trial ends before it starts.

Haya deciphers her past. She builds a file of her past. From a newspaper she cuts out an incomplete list of S.S. men, incomplete because there are more than a hundred of them with some sort of rank and terrible power from 1943 to 1945, when they are dispatched to the Adriatisches Küstenland; more than a hundred of them saunter around the unrealized dreamland of the fictitious Adriatisches Küstenland, yet the list published in the papers gives barely fifty names. Where are the ordinary soldiers? Where are the German police officers? Where are the Ukrainians? Where are the Cossacks? Where are the women and the members of their families who spend their summers and winters on the shore and in the mountains, from 1943 to 1945? Where are the Italians in the service of the Reich? Where are the civilians, the silent observers, the invisible participants in the war? And *Here, too, am I*, Haya says. *This list should be endless. This list is endless*, she says.

In the newspaper cutting Haya finds names of people she met, at whose table she ate, with whom she shook hands (*not often, thank God*, she adds), and she searches, and researches, and arranges, and stops sleeping, staring instead into the yawning jaws of the Hydra, waiting for the poisonous fumes to spew forth, and Hercules is nowhere to be found. *Oh, this eternal repetition*, she says, *can it be cut short?*

Shortcuts, Saba tells Haya's mother Ada at the Gorizia psychiatric clinic, *shortcuts are the shortest way to get from one place to the next. But shortcuts are often impassable, impassable . . .* Saba says.

And Ada, until her death repeats – *Behind every name there is a story.*

An incomplete list of the former members of Aktion T4 1943 transferred to Trieste and the surrounding areas (O.Z.A.K.)

1. ?, *Heinrich*, Linz / Österreich, ████████████, Wachmann in der "Risiera"
2. *Bauer, Erich*, Strafanstalt [penitenziario] Berlin-Tegel, ████████ Partisane-neinsatz Stationiert in der "Risiera"
3. *Dachsel, Arthur*, unbekannten Aufenthalts
4. *Dubois, Werner*, 58 Schwelm, ████████ in der "Risiera" stationiert
5. *Fettke, Erich*, 2 Hamburg ████████ Kurier in Triest
6. *von Flemming*, unbekannten Aufenthalts, Sekretärin von Wirth; wegen Schwangerschaft ausgeschieden
7. *Fischer, Helmut*, 6 Frankfurt ████████
8. *Franz, Kurt*, Untersuchungshaftanstalt Düsseldorf
9. *Frenzel, Karl*, Strafanstalt Hagen
10. *Geis, Albert*, 605 Offenbach a.M., ████████ Revierwacht-meister in der "Risiera"
11. *Gürtzig, Hans*, 1 Berlin ████████ Verpflegungswart in der "Risiera"
12. *Gley, Heinrich*, 44 Münster/Westf.
13. *Gomerski, Hubert*, Strafanstalt Butzbach
14. *Hackenholt, Lorenz*, unbekannten Aufenthalts
15. *Häusler, Willi*, 285 Bremerhaven, Bewachung des Lagers
16. *Hengst, August*, 2 Hamburg ████████
17. *Hering, Gottlieb*, verstorben (9/10/1945 Stetten i.R.),Kommandant der "Risiera" "Risiera"
18. *Hödl, Franz*, Linz / Österreich, ████████
19. *Jührs, Robert*, 6 Frankfurt a.M., ████████, Polizeioberwachtmeister
20. *Köhler, August*, 341 Northeim, ████████, Kraftfahrer und Schirrmeister in Triest; stationiert in der "Risiera"
21. *Lambert, Erwin*, 7 Stuttgart-West, ████████, baute den Verbrennungsort in der "Risiera"
22. *Linkenbach, Ilse*, ████████ 6094 Bischofsheim ████████,
23. *Mätzig, Willi*, 3 Hannover, ████████, in Castelnuovo stationiert; war
24. *Meyer, Monika*, unbekannten Aufenthalts Schreibkraft in Udine
25. *Michaelsen, Georg*, Haftanstalt Hamburg
26. *Münzberger, Gustav*, 8101 Unterammergau ████, Haftanstalt Düsseldorf Triest und Udine
27. *Oberhauser, Josef*, 8 München, ████████ Kommandant der "Risiera" als Nachfolger von Hering (Aussage Girtzig)
28. *Plikat, Karl Heinz*, Unbekannten Aufenthalts
29. *Raabe, Irmgard*, ████████, 1 Berlin 44 (Neukölln), ████████, Schreibkraft von Wirth (nur kurze Zeit))
30. *Rum, Franz*, 1 Berlin-Zehlendorf, ████████, Ordonanz in der Villa Wirths, einige Tage auch in der "Risiera". Personalangel.
31. *Schiffner, Karl*, Salzburg/Österreich, ████████, Wachmann in der "Risiera"
32. *Schluch, Karl*, 4194 Bedburg-Hau, ████████
33. *Schneider, Gerhard*, 1 Berlin 41 (Steglitz), ████████, in der "Risiera" stationiert
34. *Schöber, Edeltraut*, ████, 31 Garmisch-Partenkirchen, ████████
35. *Schubert, Helene*, 7012 Fellbach, Schreiberin von Hering, mit dem sie zusammen in einem kleinen Haus von der "Risiera" lebte.
36. *Siebert, Gerhard*, 8632 Neustadt b. Coburg, ████████, kurz in Triest
37. *Stadie, Otto*, 5949 Nordenau Krs. Meschede, ████████, "Spiess" in der "Risiera"
38. *Stangl, Franz*, z. Zt. flüchtig, Chef des Stützpunktes Udine (Aussage Münzberger)
39. *Suchomel, Franz*, 8262 Altötting, ████████
40. *Tauscher, Fritz*, verstorben offenbar als Nachfolger von Stangl, Chef des Stützpunktes Udine
41. *Unverhau, Heinrich*, 3307 Königslutter, ████████, in der "Risiera" stationiert
42. *Walther, Arthur*, 2 Hanburg-████████
43. *Wolf, Franz*, 6901 Mauer b. Heidelberg, ████████, z. Zt. Untersuchungshaftanstalt Hagen, in Fiume stationiert
44. *Wolf*, unbekannten Aufenthalts, Sekretärin
45. *Allers, Dietrich*,
46. *Siebert, Gerhard*

Gottfried Schwarz, also known as Friedl, S.S.-Hauptscharführer (head squad leader), promoted after Aktion Reinhard to S.S.-Untersturmführer (second lieutenant). Date of birth unknown. Works in mental hospitals – euthanasia centres, at the Grafeneck Castle, in Bernburg and Hadamar as "cremator", as deputy camp commander at Belzec, as commander of Sobibor. Dispatched to Einsatz R in Trieste in 1943. Killed in Istria. Buried at the German war cemetery in Costermano (grave No. 666).

Gottlieb Hering, born on 2 June, 1887, in Warmbronn, Württemberg, dies in hospital on 9 October, 1945, in unexplained circumstances. Serves for twenty years with Christian Wirth in Stuttgart criminal police, then on Aktion Tiergarten 4. Succeeds Wirth in 1942 as commander of Belzec camp. Like Wirth before him, at Belzec Hering gives himself free rein, indulging a variety of eccentricities, such as shooting at internees while galloping on horseback. About 601,500 people die and are killed at Belzec, most of them Jews. As far as anyone knows, only Rudolf Reder and Chaim Herszman survive. Like Wirth, Hering takes part after 1940 in the Nazi euthanasia programme. While Wirth supervises all six euthanasia centres in the Reich, Hering is in command "only" at Sonnenstein and Hadamer. Promoted to S.S.-Hauptsturm-führer in 1943 and made commander of the San Sabba camp, where he lives in small separate quarters with his secretary at that time, Helena Reigraf from Fellbach, whom he later marries. After Hering is admitted to hospital, Josef Oberhauser takes charge of San Sabba.

Franz Stangl, son of a night watchman, born in Altmünster, Austria, on 26 March, 1908. First works as weaver, then as policeman after 1931, S.S.-Hauptsturmführer (staff sergeant). Member of team that runs T4 euthanasia programme at Hartheim and Bernburg, Germany. Commander of Sobibor and later Treblinka, where he oversees the killing of some 900,000 Jews from 1942 to 1943. Transferred in 1943 to Italy, where he runs the R2 Zone (Udine) and organizes anti-partisan and anti-Jewish operations. The Allies capture him in 1945, but he escapes. With documents he is given by the Red Cross and with money that anti-Semitic, pro-Nazi Bishop Aloïs Hudal provides, Stangl goes to Syria, then to Brazil. Discovered in 1967 working at a Volkswagen factory in São Paulo, arrested and extradited to Germany where he is imprisoned for life. Dies of a heart attack in Düsseldorf prison on 28 June, 1971. Stangl designs and oversees the building of the fake train station at Treblinka in order to deceive future victims. For future "guests", camp painters paint words of welcome in black lettering on big backdrops: BAHNHOF OBERMAJDAN – UMSTEIGEN NACH BIALYSTOK UND WOLKOWYSK (OBERMAJDAN STATION – CHANGE HERE FOR BIALYSTOK AND VOLKOVYSK). Signs are erected to indicate a ticket window, first-, second- and third-class waiting rooms, and on the façade of the entire mirage they hang a *railway clock*. S.S.-guards stride around in uniform, pretending to work for the railway. The fake station is actually the reception for Treblinka camp. Stangl loves horses, so he rides through his camps dressed in white, as he also loves this colour.

Ask away, my conscience is clear. I was commander of Treblinka, yes, but I never had anything to do with killing Jews. My conscience is clear.

How many people were killed in a day?

A transport of thirty freight cars. Three thousand people could be liquidated in three hours. When we worked for fourteen hours, 12,000 to 15,000 people were annihilated.

I heard that Wirth visited the camp while they were building the gas chambers and he said, Marvellous! We'll try them out straight away. Bring in those twenty-five Jewish workers and pack them all into one of the chambers, so we can see how it works. That is the way they talked. All the time he'd be brandishing his whip, they said, and he beat his own men. I got there later.

Would it be true to say you got used to the liquidations in time?

Well, apparently I did.

In days? Weeks? Months?

It was months before I could look each of the future victims in the eye. I repressed the nausea: I tried to create a special place. I ordered flowers to be planted at the camp, new barracks, new kitchens, I brought in barbers, tailors, shoemakers, carpenters. There are many ways in which a person can chase away troubling thoughts, and I used them all. But in the end only drinking helped. I had a large glass of brandy before I went to bed each night.

And then it all became easier?

Not really. But I concentrated on my work. I worked hard.

And finally you forgot you were working with people?

When I was on a trip once, years later in Brazil, my train stopped next to a slaughterhouse. The cattle grazing in the pens trotted up to the fence and stared at our train. They were very close to my window, one jostling the other, looking at me through that fence. I thought then, This reminds me of Poland. That's how the people looked at me there: trustingly, just before they went into the . . . I couldn't eat tinned meat for a long time after that. Those big cows' eyes staring at me, those animals who had no idea that in no time they'd all be slaughtered . . .

So you didn't feel the camp inmates were people?

Cargo. They were cargo.

When did you begin to think of people as cargo? When you first came to Treblinka you say you were horrified by the heaps of dead bodies lying all around the camp.

I think it started the day I realized that Treblinka was a death camp, a Totenlager. Wirth was standing there, next to the pits full of blue-black corpses. These corpses had nothing to do with humanity. They were masses of rotting flesh. Wirth asked, What shall we do with this rubbish? Maybe that's when I thought, of course, they are just plain cargo.

There were many children in that "cargo". Do you know that not a single child survived Treblinka? Did you ever think, what if those were my children? Did you ever think of how you would feel in the position of their parents?

No. You see, I did not look upon them as individuals. They were always a mass for me. I sometimes stood on the wall and watched them being herded through the tube. They were naked, crowded, packed together, driven by whips, running towards the ovens . . .

Why didn't you take any steps? Why didn't you put a halt to the horror? You were high in rank.

Impossible, impossible. This was the system, and Wirth invented it. The system worked. And because it worked, it was irreversible.

Werner Dubois, S.S.-Oberscharführer, senior squad leader. Born in Wuppertal on 26 February, 1913. Raised by grandmother. Eighth-grade education. Construction and graphics worker, brush maker, farmer. Driver in the S.S.-Gruppenkommando Oranienburg, driver and guard at Sachsenhausen concentration camp, in Brandenburg, Grafeneck and Hadamar. As cremator, transports corpses and urns. Transferred as a driver in 1941 to the O.T. (Organization Todt) in Russia. In Lublin (Aktion Reinhard) in 1942, after that in Belzec until April 1943. At trial, twenty-eight years later, describes killing six people with a 9-mm Belgian F.N. Browning, and, at Wirth's command, another six exhausted Jews, who were later flung into a pit. Supervises the arrival of all transports. Transferred to Sobibor after the closing of Belzec in June 1943. In Sobibor loves shooting at inmates. Badly wounded during the uprising. After hospital treatment is transferred to Trieste as member of Aktion R, tasked with killing partisans. In May 1945 arrested by American soldiers. Released in late 1947. Works as locksmith until final arrest. At Munich trial (1963–4) acquitted of charges; in Hagen (1966) sentenced to three years in prison for participating in killing at least 15,000 people in Sobibor. Dies in 1973, before the 1976 Trieste trial. At trial for Sobibor crimes, only Dubois admits guilt: *A crime was clearly committed at the camp. I aided in that crime. I will consider it a just sentence if you declare me guilty. Murder is murder. All of us are guilty. The camp was run by a chain of command and if one link had failed, the whole system would have collapsed . . . We did not have the courage to disobey.*

Friedrich Tauscher, born in 1905, S.S.-Oberscharführer, otherwise a detective, works in Belzec as instructor for cremating corpses. From 1943 to 1945 serves in Trieste and surroundings. Commits suicide in prison in 1965.

Lorenz Hackenholt, born on 25 June, 1914. At wife's initiative, declared dead as of 31 December, 1945. Member of S.S. from 1934. Begins career as driver at Sonnenstein, then works in Grafeneck, Belzec, Sobibor and Treblinka. One of the key organizers of the euthanasia programme. Wirth's favourite. Participates in Belzec and Treblinka installing gas chambers, which he later runs. In Belzec and Treblinka they call the gas chambers Stiftung Hackenholt (Hackenholt Foundation), and on the façade of each gas chamber, at Lorenz's order, a large Star of David is mounted for all to see. In 1943 promoted to S.S.-Hauptscharführer. Serves in Italy from 1943 to 1945. Drinks heavily; loves taking photographs. A big man, more than two metres tall. In 1945 simply vanishes under circumstances that have never been explained; police and secret services search for him in vain until mid-1970s, when the Hackenholt case is placed *ad acta*. S.S.-Oberscharführer **Erich Bauer**, also stationed at San Sabba and imprisoned for life in 1950 for crimes committed at Sobibor, where more than 250,000 Jews were killed, declares under oath in 1961 that Hackenholt gets through the war alive and is in hiding using the name Jansen, Jensen, or Johannsen, working as a truck driver. Bauer also claims that Hackenholt spends the last days of the war somewhere near Trieste with a woman named Monika. The police in Trieste question all members of the R1 unit – Frau Lindner, Frau Fettke, Frau Schmiedel and Frau Allers, as well as Dietrich Allers, the final San Sabba commander – but no-one knows anything about Hackenholt being involved with any woman in Italy. They all agree, however, that Hackenholt is a common drunkard and few of them fraternized with him. S.S.-Scharführer Karl Schluch, Hackenholt's colleague from Treblinka and San Sabba, who is never convicted (after his trial in the 1960s, he is cleared of all charges), claims that Hackenholt is ruthless and brutal. S.S.-Unterscharführer Robert Jührs (cleared of all charges) is also in Belzec and Trieste with Hackenholt, and says: "He wanted to piss with the big boys, but he couldn't lift his leg."

Hackenholt is charged with participating in the murder of more than 70,000 German mentally ill patients, as well as the liquidation of more than 1,500,000 Jews during Aktion Reinhard.

Globočnik honours Hackenholt
with the Iron Cross, Trieste, 1944

San Sabba, 1944

Erich Bauer, S.S.-Oberscharführer, born in 1900. Short but strong, exceptionally cruel. Manages gas chambers in Sobibor. Stationed in Italy at San Sabba, 1943 to 1945. Arrested in 1950, recognized by chance at a Berlin amusement park by Samuel Lerer, survivor of the camps. In 1951 sentenced to death; after death penalty is abolished in Germany, sentence is commuted to life. Dies in prison in Berlin in 1980.

Arthur Daschel, guard and cremator of corpses at Sonnenstein. At Belzec and Sobibor oversees building of camps. Lives in and around Trieste from 1943 to 1945, after which all trace of him is lost.

Hubert Gomerski, S.S.-Oberscharführer. Supervisor at Sobibor, member of T4 group, spends years 1943 to 1945 in and around Trieste. In 1948 sentenced to life imprisonment, released in 1972 for ill health, but in 1974 sentenced to another fifteen years.

Karl Frenzel, S.S.-Oberscharführer. Born on 28 August, 1911. Carpenter. Member of Nazi Party from 1930. Involved in T4 programme. Arrives in Sobibor in 1942 with Stangl's crew. After Sobibor revolt, sent to Italy and subordinated to Christian Wirth. Stationed in Trieste and Rijeka. Works in theatre after the war as a lighting technician. Arrested in 1962. Charged with personally murdering forty-two and taking part in the murder of at least 250,000 Jews. Sentenced to life imprisonment, but released after sixteen years on grounds of poor health. At time of Trieste trial in 1976 under house arrest in German village of Gorben-auf-der-Horst.

Franz Wolf, S.S.-Unterscharführer, sergeant, amateur photographer, otherwise mason. Born in 1907 in Heidelberg. Works in Sobibor. Stationed in Rijeka during Einsatz R. At Sobibor trial in Hagen in 1966 sentenced to eight years in prison. After serving sentence, lives in Bavaria until death.

Erwin Lambert, S.S.-Unterscharführer, mason, member of Nazi Party since 1933. Known as "the flying architect" because he rushes from one camp to another, building, erecting, arranging, refining gas chambers. Born in 1909 in Schildow, near Berlin. Installs gas chambers at Hartheim, Sonnenstein, Bernburg and Hadamar euthanasia centres. At Treblinka and Sobibor supervises construction of barracks with gas chambers. Ends career in Trieste with introduction of crematorium at San Sabba camp. Arrested in 1962, charged with participating in the murder of an unknown number of Jews, sentenced in 1965 to four years in prison.

Ernst Lerch, S.S.-Sturmbannführer, born in Klagenfurt in 1914. Works from 1931 to 1934 as waiter in hotels in Switzerland, France and Hungary, then until Anschluss in 1938 in his father's café, Café Lerch, a watering hole for the underground Nazi movement in Carinthia. Thus Globočnik, Classen and Kaltenbrunner often stop by at Café Lerch. Lerch is a member of the Nazi Party from 1932, and is in the S.S. by 1934. Transferred to Berlin in 1938 to Central Office of Reich Security. Soon marries an employee of the Gestapo. Pohl and Globočnik are best men at his wedding. Becomes member of the Wehrmacht in December 1938; works in the Central Office of Reich security police from 1940 to 1941, then transferred first to Cracow, later to Lublin, as head of Globočnik's office and Stabsführer der Allgemeinen S.S. Lerch is one of the key people in Aktion Reinhard responsible for the "Jewish Question", that is for the mass murder and annihilation of Jews within the borders of the General Government.

After Aktion Reinhard winds down, Lerch is transferred to Trieste in September 1943, again as Globočnik's right-hand man in O.Z.A.K. (Operationszone Adriatisches Küstenland). Extensive authority in leading the anti-partisan operations in which hundreds of anti-fascists are killed. Serves several weeks as temporary chief of Rijeka police.

After Germany surrenders, Lerch flees to Carinthia, where the British Army arrests him on 31 May, 1945 with companions Globočnik, Höfle and Michalsen. During investigation conducted in prison in Wolfsburg, Lerch claims he spent only a brief time in Lublin and had nothing to do with Globočnik or the mass annihilation of Jews. Lerch is then allowed a discreet escape from prison, and hides in Austrian villages until 1950. Wiesbaden court, which spearheads the de-Nazification process of the country, sentences Lerch to two years in prison in 1960, and then in 1971, at a trial in Klagenfurt, Lerch is charged with participation in the Holocaust. Due to lack of witnesses and Lerch's insistent denials of activity in Poland, case is closed in 1976.

Until his death in 1997 Lerch runs his own café in Klagenfurt, and anyone who so desires (and knows of Lerch) can see him there, in Klagenfurt, otherwise known as Celovec, eating *Apfelstrudel* and reading the newspaper.

Hermann Höfle, S.S.-Sturmbann-führer, major. Born in Salzburg, 19 June, 1911. Member of Austrian Nazi Party from 1930. Mechanic by trade. Runs a taxi service in Salzburg. During the war a key figure in Aktion Reinhard and involved in Mielec, Lublin, Rzeszow, Warsaw and Bialystok deportations. In Eichmann's escort when Eichmann tours Belzec and Treblinka. Personally selects from transports who will work in camps. Joins Globočnik in Trieste in early 1944. Arrested in Carinthia on 31 May, 1945, with Lerch, Michalsen and Globočnik, but escapes. Lives in Italy, Germany and Austria.

Arrested again in 1961 in Salzburg and transferred to Vienna. Hangs himself in prison on 20 August, 1962.

In 2000, when certain documents from World War Two are made public, a telegram is found dated 11 January, 1943, from Höfle to Adolf Eichmann in Berlin. In the telegram Höfle lists the number of registered deaths in camps related to Aktion Reinhard. Up to 31 December, 1942: Majdanek: 24,733; Belzec: 434,508; Sobibor: 101,370; Treblinka: 713,555; total for year of 1942: 1,274,166 murdered Jews.

Robert Jührs, S.S.-Untershar-führer. Born 17 October, 1911, in Frankfurt. Eighth-grade education. Works as porter, janitor, house painter and usher at Frankfurt Opera. During war: Hadamer, Belzec, Dorhusza, Sobibor, Trieste. Task in Belzec: killing Jews who are in poor physical condition as soon as they arrive at camp. At trial, states: *I did this out of mercy. I always aimed my machine gun at the head. They died instantly. With absolute certainty I can state that none of them suffered.* Charged with killing thirty Jews. At trial in Munich in 1963–64 acquitted of all charges.

Otto Stadie, S.S.-Stabsscharführer, born in 1897 in Berlin. Before the war works as nurse. Part of T4, 1940. At Treblinka from July 1942 to July 1943 as Stangl's assistant. In Trieste, San Sabba, from 1944. At trial in Düsseldorf (Treblinka) in 1964–65 sentenced to seven years in prison. Date of death unknown.

Paul Bredow, Unterscharführer. Born in 1902. Nurse. Service: Grafeneck, Hartheim, Sobibor, Treblinka, Trieste. Hobby: shooting at live targets. In Sobibor, quota: fifty Jews per day. Has a weakness for perfumes. After the war, with colleague, Karl Frenzel, leaves San Sabba and works in Giessen as carpenter. Killed in road accident in Göttingen in December 1945.

Heinrich Unverhau, S.S.-Unterscharführer, born in 1911, eighth-grade education, works as plumber, musician and nurse at euthanasia centres of Hadamar and Grafeneck, where he takes victims to gas chambers, administers shots of sedatives; after the murders airs rooms and removes corpses. Russia: 1941–42; Belzec and Sobibor: 1942–43; San Sabba: 1943–44. Vindicated at trials for Grafeneck (1948), Belzec (1963–64) and Sobibor (1965), and released. Works as nurse from 1952 onwards, and as musician on the side. Date of death unknown.

Ernest Zierke, S.S.-Unterscharführer, born in 1905. Eighth-grade education. Worker in sawmill. Carpenter and locksmith. Member of National Socialist Workers Party, 1930. Nurse at Grafeneck, Hadamar and Sonnenstein. 1941–42 in Russia, 1942–43 at Belzec and Sobibor. Supervises escorting of Jews to gas chambers. Takes part in execution of last camp inmates as Belzec and Sobibor are closed. At San Sabba, December 1943. Acquitted at all trials due to poor health.

Karl Schluch, S.S.-Unterscharführer, born in 1905 in Lauenburg. Part of T4 programme from 1940 on. Guard. As with Unverhau, escorts victims to gas chambers and supervises cremation. Grafeneck, Hadamar, Russia, Belzec, Sobibor, Trieste – San Sabba – Aktion R. Acquitted at all trials from 1948 to 1965. Works after war as agricultural worker, construction worker, nurse.

In Belzec and Sobibor I supervised the disembarkation of the Jews from the freight carriages via the ramp. During disembarkation, Wirth told the Jews they had come there for transfer, that they would soon be travelling on further, but that they should first go to the baths and be disinfected. It was my job to calm the Jews. After they had stripped naked, I would show them the way to the gas chambers. Yes, I saw all the gas chambers. The ones in Belzec were 4 x 8 metres. They looked cheery, not a bit alarming. The doors were yellow or grey, I can't remember. The walls were painted with oil paint. In any case, the floors and walls were easy to wash. I think there were showers on the ceiling.

I believe the Jews were convinced that they really were going to the baths. After they entered the gas chambers, Hackenholt would personally close the doors and then switch on the gas supply. Five or seven minutes later, someone would look through the small window into the gas chamber to verify whether all inside were dead. Only then were the outside doors opened and the gas chambers ventilated, after which a Jewish working group under the command of their kapo entered and removed the bodies. I supervised all this. The Jews inside the gas chambers were so densely packed that they did not die on the floor but one on top of another, heaped in disorder, some of them kneeling, some of them standing, they were covered in spittle, urine and shit, their lips and the tips of their noses were bluish, some of them had open eyes. The bodies were dragged out of the gas chambers and inspected by a dentist, who removed the rings and gold teeth. Then the corpses were thrown into a big pit. Both Wirth and Oberhauser took part in these operations.

Willi Mentz, S.S.-Unterscharführer, born in 1904. Dairy farmer. Works in 1940 on farm of Grafeneck euthanasia centre, tending to herds of cows and pigs, but in his free time participates in gassings. Later, at Hadamar, he gardens, waters the flowers and cuts the grass, and also, when free, assists in killing the mentally ill. From 1942–43 likes to drink beer in the shade at Treblinka, in the open makeshift café at the entrance to the little zoo that he maintains. After Sobibor, transferred in 1944 to San Sabba concentration camp, tasked with killing partisan fighters and Italian Jews. Passionate amateur photographer, goes on outings with Kurt Franz in and around Gorizia. (And for *Kaiserfleisch* at the Trattoria Leon d'Oro on Via Codelli during the spring of 1944, when he wipes his mouth on his sleeve instead of using a serviette, surprising Haya.)

At Treblinka, under Wirth's command, Mentz lines up inmates along the edge of a pit, then shoots them in the back of the head. At Treblinka nicknamed "Frankenstein". At the S.S. garrison at Treblinka only Mentz and Kurt Franz know how to ride, so they ride through the nearby woods and enjoy the fresh air. While they ride around the camp compound, Mentz enjoys shooting at Jews who serve as live targets, so he shoots and shoots and shoots. This earns him another nickname: "Gunman". Sentenced to life imprisonment.

When I arrived at Treblinka, everything was in chaos. There weren't enough gas chambers. Afterwards we built new ones, five or six more spacious and attractive chambers. If the little chambers had accommodated between eighty and one hundred people, the larger ones could hold at least twice as many.

Otto Horn, S.S.-Untersharführer (sergeant), born in 1903 near Leipzig. Nurse. Member of Nazi Party from 1937. Sent in 1941 to Sonnenstein as member of T4 Programme, and in October 1942 to Treblinka where he supervises the Grubenkommando, whose task it is to cover piles of bodies with sand and chloride of lime. At Treblinka had reputation of a decent man who does no-one harm. Leaves Treblinka after rebellion, simulating illness. In January dispatched to Trieste, but refuses to comply and goes home. Acquitted at Düsseldorf trial in 1965.

Name?

Otto Richard Horn.

Living in?

Berlin.

Date of birth?

14 December, 1903.

How old are you?

I'm dead.

What was Treblinka?

> A camp. A death camp. They gassed people there.

Who did you report to upon arrival at Treblinka?

> The deputy commander, Kurt Franz. He sent me to the Upper Camp, the Totenlager.

What tasks were handled at the Upper Camp?

> Unloading trains and undressing.

Whom?

> Mainly Jews.

Is that all that went on at the Upper Camp?

> No. People were gassed and their corpses were burned.

Did they gas men only?

> No. Men and women.

And children?

> And children.

Who was the commander of the Upper Camp?

> Matthes.

And for all of Treblinka?

> Stangl.

Aside from the Germans and Ukrainians, were there prisoners at the Upper Camp?

> There were. About two hundred prisoners worked at the Upper Camp. Jews.

What did they do?

> They moved the corpses to the pits and burned them.

Where did they move the corpses from?

> From the gas chambers.

Were there female prisoners at the Upper Camp?

> Yes. They worked in the laundry. Six of them.

Do you remember the names of these women?

> No. But one of them testified against me at the Düsseldorf trial in 1965.

Mr Horn, how long did it take to gas a person?

> About an hour. After that the chambers were opened.

And then?

> Then the corpses were taken to the pit and burned there.

What kind of gas was used at Treblinka?

I don't know. I think that some motors produced the gas.

Mr Horn, you knew that the euthanasia programme meant killing children as well, did you not?

No, I didn't know that.

But you were present at Treblinka when they gassed children.

Yes. They killed them all – children, women, men.

And you saw murdered children?

Yes.

Where were you standing when you saw the dead children?

At the pits.

You are accused of the murder of thousands of Jews, is that right?

Yes, yes.

And some Jews came to the trial and testified against you, is that right?

Yes, but they couldn't prove anything.

What was the final verdict?

I was acquitted of all charges and declared innocent.

Completely innocent?

Absolutely. Completely.

Heinrich Matthes, S.S.-Oberscharführer. Born in 1902 in Wermsdorf, near Leipzig. Trained as tailor, later pre-qualifies as nurse. Works in psychiatric institutions throughout Germany, which makes him suitable for inclusion in T4 programme. Amateur photographer. As of 1934 an S.A., member of Nazi Party from 1937. Supervises work of gas chambers at Treblinka from 1942–43. Exceptionally pedantic and jumpy, quick on the draw. Transferred to Sobibor, then Trieste in early 1944, where he works as a policeman and guard at San Sabba. Sentenced to life imprisonment in 1965 for crimes committed at Treblinka.

What is your name?

> Eliahu Rosenberg.

How old are you?

> Eighty.

You lived in Warsaw until 1942?

> Yes.

Then on 11 July of that year you were deported to Treblinka?

> *It was summer. Very hot. As soon as they unloaded us, I heard a camp inmate say to his friend in Yiddish, Moshe, grab a broom and sweep! Sweep*

like crazy! Save yourself! Then Moshe got hold of a broom, climbed into the freight carriage which had just been emptied and started sweeping.

What did you do?

> *An S.S. officer came over. He was holding a long Peitsche, a whip, and with it he was performing acrobatics in the air. He selected some thirty men and told them, Throw down your parcels in the pile here and start sorting. We sorted shoes into one pile, children's clothes into another, gold into a third. They were huge piles, as tall as buildings. There were all sorts of things on them: toys, instruments, tools, medicine, clothing, so much clothing . . . I found a way into that group. We worked until dark.*

Your mother and three sisters came on the same transport?

> *Yes. They were ordered to go left. There was a lot of shouting on the platform. Some people were killed right there, for the hell of it.*

Did you see your mother and sisters after that?

> *No. I found out where they were buried.*

At Treblinka?

> *At Treblinka.*

What happened the next day?

The next day we sorted again. New clothing, new shoes. Then S.S.-Scharführer Matthes came and shouted, I need twenty volunteers for a light ten-minute job. I was standing right next to Matthes and I was afraid he might strike me, so I stepped forward. I was seventeen. They took us to Treblinka 1, towards a gate camouflaged with pine branches. They took us in and then we saw a pile of corpses. Then Matthes howled, An die Tragen! *but we didn't know what he was asking us to do, so we began running around the bodies. Then the Jews who were already working there told us, Two of you grab hold of a corpse and put it on a stretcher. Then we carried the bodies some two hundred metres to a mass grave and flung them down below.*

How deep was that grave?

Roughly seven metres.

And you carried the corpses that way all day?

All day. From the gas chambers to the grave.

What did you do later? You carried corpses?

And burned them. Some couldn't stand it. They killed themselves, hanged themselves with their own belts.

You witnessed the entire process of destruction?

The whole process.

Describe it briefly.

> The people walked along the famous Himmelstrasse
> from Treblinka 1 to Treblinka 2. There were S.S.
> men and Ukrainians standing along Himmelstrasse
> with dogs, whips and bayonets. People walked in
> silence. That was in the summer of 1942. They
> didn't know where they were going. When they
> entered the chambers, the Ukrainians turned on the
> gas. Four hundred people in one small chamber. The
> outer doors could hardly close behind them. We
> stood by the door. We heard screams from inside.
> Half an hour later they were all dead. Two Germans
> stood there listening to what was going on. At the
> end they'd say, Alles schläft – They're all asleep.
> Then we would open the door. The bodies fell out
> like potatoes. Bloody, covered with urine and shit.
> People bled from their ears and noses. It was dark
> inside the chamber. People would jump over one
> another to catch some air. They'd try to break
> down the door. The stronger ones would trample the
> children and the weak. Some people were unrecog-
> nizable. There were crushed children's skulls . . .

After a while they started burning the corpses?

> In February 1943.

Did any of the high-ranking officials visit the camp?

> Himmler came in January 1943. He ordered that
> the bodies be removed from the graves. We took the
> corpses out with excavators and burned them.

Did the transports arrive every day?

> Yes. Until the winter of 1943. Then they came less often. A transport would arrive every two or three days.

How many people worked on removing the corpses from the gas chambers?

> About two hundred.

Were the people who arrived at Treblinka killed that same day?

> Yes. Very quickly.

Where did the people who were killed at Treblinka come from?

> At first they came from Poland. Later from all over Europe, from Belgium, Germany, Austria, Czechoslovakia, from Serbia, from the Netherlands . . .

How do you know?

> When I carried the corpses out of the gas chambers, I saw documents falling out of their anuses and vaginas. There were those who remained alive, too.

What happened to them?

> Sometimes when we were removing the corpses we'd find a child still alive. The Germans immediately shot all survivors.

Were the Ukrainians in uniform?

       Yes.

What sort of uniforms?

       Black.

Like the S.S. men?

       The S.S. men had green uniforms. With a skull.

Were there several gas chambers in every building?

       In one there were three chambers, in another five on one side and five on the other. I remember when all the chambers were working simultaneously. In forty-five minutes ten thousand people went in. Thirteen thousand people arrived at Treblinka that day.

The gas chambers were hermetically sealed?

       Yes.

I call witness Avraham Lindwasser.

       I am Avraham Lindwasser.

How old are you now?

       If I were alive, I would be eighty-seven.

On 28 August, 1942, you arrived at Treblinka from Warsaw?

       Yes.

Was there a sign at the station, in German and Polish?

Yes.

What did it say?

It read: after you have bathed and changed your clothes, your journey will continue to the east, to work. *But then they opened the freight carriages and started shouting, Get out! Get out! and they beat us with their clubs. We didn't understand what was happening. We were chased to the square and ordered to hand over our money and jewellery. We were told to take off our shoes. Then they lined us up in threes and went on beating us. Then a man with stripes appeared, I later learned he was called the Hauptmann with spectacles, and he began asking us one by one what our professions were. When he came to me he looked at me – I also wore spectacles, in a golden frame, he came up close and asked, Is that frame made of gold? and I said, It is, it is gold, and he then said, Do you know what gold is? Do you know what silver is? Do you know what jewellery is? and I said, Yes, and he struck me again with his club. Then he told me to step forward. A Jew was standing next to me, an electrical engineer, and he was also ordered to step forward. We were the only two to step forward from the line.*

How many people were there in that transport?

More than a thousand.

When you came, did you know where you were?

No. Only that we had arrived at Treblinka.

You had heard about Treblinka in Warsaw?

We had heard.

Did you know that Jews were being exterminated at Treblinka?

We did not believe those stories.

You did not believe?

One simply could not grasp that it was possible – extermination. But when we set out from Malkinia towards Treblinka, I saw the Polish railway workers making signs at us – they were drawing their fingers across their throats. I remembered that later.

Did you see corpses when you got off the train?

Yes.

And?

At first I thought they were the corpses of those who had died on the trip, that they would be bathed and buried. Then Matthes took me into a building at Treblinka 2 and ordered me to begin dragging bodies towards the graves.

In the evening, you again came across the Hauptmann with spectacles?

Yes.

What did he say when he saw you dragging bodies?

He asked why I was dragging bodies. He said, After all, you're a dentist, you shouldn't be dragging bodies.

You are a dentist?

No, I am not.

And?

He pulled me by the sleeve, seized me by the hand, dragged me by force, again with blows to the back – I want to stress this – he kept hitting me, and he brought me to a well. Next to the well there were basins with gold teeth and also pairs of forceps for extracting teeth. He said, take the forceps and start extracting teeth from those corpses over there. The corpses were lying by the back exit of the gas chambers.

From where they took them to the graves.

Yes.

And you extracted their teeth?

I did.

You extracted teeth from corpses until the revolt?

Not exactly. I extracted teeth for about a month, a month and a half, until I recognized my sister's body.

She was lying there, among the dead?

Yes. Then I told the group commander Dr Zimmermann to give me another job. I told him I couldn't go on with that one.

Who was this Zimmermann?

Dr Zimmermann was the kapo of the dentists.

A Jew?

Yes. I asked him to take me off teeth extraction and put me on cleaning the teeth in the cabin where we lived.

Teeth were being cleaned there?

Teeth were being cleaned there.

How much gold from extracted teeth was sent out of Treblinka each week?

Two suitcases, each weighing between eight and ten kilograms.

Where were the suitcases sent to?

Matthes, one of the camp commanders who also supervised our barracks, said they were dispatched to Berlin.

Did they only contain gold teeth?

Gold teeth and also false teeth removed from bridges. Porcelain teeth.

What did the Germans call the transports of Jews?

> *They called the bodies* die Figuren, *as if they were dolls, and the actual transport they called* die Scheisse, die Lumpen *and other insulting names. It was forbidden to mention victims or corpses or bodies.* Everything was secret. *When Matthes came down with typhus, he raved in a delirium about the burnings and the gas chambers, so they posted a guard by his bed to silence him if necessary.*

Gustav Münzberger, S.S.-Unterscharführer, born on 17 August, 1903. Works as a carpenter, first at his father's firm, then at a paper factory, and then in the euthanasia centre at Schloss Sonnenstein where he helps in the kitchen as well, so becoming a cook. Was in the S.S. from 1938, in Lublin in 1942, at Treblinka 1942–43 assists Heinrich Matthes in managing gas chambers. Member of team for transporting corpses. In Trieste and Udine in November 1943. Arrested in 1963 at first trial for crimes committed at Treblinka in 1965; sentenced to twelve years in prison. Released for good conduct in 1971. Dies in 1977. His son Horst remembers him as a tender father.

August Miete, S.S.-Unterscharführer. Born in 1908, member of the Nazi Party from 1940. Part of T4 (Grafenek and Hadamar) 1940–42. Treblinka: June 1942–November 1943. Nickname: "Angel of Death". One of cruellest S.S. men. Shoots without remorse, straight at head, whenever moved to do so. Sentenced in 1945 to life imprisonment. Dies in prison.

Josef Hirtreiter, S.S.-Scharführer, born in 1909. Nickname: "Sepp". Low I.Q. Held back twice in elementary school; fails locksmiths examination. Finds work as labourer at construction site. Member of Nazi Party from 1932. Hadamer 1940 (washes dishes); Sobibor and Treblinka 1942–43. Speciality: killing one- and two-year-old children: when transports are being unloaded, grabs children by the legs and smashes them against a freight car. The children expire instantly, their skulls crack open. In October 1943 transferred to anti-partisan unit of Trieste police force. Arrested in 1946. Sentenced in 1951 to life imprisonment at the Frankfurt trial. Released in 1977 due to illness and dies six months later in old people's home in Frankfurt.

August Hengst, S.S.-Unterscharführer, born in 1905 in Bonn. Cook and pastry chef. Member of Nazi Party from 1933. Member of T4 from 1940. Installs kitchen at Brandenburg euthanasia centre and cooks there. Also cooks at Treblinka before 1943, then transferred to Udine, and on to San Sabba, where apart from cooking up swill for camp inmates, he bakes cakes for the commanders. Rainer adores his poppy-seed cakes and strudels. After the war Hengst opens a bakery near Hamburg and local housewives fight over his butter rolls. Closes bakery due to illness and finds work as courier in the port of Hamburg. Likes to wear wide-brimmed hats. Date of death unknown.

Karl Schiffner, S.S.-Unterscharführer, born as Karl Kresadlo in 1901 in Weisskirchlitz, now Novosedlice, the Czech Republic. Trained as carpenter and tradesman. Serves in Czech Army 1921–23. After Czech occupation joins S.A. and later the S.S. troops "because the black uniforms look better". Works at Sonnenstein euthanasia centre until 1942. In Lublin, Belzec, Sobibor, Treblinka until late 1943, when he is transferred to Trieste to an anti-partisan police unit. After the war flees to Carinthia, arrested and held by the British Army at Usbach camp until October 1945. Leaves the camp to go to Salzburg.

Fritz Küttner, S.S.-Oberscharführer, born in 1907. Sentry for many years in German police, supervisor in Camp 1 at Treblinka. Despised by camp inmates. A snooper. Follows and searches inmates, beats them ferociously, then flogs them with a long whip and takes away the smallest piece of personal property they have (family photographs, letters, money), then sends them to infamous Lazarett. Nickname: "Kiwe". Takes advantage of the helplessness of certain inmates and turns them into informers. Dispatches children to gas chambers without blinking. After Treblinka transferred to Trieste. Dies before trial begins.

Fritz Schmidt, S.S.-Unterscharführer, born in 1906 in Eibau, Germany. Guard and chauffeur in Sonnenstein and Bernburg 1940–41. Chauffeur and head of garage at Treblinka in 1942; looks after equipment for gas chambers. In Trieste in 1943. Arrested by the Allies in Saxony. In December 1949 sentenced to nine years in prison, but escapes to West Germany and no-one cares. Dies in 1982.

Albert Franz Rum, S.S.-Unterscharführer, born in 1890 in Berlin. Nightclub waiter and policeman. Member of Nazi Party from 1933. Stationed at the Berlin T4 headquarters after 1934, works there as photographer. Treblinka 1942–43. When Treblinka is dug up and the camp closed in autumn 1943, Kurt Franz orders him and Willi Mentz to kill the last thirty Jews, which they do, of course. After Treblinka transferred to Trieste as Wirth's orderly. Sentenced to three years in prison in 1965, but dies before verdict is announced.

Franz Suchomel, S.S.-Unterscharführer (sergeant), born in 1907 in Krumau, today's Czech Republic. Tailor. From 1940 to 1942 part of the T4 euthanasia programme in Berlin and Hadamar (department of photography). Treblinka 1942–43. Assigned to Treblinka "railway station" where he supervises the processing of women (stripping, gynaecological examinations, shaving of hair) before they are escorted to the gas chambers. Later runs section of "Goldjuden", in which some twenty inmates – Jews, mostly goldsmiths, watchmakers and bankers – are assigned to collecting and sorting confiscated money and jewellery. In October 1943 sent to Sobibor, then to Trieste. Arrested in 1963 and at first trial for crimes committed at Treblinka in 1965 sentenced to six years in prison. Released in 1969. Dies in 1980 with a relatively clear conscience.

So, in 1976 Haya makes a little file, utterly pointless. She writes out notes, arranges them, rearranges them, as if shuffling a pack of cards. *I could play solitaire with these notes*, she says, which, in a sense, she does. This dog-eared file, full of cracked photographs of people, most of whom no longer exist, becomes Haya's obsession; over the year she supplements her collection, slips into it little oddities, terse news items which after two, three, four decades she digs out and peruses, as if grabbing at dry dandelion fluff, as if catching eiderdown in a warm wind. Pointless, pointless. Forgotten dossiers, sealed archives open slowly, slowly, and what emerges is no more than water dripping from cracked sewage pipes. During the Trieste trial in 1976 only two "big fish" remain: Josef Oberhauser,* brewer in Munich, former San Sabba commander and – from 1941 to the end of the war – Dr Dietrich Allers, a high-ranking official, one of the executive directors of the T4 programme, a lawyer and S.S.-Obersturmbannführer

---

* *Josef Oberhauser*, S.S.-Oberscharführer, born in 1915 in Munich. Seventh-grade education, farm worker. Joins S.S. troops in 1935, joins the T4 programme in 1939. Works as cremator at Bernburg, later at Grafeneck, Brandenburg and Sonnenstein. In 1941 goes to Lublin, becomes Globočnik's officer for communication and Wirth's faithful escort during tours of Belzec, Sobibor and Treblinka. Transferred to Trieste in autumn 1943, where after Wirth's death he is in command at the San Sabba camp. Sentenced to fifteen years in prison in Magdeburg in 1948, but amnestied in 1956. Nine years later on trial in Munich, sentenced to four and a half years in prison and released after two. For crimes committed in Belzec, where 600,000 Jews were murdered, only Josef Oberhauser is convicted. Most of the S.S. men stationed at the death camps in Aktion Reinhard were never brought to trial.

(approximately a colonel). But Allers dies a year before the trial, in 1975. Born in 1910 in Hamburg, Allers works as an attorney until 1968, when he is sentenced to eight years in prison, which he does not serve out. So all the fuss, all the pursuit of justice – for nothing. The Italian judiciary does not call for Oberhauser's extradition, because according to the agreements in force at the time between Italy and Germany, only those suspected of crimes committed *after* 1948 may be extradited. The trial goes on literally in a void: no defendants sit in the courtroom, the judges natter on, journalists snap their cameras – at no-one. In a solemn voice the judgement is read out to unschooled farmer Josef Oberhauser, but Josef Oberhauser is nowhere to be seen, so to whom is the judgement read? Oberhauser is sentenced in Trieste to life imprisonment, yet in Munich he goes on selling beer, especially during the Oktoberfest, when he is in particularly fine fettle. Three years later, in 1979, fat Oberhauser dies of a heart attack.

There is one dossier Haya never gets around to closing. One name she skips over. Thirty years have passed. The name, printed next to the number eight on the newspaper clipping, looks wholly innocent, a cluster of letters arranged in two short words: *Kurt Franz*. Kurt Franz. Letters that elude harmony; letters that zing in staccato out of their context and slam into Haya's temples like bullets. Kurt Franz watches Haya, Haya watches Kurt Franz, and then, in 1976, under him, under her, all around, gapes a chasm into which Haya strides, into the forecourt of Hades.

Who is Kurt Franz?

Kurt Franz cannot be put into Haya's archive. His story doesn't end in 1976. Kurt Franz's story doesn't even end with his death, furthermore with Kurt Franz's death the story of Kurt Franz, the story *about* Kurt Franz, spreads, flows into waiting, into Haya's wait, today's, into our wait.

It was late summer or the beginning of autumn 1942 when I came from Belzec to Treblinka. It was night . . . Everywhere in the camp there were corpses. Bloated corpses. The corpses were dragged through the camp by working Jews, and these working Jews were driven by the Ukrainian guardsmen and also by Germans . . . I reported to Wirth in the dining room. Stangl and Oberhauser were with him . . .

Kurt Franz, S.S.-Untersturmführer, was born on 17 January, 1914, in Düsseldorf. A cook. Trained at Restaurant Hirschquelle, then at Hotel Wittelsbacher Hof, but does not pass his final examination. Serves in the army from 1935–37. Joins the Waffen-S.S., given number 319,906. Begins his career in late 1939 as a cook at the Grafeneck euthanasia centre, and later, when the job at Grafeneck is done, Kurt Franz moves to Hartheim, then to Sonnenstein, and then to Brandenburg, and he cooks less and advances more.

Grafeneck is a medieval castle located in the state of Württemberg on a hill overlooking the town of Marbach, where Schiller was born, so there is a Schiller Museum in Marbach and a rich literary archive. The air is fresh at Grafeneck; the nights are chilly. In the early 1930s a samaritan organization turns the castle into an institution for the mentally handicapped. Then S.S. men come in the late 1930s, members of Aktion T4 arrive, headed by Viktor Brack, to have a look at the castle, to see whether it suits them; the natural surroundings are beautiful, and the *software* is already there. So the S.S. elite requisition the castle with all the patients and throw themselves into work. The castle is adapted for the personnel. A small settlement of barracks goes up nearby. The barracks are surrounded by a four-metre wall. The patients sleep in the barracks and are killed in the barracks by S.S. men. The S.S. men are playing. Experimenting. At one of the barracks S.S. personnel install two mobile crematorium ovens, which dangerously heat the roof, so they remove the roof, and into the sky goes the smoke, turning nature black, the trees, grass, flowers, the sky – everything is black. Even when the sun shines the environs are black. Even the birds are black. This primitive gas chamber (gas chambers will be perfected later), this barrack, has a capacity of seventy-five people per session. The entire castle is surrounded by barbed wire and guards. And dogs. Expert personnel work at Grafeneck, twenty-five female and male nurses, Dr Horst Schumann is there with his colleagues, and Christian Wirth becomes head of administration.

In January 1940 Dr Horst Schumann, S.S.-Sturmbannführer (major), runs the Grafeneck euthanasia "institute". Once the work is up and running, Dr Horst Schumann transfers to Sonnenstein "institute" in Saxony, in order to start up a new euthanasia programme. Schumann is, otherwise, a member of a medical commission, the task of which is to dispatch ailing camp inmates from Auschwitz, Buchenwald, Dachau, Flossenburg, Gross-Rosen, Mauthausen, Neuengamme and Niederhangen to the euthanasia centres which are beginning to flourish all over the Reich.

Dr Schumann arrives at Auschwitz in June 1941 and selects 575 prisoners whom he sends to Sonnenstein where the guards inject them straight into the heart with super-toxic phenol. Schumann returns to Auschwitz to try out a "cheap and effective" method of mass sterilization of women and men using X-rays. Hardly any of his guinea pigs survive. They die of internal haemorrhaging, of burns. They die after additional "operations", meaning the removal of ovaries and testicles. They die of exhaustion and shock. At Auschwitz, and maybe later as well, Schumann examines the efficiency of devices he never patents – ah, events follow one upon another with such speed, devices that serve for the experimental harvesting of sperm, a small rectal insertion to stimulate the prostate and ejaculation. Dr Schumann leaves Auschwitz in 1944. A Dr Schumann, such a nice name, shows up in October 1945 in Gladeck, a small industrial town in the Ruhr region, where the local authorities employ him as a sports doctor. Somewhat later, Dr Schumann opens a private practice that prospers for him until 1951, until someone – Lord, such a classic! – someone identifies him as a war criminal. Dr Horst Schumann vanishes, of course. He works for three years as a doctor on a transatlantic ocean liner, then travels to the Sudan and is joined there by his wife and three innocent, golden-haired children. Four years later the happy family hurry through Nigeria and Libya to Ghana. In fact, Dr Schumann does end up in prison around 1966 after President Kwame Nkrumah dies. Nkrumah thinks highly of Schumann for all he does for the people of Ghana, because this tall, well-built man with elegant hands and long artistic fingers, this man who is nearly a saint, living in a damp Ghanaian province where malaria rages, the rains never cease, the tropical heat steals the breath, the poverty is immense, this humanist, in his (Nkrumah's) African backwoods builds a hospital with forty beds and lives there with his family in a modest bungalow, three day's trek from the nearest town, because the roads are so ghastly and no white men anywhere, and if someone, a white-skinned visitor, happens to stumble across him, Dr Schumann brings the guest to the humble clinic and shows him the charters from the World Health Organization hanging there, clearly visible, reads them to the visitor so that the visitor remembers that it is the duty of every doctor to furnish mankind with the best possible conditions for a healthy and happy life.

Once Nkrumah is no longer there to protect him, Dr Horst Schumann leaves Ghana handcuffed to two detectives. Ah, happy days, *schöne Zeiten*. Dr Schumann will remember his African interlude; so many old acquaintances from Hitler's Chancellery, the occasional encounters with Dr Helmut Kallmeyer, for example, the exotic *hors d'oeuvres* . . . perhaps it is better not to remember. Detained in 1966, Dr Schumann appears before a court in 1970 and then announces he is not well. He's troubled by high blood pressure. He collapses at trial (this turns out to be a feigned heart attack), so the administration of the prison, humane to a fault, releases him for treatment. No-one protests, not the public or the media, and for twelve years thereafter Dr Horst Schumann lives in Frankfurt, attends the Frankfurt Book Fair, goes to concerts (Frankfurt has a passable symphony orchestra). He strolls in spring through the streets, but he does not leave town on outings, because Sachsenhausen is nearby, and Dr Schumann is not eager to see Sachsenhausen, as his blood pressure might skyrocket. Now and then Dr Schumann enjoys a frankfurter, and this ultimately kills him: he dies on 5 May, 1983, just after his seventy-seventh birthday.

The killings at Grafeneck last until mid-December 1941. Then they stop abruptly. There are no handicapped and retarded left; they have all been successfully executed: 10,654 people. Grafeneck and its surroundings are now cleansed, and so much the healthier. Grafeneck is dropped from the euthanasia programme. All traces are erased, the walls and the wire; the natural surroundings revert to green; the staff go on holiday. It is nearly Christmas, and so begins the season of goodwill and endowment. With the new year comes a new location: Hadamar. At Hadamar 10,824 patients are gassed. After the war, of the hundred or so staff members who run the Grafeneck euthanasia programme, eight are charged and three receive prison terms ranging from eighteen months to five years. Fifty years later, in 1990, a memorial is raised at Grafeneck listing the names of the patients who were killed, and the "patients" who killed them.

Yes, Kurt Franz. Kurt Franz still works as a cook at Buchenwald; then in 1942 he goes to Belzec for a time, then on to Treblinka. Treblinka becomes his kingdom. After the revolt in August 1943 Kurt Franz is made camp commander. He oversees the last "gas operations" and finally shuts down Treblinka.

> *That's not true! I was not commander of the camp! I had the rank of Oberscharführer at Treblinka, and as a member of the Waffen-S.S. units I was responsible exclusively for the camp guards. The Oberscharführer is technically a sergeant, not an officer. My conscience is clean.*

At Treblinka Kurt Franz struts about, rides, goes off for a morning jog, sings, sings a lot (Kurt Franz loves music, especially orchestral music), keeps himself in shape, keeps his beautiful body trim, and faithful Barry is always at his heels. At Treblinka Kurt Franz lets his imagination run wild, he comes up with little extravagances, he plants flowers.

> We planted flowers in the end, when we were getting ready to leave. I ordered the excavators to level off the camp. We planted lupins. What? Lupins are perennials, lovely flowers, spectacular floral candles. Against an attractive leafy background they create a stunning floral landscape. Lupins are ideal for planting in colourful clusters in full sun. I love flowers. I have a well-tended garden.

Before closing down the camp, Kurt Franz kills time by killing people.

> Lies, all lies. I heard with my own ears how Wirth, in quite a convincing voice, explained to the Jews that they would be deported further and before that, for reasons of hygiene, they must bathe, and their clothes would have to be disinfected. Inside the disinfection barrack was a long wooden counter for the deposit of valuables, jewellery, money and such – small things. It was made clear to the Jews that after the bath their valuables would be returned to them. Then the Jews applauded Wirth enthusiastically. Their applause is still ringing in my ears. So, the Jews believed Wirth.

In late 1943 Kurt Franz is transferred to Trieste and tasked with killing partisans and Jews. From Trieste he flees to Austria in April 1945, but American soldiers catch up with him and put him behind bars. Big and strong, Kurt Franz escapes from prison. He goes back to his native Düsseldorf and, using his own name, works first as a labourer at a building site, then returns to his old profession, cooking. For fourteen years Kurt Franz goes fishing, tells his children all sorts of fairy tales, plays football on Sundays, compiles new albums of colour photographs of nature, friends, animals, soon loses his hair and puts on weight. Still, it's as if the happy days are here again. Then in 1959 Kurt Franz is arrested once more and on 3 September, 1965, at the first Düsseldorf trial for crimes committed at Treblinka, he is charged with murdering at least 139 camp inmates and participating in the killing of more than 300,000 Jews, and sentenced to life imprisonment. During the trial, as evidence, the police present a photographic album they find in Kurt Franz's garage behind empty, dusty wine bottles and the muddy rubber boots Kurt Franz wears when he waters his garden flowers. On the album in large letters are the words *Schöne Zeiten*, which would be "The Good Old Days" or "Happy Days" or "The Joy of Life", ah, the age of ignorance.

This much Haya is aware of in 1976. Only later, only now, in 2006, according to the surprises that life serves up to its drowsy consumers, only now does Haya learn that in 1993 Kurt Franz is released from prison and dies in an old people's home in Wuppertal on 4 July, 1998, when the Red Cross send her a photograph of a fat bald man, a doddering old geezer, actually, sitting hunched over a wooden table, and next to him an elderly woman in a rumpled house dress, dishevelled, obese, sagging and slovenly. The wall behind Mr and Mrs Franz is covered in paisley wallpaper, and on it hang a number of small trophies, hunting trophies, and insignia that look like medals. This photograph does not hold Haya's interest. By then, in 2006, she has a thick file on Kurt Franz, a file which lies like a memento at the bottom of her red basket, like a deep blue tattoo on her bosom, like a shroud under which her brain pulses more and more feebly, relegated to the past.

The Red Cross is always late or never gets there at all. The Red Cross is so busy everywhere in the world. The Red Cross is caught up in a broad range of activities, chiefly humanitarian, so it has trouble concentrating on individual activities, so its work is dispersed, aflutter and *it never takes sides*. The imperative of the Red Cross is to sustain a universal, global neutrality. In terms of history and people. The Red Cross has been reminding Haya for six decades, every 8 May, of its day, thanking her for the trust she has shown it, the Red Cross, of course, hoping that soon it, the Red Cross, will contribute to solving her "case", regardless of the fact that, of course, Haya Tedeschi may no longer be alive by then. Haya, on the other hand, does not think of the case of the disappearance of her son

Antonio Tedeschi on 13 April, 1945, as hers, because she did nothing to bring about the disappearance of her son Antonio Tedeschi, it was due to, let's say, historical circumstances. The Red Cross has contacted Kurt Franz, in and out of prison, but Kurt Franz knows nothing of an Antonio Tedeschi, and *the name Haya Tedeschi is completely foreign to me*, Kurt Franz says, he holds and fiddles with a copy of the birth certificate that the Red Cross workers have given him to inspect. *And besides,* Kurt Franz says, *Tedeschi* ist ein jüdischer Name. *You don't think that I would risk my life for a Jewish woman, do you?*

North-west of Kassel and east of Dortmund is the little town of Bad Arolsen. In a baroque palace in the middle of a dense forest – deliberately hidden, one might suppose, from the eyes of the public – at Grosse Allee 5–9, is housed the largest archive for World War Two. For fifty years now in this stately home an army of 430 people arranges, copies, digitalizes, registers, analyses and classifies the documents of the Third Reich in the forlorn hope that here, maybe now, sixty-plus years after the fact, they will contribute to picking apart and laying bare at least one little piece of the past. The International Tracing Service is in Bad Arolsen, and they still receive almost half a million enquiries annually regarding the missing and the dead, those torn violently from their families, the uprooted, robbed and murdered; enquiries pertaining to children and adults, as if people do not die, as if people do not give up, as if the past doesn't wear thin (it seems not to) the nightmares of the dead times continue to circle the world.

Few people know of Bad Arolsen's vast functional archive, which could bring succour to millions and disturb millions were it made available to the public. Every day through the fingers of the officials of the International Tracing Service slip human lives with names, both real and fabricated, with names added or erased, lives with identities or without them, lives with meaning and those bereft of meaning, regardless, lost lives. Mislaid lives. At the baroque palace in Bad Arolsen, on huge sliding shelves marked with the names of the camps, cities, battles, regions, in alphabetical registers, lurk unfinished stories, trapped fates, big and little personal histories, embodied histories, there are people huddled there who languish, ghost-like, and wait for the great Mass of Liberation, the eucharistic celebration after which they will finally lie down, fall asleep or depart, soaring heavenward. Bad Arolsen, this vast collection of documented horror, preserves the patches, the fragments, the detritus of seventeen, yes, in digits, 17 million lives on 47 million pieces of paper collected from twenty-two concentration camps and their satellite organizations; from factories, from an array of institutions, from ghettos, from prisons, from these commands and those commands, from hospitals and hospital files (medical records), from the laboratories (experiments), from institutes, local archives, the police and police files; there is information here about executions, political, criminal and racial, about murders "for reasons of health", everything is here that the Allied Forces collected when Germany surrendered, first to be warehoused in London, then in Frankfurt and, in 1952, finally, in Bad Arolsen.

In Bad Arolsen, in this "library" of horrors, in this alchemist's kitchen of maniacs, little lives of little people have been foundering already for sixty years; they are waving their deportation I.D.s, their brittle, faded and cracked family photographs, their hastily penned letters, diaries, their birth certificates and marriage licences, their death certificates, sketches, poems, their coupons for food and clothing, anything that can supplant their cry, they are waving: *Here we are, find us.*

Information about missing children is collected and preserved in a special department in Bad Arolsen. Missing children from World War Two. The 250,000 children who went missing during World War Two. Fewer than 50,000 of them have found their families to date, what is *left* of their familes, their – roots. And so about 200,000 people (an entire medium-sized city) have no notion of who they are; some of them wonder, some of them wonder where they are from, while others live thinking they are someone they are not, and they do not ask themselves any questions, and they do not wonder if they might be someone other than who they are, but actually they are the very person they think they are not, a person who is altogether strange and foreign to them, until one day, sometimes after two, three, four, five, six decades, when these children are no longer children and are getting old, one day a warm breeze wafts the "happiness", the "realization", a white sheet of paper, a document, a stamped certificate (from Bad Arolsen) to one of these elderly children, which declares that they do not exist at all, because who they thought they were, they aren't, they are someone else, someone who has, as far as they are concerned, never existed, and then overnight the person who has never existed for them becomes who they are. In Bad Arolsen, in that special department, they keep information about children (and infants) who were killed or taken from their non-Aryan parents to be given to "pure Aryans" to be looked after and raised. About children who are lost forever to their parents, most of whose parents no longer exist, just as these children are now non-existent for themselves.

The baroque palace in Bad Arolsen preserves, cleans, cleanses, fine-tunes in its belly a city of paper, a paper city, a *papier-mâché* model of Europe, of life, of compacted tragedies, gigantic tragedies squashed on to yellowed slips of paper.

But. The information kept in Bad Arolsen is accessible only to those who sit in the baroque palace in Bad Arolsen, and the staff of the International Red Cross, who have been permitted, – and only they, in the name of the victims and their children – to stroll through the renovated rooms of the International Tracing Service and nibble at warm cakes in the small cafés scattered here and there for atmosphere and increased staff productivity. The Red Cross is slow, just as the United Nations is slow, and not so very united. It takes the Red Cross between three and thirty years to find a concrete piece of information, confidential information that often leads nowhere. But they send out their cards wishing everyone a Happy 8 May, Red Cross Day, without fail, in perfect order, to those they know and those they do not, to the living and the dead, potential and genuine consumers of the services of the International Red Cross, like a little reminder, like a slogan – *we are thinking of you, we are working for you*. To all others, to historians, journalists, sociologists, writers, to everyone, and especially to those with a personal stake in this, whose wanderings through the historical twilight might lead them to an occasional lit path, to all of these, access to the baroque palace in Bad Arolsen is forbidden. Out of the question. The baroque palace in Bad Arolsen is fiercely guarded. With the excuse of protecting the privacy of the victims, Germany has been protecting its own reputation for fifty years. Italy's as well. And countless other big and little, powerful and powerless countries scattered across all the continents of the planet.

Now and then a curious piece of information leaks from the palace in Bad Arolsen to the public. For example, while they were looking for the family of a Mr Weiss, workers at the International Red Cross stumbled upon the Mauthausen "Book of Death" in which it states that on 20 April, 1942, at a special celebration in honour of Hitler's birthday, an additional 300 people were put to death at the camp, after which the guests enjoyed a festive meal.

Germany resists the opening of the Bad Arolsen archive for twenty years. The International Red Cross declares with pride that it opened its archives to the public ten years earlier, without mentioning the *secrecy* of the fifty years before that, during which there was time to "reorganize" the data, erase and destroy evidence that might compromise the war (in)activity of the International Red Cross. All parties protect their asses as much as they can, and so does the International Red Cross. And so does the Church, particularly the Catholic Church.

Then there is a change in April 2006. After years and years of negotiating, Germany, the United States, France, Belgium, Great Britain, Israel, Greece, the Netherlands, Poland, Luxembourg and Italy, the eleven countries which signed the agreement on establishing the protected archives of documents captured from the Third Reich in 1946, come much closer to reaching a consensus. Germany agrees that the Bad Arolsen doors should be opened, though not straight away. They call for additional meetings, more consideration, further assessment.

Haya comes across the news of the opening of Bad Arolsen in the newspapers *L'Unità* and *Corriere della Sera*. It is a small news item, appearing at the bottom of the fifth and sixth page, respectively, of the newspapers Haya regularly reads. Haya reads many papers. By this time she has experience with newspapers. Haya snips out the article about the opening of the German archives and places it on the desk by the window. *Soon*, she says. *Soon it will be time to go to Bad Arolsen*. There is no-one around to tell Haya, *Take it slow, Haya. It is too soon to start packing. Bad Arolsen is not yet open, and you are old.*

Anyway. After the news that the Bad Arolsen archive might soon be opening its doors, Haya decides: *I am coming back among people. It is springtime. I will hold a little dinner party for my closest friends.* Yes, Haya is old. The preparations for the dinner take a long time. For a week Haya brings home food supplies, bottles of Merlot and Picolit, fresh vegetables, strawberries are available, she gets *prosciutto, prosciutto di San Daniele*, she has no flour at home, no sugar, she buys asparagus, *gli asparagi della Bassa friulana*, she has no cooking oil, she buys spring beans and potatoes, *i fagioli e le patate della Carnia*, she buys cheeses, especially *formaggio Montasio*. Haya doesn't eat much, mostly *Zwieback*, on the day of her dinner Giovanni the fisherman leaves at her door trout he has just caught, lovely, plump trout, *le trote del Natisone*, oh, it will be a feast, a real feast after so many years of fasting. Haya gets out her fine glasses, the ones with the gold rim. She washes them so they glisten. She takes out her special tableware. Carla comes over. Carla cleans the house. The windows gleam, the floor gleams, there is a sense of gaiety in the air, a long-since-vanished gaiety that now sticks to the sun's rays, and prances with them, prances like flies driven mad by impending rain. And Freddy, Freddy comes over, to braid a black velvet ribbon into her heavy grey hair.

No-one comes.

Everyone is busy. They all apologize. *We're busy*, they say. Fanny is busy, Igor is busy, Albina is busy, Frau Helga, nicknamed "Hitlerchen", is also busy, Don Sebastian is busy, Olga is busy. Who else had she invited? she can't remember just then. She invited Roberto. She invited Roberto, and Roberto is busy. All her guests, all *twelve* of her guests are busy. They have more pressing things to see to. Haya can't remember what these things are, pointless things, yes, she doesn't remember *what* they are busy with, *who* they are busy with. No-one comes to her little party, to the last dinner of her fast, to her return to the living.

So what? That's fine. Bad Arolsen will open and she will go there.

Arolsen will open and I will go to Arolsen, Haya says. And further she says, *I would like my name to be Babette. Babette knows about feasts. Eating and celebrating are ordinary deceptions*, she says. *Waiting lasts, waiting endures.*

What's with Zion? Divine salvation? Ridiculous. What does he have in mind, this God, this god of the Jews, this god of the Christians, that a feast can bring salvation, that one little feast can overpower death, plough up the cemetery in her breast? Ha! Reconciliation? One big or little bash, either way, will that bring liberation? How, on a platter?

> *Listen, Haya, I know something about this. It's true, salvation is, in human terms, absolutely unattainable; but everything is possible for God! This is a struggle of faith, which, if we can say so, fights madly for possibility. Possibility is the only force that saves . . . At times the inventiveness of the human imagination may be enough to create possibility, but ultimately this means when one should* believe, *the only thing that helps is that everything is possible for God.*

Leave me, Kierkegaard. I don't feel like talking. This little gastronomical defeat is an ordinary "decoration". There is no despair in it. I am too old for new despair.

> *Despairing is not a trait of the young alone. No-one outgrows the way that one "moves beyond an illusion". But an illusion cannot be outgrown and*

no-one is so mad as to believe that. Indeed, we will often run into men and women and the elderly who have more childish illusions than any young man or woman. But we forget that illusion has essentially two forms: the form of hope and the form of recollection. Youth has the illusion of hope, age – the illusion of recollection.

My recollections are not illusions. They are not the past. My memories are my present.

This past-present of yours is perhaps something that remorse, in fact, should be dealing with. But for there to be remorse, one must first reach the ultimate point of despair, and spiritual life must reach its foundations. This is difficult. Young people despair for their future as a present in futuro. *You despair because of the past as present* in praeterito.

I despair because I remember. Leave me, Kierkegaard. Don't you see that time has arranged itself in circles? The past is reality. The past is a factual state. The past is a fait accompli. But the future offers branching possibilities. Think a little about temporal logic. I am fine with my despair. As with my solitude.

Yes. Only the breed of incoherent, talkative people, this herd of the inseparables, feels no need for any kind of solitude, because they, like little parakeets, die immediately, as soon as they are for a moment left alone. Preserve your despair.

I know. You keep saying that. "Despair – a sickness from which one languishes but does not die. Sickness unto death." You talk too much, Kierkegaard. I don't need language any more. Numbers and a few letters suffice, because everything is in formulas, everything.

May I say something?
Who are you?
Pound, the crazy poet

Speak, Pound, tell Kierkegaard.

And the betrayers of language
          . . . . n and the press gang
And those who had lied for hire;
the perverts, the perverters of language,
          the perverts, who have set money-lust
Before the pleasures of the senses [. . .]
The slough of unamiable liars,
          bog of stupidities,
malevolent stupidities, and stupidities,
the soil living pus, full of vermin,
dead maggots begetting live maggots,
          slum owners,
usurers squeezing crab-lice, pandars to authority,
pets-de-loup, sitting on piles of stone books,
obscuring the texts with philology,
          hiding them under their persons,
the air without refuge of silence,
          the drift of lice, teething,
and above it the mouthing of orators,
          the arse-belching of preachers.
          And Invidia,
the corruptio, fœtor, fungus,
liquid animals, melted ossifications,
slow rot, fœtid combustion,
          chewed cigar-butts, without dignity, without tragedy,
. . . . . m Episcopus, waving a condom full of black-beetles,
monopolists, obstructors of knowledge.
          obstructors of distribution.

So it is that in 2006 Haya largely stops speaking; she mainly listens to ghosts. And waits.

I stand at the door to the "baths"; under a tree I see a small orchestra: three Jews, yellow stars on their chests, are singing, and three are playing instruments. They have a violin, a mandolin and a flute. The S.S. men like music. They love it when there is playing and singing. They dance at night in their club. The club at Treblinka is called "Casino". A little orchestra plays the latest hits. Artur Gold performs his popular tango "Autumn Roses". In the rhythm of autumn roses people go off to the "showers". They march to the sounds of the violin. The S.S. men smile wistfully.

It is 1942. The anniversary of the outbreak of war is being celebrated at the camp. All night between 31 August and 1 September Jews sing and dance for the Germans. The next day these Jews are no more. They die with a song on their lips. I am Abraham Krzepicki. I escape Treblinka in late 1942. Later I am killed in Warsaw, in 1943. I am twenty-five years old.

There are many musical instruments at the camp, but not enough musicians. Musicians disappear into the "showers". S.S.-Hauptsturmführer Stangl loves jazz, so he decides to form an orchestra. When he returns from his vacation, he brings back a collection of cymbals. Kurt Franz orders the tailors to make white suits for the members of the orchestra with shiny, blue lapels and collars and giant, monstruous, blue bow ties of the same fabric. Gold trots out on to the stage in a white tuxedo jacket. He is wearing a white shirt, perfectly pressed trousers, patent-leather shoes. His blue lapels and blue collar glitter in the spotlights. As if we are in a Warsaw cabaret. The S.S. men love Gold. And the camp inmates love Gold. For his forty-fifth birthday they throw him a little party in their workshop. That same evening Gold plays for the S.S. personnel in their casino. Then Kurt Franz orders: Compose me an anthem for the camp. *Gold writes the melody; the Czech, Walter Hirsz, writes the words. Afterwards both are killed. The anthem is called "Fester Schritt". The anthem is played during evening roll-call, while S.S. men whip disobedient inmates, and it is played most often when the inmates do exercises in the yard. At the end of roll-call the inmates sing their hymn once more and Kurt Franz shouts,* Lauter, lauter! *Kurt Franz loves music at Treblinka. Life was lively at Treblinka.*

By the way, my name is Oscar Strawczynski. I arrive at Treblinka on 5 October, 1942. I am a smith and there was work at Treblinka for smiths. When I wasn't working as a smith, I sorted stolen clothing. I took part in the revolt. I saved my brother and sister. Everyone else from my family was killed, my mother, my father, my grandmother, my grandfather, my uncles. Everyone. Some at Treblinka, some at Auschwitz. After escaping from Treblinka I joined the partisans. I testified in Düsseldorf in 1965. I died in Montereale in 1966.

I killed myself.
My name is Richard Glazar. I killed myself in Prague in 1997.
I survived the camps. The Americans liberated me. I testified at the trials of Kurt Franz, Stangl, and his companions. I studied in Prague, Paris and London. After the Prague Spring I left Czechoslovakia and lived for a long time in Bern.

In the spring and summer of 1943 there were fewer transports. One evening at roll-call, Kurt Franz said, Sundays in the afternoon we won't work. We'll have some fun. We'll have a cabaret. We'll play music. We'll sing. We'll perform sketches, and sometimes we'll box, *that is what he said. Kurt Franz loved boxing.*

Let's box a few rounds, Kurt Franz said to an inmate. We called Kurt Franz "Lalka". In Polish lalka *means doll. This inmate was a professional boxer from Cracow. He was about twenty years old. The soldiers tied the gloves on to the inmate. Lalka took only one glove, the right one. In that glove he tucked a small pistol and grinned.* Go! Now! *shouted the S.S. men from behind Lalka's back. With one hand raised, with the hand in the glove, Lalka stepped up to the inmate as if he were ready for a fight, and then he shot the man between the eyes. The boxer fell dead on the spot. That is how Franz boxed. My name is Jacob Eisner.*

This is Strawczynski. I'd like to add something. Do you remember Wolowanczyk? He was the terror of the Warsaw underground. Tall, blonde and robust, stronger than Franz. A dangerous man. He wasn't more than twenty. He was killed afterwards during the revolt. Once Franz – Lalka – started boxing with him, but Wolowanczyk, quick on his feet and spry, kept evading him. Lalka got dangerously angry. He grabbed Wolowanczyk by the shirt and tried to punch him in the head, but the boy flung himself on the ground and Franz missed, lost his balance and fell right next to Wolowanczyk. Then he really went wild. He flung bricks and stones at the boy, threw him to the ground again, kicked him hysterically and flogged him. I watched it all from the roof of the barrack and I was sure Wolowanczyk was dead, that Franz had killed him. But no. Wolowanczyk got up, brushed off the dust and walked away as if nothing had happened. Go on, Glazar.

Concerts were rehearsed in the hallways in front of the gas chambers. One sunny afternoon we gathered around the ring. The S.S. men, trim in their uniforms, sit in a semi-circle. We stand behind them, our heads shaved, in rags; the guards, the body carriers, the tailors, the cobblers, the uphol-sterers, the cooks, all stand, the washers, clerks, accountants, doctors, gravediggers. We inmates stand behind the S.S. men, and our backs are guarded by soldiers with guns at the ready. Artur Gold and his boys, all in white jackets with broad blue lapels, play a march, after which "the show may begin". Stangl, head of the camp, sits in the middle. He keeps the beat with his foot and light flicks of the whip to his polished boot. Salwe comes onstage and plays an Italian tarantella. After him, one of the best Warsaw tenors performs an aria from Tosca, the music ascends heavenward, above the barracks, above the gas chambers, disappearing into the pine trees. Then Salwe sings. Salwe sings an aria from Halevy's opera La Juive. He sings "Rachel, quand du Seigneur", and we look on, frozen. The S.S. men do not react. Only Stangl turns.

Artur Gold and his brother Henryk were Polish musical stars, especially Henryk. He survived. They performed with their eight-piece jazz orchestra at the Café Bodega in Warsaw. At first they played ragtime, then later waltzes and tangos. They cut

records for Syrena, Electro and Columbia. Jerzy
Petersburski played with them, author of the hits
"O, Donna Clara", "The Last Sunday". There were
quite a few musicians at Treblinka. The Schermann
brothers were there, and little Edek who played the
accordion . . .

One day in October 1942, while I was taking bodies
out of the newly constructed gas chambers, a kapo
came up to me with a violin in his hand and asked,
Do you know anyone who can play? I know, *I*
said, I play.

    They immediately moved me into the kitchen to
peel potatoes. There were six of us. One was Fuchs,
who played the clarinet and who had worked for
the Polish Radio before Treblinka. At first just the
two of us played, Fuchs and I, from time to time
during roll-calls. Then we were joined by a pianist
and composer from Warsaw who played the accor-
dion, and from that time we were a trio. The most
popular song was the love song "Tumbalalaika".
That spring an S.S. man often came by whose
nickname was "Blackie" (der Schwartze). He would
sit himself down on a chair near the well and order
us to play for him. He'd say, Play one for my soul.
At Treblinka once we played at a Jewish wedding.
That day there was a lot of dancing. Then the
happy couple was led to the "showers".

    My name is Jerzy Rajgrodzki.

        Lager zwei ist unser Leben, ay, ay, ay!
        Lager zwei ist unser Leben, ay, ay, ay!
        we sang in chorus, on the open area between the gas
        chambers and the mass graves. I am a singer and
        actor from Prague. My name is Spiegel. I died, too.

Pause.

It will be summer soon. Haya goes out for walks again.

The shop windows are full of women's suits in pastel hues. Haya looks at them. *The skirts are too short*, she says. *Women have fat knees. The suits close the construction and express a function as a power series of the argument* x *with the assumption that the function is infinitely differentiable at* 0. *That would be a Maclaurin series. In a Taylor Series, the function* y = f(x) *is expressed as a power series in a neighbourhood of point* a, Haya says to a woman who is also standing in front of the display window.

I don't understand, the woman says.

I'm not surprised, says Haya and walks on. Haya walks slowly. Her step is not unsteady. Haya is a hale old woman.

Haya walks and hums. The noise levels are mounting in Gorizia. *Gorizia is loud*, Haya says. Whenever she goes out, Haya senses more noise. The noise sits on her brow and weighs down on her head. Gorizia is full of exhaust fumes today. There are new cafés. Haya goes to the park. The greenery at the park is intense; it soothes her eyes. Haya sings to outnoise the noise rolling down the Corso. If she could, if she were younger, she'd chase the noise; she'd say to it *Shoo!* or maybe she'd say to it *Come, lie on my bosom*, because there is too much quiet in her breast. She is not younger. What can she do about that? Haya hums. How is it that Haya hums when she isn't particularly happy? Generally when they sing people feel glad. They probably first feel glad, then they think, *Ah, I'm filled with gladness*, and then they sing. Is that it? But what if the songs people sing when they are glad, what if these songs are sad? It must be that they are moved then by a sorrow that mingles with their happiness. As with mathematics. Formulae. Planes interweave. Planes of sorrow and happiness melt to zero, to nothing. *What is going on?* Haya says, surprised. *Nothing is coming out of my breast*, she says. *A big immobility is crouching inside.* By the time she died Ada could no longer sing; something had happened to her voice box. When she tried to sing, though seldom, as she neared death, she could only squawk. She'd look at Haya and say, *Something's broken*. She died wearing a yellow, short-sleeved blouse with Richelieu embroidery and red wine stains that had gone dark blue. A beautiful blouse. *This is the blouse my mother wore when she brought the soldiers their macaroons*, Ada told Haya, then she died. In that hospital. In Dr Basaglia's ward. Haya did not bury Ada at Valdirosa. When Ada died the Valley of the Roses was in another country. Haya put Ada in a little niche, here, at Gorizia cemetery. There are poppies with silk petals in front of the niche. Now that they are sewing Gorizia back together again, Haya might be able to move Ada. She won't. There is nothing left to move. Ada is now little more than a handful. It seems silly to move little objects, little things. Little things can be carried in the pocket; they go with us.

The weather is getting warmer.

A small white cat with one eye and no nose creeps by Haya's feet at the Parco della Rimembranza. And breathes its last. Here, right at Haya's feet. *Deterioration lies everywhere*, Haya says. Haya looks a little at the dead kitten, a little at her shoes. *My shoes are so unsightly*, she says. *I won't buy shoes with round shoelaces any more. Round shoelaces always come undone. I could play bridge. With whom?*

Haya closes her eyes. There on the bench at the Parco della Rimembranza beneath her eyelids surfaces the large eye of an ox, a wrinkled eye, a horrible, open eye. There is no person who can gaze like that, that way, like an ox. The huge eye watches Haya from the inside. It draws itself in, squints, then opens even more. *How unpleasant*, says Haya and gets up. *What will I do with my time?* wonders Haya, then sits again. *I am dragging time along like a dog on a leash. This is becoming an effort.*

A woman walks by with a dog. The dog wags its tail. It wants to go to Haya. In a high voice the woman says, *Be good! DON'T bother the lady*. The woman has narrow hips. Women with narrow hips have more trouble giving birth. Haya has broad hips. Mothers talk to their children, especially in parks where the children like to explore, they tell them, DON'T *bother the lady!* Children do not bother Haya. Even dogs do not bother her. But the people in charge boss around children and dogs – DON'T *be a bother!* In general, they speak with dogs and children the same way. *That's a no-no, nasty!* they tell them. *Maybe I should go mushrooming?* wonders Haya. *Collect medicinal herbs, brew herbal teas?*

In Berlin once, many years before, Haya got to know Jarmušek, a painter, who brewed her berry teas. Red teas and purple teas, nearly black. In Berlin that year, at a flea market, Haya bought an old doll whose eyes wouldn't close. Jarmušek told her, *Dolls keep secrets even when their eyes are open.* Then Haya and Jarmušek went to Nuremberg. *Let's go to Nuremberg,* Jarmušek said. *Nuremberg is the city of toys.* So Haya and Jarmušek went to Nuremberg in 1968 and looked at the toys, though they were already adults, over forty.

While in Nuremberg Haya studies the city. It is a green city; it has a lot of greenery. In Nuremberg Haya and Jarmušek discover stories about dolls. Nuremberg is an old city, almost a thousand years old. For seven hundred years people have been making dolls in Nuremberg; first little ones, then big ones. The little dolls are old, they are white clay dolls the size of a finger, they are little women and little men, little horsemen, little monks and remarkably little babies, who are little anyway. *I would like to have a doll like that,* says Haya, *a little white baby.* At the exhibition of dolls and toys someone says, *Only Strasbourg dolls from the thirteenth century are older than the Nuremberg dolls.* At the doll exhibition Haya and Jarmušek listen to the story of Nuremberg doll-making.

I don't know whether we need this, this history, Haya says.

There are terrible dolls, Jarmušek says.

That is how Haya and Jarmušek learn that more than six hundred years before, two doll-makers – two *Dockenmacher* – live in Nuremberg, and that wooden dolls follow the clay dolls, and later there are dolls made of alabaster, wax, rags; there are colourful dolls and dolls dressed in the fashions of the day. They learn that toy production in general follows the making of dolls; that Georg Hieronimus Bestelmeier, a Nuremberg merchant and shop owner in the centre of the Old City, in his catalogue for 1798 lists 8,000 items produced in the Nuremberg workshops, including rocking horses, wooden blocks, doll's houses completely furnished, kitchens for dolls with all the equipment, miniature shops, an array of pewter animals and other wind-up figures, children's musical instruments and all sorts of other wonders.

They are making little worlds of the dead, whispers Haya to Jarmušek.

Worlds for fun. Worlds people play with, Jarmušek says.

In the eighteenth century the so-called *Papierdockenmacher* make dolls, animals, *papier-mâché* masks, or only body parts, which are then glued or sewn onto a stuffed leather torso. In the second half of the eighteenth century the Hilpert, Ammon, Heinrichen, Allgeyer and Lorenz families dictate the production of pewter dolls. Shops and children's stores are inundated with an exotic (pewter) animal world, with mythological characters and medieval knights. In the nineteenth and twentieth centuries the Trix, Schucho, Bub, Fleischmann, Arnold, Plank, Schoenner and Bing companies become synonymous with the desirable toy. The number of people involved in designing and producing toys keeps growing. While, for example, 1,366 people work on making toys in 1895, ten years later there are more than 8,000 of them, and 243 companies or small toy factories are at work in Nuremberg in 1914. And so, the Nuremberg world of imagination grows and grows and travels everywhere, especially to the United States. Toys feed Nuremberg and Nuremberg feeds on toys.

Then comes World War One, and with World War One begins the quiet demise of Nuremberg toys. Instead of toys, weapons are produced. Instead of little varnished, mechanical cars, big olive-drab caterpillar tanks are produced. Instead of swift electric trains that circle through mountain landscapes in elegant salons and spacious children's bedrooms, the hit is Big Bertha. Then, from 1933 on, Jews, the majority owners of the factories begin to disappear from Nuremberg at a dizzying rate, so the toys disappear, too. In the summer of 1943 Hitler announces a ban on manufacturing toys, all toys. Hitler advises children to *Play at the arts of combat and sing war songs, marches.*

At the doll and toy exhibition Haya and Jarmušek look at a photograph beneath which there is a pile of old toys, stained and broken. The picture shows first-grade Nuremberg pupils from the Jewish elementary school located at the time at Obere Kanalstrasse 25. The picture is dated 1936. Each child in the picture is holding a toy. The boys hold a paper cone of some sort in which there might be sweets, models of little metal automobiles in lively colours, perhaps a small train, a tin soldier or a miniature tank. Most of the girls are holding dolls.

But by 1943, when Hitler puts a stop to toy manufacturing, the children in the picture no longer exist. Four of them (numbers 10, 18, 32 and 33) are deported to Poland with their families in 1942, to Izbica, the packed departure lounge for Belsen. Their teacher is taken to Krasniczyn. No-one knows who the children marked 2, 8, 9, 12, 14, 15, 16, 19, 24, 28, 30, 31, 35 and 36 are, where they have gone or what has happened to them. Perhaps they are riding along on a moveable shelf in Bad Arolsen, which Haya knows nothing about at that point, though she might have known. But no matter where the children from the picture went, no matter where they were taken, in 1942 they probably carried a toy with them. They were the children of Nuremberg, connoisseurs when it came to dolls, trains and automobiles.

When Birkenau was liberated, aside from the gold teeth, the hair and clothing, the piles of bones, dolls were also found, many of them from Nuremberg. Their hair pulled out, naked, with no limbs, often with eyes missing, so similar to their little owners. In camps, objects and people merge. In camps, objects and people become symbiotic.

These camp dolls are like Bellmer's, but smaller, Jarmušek says.

Bellmer who? asks Haya.

Three years before the picture of the first-graders of the Jewish elementary school was taken in Nuremberg, in Berlin Hans Bellmer fashions his first life-size doll, as if mocking the future Borghild. Afterwards, Bellmer makes many more "sick" *Puppen* in Paris. He makes *Puppen* with moveable pubic bones, with mobile, twisted limbs, with extra limbs; *Puppen* with feet in white socks and children's shoes, their private parts without pubic hair; gigantic monstrosities of immature adults who mock the impeccably modelled, muscular bodies which Leni loves photographing and Adolf loved watching. Bellmer's *Puppen* were monster *Puppen*, huge mirrors reflecting history and its *Macher*.

Albrecht Dürer was born in Nuremberg, Jarmušek says.

And Hans Sachs, Haya says.

The first pocket watch was made in Nuremberg, Jarmušek says.

The first European railway line was built in Nuremberg, Haya says.

The Nuremberg laws were adopted in Nuremberg.

There were trials in Nuremberg.

Nuremberg was reduced to rubble by bombs. Nuremberg was a rubbish dump with 100,000 people left homeless.

Nuremberg has a promenade along the River Pegnitz. Let's go for a walk along the Pegnitz, Haya says. *Are there any Jews in Nuremberg?*

We learned a lot about Nuremberg, Jarmušek says.

Yes. Nuremberg is a green city, Haya says.

Later, Haya left, Jarmušek flew away. Like a blonde angel Jarmušek flew over Berlin, and Haya went back to Gorizia. *I cannot fly with you,* she said. *I cannot.*

Do birds chirp in flight? Haya asks a woman who is sitting next to her. The woman who is sitting next to Haya is elderly, about seventy, and she appears to be agitated.

It is a crime to catch song birds and cage them, says the lady sitting next to Haya. *That's what my neighbour does. My neighbour has nine caged birds, which no longer sing*, she says.

We started out down Himmelweg.

To paradise?

To the chirping of birds.

What is your name?

Rajzman, Samuel Rajzman.

What did you do before the war?

Before the war I was an accountant at an export firm.

When did you turn up at Treblinka and how did you get there?

In August 1942 they picked me up in the Warsaw Ghetto.

How long were you at Treblinka?

For a year. Until August 1943.

Describe the Treblinka camp.

Trains arrived every day, sometimes three, sometimes four, sometimes five of them. All the travellers were Jews. Jews from Czechoslovakia, from Germany, from Greece and Poland. As soon as the trains stopped, the people had to disembark at once, within five minutes. On the platform they were sorted into groups, men in one group, women in another, children in a third. Then they ordered them to take off their clothes. While the people hurried to strip off their clothing, the German guards snapped their whips. Then the old camp inmates would come. They would collect the clothing and take it to the barracks. The people walked naked along a special path to the gas chambers.

What did the Germans call the path?

Himmelfahrtstrasse.

The Street of the Heavenly Path? The Road to Heaven?

Something along those lines. I can draw you where the path went.

No need. How long did people live after they arrived at Treblinka?

Not long. From when they stripped off their clothes to when they arrived at the gas chamber, at most ten minutes. The men. Fifteen minutes for the women, because first they had to have their hair cut.

Why did they cut the women's hair?

There was talk that they were using the hair to make mattresses for German women.

I cut women's hair.

You are?

> Abraham Bomba. I was a barber before the war. At Treblinka
> I cut men's and women's hair, mostly women's. After the war
> I opened a hair salon in the basement of New York Grand
> Central Station.

Where did you cut the women's hair?

> First in the gas-chamber, before they gassed them, later in
> the undressing barracks. When they stripped them naked the
> women were first examined, then sent to us for a haircut. The
> women were always naked when we cut their hair.

How were they examined, by whom?

> They were laid on tables and their intimate parts were exam-
> ined. Those were not professionals, not doctors. They were
> supposed to find out if the women hid any valuables, gold,
> money, jewellery, in their vaginas. These men used leather
> gloves for their examinations, so the women bled terribly.

How many barbers did the work?

> I don't remember precisely. Some were professional barbers,
> others were not. There was this Jewish Camp Elder, engineer
> Galewski. He told us what to do.

What did he say?

> He said we should make believe we're giving the women a real
> haircut, so they wouldn't know they were going to be gassed,
> so they would believe that after the haircut they were going to
> take a shower. He said, don't make them look like monkeys.

How much time did you have for each haircut?

> Two minutes. It was very painful. Some barbers recognized
> their wives, their mothers, their grandmothers, and they just
> had to go on cutting. And they weren't allowed to say a word.
> Not even hug before their dear ones were to be gassed. It was
> very hard to watch. It was horrible. It was awfully painful.

Rajzman, describe the railway station at Treblinka.

> At first there were no signboards whatsoever at
> the station, but a few months later Kurt Franz, the
> camp commander, ordered they be put up. The
> barracks where the clothing was stored had signs
> reading "RESTAURANT". Then there were signs
> for "TELEPHONE", "POST OFFICE", "WAITING ROOM".
> There were even train schedules for the departure
> and arrival of trains from, say, Vienna and Berlin.

How did the Germans at Treblinka behave with the victims?

> They each had their duties. For example,
> Scharführer Mentz, Willi Mentz, was in charge of
> the Lazarett. Weak women and children who
> couldn't make it to the gas chambers on their own
> were killed at the Lazarett. There was a Red Cross
> flag flying at the Lazarett entrance. Mentz special-
> ized in killing and he didn't let anyone replace him
> when there was killing to be done. Mentz loved
> to kill. I remember, they brought him two sisters,
> one ten, the other two years old. When the older
> girl saw that Mentz was pointing a revolver at her
> sister, she threw herself at his feet and pleaded
> with him not to do it. Then Mentz didn't kill
> the two-year-old, he flung her into the oven alive

and shot the older one. Once they brought to the Lazarett *a woman and her daughter who was about to give birth. They laid the pregnant woman on the ground, and around her gathered S.S. men to watch her labour. The birth lasted about two hours. Then Mentz asked the baby's grandmother whom he should kill first, her or the baby. The woman said,* Kill me. *She pleaded with Mentz,* Kill me. *But of course Mentz first killed the baby, then he killed the baby's mother, then in the end he killed the grandmother.*

Do you know who Kurt Franz was?

Unfortunately, I do. I also know his dog Barry. Kurt Franz was a savage murderer. One of the worst in the camp.

Substantiate that statement.

The train from Vienna arrived. I stood on the platform as people were led out of the wagons. An older woman approached Kurt Franz, produced an identity card and said, I am Sigmund Freud's sister. Assign me to office work. I am frail and old, *she said. Franz studied the card very thoroughly, and then said,* Yes, ma'am. This is an error. Look, *he said,* here is the train schedule. You have a train to Vienna in two hours. Leave all your valuables and documents, *Kurt Franz said,* and go and take a shower, *he said.* When you get back your ticket to Vienna and all your things will be waiting for you. *Naturally, the woman went into the bathhouse and never returned.*

You were saying, Glazar?

Tölpel. His name was Moritz Tölpel. He was very short, nearly dwarf-like, almost completely bald and a bit of an oddball. So, Moritz Tölpel stands there during roll call, his trouser legs dragging on the ground. He stands there, cringing. Kurt Franz – Lalka – takes his measure, and says: Yes, you're the one. A Ukrainian guard manages to dig out a smelly old robe from the grisly pile of clothing belonging to the men, women and children who had already been murdered, and tells Tölpel, Put that on. The garment drags on the ground. Tölpel can't even take a step. He trips, falls, gets up, falls, and Lalka howls, Step, march, one-two! and keeps snapping his whip. Then a guard digs out a black hat that used to belong to a rabbi long since dead, a grimy Halbzylinder, pins a shiny half-moon onto it, then into the tiny hand of dwarfish Tölpel he thrusts a heavy club. A sign will be put on each of the latrines, Lalka says. "TWO MINUTES FOR SHITTING. WHOEVER TAKES LONGER LIVES A DAY SHORTER" Then Bredow hangs a large kitchen clock around Tölpel's neck and says, Here he is, our Treblinka "Scheiss-Meister", and Lalka howls: From now on you are Commander of the Shit! You are now the grand sovereign over everyone and their shit. Anyone who takes longer than two minutes, do with them what you will!

I am Strawzcynski. Once Lalka was out walking with a camera in one hand and a gun in the other. He didn't know whether he'd rather be snapping some pictures or doing some shooting. Then he spotted Sztajer, whose back was turned to him. Sztajer was my neighbour from Czestochowa. Lalka took aim and shot Sztajer in the buttocks. Sztajer screamed and fell to the ground. Lalka came over, beaming. Get up and drop your pants, he said.

The man obeyed. He was barely conscious, blood gushing from his buttocks. Lalka scowled, shrugged and said, Fuck it. I missed your balls. *Then off he went looking for another target.*

Rajzman, how did you manage to stay alive?

> *There were about eight thousand Jews in my transport, brought from Warsaw. I had already undressed and was heading towards Himmelfahrtstrasse when Galewski, a friend of mine of many years, noticed me. He whispered,* Go back. Go back quickly. *He said,* They need a translator for Hebrew, French, Russian, Polish and German, and I convinced them to let you go. *Galewski was in charge of a group of camp workers. He took part in the revolt. He was killed. I was assigned to the job of loading. Onto trains I loaded bundles of clothing belonging to people who had been killed. After two days, from a small town near Warsaw, they brought to Treblinka my mother, sister and two brothers. I watched them being taken to the gas chambers. Then, while I was loading clothing, I found my wife's documents and a photograph of her with our child. That is all I have left of my family. That photograph.*

On average, how many people were killed every day?

> *Between ten and twelve thousand.*

How many gas chambers were there?

> *At first there were only three. Then they built another ten. They were planning twenty-five.*

How do you know?

> *I know. There was construction material on the*
> *small square. I asked someone,* What's that for?
> There aren't any Jews left. *Then someone said,* There
> will be more. We still have plenty of work to do.

Have you heard? says the woman who is now sitting very close to
Haya and makes no effort to leave. *Have you heard? A bedridden little*
old lady on Via dei Magazzini was eaten by rats? she says. *Do you have*
a dog? A person needs a dog. Dogs protect us from rats and loneliness,
says the lady sitting next to Haya. *My dog died recently. Ever since my*
dog died I haven't been sleeping well. I listen. I do a lot of walking. I had
a nice dog, a golden retriever, she says.

They call the new Pope "Rottweiler", Haya says. *The definition of*
hyperbolic functions is:

$$sh\ x = \frac{e^x - e^{-x}}{2},\ ch\ x = \frac{e^x + e^{-x}}{2},\ did\ you\ know\ that?\ The\ Panzer$$

Pope Rottweiler.

The lady sitting next to Haya on a bench in the Parco della
Rimembranza *pretends* not to hear what Haya has said about the
new Pope, because she *has* heard. A little later it will become clear
that the elderly woman has excellent hearing. *Have you read?* asks
the lady sitting next to Haya, right next to her, on the same bench in
the Parco della Rimembranza, their shoulders *nearly* touching, but
not touching, for had they touched Haya would have moved away,
that's for certain, she would have slipped off the end of the bench,
Do you know that postmen in Germany have recently been attending
workshops on canine psychology? asks the lady next to Haya. *The*
German post office is offering classes on canine psychology to all their
staff the lady says to Haya. *The heads of the post office insist,* says the
lady sitting next to Haya in the Parco della Rimembranza, *that dogs*
continue to attack postmen because postmen are particularly attractive
to dogs, the lady says, *but ever since the German post office has been*
offering these workshops, the number of attacks has dropped drastically,

or so says the post office spokeswoman, a certain Sylvia, says the lady sitting next to Haya. *The number of attacks has dropped by half, says Sylvia,* says the woman next to Haya, *and that has been happening ever since the postmen were advised at the workshops not to run when they see a big dog coming at them. The spokeswoman says,* says the lady next to Haya, *that some eighty thousand postmen and postwomen attended the workshops on canine psychoanalysis this year,* she says, *and the exercises included theoretical and practical advice, and the psychologists explained to the postmen that they must not rely on their bicycles, because one cannot escape a chasing dog even on a bicycle, so says Sylvia, the spokeswoman of the German post office,* says the woman next to Haya. *So the postmen said,* Buy us vespas, or mopeds at least, says the woman next to Haya, *but Sylvia the spokeswoman tells them that is out of the question.*

What is your name? Haya asks the woman sitting next to her.

Aurelia.

And just now, on Tuesday, a boy was attacked by a pack of dogs. The boy was on his way to kindergarten, the police reported, says Aurelia. *Three dogs attacked the boy not far from the house where he lives, where he lived, and there wasn't anyone on the street to help him, so the police say,* says Aurelia, *and the boy died. The police say it still isn't clear why the dogs attacked the boy,* says Aurelia, *and now the spokesperson for the police is saying,* We locked up the dogs, and we'll speak to the owners, *because, so the spokesperson says, in this region alone dogs bite at least thirteen thousand people every year. Do you have a dog?* Aurelia asks Haya. *One should have a dog,* she says. *Dogs protect us from rats and loneliness,* says Aurelia. *My dog died recently. I had a nice dog, a golden retriever,* she says.

The dog was called Barry.

Barry was a nice dog. A black-and-white dog. A big one.

Barry belonged to Kurt Franz.

Kurt Franz was called Lalka. In Polish "*Lalka*" means "doll". Kurt Franz was a handsome man, tall, big and strong. A blond man, blue-eyed.

The dog Barry was a trained dog. The dog Barry was trained to attack camp inmates, especially their genitals.

The dog Barry attacked inmates when ordered: *Man, grab that dog!* The dog Barry lived at Treblinka.

What is your name?

> Ya'akov Wiernik

When were you deported to Treblinka?

> *23 August, 1942.*

How long did you stay at Treblinka?

> *Until 2 August, 1943.*

How old are you?

> *I'm dead.*

Do you recognize the person in this photograph?

> *Even if I were on my deathbed Kurt Franz's name would make me tremble.*

You said that Franz amused himself with the prisoners. How did Kurt Franz amuse himself?

> *He had a big dog he called Barry. When Franz ordered,* Mensch, schnapp den Hund! *the dog would attack people and tear off pieces of their flesh.*

You are Kalman Teigman?

> *Yes.*

You live in Israel?

> Yes.

How old are you?

> Eighty-four.

You were deported to Treblinka from the Warsaw Ghetto. When?

> 4 September, 1942.

Do you remember the late Dr Chorazycki?

> Yes, very well.

Who was Dr Chorazycki?

> A physician from Warsaw. At Treblinka he treated the Ukrainians and Germans. Once the deputy camp commander Kurt Franz searched him. I don't know why. Maybe someone snitched on Dr Chorazycki. Maybe it was a routine search. I don't know. And Kurt Franz discovered that Chorazycki was hiding money in his clothing. Chorazycki knew what would happen to him. People were hanged or shot for that.

Why was Chorazycki hoarding money?

> He belonged to a group that was planning an armed revolt. Chorazycki didn't hesitate. He rushed at Franz. He was already old, while Kurt Franz was young, tall and strong. Then he spun around and ran towards his barracks. He didn't get far. After a

few metres he dropped suddenly to the ground.
Clearly he had taken poison of some kind. Then
they called us to the scene, prisoners and personnel
alike, to watch how they pumped Chorazycki's
stomach to revive and torture him. Franz's faithful
assistant Rogozo, a Ukrainian who had worked for
the railways, grabbed a hook and with it drew out
Chorazycki's tongue. Franz poured water from a
filthy bucket in to the man's mouth, and then like
a madman he began to jump all over him. Then
the guards turned Chorazycki upside down, but
nothing. By then completely and utterly dead,
Chorazycki was stripped and beaten savagely
with thick poles. Later they carried him off to the
Lazarett *on a stretcher.*

Who is in this photograph?

Kurt Franz and his dog Barry.

What do you know about Barry?

Barry arrived at Treblinka in late 1942. He was
as big as a calf. He was white with dark spots. He
was a mongrel, a lot like a St Bernard. Whenever
Franz went out to tour Treblinka 1 and Treblinka 2,
Barry went along. Without any reason whatsoever,
Franz would order Barry to attack prisoners. Go,
man, bite that dog! *he'd howl:* Mensch, beiss den
Hund! *But Barry didn't have to wait for the order.*
He'd pounce on the inmates as soon as Franz raised
his voice. Barry was so big that his head came up
to a person's thighs, so the first thing he went for
were a man's privates. He'd bite like crazy. He
managed to bite the penis off several inmates; blood

gushed everywhere. Barry knocked others over on to the ground and mutilated them. Until they were unrecognizable.

You are?

Henryk Poswolski. I watched S.S.-Hauptscharführer Küttner toss a live infant into the air as if it were a clay pigeon, and Kurt Franz "picked it off" with two bullets. Then they went for a beer at the zoo.

What is it, Zabecki?

Once, when Kurt Franz was making the rounds at camp, Barry drew him off into some bushes. We were standing to the side. Franz parted the branches and saw a woman on the ground with a very small baby, only a few months old, lying on its mother's breast. Apparently the woman was dead. Barry yanked free of the leash, went over to the baby and lay down next to it. Then the dog began to whimper and lick the baby's hands and face. Franz went over to Barry and held his gun to the dog's head. Barry looked up at his master and wagged his tail. Just then Franz, cursing loudly, whacked Barry on the back with a pole. Barry fled. Franz kicked the dead woman several times, then he started kicking the child and stomping on its head until it died. Then he continued his walk through the woods, calling the dog, but the dog played deaf, though he was nearby. We saw Barry lurking in the bushes and whining softly, as if searching for someone. After a while Franz went out on to the road and Barry came trotting over to him, but Franz started beating him with such violence that it was as if he'd lost his mind. Barry snarled and barked, and he even lunged at Franz's chest, we thought he'd gone mad, but when Franz ordered him to sit, Barry sat. Then Franz shouted, Lie down! and Barry lay down. Then Franz shouted, Stand! and the dog stood and began licking his master's boots, splattered with the baby's blood. Franz fired several shots into the air and sent Barry after some Jews who were trying to escape from the railway station.

I heard that after the war Barry ended up with a family, and that he became a docile, tame household dog. That he adored children.

I don't know how he was with children, but he was docile. After Treblinka closed, Barry was taken in by a Nazi physician and in 1944 the doctor sent Barry to his wife in northern Germany. Several years later they put Barry down, because he was old and feeble. Later, in 1965, veterinarians and psychologists from Düsseldorf asked the famous behavioural scientist Konrad Lorenz to shed some light on the dog's behaviour. Lorenz told them that such behaviour in a dog is altogether plausible; that a dog's behaviour expresses the subconscious of the dog's master, as Lorenz put it. If he has an aggressive master, the dog will probably attack other people, Lorenz said, and if the behaviour of his master changes, the dog's behaviour will change as well, Lorenz said, and Lorenz can be believed, because during the war he was a loyal Nazi who "changed masters" after the war and was given the Nobel Prize in 1973 for his research into animal and human behaviour.

Oh keep the Dog far hence, that's friend to men,
Or with his nails he'll dig it up again!

I would add something.

Please do, Pound.

> *See, they return; ah, see the tentative*
> *Movements, and the slow feet,*
> *The trouble in the pace and the uncertain*
> *Wavering!*

> *See, they return, one, and by one,*
> *With fear, as half-awakened;*
> *As if the snow should hesitate*
> *And murmur in the wind,*
> > *and half turn back;*
> *These were the "Wing'd-with-Awe",*
> > *Inviolable.*

> *Gods of the wingèd shoe!*
> *With them the silver hounds,*
> > *sniffing the trace of air!*

You have something against the Pope? Aurelia, who no longer has the golden retriever, asks Haya. *People love the Pope,* she says.

There is a kind of sausage called Ratzinger, Haya says. *Or is it Rottweiler? I've forgotten. Birds don't chirp while they fly, that much is certain; while they fly, birds do not chirp. Ah, Aurelia,* Haya says, and then again she says, *Ah, Aurelia!*

Haya wants to talk, but she cannot. The year is 2006, it is the spring of 2006. In her purse Haya carries a newspaper article from the *Corriere della Sera*, wrinkled and tattered, stained, creased in several places, which was published on 28 December, 2005, and which for months she has been unfolding and refolding, reading and rereading then reading it again, and by now, of course, she knows it by heart. Haya would like to show this, this article, to Aurelia, who is so fond of the Pope and who is grieving the passing of her retriever.

Alfonso Morelli of Bologna says that he found a document in the archives of the French Roman Catholic Church dated October 1946 in which Monsignor Angelo Roncalli, papal nuncio to France and future Pope John XXIII, is ordered to keep track of the fact that the Church must retain supervision and guardianship over Jewish children who were baptized. *In this document,* Morelli declares, *it says that children who have been baptized must under no circumstances be handed over to Jewish agencies with responsibility for the care of children, because these agencies cannot guarantee the further Christian upbringing of these Jewish children, who were saved by the Church during the war and were Catholicized with such benevolence and salvation, especially if these Jewish agencies are handing these, during the war, benevolently Catholicized children back to the Jews, the document says,* writes Morelli, *and the Jewish agencies can do even less to guarantee anything regarding children Catholicized during the war if the children are given back to their parents, who are searching for them frantically, who pound urgently on the heavy door of the Catholic Church. Further, the document states,* Morelli quotes, *such children, who have been baptized, should be kept at all costs within the embrace of the Catholic Church, even if their parents are found, even if their parents* demand *that their children be restored to them. In closing, the document states that this decision, or rather this order, is* "confirmed by the Holy Father", *meaning Pope Pius XII, born Pacelli,* as Alfonso Morelli from Bologna writes, *and Cardinal Angelo Roncalli, future Pope John XXIII, known as* "il papa buono", Morelli writes, *had been deeply concerned about the fate of the Jews, because he knew everything about what was going on, because he kept track of what was going on, because he listened to what people told him, among them some Catholic priests as well, and for that reason,* Morelli writes, *precisely for that reason, after the war Cardinal Roncalli does all he can to reunite the Jewish children, the Jewish children hidden during the Holocaust in Catholic monasteries and various Catholic institutions, to reunite those very children with their parents and their families. The document states that the children who have been baptized,* Morelli writes, *cannot be handed over to families who will not see to their Christian upbringing.*

Parents who entrusted their children to the Church, as it also says in the
document upon which I stumbled in the archive of the French Catholic
Church, quite by accident, since all Catholic Church archives are well
guarded and absolutely inaccessible, especially the one in the Vatican
called Archivum secretum *apostolicum Vaticanum,* writes Morelli,
those parents who entrusted their children to the Church and are now
asking for the return of their children, says the document, which is
actually less a document than a directive, writes Morelli, *it says "these*
children" as if they are gifts of God, but they are not, they are someone's
children, writes Morelli, *it says* these *children could* only *be returned*
if they were never baptized; if they were baptized, then there is no
chance of returning these *children to* these *parents. The directive also*
stipulates that the Church will consider each case relating to the return
of children on its own merits, and issue a final decision, whether to
return the child or not, and further, the directive orders that the
Church must never under any circumstances *respond to official Jewish*
enquiries in writing. Secrecy *and* mystery *are the underpinnings of the*
ideology of the Catholic Church, writes Morelli. *Since the document*
which I stumbled upon is a legal Church document written in the spirit
of the general principles of the Catholic Church and its policies, and
since this document actually forbids *the return of children to their legal*
parents, and as such is approved by the highest Church authority, Pope
Pius XII himself, one can assume, writes Morelli, *that the order was*
to be implemented throughout Europe. After this discovery, of course,
Morelli continues, *the canonization of Pius XII, about which so much*
has been written and said these past few months, is now in question.
My colleagues, journalists and historians, writes Morelli, *but also*
some institutions, he writes, *are asking the Vatican to establish a fully*
autonomous international commission, which they will finance in full,
to establish a commission staffed with historians, ecclesiastical officials
and forensic experts in order to ascertain how many *European children*
the Church kidnapped. *Some estimates posit the number as high as*
eight thousand. The commission would have to have free access to
all *Church institutions,* writes Morelli, *and complete access to* all
documents. But, writes Morelli, *the diaries of Angelo Giuseppe Roncalli,*

Pope John XXIII, are soon to be published, and it may be possible to learn more regarding this question, the question of the children kidnapped all over Europe. I am appalled at the language in which this document-decree is couched, my friend Leo Levi, president of the Union of Italian Jewish Communities, tells me, writes Morelli, *because this document is addressing a serious question, a very painful question, in a manner that is utterly bureaucratic, as Leo Levi tells me,* writes Alfonso Morelli. *This document makes no mention of the extraordinary historical circumstances under which the Catholicization of Jewish children went on, circumstances in which all these children came under the protection of the Catholic Church, Leo says,* Morelli writes. *In this directive the Holocaust, which is what led to the baptizing of the Jewish children,* in this decree, *the Holocaust is never mentioned, Leo Levi says. And furthermore, when the document, or better yet – directive – was written in October 1946, memory of the liberating of Auschwitz was still fresh, Auschwitz had been liberated only a few months before this high-level Church decree was penned, but in it, in this decree, Auschwitz is never mentioned, nor is the Holocaust, Leo Levi says,* writes Alfonso Morelli. *However,* writes Alfonso Morelli in *Corriere della Sera* on 28 December, 2005, *we still don't know how far Roncalli and other Church functionaries went in implementing the Vatican directive, since all documents pertaining to Church policy are* sequestered *either in the Vatican archives or in the archives of national churches. It is known,* writes Morelli, *that at the time of the war many children found shelter in Catholic monasteries, in boarding schools and in schools, but* not at the behest of the Pope, writes Morelli. *It is well known that after the war the Jews who survived had serious difficulties locating their children,* retrieving *their children from Catholic institutions,* writes Morelli, *but until now it was only possible to* surmise *that the Church was systematically* stealing *Jewish children in order to indulge Jesus. For sixty years the Church and its "servants" have been striving to prove to the world that they have no blemish on their conscience for their activities as far as World War Two is concerned,* writes Morelli. *For sixty years the Church has been trying to prove the innocence of Pope Pius XII and many of his bishops and priests. If there is anything that has been preserved with dedication and* faith, *anything that has been* sacrosanct *in the church books, then it is the dates of baptisms and deaths*, writes Morelli, *so it wouldn't be difficult to ascertain what happened to the baptized Jewish children. If Switzerland, so-called* neutral *Switzerland, has mustered the strength to set up the Bergier Commission, the I.C.E. – an independent commission of experts – though only on 12 December, 1996*, writes Alfonso Morelli, *to prove the ties between the Nazi regime and the Swiss banks who had at their disposal vast quantities of stolen Jewish property; if Australia has spoken out about the children kidnapped by their authorities,* stolen *from Aborigines during World War One*, writes Morelli, *then instead of obscuring history, the Catholic Church can get off its arse and throw open its archives. And not only that*, writes Morelli. *It is time for the Church to stop pretending, to stop lying about how its greatest crime during the war was* inadequate involvement *in saving Jews*, writes Morelli, *it is time for the Church to stop believing that it is enough for it to launch* anaemic *apologies for its* "inadvertent" *lapses, these ecclesiastical apologies, which are becoming more and more revolting over time, truly disgusting, insipid*, writes Alfonso Morelli, *because*, he writes, *it is reasonable to deduce that this letter written to Cardinal Roncalli is not the* only *incriminating document hidden in the vast* secret *archives of the Catholic Church. We are hopeful it has become clear by now*, writes Morelli, *that the Church should slow things down a bit as far as the panicked, nearly hysterical race to beatify, canonize, whatever, Pius XII, who, ah, now this is something that is widely known*, writes Morelli, *was at the head of a Church which was openly championing anti-Semitism at a time when the Nazis and Fascists were persecuting and murdering Jews on a grand scale. He, Pius XII, led a Church in which many German priests abused church birth registers in order to help the Nazis determine who should be first to wear a yellow star – and then be killed, and some German priests kept right on doing this* officially for an entire decade after the Holocaust ended, *in order to convince those Jews once and for all that they were guilty of murdering Christ. Just as a reminder*, writes Morelli, *the* "Reichskonkordat", *a concordat signed on 20 July, 1933, between the*

Holy See and the Reich, is in force in Germany to this day. During that time, Eugenio Cardinal Pacelli, the future Pope Pius XII, is Secretary of the Vatican, and he is the one who signs this concordat, while Cardinal Michael von Faulhaber, writes Morelli, *in a sermon given in Munich in 1937, says, "Now, when the leaders of the greatest world nations observe the rise of the new Germany with a dose of reservation and much scepticism, the Catholic Church, this greatest moral force on earth, is showing its trust in the new German authorities through this concordat, which is an act of vast significance, because it contributes to the strengthening of the renown of the new authorities throughout the world," says Faulhaber,* writes Morelli. *Abe Foxman tells me,* continues Morelli, *and Foxman is director of the Anti-Defamation League,* writes Morelli, *that they placed him, Foxman, with a Polish family and his nanny had him* secretly *baptized, and later there were terrible problems, all sorts of complications, before he was returned to his parents. I believe that today there are tens of thousands of Jewish children in the world who were saved and then baptized, Abraham Foxman tells me,* writes Alfonso Morelli, *children who do not know to this day of their origins, nor will they ever learn of them, says Foxman,* writes Morelli.

When I was young I used to go mountain climbing, Aurelia says. *Mountaineering is good for breathing. And it fortifies the will,* Aurelia says.

In the coordinate system the parabola may hold an interesting position, Haya says. *The ordinates of a parabola may be positive, plus and negative, minus, if the sign of the derivative of the parabola is only positive or only negative in a neighbourhood, then no extreme values can exist in that neighbourhood. Don't mention mountaineering, that mountain discipline,* Haya says. *I do not like disciplines. I don't even like cycling anymore.*

The days do not unfurl, but neither do they trip over one another. Strangely, Haya does not get ill. Haya is a hale old woman. A small dental bridge with the upper-right first and second molars, (the other teeth are hers); cataract surgery on both eyes; her gall bladder removed; mild bronchial asthma (in spite of which she continues to smoke some fifteen cigarettes a day); a fractured tibia thirty years ago – that would be it. Of course, the functions of her body are slowed, diminished and brief, and a nasty itch plagues her in the early evenings: lower arm, upper arm, the left lower arm, then the right, Haya scratches and scratches and scratches, she holds her arms under a stream of cold water and looks, aghast, at the tracks of her fingernails on her thin, dry skin. *Am I disappearing?* she asks. Her sleep is light, her bloodflow inaudible, the beats of her heart short, like her steps; her vision and her dreams, yes, her dreams, are melting; only Haya's wait grows and she is frightened that this wait of hers will spill over into nothing; that it will drain away, that soon it will whisper to her *I am the wait that got tired, I am your lifeless wait and I'm off now, ciao.*

HURRY UP PLEASE IT'S TIME

Though she has had a computer for fifteen years now, Haya uses the Internet at the city library, it costs less. *It's all so simple, this Internet,* Haya says to the librarians, who are surprised; she cannot see why the librarians are surprised. And so, three times a week, from eight to ten at the city library, Haya reads the newspapers on the Internet (mostly German, Italian and Slovenian), and sends letters to the International Red Cross, the Italian Red Cross, to the state and city and tracing services at home and abroad. Slightly hunched, bent at the waist, petite, grey-haired, with spectacles perched on the tip of her nose, her lips pursed and her chin held high, she peers at the monitor as if looking for spots to wipe away with a moistened finger. But they can't be wiped away. What she comes up with, what she sees while she writes her electronic missives to known and unknown witnesses scattered around the world, to the tracers who are like truffle-hunting dogs, like burrowers through the past, becoming one herself, a bloodhound riffling through the rubbish heap of time, are nothing but gleams of lives among which is hers, gleams reduced to embers under the ashes of which writhe small truths, no longer needed by or essential to anyone. And, while Haya taps at the keys, Gorizia whispers *Crazy Haya*. And Haya asks, *Is it time?*

In June 2006 Haya is visited (after all) by a little dream, a quiet dream, so small and so quiet that Haya barely recognizes it.

on the street, barefoot and in the dark, haya goes to a public toilet. the floor of the toilet is awash with urine and faeces, she has nowhere to go, behind her the ground is caving in. to get to the toilet seat, haya wades through the excrement and stares at her belly, which swells before her eyes. i am calm, she says, although no-one knows who the father is, she says. later, haya returns to an old abandoned flat, then a man with a camera around his neck runs in to the flat and says: i am a spy. it is alright, i am pregnant, haya says, i'll lean on your chest, she says. light brown freckles come out on her temples and forehead. ada springs up from somewhere, all dripping in urine. haya says, mama, now we look alike, but ada only smiles and jerks her head. then ada says, here, haya, read this. on a page torn from pravda *are written the words,* józsef nagy: *"the truth is hard to find"*

On Monday, 3 July, 2006, Haya receives a letter from the International Red Cross, or rather the International Tracing Service (I.T.S.) in Bad Arolsen. This letter, as Haya realizes immediately, is not a Christmas or New Year's card, because it is not winter but summer. The Red Cross, in fact their tracing service, in fact Mrs Helga Mathias, who signs the report, informs her that a copy has been found in Bad Arolsen of a baptism certificate which matches the one Haya sent them with a black-and-white photograph of an infant, on 2 February, 1946, asking for their help in finding her son Antonio Tedeschi, born 31 October, 1944, in Görz, then part of the Adriatisches Küstenland, within the borders of the Third Reich. Helga Mathias writes that in this letter Haya describes how her son Antonio Tedeschi disappeared on 13 April, 1945, but Haya cannot grasp why Mrs Helga Mathias is repeating what Haya wrote sixty years before, because Haya remembers every word of what she wrote to the International Tracing Service sixty years before; after all, children do not go missing every day, the disappearance of children is not such a commonplace event. The disappearance (of children) is something one remembers for a lifetime, isn't it? *Despite the fact that the baptism certificate is incomplete*, writes Helga Mathias, *and as the mother of the child, Haya Tedeschi, which we are assuming to be you, was not wed to the father of the child, S.S.-Untersturmführer Franz Kurt, born on 17 January, 1914, in Düsseldorf, we gave your petition serious consideration*, writes Helga Mathias from the International Tracing Service in Bad Arolsen. Helga Mathias adds that the petition was in a misplaced box with documents, untypically preserved, about the *secret Lebensborn* project, with it a letter from Father Carlo Baubela from Görz, today Gorizia, who baptized the child and then handed a copy of the document about the birth of Haya's son to an unknown person, and that with the letter from Carlo Baubela they found an *official order* from the Central Office of Reich Security under the supervision of the Ministry for Internal Affairs in Berlin (Reichssicherheitshauptamt, or R.S.H.A.), signed by Heinrich Himmler, Reichsführer-S.S. and Minister, who was in charge of the Ministry at the time. *Apparently, according to Heinrich Himmler's directive*, writes Helga Mathias, *"a male child of Aryan descent, with the temporary name of Antonio Tedeschi is to be sent to Schloss Oberweis near the town of Gmunden, region of Traunsee, in the former Austria"*. *Since most of the files holding documentation from most of the* Lebensborn *homes throughout the former Third Reich were destroyed just before the capitulation of Germany*, Helga Mathias writes, *it is highly unlikely that we will find any information pertaining to Schloss Oberweis. For now we are assuming that your son was given up for adoption to a German or Austrian family, and that his name was changed at the time. For additional information,* writes Helga Mathias, *please contact the Red Cross of your country at CROCE ROSSA ITALIANA, Servizio Affari Internazionali, Ufficio Ricerche, Via Toscana 12, 00187 Roma.*

For sixty-two years she has been waiting.

If she knew how to pray, Haya would now say to the sky:

Thou bringest all who are dispersed by war
The sheep thou bringest home, to rest:
the child thou bringest to the mother's breast.

but Haya does not know how to pray,

> *O Lord Thou pluckest me out*
> *O Lord Thou pluckest*

so all she says is

HURRY UP PLEASE IT'S TIME

Haya sits and rocks by a tall window in a room on the third floor of a building from the time of Austria-Hungary in the old part of Old Gorizia. The rocking chair is old and as she rocks, it whimpers.

Is that the chair whimpering or is it me? she asks the deep emptiness, while she turns over the letter from Helga Mathias, and lying around her everywhere are lives which have dropped like old L.P.s that have played what they have to play. Photographs, papers, posters, letters and little objects from which oozes a thick, sticky silence. And the sole remaining snapshot, cracked, on which the infant Antonio Tedeschi's face is fractured, as if in a broken mirror.

Then Haya says, *The red basket is empty. I have cleared out the years. I see the bottom.*

Space has turned into time – Zum Raum wird hier die Zeit. *Oh, daughters of the Soča, the essence of reality lies in its multiplicity. Every* *convergent series is limited. The number **a** is the limes, the border value of the function **f** when **x** tends toward **a**, lim (**x**) = A, oh yes.*

> *What are the roots that clutch, what branches grow*
> *Out of this stony rubbish? Daughter of woman,*
> *You cannot say, or guess, for you know only*
> *A heap of broken images . . .*

Yes, a heap of broken images.

So, Don Baubela did not keep his word. He betrayed Haya's secret; which may turn out to have been for the best in the end, which may have pointed to a trace, which may have contributed to the end of the story. For sixty-two years Haya Tedeschi has been waiting.

On Via Aprica, where until recently there was a butcher's shop, a café bar called Joy has opened facing the building in which Haya lives. *What a coincidence*, Haya says, while through the window she sees the first guests nibble at their *antipasti* with slivers of salmon and beads of black caviar. Her stationery shop Gioia, this café Joy, the letter from Mrs Helga Mathias, as if the path is narrowing as it approaches the jumping-off point from which a person vanishes.

haya is riding a bicycle through the woods. the green leaves shine so brightly that beams bounce off them and penetrate her skin, crawl under her eyelids and pour over her ageing organs, wrap them in the fragrance of the soča. the wheels spin ever faster, her eyes fill with wind, a strange song floats in her head, a chorale soft and sunny. what a stupid song, says haya, angels don't exist. she keeps missing the pedals, a fist in haya's breast tightens while she clutches the handlebars, the path is white and uneven, the wheels spin quickly, quicker and quicker. haya lets go of the handlebars, haya flings her arms open in the wood, lifts her feet from the pedals, spreads her legs towards the woods, raises her head to the sky, flies, she flies through the rhomboid images of a kaleidoscope. there in the corner, squinting through this cardboard box of interwoven charms, haya sees her life as it crouches and waits, as it stares at her with dry, wide-open (lidless) eyes. commotion, in her head commotion.

via aprica narrows to a glowing arrow. the arrow flies and embeds itself
in Haya's eye, turns into a tiny globe reflecting the sign: Joy

Those roads were echoes and footsteps,
women, men, agonies, resurrections,
days and nights,
half dreams and dreams,
every obscure instant of yesterday
and of the world's yesterdays,
the firm sword of the Dane and the moon of the Persian,
the deeds of the dead,
shared love, words,
Emerson and snow and so many things.
Now I can forget them. I reach my centre,
my algebra and my key,
my mirror.
Soon I will know who I am.
I squeeze shut my lidless eyes
and wait.

HURRY UP PLEASE IT'S TIME

On Friday, 30 June, 2006, I leave Salzburg for Gorizia.

It is night. The train glides along, lit from the inside and nearly empty. I move through the black silence, through the fragrance of summer, through a silence which envelops itself, which pours slowly and lazily across the earth and sky, everywhere around us.

A woman sits opposite me, smiling as she looks out the window into the dense nothing glued to the windowpane, into a breath that sways behind us, which follows us like a wind-borne shroud. *Going to Gorizia?* the woman asks me. *Why?*

I say nothing.

The woman has on heavy shoes, winter shoes, she is wearing them on bare feet with no laces. The woman has firm hands, thick hair, black, and she's about forty. There is neglect on her face.

I have four voices I recognize, the woman says, *three which are someone else's and one which is mine.*

Oh, I want to say, just don't speak of voices, not of voices.

Now my voices are quiet, the woman says, *so we can talk*, she says, but I don't feel like talking, in my lungs, like colourful ribbons, *my* voices are dancing mischievously, thin, wheezy and cacophonic voices, which clench my breathing, and I feel like beating myself hysterically on the chest in order to dislodge these intruders and send them fluttering off into the night. *I am not in the mood to talk*, I say.

Are you originally *from Gorizia?* continues the woman, as if she doesn't hear what I am saying, and I tell her I don't know. *I don't know*, I say to the woman who is sitting opposite me and travelling with me to Gorizia and who irritates me, because I don't want to talk, I don't feel like talking, and this woman keeps asking, she keeps asking, *It remains to be seen whether I am from Gorizia or not*, I tell the woman, and she goes on as if I hadn't said a word. *If you are from Gorizia*, she says, *I may know you. Many people in Gorizia know each other*, and I tell her that I doubt it, that I truly doubt our paths have ever crossed anywhere, at any time. *I doubt it*, I say, and she concludes philosophically, *Reality is intertwined and boundless, reality is indivisible like my voices. And coincidences are rare*, says that woman on the train to me. *Reality is a skein that knits us in, entangles us*, says this woman who is bothering me by this time, and then, thank goodness, we arrive in Gorizia and I bid her goodbye.

I stay at the Palace Hotel at Corso Italia 63, for 31 euros a night. The row of trees my window looks out on is dense and deeply green. I ask them to bring to my room a portion of *gubana goriziana* and a bottle of Picolit. I will lie in the half-dark and caress the golden-yellow thickness with my tongue, the fragrant heft of that discreetly chilled, discreetly dignified Picolit, which they bring me, this is what I have in mind. The taste and fragrance of dried figs, honey, vanilla, wild flowers, peaches, acacia, red and black berries, the warmth and softness of dry-sweet acidity, the tartness of the little oak barrels in which the hundred-year-old fragrance of the Gorizia forests will course through my body, slide to the tips of my toes and back into my breath, to the depth of my eye sockets in which waters of the past are sloshing like blurry mirrors with portraits of my unknown ancestors. Picolit is a miraculous wine. One shouldn't drink it frequently. Picolit is a delicate wine, a wine of the European nobility, the exclusive nectar of meditation, always produced in small quantities. Picolit is an ancient wine born during the Roman Empire, and it preserves its history in the records of Antonio Zanoni from 1767. I know all sorts of facts about Picolit, a heap of useless details. Later, Picolit imparts serenity and a quiet joy to the already peaceful aristocracy of Germany, France and England. Picolit is an ever-changing but perfect symphony, a unique jewel, which will bring me, I believe soundlessly, painlessly now, after such a long wait, to the scarred past, mine and that of my family, so alien to me. Picolit must be imbibed in solitude, because Picolit is made by courageous vintners for refined palates. So much for Picolit.

My name is Hans Traube.

I was born in Salzburg on 1 October, 1944.

All my documents say my name is Hans Traube, and they say I was born in Salzburg on 1 October, 1944. When someone says "Hans", I look up. That's what I've always been called: Hans. Ever since I can remember people have called me Hans. People I know well and people I do not know well call me Hans, for myself I am Hans, too, who else could I be but Hans, when I botch something, I say, *Oh, Hans, Hans, what a mess you've made.*

Oh, Hans, Hans, my mother said to me on her deathbed *once you were called Antonio.*

Ever since then, since the moment my mother Martha Traube moaned *Oh Hans, Hans,* and that was on 20 April, 1998, I have been searching, looking for this Antonio who has been lost, but who isn't lost, who was in hiding for half a century, yet he wasn't – all the while this Antonio has been crouching inside me watching, breathing with me yet listening to me breathe, dreaming with me while stealing my dreams, and I knew nothing about it until my mother Martha Traube, as she was dying, said, *Oh Hans, you were born Antonio.*

In Gorizia the search is over. After eight years *I think* the search is over. *I believe* I know the essential facts of my life, and since these essential facts are now known to me, *I am convinced* they will no longer matter, they will soon become *completely unimportant and unnecessary* facts, all those details I have been researching like a lunatic for eight years, digging frantically through archives in a number of cities, in a number of countries, examining countless details, now I see – utterly pointless details, that is why I actually *know* that soon, just as Thomas (Bernhard) said when I last photographed him in 1988, I believe I will say, *Servus, now nothing matters.*

I photographed Thomas in Gmunden, where he was living at the time, and where he died soon after we took some wonderful pictures of him, Thomas, and of Gmunden with the places where Thomas often walked. I am a professional photographer. I work for magazines and exhibit all over the world. Sometimes I write. That is why I went to Gmunden. Gmunden is a little town. It has about 13,000 inhabitants and very fresh air; since 1862 Gmunden has been known as a *Luftbad*. Today Gmunden is a tourist town through which tourists stroll in packs, passing thus by Bernhard's house, too, though most of them who pass by his house have no idea who Bernhard is and probably will never read what he has written. Gmunden is located in a charming spot, on the northern shore of Traunsee, surrounded by woods. Today Gmunden also has a hospital, a small theatre, an observatory and the oldest electric tram in Austria (introduced in 1894). There are several secondary vocational schools in Gmunden, two gymnasiums and a *Mädchenpensionat* for the Sisters of the Holy Cross. Pottery from Gmunden is valued highly, as is Gmunden porcelain. Gmunden has several baroque and Gothic churches and monasteries and an interesting cemetery.

There are many paper mills in this area, Bernhard told me, *and thus a lot of cripples because of the machines,* he told me, *which cut off their fingers or arms, or even their ears.*

We walked by Schloss Oberweis and I took several pictures of the *charming building,* as Thomas called it, owned at one time by a Jewish family which disappeared, *and today Oberweis is once again in private hands,* Bernhard said, *and it is* inaccessible, he stressed, though  this did not upset me, because I had no inclination to go inside anyway. *Unlike Schloss Oberweis, which was designed to be grandiose,* Bernhard said, *my farmstead here was an ordinary barn, nothing but a ruin, rotten and in a state of utter decay, but I liked that, I liked bringing such a rotten state into some sort of acceptable order,* he said, *so I decided to* restore *this ruin as much as that was possible, although it remains questionable to what degree fundamental rot can be fully salvaged. I did all this with a man whose name was Ferdl and whom we buried the day before yesterday,* said Bernhard then, in 1988. *Ferdl was my dearest friend here,* he said. *A small, gaunt old man,* he said, *who died the day before yesterday of stomach cancer. For two years Ferdl had been saying: "Something's eating me up, something from* inside," said Thomas, *so one day I'll write a book called* Ferdl, he said.

From a polite distance we looked at that castle, that Schloss Oberweis, a large two-storey building surrounded by a well-tended lawn, surrounded by what are actually *fields* of dense, impassable grass, by what is actually a park with a fish pond. Why Bernhard didn't tell me then, in 1988, the most important fact about Schloss Oberweis, I don't know, but I suppose everything has its time and place. He said, *It became apparent long ago that what they taught us was a deception. I couldn't penetrate before into the everyday, lethal game of existence, I didn't have the spiritual or physical wherewithal to do that, but today the mechanism moves forward on its own,* he said. *This is a daily alignment, a tidying of the mind: every day every thing must be set in its place,* he said. And then, ten years later, when my mother Martha Traube said, as she was dying, *We took you from Oberweis,* I watched that lethal game of existence begin, I saw *my* game of existence begin, how just as it began, this game of my existence, it started moving in a downward trajectory towards its end. I watched how the mechanism sets itself in motion and how my life, of its own volition, is sliding into a one-way current, as if willingly heading for the gallows; how before it becomes extinct it is setting itself to rights, sprucing itself up, as if *closing* at one moment and *opening* the next like a fluttering figure of origami.

I sat in my hotel room in Gorizia surrounded by papers, archival documents, letters, photocopies, photographs, books, everything I had amassed over the eight years of searching and once again I arranged and rearranged my treasures, leafed through them, *read* them, repeated the facts as if I were preparing for an operation after which I would *see* once again. But games with eyes are deceptive games. The eye is a soft organ, which sees and does not see, depending on how you look at it. The eye is a sensitive organ, it wells often with tears; when it rebels, it calms quickly, it darkens, as if to say *I won't watch*; it succumbs without a struggle to external and internal pressures, moreover the eye is easily destroyed and is particularly attractive for certain animals, which like to feed on it, on the eye, who knows why. There was once a woman whose eye was operated on and she convalesced in hospital with a bandage over the *operated eye. This eye that you operated itches me terribly*, said the woman to the doctors, but the doctors ignored her. The woman complained so bitterly – more each day, not only of the itch, but of unbearable pain – that the doctors decided to remove the bandage and inspect her eye. When they *uncovered the woman's eye* they saw that the eye had become totally dead and useless, because inside it an *ant colony* had made a big hole and from the hole the ants were streaming out and crawling all over the woman's face. Another woman complained of terrible headaches for months, but doctors found no medical anomalies. In the end she went to have her eyes examined. In one of her eyes medical experts discovered a twenty-centimetre-long worm that had coiled around her eyeball and was poised to *enter* the eye. The doctors drew the worm out of the woman's head slowly and cautiously, so her eye wouldn't be damaged, but the eye was already dead. I cannot say whether it is a coincidence that the victims of predators, which are largely benevolent, tame and docile creatures, not usually *ocular predators*, are in harmony with their natural environment, part of Nature, close to the ground, I cannot say whether it is a coincidence that the victims were women, or rather women's eyes. Perhaps these horrors could have happened to two *men's* eyes and may well have, but this is how the stories go.

Schloss Oberweis was called Alpenland between 1943 and 1945, and children lived there, mostly small children, mostly children who had been stolen, mostly, I later learned, children stolen from Yugoslavia and the Adriatisches Küstenland. At Alpenland, at Schloss Oberweis, that is, there were also children from Poland, but these were merely a *vestige* of stolen Polish children, because about 250,000 stolen children had already been placed in some twenty *Lebensborn* homes throughout the Reich, and in the General Government, of course, in Cracow, in Otwock and in Warsaw, from where the little blonde, blue-eyed Poles were sent for brainwashing to the hell of total Germanization, for adoption with trusted Aryan families or – if these stolen children did not meet the strict selection criteria – they were shipped off to concentration camps for lethal injections by Himmler's tried and true physicians.

I grew up the way most children do, in an ordinary, routine and relatively boring way. Of course, the details of the big Third Reich *secret*, of the population project designed to boost and spread the *Übermensch* species, of that *Lebensborn* plan, I learned only once I'd begun researching, and I started my research after that (then) devastating sentence from my mother, Martha Traube, *I did not give birth to you.* My father Jürgen Traube was already dead when Martha Traube said, *Now I'll tell you everything I know,* but it turned out that she knew very little, that she actually knew nothing, or pretended to know so little about me, about Austria, about the war, about the Nazis, because the war and post-war doubts of my parents Martha and Jürgen Traube (if they entertained any) ended in 1946. I knew I had a brother named Gottfried, Jürgen and Martha Traube's son, because there was always talk of Gottfried in the house, while almost nothing was said of the war and National Socialism, at least not by the time I was old enough to remember such conversations. Gottfried had been killed as a soldier of the Wehrmacht on 24 November, 1942, at Stalingrad, when he was not yet twenty. The album with Gottfried's photographs, a reliquary, lay in a small niche by the living-room window and I leafed through it, especially during my childhood, and whenever I leafed through it I'd ask my mother Martha, *Where am I when I was little?* Mama Martha would say, *We lost one of the albums when we moved here, the album with your baby pictures taken before the pictures in this album which, as you see,* wasn't *misplaced,* and then I looked at myself in the second album in which I was already eight months old on the first page and sitting up. *The war was nearly over*, Martha said on her deathbed, *and the Oberweis home was about to close. At Alpenland they told us that your father had been killed somewhere in the Adriatisches Küstenland*, Martha said, *that your birth mother died when partisan bands bombed Casa Germanica in Trieste*, she said, *and that German troops found you at a nursery for German children which was reduced to rubble. You can be sure, they told us at the Salzburg Lebensborn, this is a child of German blood, they said, although we hadn't asked. You see, they told us at Schloss Oberweis, see how blonde and blue-eyed the child is and how tall for his age, they told us*, Martha said, *and besides, the child was examined thoroughly at the Race and Settlement Office, R.u.S.H.A., so there could be no doubt, they said. Everything happened at lightning speed. Our petition for adoption had been waiting for six months at the Salzburg Lebensborn, but then they called from Oberweis on 21 April, 1945. Come right over, they said, we have a child. The next day we wrote to R.u.S.H.A. in Salzburg. We asked them whether they had any new information regarding your background. Herr Obersteiner answered us personally. Herr Obersteiner was the chief of police and a high-ranking S.S. official of the Salzburg R.u.S.H.A. office*, Martha said. *Here is the document. Look, on 27 April Herr Obersteiner writes, We still have no reliable information on the background of your child, so we ask for your patience. We are hard at work on this case, writes Herr Obersteiner. We will contact you as soon as we have relevant information regarding the child. I hope your little Hans will bring much joy to your lives. See here? Herr Obersteiner writes*, Martha said. *We had no word from them after that. On 4 May the Americans enter Salzburg and immediately bomb Hitler's "nest", Berchtesgaden, chaos erupts. Thousands and thousands of Nazis from Germany pour into town and shout, Don't you worry, in two weeks' time victory will be ours! Still, they strip off their uniforms and in worn* Lederhosen, *carrying rucksacks, they leave to yodel in the fresh mountain air. Pitiful phantoms wander the streets, Germans and Austrians dressed in weird combinations of grimy, tattered uniforms of the Hungarian, Czech, Yugoslav and Italian armies, in the hope of saving their skin. The Salzburg Nazi government slinks off into the underground, burns documents, steals supplies of food and weapons, and flees. And we didn't care*, Martha said as she was dying, *we only wanted a little Gottfried and that was that*, Martha said. *They didn't send us anything, any documents, because the home at Oberweis was closed soon after that and the children vanished. Where they went to I don't know*, Martha said. *When they handed you to us on 21 April, 1945, at Schloss Oberweis they said, Here is a new birth certificate, an absolutely valid birth certificate, a government birth certificate, they said, and on it we will write your last name and your child's name. Hans, you say? they asked. So that's it, Hans*, repeated Martha as she was dying. *For many years, Hans*, Martha also said, *this unspoken truth has been eating me up. From inside*, she said.

Just like Ferdl, I said.

There was always chocolate in the house. There were chocolate balls and chocolate bars even when there was no meat, because my father Jürgen Traube worked first at the Café-Konditorei Fürst in Alter Markt, at Brodgrasse 13, where Paul Fürst began making his *echte Salzburger Mozartkugeln* by hand, where manufacture by hand continues to this day. Later, when Mirabell splits off from Rajsigl, a famous Salzburg chocolate factory, and Fürst builds his own plant in Grödig near Salzburg, Jürgen Traube works in the sales department at Hauptstrasse 14 and still brings home *Mozartkugeln*, which Mirabell may not have made by hand, but they were still authentic. So, probably for lack of other stories, *Mozartkugeln* and their authentic production by hand became, aside from Gottfried, the foundation of our family life.

Former chocolate magnate Felix Rosenzweig propels Jürgen into the chocolate industry in the late 1950s. Felix Rosenzweig is one of the pre-war owners of Rajsigl and Hofbauer and he flees Austria in 1939, only to return in 1950 with nothing but the shirt on his back, yet nevertheless alive and with some of his connections and company shares awaiting him, confiscated, in the vaults of Swiss banks. Felix Rosenzweig brings his wife Isabella Fischer with him to Salzburg, and she opens a small photography studio with a darkroom on the ground floor of a building that had originally been owned by the Rosenzweigs, but was confiscated in 1940, and, with the approval of the regime, some suitable people had moved in during the war. These same people generously rent Felix Rosenzweig his own premises in 1950, so that he can set up the photography "salon" for his wife Isabella Fischer, and for the whole time the civil court suits are going on, dealing with the (partial) return of Felix Rosenzweig's property to Felix Rosenzweig, these people collect rent for Isabella's photography salon. The reinstatement of the Rosenzweig family property to its members takes an unreasonably long time, partly because the *other members* of the Rosenzweig family who are holders of this property never show up, because, it seems, they are no longer around, and at that point, in 1950, it is difficult to prove where and how they met their end, because then (and even later, and even, to some degree, today) the Austrians stubbornly insist that they were the first victims of Nazism and that they haven't a clue about anything, all they know about is their own losses, their own victims, their own vast suffering. My parents Martha and Jürgen Traube offer Felix Rosenzweig and Isabella Fischer (Rosenzweig by marriage) a small flat in the attic of the building where we live, until they find their feet, and are surprised and almost offended that Felix and Isabella bring up their Jewish background. *Nonsense*, Jürgen Traube says, *Jews are people, too.*

I develop my first photographs as an elementary school student in the back room, in the makeshift darkroom of the Isabella Photo Studio, following the instructions and advice of its proprietress, Isabella, who tells me war stories, always in a whisper. While my parents seem to know nothing of the war, for Isabella the war never seems to have ended. Felix Rosenzweig dies in 1978, and Isabella leaves Austria and moves to Yugoslavia, to the little port of Rijeka. Why, for what reason, she never says, though I visit her at least once a year until 2000, when I learn that she has hanged herself in the attic of a building near the train station. My father Jürgen Traube, as set out in Felix Rosenzweig's will, was "to send a quantity of chocolate truffles to Isabella on a regular basis, no matter where she was living, and if he, Jürgen Traube, should die before Isabella, then his son, Hans Traube, will assume responsibility for supplying the truffles". So after my father dies in 1980 I send Isabella Fischer chocolates in numerous shapes and sizes made by the most famous chocolatiers. I send her confections from Manner, Lindt, Droste, Suchard, Nestlé, Milka, Neuhaus, Cardullos, La Patisserie, Asbach/Reber, Biffar (the only selection of candied fruit – the rest were all chocolates), Hacher, Underberg. I discover there are truffle balls called *Joy of Life* and *Karl Marx Kugeln*, so I send Isabella those, too. The most expensive chocolate truffles are, of course, the Austrian ones from Salzburg. By sending them I hope to delight Isabella. They are Strauss balls, actually praline cubes, and *Constance und Amadeus* balls by Reber, also previously co-owned by Felix Rosenzweig. I mention Isabella Fischer, because she is a source of key information about my possible origins.

"*Lebensborn*" means fount of life. As a registered society (Lebensborn Eingetragener Verein) *Lebensborn* grew into a *secret* Third Reich project for preserving the racial purity of the German nation. It was S.S.-Reichsführer Heinrich Himmler who designed the project and brought it to life. A shy and sensitive, restrained and modest man, not tall, he rather resembled a subservient, pedantic bank clerk than the head of the state police. Himmler suffered from migraines and stomach cramps, and nearly fainted when they killed some one hundred Jews in his honour at the Russian front. That was when he called for the use of "more humane methods" of execution, which meant introducing gas into special chambers fitted with showers.

For many, *Lebensborn* ended in a nightmare; some came out of *Lebensborn* decapitated, cloned. Founded in 1935, the Lebensborn Project was designed at first to care for "racially and biologically quintessential" pregnant women, who would give birth to racially and biologically quintessential sons of the homeland, perfect stallions at least one metre eighty centimetres tall, blonde and blue-eyed, muscles bulging, and sleek, disciplined Spartans.

There are absolute and unquestionable principles which every S.S.

man must uphold, shrieks Himmler before his companions in Poznan in 1943. *One basic principle must be an absolute rule for S.S. men: we must be honest, decent, loyal and comradely to members of our own blood and to nobody else. What happens to a Russian, to a Czech, does not interest me in the slightest. What other nations can offer in the way of good blood of our type, we will take, if necessary, by kidnapping their children and raising them here with us. Whether nations live in prosperity or starve to death interests me only so far as we need them as slaves for our culture; otherwise, this is of no interest to me. Remember, we will be unfeeling and rough only as much as this is necessary. We Germans are the only people in the world who treat animals decently, and we will treat this human animal kind courteously and humanely.*

Himmler opens the first *Lebensborn* home in Steinhöring near Munich in August 1936. At Steinhöring certified Aryan women can give birth to their illegal children *in secrecy*, most of them hand their children over to the S.S. officials after shedding a few tears, or simply abandon them. The children who are ill, who are mental or physical invalids, are sent off to the paediatric ward of the Leander Institut at Brandenburg-Gorden near Berlin, where under the guidance of Dr Hans Heinz, "expert in child euthanasia", they are first *killed*, and then their brains are *examined*.

I was born at Steinhöring, Olaf told me. I met Olaf at one of the meetings to which people go looking for their lives. First they seek themselves, then they seek forgiveness for the sins of their fathers. Confused and angry people attend these meetings. The descendants of well-known and not so well-known Nazis attend, as do the descendants of those who disappeared in concentration camps. At these meetings the Nazi descendants vomit up hatred and impotence; they excavate long years of silence, feelings of guilt and a plea for forgiveness which ends in unthinkable embraces and timid friendships. At these meetings people try to heal wounds that, like cancer, invisibly take over the body and eat it from *inside*. These meetings are interesting meetings. Those who do not go to such meetings write books.

I was born at Steinhöring in 1942, said Olaf, who is taller than I am, and I am quite tall, 190 centimetres. *I was very good looking*, he said.

I was good looking, too, I said. When we stand next to each other, it's as if we've stepped down off a macho billboard, as if we were Hollywood actors, although both of us are greying.

If Hitler were alive, Olaf said, *he would be pleased. I was one of the 2,800 babies born at Steinhöring*, he said, *at the Hitler-Himmler fertility clinic, at the breeding ground of Nazi Aryans*, he said. *I haven't told anyone about this*, Olaf said at the meeting. *At school they didn't teach us about* Lebensborn. *It was never mentioned. When I turned five my mother told me I was special*, Olaf said. *You are absolutely exceptional, she said. You are Hitler's boy, and as Hitler's boy you were born at a special clinic, my mother told me*, Olaf said. *I worked at the hospital, she said. I asked for a job at the hospital so I could serve the Third Reich, my mother told me*, Olaf said. *I was a member of the Nazi Party. I was an aide to a very powerful man and I always wore the party badge on my chest, my mother said, and to this day I am a believer, and I will remain a Nazi until the day I die, my mother said. She died in 1976*, Olaf said. *And my father stayed a fervent Nazi to his death*, Olaf said. *They were both attractive, my mother and my father, but they didn't live together. I saw my father only a dozen times. The Nazis had guards around the hospital, my mother said, because the local people of Steinhöring threw stones at the women from the centre and called them whores, she said. But we were serving Germany and Hitler, she told me*, Olaf said. *My mother hit me whenever I cried. Stand up straight! she shouted. Straighten up! You are a soldier of the homeland! One day you will rule the world! she said. The more she loved Nazism, the more I despised it. It's a lucky thing that her dreams did not come true*, Olaf said. *When she realized Hitler was gone and there was no new Hitler in the offing any time soon, my mother came to despise me, she rejected me. It would be better if you'd never been born! she shouted*, Olaf said. *Then I joined the ballet*, Olaf said. *Then I became a homosexual*, he said, *but my mother said, If Hitler were alive, you would have ended up under the gas showers. I danced for three years in Paris,* Olaf said. *We toured Europe,* he said, *then I went to Israel. There I explained to people what had happened to me. They said, Don't worry, it's OK. My mother hates Jews, I said to the Jews in Israel. And my father hates Jews, I told them. When he came back from the Russian front, my father hid, changed his name, changed his identity, and he never worked, he just drank and took drugs. He died at the age of sixty-three, homeless,* Olaf said. *The last time I saw my father he was lying drunk on the pavement,* he said. *Many* Lebensborn *children live today in Canada, England, America, Australia, Norway, Sweden. They are everywhere,* Olaf said, *and we correspond, now that we're old. Now that our parents are dead it is too late to disown them, or spit in their faces,* Olaf said.

Counting on the high fertility of the German woman, Himmler opens centres all over Germany, and when he decides there are enough there, he proceeds to Norway, where the women are also blue-eyed and blonde and where so many pure-blood German soldiers are stationed. They adapt hotels and villas, castles and ski resorts, some of them donated, many taken from Jews. Medical and administrative personnel are first checked, then hired. The food is good, the rooms are light and decorated with German symbols, the air is pure, the natural surroundings are beautiful and the care is first-rate. The war is going on somewhere far off and – for these select children – it is inaudible. Himmler spares no expense in equipping the *Lebensborn* homes, he takes as much as he needs, dipping chiefly into funds from confiscated Jewish property.

So from December 1935 to April 1945 it is lively at Heim Hochland in Steinhöring. There are 50 beds for mothers and 109 beds for children in Heim-Hochland. The building, previously the property of the Catholic Church, had been used as a hostel for retired priests. Himmler gives the Church 55,000 Reichsmarks for the building, and then invests another 540,000 in it so that the facility can house his dreams. Then, in 1937, Heim Harz is furnished in Wernigerode with 41 beds for mothers and 48 beds for children. That same year Heim Kurmak is set up in Klosterheide – 23 beds for mothers, 86 for children. From 1938 to February 1945 Heim Pommern is built in Bad Polzin (today in Poland) with 60 beds for mothers and 75 beds for children. Only 217 babies are born at Heim Friesland near Bremen with its 34 beds for mothers and 45 beds for children. Heim Friesland ceases to operate in January 1941, because at the time a small allied bomb attack begins on Bremen and the surrounding areas. So the children and mothers are sent to other homes, and the head nurse comes to Norway to set up the Norwegian *Lebensborn* homes in which the S.S. will accommodate the sons of the homeland. Not four years later these sons become *nullius filii*, needed by no-one, forgotten. Heim Friesland was the most luxurious within the *Lebensborn* organization, having previously belonged to the Lahusens, a wealthy family, industrial magnates from Bremen and the surrounding area, but the Lahusen family declared bankruptcy before the war and sold their property, and Himmler immediately nabbed the estate for his project of the sweeping Germanization of select European peoples.

From 1939 to March 1945, Kinderheim Taunus was up and running in Wiesbaden with 44 children's beds; Kriegsmütterheim opened at Stettin in 1940, followed by Kinderheim Sonnenwiese in 1942 in Kohren-Sahlis near Leipzig, with 170 children's beds, where the "aunties" took the children out for walks each day to make them strong and fit for adoption, for a better life, stable, planned and set, for a life full of the love that had been stolen from them, from which they were stolen. Heim Schwarzwald opens in 1942 in Nordrach near Baden, and a little later Kinderheim Franken I and Kinderheim Franken II are adapted at Schalkhausen near Ansbach, and then the S.S. confiscates the villa belonging to the Mann family in Munich, on Poschinger Strasse, and houses newly obtained children there.

In Austria at Pernitz-Muggendorf, today a suburb of Vienna, Wienerwald House opens in 1938 with 49 beds for mothers and 83 beds for children, and in 1943 "my" house, Alpenland, opens at Schloss Oberweis near Gmunden, where they change my identity and hand me over to Martha and Jürgen, having done a superficial *screening*, sloppy and hasty. By then the S.S. are in a big rush, because the house is about to shut down, because Himmler will soon be biting into his cyanide capsule, because cinders are all that is left of his magnificent dream of cloning a super race, a superman of a new race. In Austria there is another *Kinderheim* at Neulengbach near St Polten, about which I have no information. I might have ended up in Luxembourg at Heim Moselland in Bofferding, because mainly stolen children are accommodated at Moselland. After all that searching I finally ascertain that I, too, was *stolen* from the Adriatisches Küstenland, not *saved* after my parents were killed, as Martha Traube told me on her deathbed. Isabella Fischer (Rosenzweig by marriage) tells me in 1999 that *there were about a hundred, roughly one hundred high-level S.S. officials milling around the Adriatisches Küstenland, so go to the Berlin archive and search through their dossiers.* By digging through all the local and central Church and city archives of Germany, Austria, Italy, Slovenia and Croatia, I discover precisely 1,532 male children with the name Antonio born in the Adriatisches Küstenland in the second half of 1944.

Let me finish with the homes.

Belgium: the Ardennen in Wegimont near Lüttich (from 1943 to September 1944) for mothers of German blood, fertilized by S.S. soldiers.

France: the Westland in Lamorlaye near Chantilly.

The Netherlands: the Gelderland in Nijmegen with 60 beds for mothers and 100 beds for children, and, finally,

Norway, where this was a flourishing activity and from whence today there is a little army, not of *baby boomers*, but of *baby doomers*, about 12,000 all told, born between 1942 and 1945:

Heim Geilo (1942), 60 beds for mothers, 20 for children.

Kinderheim Godthaab near Oslo, opened in 1942.

> *My name is Ester, today. I was born at Kinderheim Godthaab as Gisela. When I turned two my mother advertised in the local newspapers that she was*

putting me up for adoption. I had blonde curls and I was pretty. When the people who adopted me found out my father was German, they returned me to my mother and drew a large swastika on my little rucksack. Then another family came forward and my mother told them the truth. They were wonderful parents, but they never told me I was adopted. When I turned forty-three a woman called and said, For years I have been shadowed by a little girl with blonde curls and a swastika on her rucksack. I am your mother.

Twenty-seven children from Kinderheim Godthaab were declared mentally retarded and consigned to institutions for the retarded throughout Norway. Many of them spent their whole lives there. Some thirty children were secretly sent to Sweden. In Sweden their names were changed and they were put up for adoption. Those who adopted them were told they were children of members of the Resistance who had been killed, or Jewish orphans. Most of these people don't know to this day that they are not the people they believe themselves to be. Most of them have no idea they are someone else. I only found my German relatives in 1995.

I, too, lived at Godthaab. I was assigned number 603. My mother brought me there and left right away. The discipline was rigorous. The nurses had white, starched uniforms and spoke only German. Then in 1946 they moved me to a lunatic asylum. I almost went mad with terror. Inmates were bound with chains. Some defecated in their clothes. Wherever. They screamed. I was five. When I turned twenty-three they released me. They said,

You're free, good luck. I was fortunate, however.
No-one ever raped me. I completed two grades of
elementary school. I worked in a factory at the
hardest physical jobs. I tried to kill myself, shoving
my arms into a machine for cutting waste, but I
survived. My name is Hansen. I found my mother
in 1970. She said, Get out of my sight. She said,
Your S.S. father croaked in 1953.

I was born in 1943. My father died that same year
and my mother was too ill to look after me. They
sent me to Godthaab when I was six months old. At
the end of the war they decided I was mentally
retarded. At the age of seven I was sent to the Emma
Hjorth mental hospital where they put me in a
straightjacket at night. When they released me I got
a job as a housecleaner. I don't know who my
mother was. I don't know who my father was. I am a
member of the society of Lebensborn *children who*
are demanding compensation from the Norwegian
government. I know Hansen. After the war they had
to hate someone, so they hated us, the children of
German soldiers. But there was no talk about us in
public. We are a footnote to a history which Norway
would like to expunge. After the war they tried to
send us all to Germany, but Germany at that point
was poor and devastated and couldn't take us in.

Then the *Lebensborn* home in Trysil, then
    the Hurdalsverk, opened in 1942, with 40 beds for mothers and
80 beds for children.
    The Klekken opened in 1942.
    Heim Bergen in the town of Hop near Bergen opened in 1943.
    Kinderheim Stalheim opened in 1943, could accommodate one
hundred children.

I lived at Stalheim. When the war ended they returned me to my mother, who didn't want me. My mother sent me to a home. I sat in a doctor's office with six doctors who confirmed I was mentally retarded and that I must never have children. Two staff members from the social welfare centre abused me with oral sex and told me this was obligatory therapy. I was five. I spent twelve years in the Merchant Marines. In 1996 I had a nervous breakdown. My wife left me. I spent a year being treated for manic depression at a psychiatric clinic. My mother died in 1988. I found my German father in 1997 and in 1998 he, too, died. I am sixty-five. I am an empty man. My name is Karl Otto Zinken.

Stadtheim Oslo in downtown Oslo opened in 1943. That same year, another state home opened in Trondheim.

I was born at the Trondheim home. My mother was one of the 14,000 who got pregnant with an S.S. man, one of the 5,000 women who were sent to work camps after the war, and before that their hair was cut on the main square in Trondheim. I was one of the 12,000 children who posed a threat to Norwegian society. When I turned two they gave me to a family for care and the family kept me chained in the yard with their dog. When I turned six a man threw me into a river, shouting, Let's see if the witch sinks! When I was ten, drunken villagers from Bursur near Trondheim branded my forehead with the shape of a swastika using bent nails, and howled, Now we will rape you! I was saved by a woman. Afterwards, I used sandpaper to rub at the swastika on my forehead to remove it. When I turned thirty I wrote a book called The German Child. *Then I found my mother.*

My mother's name was Synni Lyngstad. My mother fell in love with Alfred Haase, a married S.S. sergeant. During World War Two, from 1940 on, once Norway had been occupied, there were about 350,000 German soldiers roaming around Norway. My mother was eighteen when she fell in love with S.S. Sergeant Alfred Haase. I was born in Ballangen, near Narvik, on 15 November, 1945, a bastard. In early 1946 my mother, grandmother and I moved to the little town of Eskilstuna in Sweden. We were safe there: no-one knew of my mother's past. At Eskilstuna in Sweden no-one would say to my mother after the war, You are a Tyskerhor. *You are a German whore, a traitor of Norway. No-one shaved my mother's head in Sweden, nor did they send her to a work camp. They did not consign me to an orphanage or a mental hospital, nor did they ship me off to Germany or overseas to get rid of me. We were safe in Sweden. Sweden knew who we were, but kept quiet. That was the agreement between Norway and Sweden, that Sweden would keep quiet. Sweden agreed to receive several hundred children like me, several hundred half-German, traitorous children who are sixty-year-old Swedes today. My mother Synni died in 1948 of kidney disease, and for thirty years I believed that my father had been killed at the end of the war on his way back to Germany from Norway. That is what my grandmother told me, Your father is dead, she'd say whenever I asked. Then in 1977 a German magazine published a story about my background and claimed that former S.S. Sergeant Alfred Haase was alive. So I found my father, who came to*

Sweden to meet me. It was difficult to talk with him. He was an elderly S.S. man and a retired pastry chef. I don't believe he was a war criminal; he was never taken to court. The two of us are physically similar and this disturbs me. My name is Anni-Frid Lyngstad. I was a singer in ABBA. The brunette.

My uncle breeds dogs, so he trained me as if I were a dog. My aunt recently said to me, I won't leave you anything when I die, because you are an S.S. bastard. I am sixty-three.

For fifty years they were putting us down. For fifty years what happened to us had been a taboo. Nothing was said about us until 1990. We didn't exist. But our dossiers are still open. In them crouch ruined lives. We, the children of Lebensborn, are already old. Many of us will never learn who we are. We started searching too late. They doused me with scalding water at the orphanage. This is how filthy German children are washed, they said. A teacher abused me sexually. A priest said, I recommend sterilization.

I changed orphanages twenty times. They locked me in a pantry because I "stank". They scrubbed me with ammonia; the older boys raped me; the teacher pretended not to see what was happening. They force-fed us swill until we vomited, and then made us eat the vomit. The Ministry of Defence and the C.I.A. took some of us for experimentation with L.S.D. Four of the children died, six killed themselves. One boy was raped by nine men, and afterwards all nine of them urinated on him "to wash away the S.S. disgrace". For sixty years they

called us Tyskerbarna, *German bastards. We sued*
the Norwegian government. Then the Norwegian
government apologized in 2001 to the "German
bastards". We have barristers helping us obtain
compensation, which, I hear, will be $3,000.

At all *Lebensborn* homes the files with information about the mothers
and their children were closely guarded under lock and password,
and this information is not entered into the municipal or Church
records. But something somewhere fell flat. Despite Himmler's
generosity, only about 8,000 babies were born throughout the war
as part of the initial *Lebensborn* project. New solutions had to be
devised.

Apart from the German children born there, children collected
by Himmler's activists from orphanages throughout the Third Reich
are also placed in *Lebensborn* homes where they are trained, brain-
washed, fed with Nazi stories about the greatness of the German
nation, about the need to bow down to Adolf the god, and once they
are prepared, shaped, turned into marionettes, they are sent to
ideologically acceptable adoptive families. Decades after the war had
ended these children still did not know what happened to them,
what Himmler's officials did, especially the children in what was
then East Germany, who also had no inkling that their parents
were not their parents. There were many such children, thousands.
Some learned only forty years later about Hitler's and Himmler's *top
secret* pro-Aryan *Kinder*-swindle, while some do not know even to
this day, because the Communist authorities held this little truth,
meaningless to them, this piddling episode of historical reality, in
such *secrecy*. The *secret* archives with information about the birth
of the *Lebensborn* children, with information about those put up for
adoption, the files listing the changed names, are shunted during the
war from one centre to another, and after the war many of these files
are destroyed, some intentionally, some not. When the Allies start
milling around Germany in the spring of 1945, the staff burn records
and abandon most of the *Lebensborn* homes in panic. And so it is

that the identities of thousands and thousands of people disappear forever in flames, which still does not mean that these people did not exist and that they don't have other interesting, alternative, replaceable identities, as do I. At the end of the war, registers surface in Steinhöring with detailed information on 2,000 children stolen, adopted, displaced in orphanages, while the Federal Archive in Berlin makes public in 1999 that they have come upon a set of files with information about an additional 7,000 children, which profoundly disturbs the lives of some of these former children, who decide to dig through the files and through their genes. In the information at Steinhöring there is no mention of me.

Files found in Heidelberg and information preserved (and hidden) in the former East Germany are also in Berlin, and the only ones with access to this archive, once they have overcome the numerous bureaucratic hurdles, are those who hope to find a lost piece of themselves among the boxes on shelves resembling the shelves in Bad Arolsen.

I was in Ludwigsburg, near Stuttgart. At a former women's prison in Ludwigsburg is the Central Office of the State Justice Administrations for the Investigation of National Socialist Crimes (Zentrale Stelle der Landesjustizverwaltungen zur Aufklärung von N.S. Verbrechen). The Office opened in 1958 and to date they have investigated more than 7,000 cases with more than 100,000 suspects. Ludwigsburg is a picturesque little town on the outskirts of Stuttgart. The Dukes of Württemberg used to spend time in Ludwigsburg. Schiller was born there; in the house where he was born there is now a restaurant, one of the Wienerwald chain, and right next to the Wienerwald restaurant they sell McDonald's hamburgers. The Duke of Württemberg's financial adviser, a Jew named Süs, was hanged there in the eighteenth century, and at the entrance to the Duke's palace stands a plaque which says, *This castle shows its bright and cheery face. Its lively, liberal atmosphere is visible even today, as long as one is prepared to visit the other parts of Ludwigsburg, and not just its palaces and parks.* Next to the Central Office is a seventeenth-century fortress which housed a prison until 1990; the oldest prison in Germany, now in the fortress, is a museum of crime.

I was at the museum in Ludwigsburg, Ian Buruma told me. *The boy who brought me in smiled and enumerated the museum's treasures,* Buruma said. *This is a guillotine that was in use until the late 1940s, the boy said, these are thumbscrews, here, these are the uniforms, ropes and belts they used to hang prisoners, here are the renovated death cells, here, the boy said, is the executioner's axe,* Buruma said, *then he showed me lively copper etchings with torture scenes, and the menu for Süs the Jew's last meal,* Buruma said. *Süs the Jew was given bouillon, stewed veal, beans and white bread.* Then Buruma told me of a taxi driver who had brought him to the Central Office for Investigating Nazi Crimes, when Buruma was looking for something or someone there. He told me how the taxi driver first claimed he didn't know where the Office was. *No clue,* the taxi driver said, and went on to say, *that office should be scrapped; it's high time for us to forget those old tales about the Nazis,* that is exactly what the taxi driver said, *those old tales, as if there aren't more important things to be doing, as if the Communists weren't every bit as bad,* the taxi driver said, *and so on and so forth, repeated the taxi driver,* said Buruma.

The Office in Ludwigsburg is the brain, a paper memory, a bureaucratic memory of the Nazi past. In the Central Office, as in Bad Arolsen, lost lives huddle in steel cabinets. At the Ludwigsburg Central Office, filed tidily in alphabetical order, are more than 1,400,000 testimonies of witnesses and victims, various dossiers, Gestapo documents, archival court transcripts, not just from Germany but from everywhere – Poland, the former Soviet Union, France, Romania, Hungary and the Netherlands (Buruma is from the Netherlands), *and so forth,* as the taxi driver would say. Lord, it's as if all of Germany is crisscrossed with hidden, underground water-ways, subterranean conduits of lamentation, woe and oblivion, the inexhaustible Acheron, the Cocytus and the Lethe.

I was at the Berlin Federal Archive – the largest Nazi archive there is, with more than 50 million pages registered, including the originals of the personnel files of members of the National Socialist Party and S.S. officials – and there I stumbled upon a little clue that took me further. Later, when I established that my genetic father might have been S.S.-Untersturmführer Kurt Franz, I went back to the Berlin Archive and leafed through his past, which was a source of incredible distress to me, in fact, of *physical revulsion*, though I kept telling myself I had no tie to this man, which was not, of course, true. In Kurt Franz's dossier there were photographs, especially from Treblinka, showing Kurt Franz riding, or in white sports shorts, running through a lovely, dense forest, Aryan and sexy, all the more nauseating. The Berlin Federal Archive, like the International Tracing Service in Bad Arolsen, is in a dense forest. But unlike Bad Arolsen, which is completely *hidden*, the Berlin Archive is not far from downtown Berlin, though both buildings – the main building in Bad Arolsen and the one in Grunewald on the outskirts of Berlin – used to belong to the Gestapo, which can be quietly chilling for the visitor.

Aud Rigmor Harzendorf from Kohren-Sahlis told me that they never spoke of the past in East Germany before 1989, and I told her that in West Germany they didn't speak of it either, nor did they in Austria, though, of course, they talked a lot about the more *distant* past, they spoke of *several* distant pasts, the more distant the pasts were, the greater the detail in which they spoke of them, but there was very little talk, only quiet and *secretive* talk, about the *recent* past, on the basis of which one might conclude that the recent past was quite a dirty past. Then I learned that in East Germany there was a major *secret* scam perpetrated with the names of the *Lebensborn* children, which was why the whole story had been *unknown* there until recently. The Stasi needed new names for its spies, so they stole the original identities of the *Lebensborn* children who had been given up for adoption, meaning their real names, and if these children decided to poke around the archives later, they would come upon a whole heap of alarming political and police hurdles. *My adoptive mother told me I have no parents, that I was left with no parents. You were left without both parents, my adoptive mother said,* Aud told us. *And that is why they gave you to me, said my adoptive mother, whom I loved as if she were my own, and that is absolutely all she said,* said Aud, *but we lived five hundred metres from the former* Lebensborn *home in Koren-Sahlis, and I had no idea what kind of a home it was, what went on there, I didn't know I was born inside. Today there is a children's nursery school in the building, it is very cheery, but I still don't know who gave birth to me or what her name was,* Aud told me when I met her at a gathering of other children who are searching for themselves, frantically, and who are no longer children, of course, some have children of their own, grown children, some even have grandchildren, like me, for example. I am sixty-two and I will have to tell my children, my grandchildren, everything I have discovered in the course of my eight years of searching, which will confuse them, because everything I have come across since 1998, when my mother Martha Traube told me *You are not Hans Traube* as she was dying, until today, 3 July, 2006, all of this sounds incredible, and I will have to speak with them about it, and they will have to drag this shit around with them for years, decades, like a punishment, a curse, and they will forever be wondering *What is hidden in my genes?* and I will tell them and I'll say it over and over: Your genes contain the genes of a member of the S.S. and a war criminal and the genes of a Jewish woman. I will have to tell them, and they will have to find a way of dealing with it. History, history which we Germans (and Austrians) have repeatedly mucked up, as Grass says, is a clogged toilet. We flush and flush, but the shit keeps coming up.

Then Aud showed me this photograph, which her adopted mother had been hiding for fifty years, a picture from the *Lebensborn* home at Kohren-Sahlis, and in it is Aud, of course, and then Aud told me, *Look, that's us, Hitler's children.*

There were various ways of bringing children to the *Lebensborn* homes. Other than the German children, there were children who had been stolen from the occupied countries of the Reich. Little Poles were the largest number to stay at the *Lebensborn* homes, about 250,000 little Poles, but there were children stolen from Ukraine (about 50,000), the Baltic countries (about 50,000) and Yugoslavia (600 children are known to have been taken from Slovenia alone). There were many children from different places, much like the little fair-skinned, blue-eyed German children of pure German blood. Even French children weren't spared, and Norwegian children. Today only 50,000 of these children know of their origins and who their parents were or are.

Himmler adored *Lebensborn* homes, over which special *Lebensborn* banners flew, in which they used special *Lebensborn* dishes and special *Lebensborn* cutlery on which there was a special *Lebensborn* stamp (today the cutlery goes for a lot of money at auction). The bedding and table-cloths and towels had *Lebensborn* monograms, and the staff wore a special *Lebensborn* pin on their chest, so that everyone would know.

Every single object at the *Lebensborn* homes was marked with little runes resembling a hissing stroke of lightning: S.S. Himmler loved making the rounds of "his homes", so that he could be sure the Germanization of the right sort of children was progressing at a desired pace, and sometimes he would be present at the ceremonial rite of pseudo-Christian baptism under the Nazi flag, during which the newborn would be given candlesticks made by camp inmates from Dachau.

Himmler's favourite child, Gudrun, her father's "Puppi", who grieves even today for her fanatically Catholic and equally fanatically racist father, had the opportunity to ascertain personally how creative the Dachau prisoners were when, at the age of twelve, she wrote in her diary after a visit to the camp in 1941: *Today we visited Dachau S.S. concentration camp. We saw everything there was to be seen. We saw the tended gardens, we saw orchards, we saw beautiful paintings made by the prisoners. And after all that, we had a lot to eat . . . it was wonderful.*

During a baptism, an altar would be draped with a cloth embroi-dered with a swastika, the baby would be laid on a pillow in front of the altar, and then a Nazi would read excerpts from *Mein Kampf*, then Haydn's *Variations on the German National Anthem* would reverberate throughout the room, a uniformed S.S. man would bless

the (male) child by holding an S.S. "honour dagger" to its brow, a second S.S. officer would give a brief speech, the child would be given a name, and they all would sing.

Himmler gave the children born on his birthday (7 October) special gifts. *I think it entirely right that we are taking little children from Polish families*, writes Himmler in 1941. *We are placing these children in special homes and schooling them*, writes Himmler, *because these are children with particularly robust racial characteristics. I order that after six months every child who has proved to be acceptable be furnished with a new family tree with valid accompanying documents*, orders Himmler, *and that after one year of observance, those children be given for adoption to racially authenticated parents with no children. Because among so many people there will obviously be some persons of high racial quality*, writes Himmler. *Hence our task is to remove these children from their environments, if necessary by violence and theft, because*, Himmler writes, *either we will keep all the good blood for ourselves . . . or we will destroy that blood.*

Racial selection of stolen children was stringent, entailing medical examinations and tests: they measured the head, its size and shape, the limbs, their length and girth, the structure of the female's pubis, the coordination of movement, the intelligence, the shape of the nose, fingernails, mouth, eyes, all of it was regulated and explicit. Top-category children went off to famous, wealthy S.S. families; second-category children qualified to receive social and financial aid; the less valuable children were sent to orphanages. It was known exactly what perfect German babies should look like.

Ḩerzliche Glückwünsche
zum Geburtstage

Photographs of perfect German babies began cropping up everywhere. They were used in advertisements and on propaganda posters, on food labels, in school textbooks. Thanks to Himmler's obsession with the need to produce as many perfect Aryan children as possible, competitions for the most beautiful, perfect Baby of the Month, Year and Nazi Eternity were regularly announced, just like similar ghastly competitions the world over today, filling the pages of cheap newspapers with their ads. It so happened in 1935 that the title of Most Beautiful Aryan Baby of Berlin was won by Hessy Levinsons, whose parents had brought her to a prominent Berlin photographer to have her picture taken. Several months later, this photograph of Hessy Levinsons appeared on the front page of the magazine *Sonne ins Haus*. Jacob and Pauline Levinsons, who were both famous opera singers, originally from Latvia, froze when they saw the front page. They went to the photographer to ask how it had happened, and the photographer confessed he had known Hessy was a little Jewish girl, but he had *deliberately* submitted her photograph in order to prove that the racist Nazi theory of blood and soil was plain nonsense, confirmed by the fact that Hessy had been chosen in fierce competition with pure-bred German babies. The picture was printed on postcards. Hessy was sent out as a birthday greeting to travel all over Germany, and perhaps beyond as well. In

1939 the Levinsons decided to flee the Third Reich, first to France, then over the ocean to Cuba, and finally on to New York.

Nazi family pasts are hard to expunge. Now, as the next generation is already ageing and on its way out, Nazi family stories are winging their way into the homes of the third generation and wreaking havoc there. Compared to me, Sam Thacker is a mere kid at thirty, living in England. Pasts are free-thinking, pasts like to roam, pasts traverse borders, glittering gaily, pasts are bold travellers, sliding through their own molehill-like labyrinths. Recently, among mislaid, discarded family documents, Sam Thacker's mother comes upon several un-developed rolls of film, which her father, Sam's grandfather, a member of an elite unit of the Waffen-S.S., the Leibstandarte S.S. Adolf Hitler, and decorated with the Iron Cross for his merits, brought back from the front at some point. In these pictures life is so lovely and so ordinary. In special combat gear the young S.S. men tour the sites of Paris, they swim, attend football matches, visit the military cemetery at Verdun, sit in bistros in the company of three lively French women; nothing inhumane, nothing monstrous on the faces of the young men who are serving their leader and their homeland. But Sam Thacker is disturbed. Photographs testify. The Nazis cultivated a special weakness for the amateur photographer snapping shots with expensive photographic equipment. Photographs, of course, can be burned, but that doesn't often happen. When photographs are burned, crumbs of memory remain from which sprout fear and shame, the sins of the fathers and grandfathers are difficult to eradicate. The children of these fathers and grandfathers are still tiptoeing through their own minefields today. And once they step into the field of anger and condemnation, once they cross it, a heavy cloak of pain settles upon them. And small, though dangerous, geysers of the past continue to erupt unexpectedly under their noses, until these descendants, and they are many, these descendants of big and little Nazis rub their family excrement deep into the pores of their own bodies, after which they will at last be able to rinse themselves clean. History, an ornate lady who does not die easily, dresses again and again in new costumes, but keeps telling the same story. History as Dracula, History as the Vampire, the vampiric fate of history, History the Bloodsucker, that great mistress of humanity.

Whenever the quota of children at homes and orphanages got low, the Nazis kidnapped children from streets, playgrounds, parks; they tore children from their mothers' arms, which is what happened with me. A week before I left for Gorizia on Monday, 26 June, 2006 I received a letter from the International Red Cross, or rather from the I.T.S. (International Tracing Service) in Bad Arolsen, in which that organization – or rather a Mrs Helga Mathias – informs me that they have found a copy in Bad Arolsen of a baptism certificate which matches one sent to them on 2 February, 1946, with a black-and-white photograph of a three-month-old infant by a Haya Tedeschi of Gorizia, asking for their help in finding her son Antonio Tedeschi, born 31 October, 1944, in Görz, then part of the Adriatisches Küstenland. *The baptism certificate,* writes Mrs Mathias, *says that the father of child Antonio Tedeschi is S.S.-Untersturmführer Kurt Franz, born on 17 January, 1914, in Düsseldorf, where he died in 1998.* Helga Mathias adds that they compared the photograph, which I, Hans Traube, born in Salzburg on 1 October, 1944, sent them on 23 January, 1999. *We compared the picture on which you are, as you say, about eight months old,* writes Helga Mathias, *with the picture of the three-month-old infant sent to us by Mrs Haya Tedeschi of Gorizia,* writes Helga Mathias, *and we ascertained that the similarity is striking. In a displaced box, among the rare documents preserved about the* secret Lebensborn *project,* Mrs Mathias writes further, *we found a letter from Father Carlo Baubela of Görz, now Gorizia, who baptized the child and then handed over to an unknown party a copy of the document about the birth of Mrs Haya Tedeschi's son, being Antonio Tedeschi, who could be you. With the letter from Carlo Baubela,* writes Helga Mathias, *we found an official order from the Central Office of Reich Security, signed by Reichsführer-S.S. and Minister Heinrich Himmler, who was in charge of that ministry at the time, an order to send the male child of Aryan descent with the temporary name of Antonio Tedeschi to the Alpenland* Lebensborn *home, to Schloss Oberweis near the town of Gmunden, region of Traunsee, in Austria.*

Since the registers with documentation of almost all the Lebensborn *homes throughout the Third Reich were destroyed just before Germany surrendered,* writes Helga Mathias, *we are unlikely to find any information pertaining to Schloss Oberweis.* I had a week to learn the details of the life of S.S.-Untersturmführer Kurt Franz, though he was already in my private archive, among the officials who were stationed then, between 1943 and 1945, in the Adriatisches Küstenland.

Before I left on my trip, I got in touch with several acquaintances, I can call them friends and fellow sufferers, who have gone through or are still going through the hell I had been going through for eight years, people I met at various gatherings and workshops at which one practises breathing in the truth and at which there is a lot of weeping. Aloizy Twardecki (the Nazis kidnapped him too and changed his name to Alfred Hartmann, then gave him up for adoption to a German family) told me, *Come on, perhaps this is the end, though I doubt it.* After the war Aloizy was repatriated to Poland and today he teaches at the University of Warsaw. I got in touch with Don Alexander Michelowski, who was ten in 1942 when he was kidnapped from his home and his name changed to Alexander Peters. He knocked around orphanges for years because he was too old for adoption, and later, as a Catholic priest, served the Polish Diaspora in Newcastle. Alexander said, *Even God didn't help me.* Helena was adopted by a German policeman and his wife, a seamstress, but after the war she was returned to Poland, and today she is a judge in Warsaw. Helena told me, *Write a book, maybe it will heal you.* It was hardest to talk with Ingrid von Oelhalfen. Ingrid was stolen as an eight-month-old baby from Slovenia. *They kidnapped me in Celje,* she said. She was taken to Germany and never returned, and she never found any of her family; she only found this small and useless fact stating that she is not Ingrid von Oelhafen.

> *My name is Ana Johnson. I was born on 3 March, 1946, in Reutlingen, Germany. Because of an illness of the joints and bones I took my first steps only at the age of two. When my mother Mary Božić tried*

to board a ship for Australia in 1946 they stopped her. You cannot leave Germany without your child, they said. So Mary waited for me to walk. We arrived in Australia in 1948 and Mary immediately left me at St Therese's Orphanage in Essendon. On 16 December, 1984, I was found by the Federal Police. Mary Božić has less than a month to live, said the men from the Federal Police. Mary Božić has cancer of the large intenstine and she wants to see you, repeated the Federal Police. We will take you to Mary Božić, they said three times. Then I saw my mother after thirty-six years and I had no recollection of her, so I thought right away that maybe she wasn't my mother. I nursed Mary Božić and she told me the story of her life as she was dying. On her left arm Mary Božić had a tattoo of a swastika and the number LB 0097. I was a Lebensborn *slave, she told me. I worked at the munitions factory in Reutlingen. We produced rockets and rounds for the German Army, she said. There were many S.S. men there. I was beautiful. The S.S. men raped me whenever they felt like it. There were many S.S. men. They raped me often. I was beautiful, she said. Luckily you were born on 3 March, 1946, she said, because had you been born on 3 March, 1945 you would not be alive today. They would have killed you, because Hitler wanted as many male children as possible. I spent my whole life in fear, my mother Mary Božić said, as she lay there dying in Australia, and I told her that I had constantly felt guilty, but didn't know why. They moved me from orphanage to orphanage, I told my newly discovered mother, Mary Božić, then they sent me to reform school. To this day I don't know why, because I never had any reason to reform. I was quiet and obedient, I told her. My mother, Mary Božić, died on 2 February, 1985. We talked for a month, for a month we were together. This was a great joy for me. I got in touch with the Red Cross. I hoped the Red Cross would help me find out my grandparents' names. I might have relatives. I might have nephews. My mother had six brothers. My grandmother was a Gypsy from Hungary and my grandfather was from Yugoslavia. I believe I have hundreds of brothers and sisters. Who knows how many women he slept with, the man who got my mother pregnant? Mother never told me my grandmother's name. I am German property, because I was made in Germany at the behest of Heinrich Himmler. I was born in Germany, but when the war ended they forced Mary Božić to take me with her, because they wanted to forget I existed. They did not want to see me. They wanted to forget I had ever lived, but I'm not giving up. Germany owes me an apology. It owes me compensation. Me and my mother Mary Božić. I must find out who my family are and where my grandfather and grandmother are buried. Thank you for hearing me out.*

At Nuremberg, for crimes against humanity, for the theft of children, for *Lebensborn* manipulations, the following people were brought before the court, and sentenced or released:

Ulrich Greifelt: life imprisonment
Rudolf Creutz: 15 years
Dr Konrad Meyer: released
Otto Schwarzenberger: released
Herbert Hübner: 15 years
Werner Lorenz: 15 years

Heinz Brückner: 15 years

Otto Hofmann: 25 years

Richard Hildebrandt: 25 years

Fritz Schwalm: 10 years

Gregor Ebner: two of the charges dismissed, convicted of the third charge, but released on account of time served

Max Sollmann: released

Gunther Tesch: released

Inge Viermetz: released

My situation is complicated many times over. I was stolen. I am a *Lebensborn* "child". I was raised by former supporters of Nazism, Jürgen Traube (who never, thank God, sullied his hands) and housekeeper Martha Traube, who also, thank God, renounced her "support". I still consider Jürgen and Martha Traube to be my parents. I would like to disown them, but I cannot, because they were good and tender parents, they were *permissive* parents, though they were Catholics, I mean they were not *fanatic* Catholics, because fanatic Catholics are the worst Catholics, just as all fanatics are horrible and dangerous people. As *tolerant* parents, Martha and Jürgen Traube took my pronounced anti-fascism in their stride, my anti-Nazi photographs and exhibitions, my often uncontrolled outpourings of fury and, for me, not the least bit benign *ressentiment* of Austria's part in the war. They put up with my disgust at Austrian silence, at Austrian blindness bound to Austrian Nazi history. They listened to what I told them and when I married Rebecca they said, Rebecca, you are ours as much as Hans is. But then into my life crept that murderer, S.S.-Untersturmführer Kurt Franz and that Jewish woman who spread her legs for him, for the blonde angel of death, the admirer of music and nature, the bad amateur fanatic photographer, the baby-faced executioner, she spread her legs while trains rumbled past, right there in front of her nose, on their way to killing grounds all over the Reich. At first I was sorry that S.S.-Untersturmführer Kurt Franz was dead, I wanted to shake him up, though his story didn't interest me, I didn't want to hear it, because the story was clear to me and for me the story has no inside or outside, it is a monstrous story, full stop. Maybe I would have killed him, S.S.-Untersturmführer Kurt Franz, believing that I was thereby destroying, expunging, *exterminating* all the dirty genes that are planted inside me. Today *nothing matters*. I wanted to hear out the woman who gave birth to me, I wanted to forgive her, because she might be able to bring to life the little man, the stunted midget, Antonio Tedeschi, who has been waiting inside me for sixty-two years to grow up, to obtain some kind of a biography, no matter how dull and defective. This Haya Tedeschi could inscribe a history onto my minuscule, half-dead double, this foetus inside me, after which he, Antonio Tedeschi, would open his glued-shut eyelids, straighten up and maybe go his way, leaving me in peace.

I know, there are more stories like mine.

Ah, said my wife Rebecca, *relax. The world is full of horrors and life is unpredictable. Look what happened to Beate Niemann, the protagonist of that documentary* My Father the Murderer.

I know the story.

Beate Niemann was born in 1942, but it was only in 1997 that she set out to search for her father, which seems both comprehensible and incomprehensible, reasonable and unreasonable, courageous and cowardly. But who am I to judge?

Beate Niemann looked for a father she could be proud of, but she found a murderer. She found S.S.-Major Bruno Sattler up to his elbows in blood. She traced a life shadowed by her mother's lies, by lies never renounced or denied. Only a few weeks before Beate Niemann was born, Bruno Sattler grouped gassing trucks around Sajmište concentration camp on the outskirts of Belgrade, he assembled lorries for the gassing of women and their children. Bruno Sattler was killing women and children at Sajmište concentration camp and sending his pregnant wife little love letters, photographs from *the field*, photographs of *nature*. Beate Niemann's father, S.S.-Major Bruno Sattler, had ordered the shooting of several tens of thousands of Jews in Smolensk and near Moscow. They say that Beate Niemann's father, S.S.-Major Bruno Sattler, took part in the liquidation of 500,000 Yugoslav partisans, Jews, Gypsies and others.

Poor Beate Niemann. Born in Nazi Germany which after the war has for decades *publicly*, persistently, even courageously, been uncovering the dangerous refuse of its past, Beate Niemann, fifty and something years later decides to start digging through the secrets of her own family, utterly shaken with and surprised by what she finds. Where had the loads of logical doubts been hidden? Which waters did they flow into? Where were her parents' monstrous truths stored? In tightly packed bundles of hatred which will, covered by layers of mould, of deposited dirt, spontaneously dissolve?

Thus, when in her sixties, when body, but also spirit, become weaker, Beate Niemann, as if stepping on a land mine, faces the truth that additionally crushes her.

After World War One, during the 1920s, Bruno Sattler sells jewellery at the Wertheim department store in Berlin. The proprietors of the store were members of the Wertheim Jewish family, Sattler knows that, so he quickly joins the Nazi Party and becomes a policeman, then advances further and further, until he finally arrives at the Gestapo. Then he moves to the secret service of the S.S., then to the Einsatzgruppen who kill more than a million and a half civilians in the Soviet Union before the butchers and slaughterers of Auschwitz and Treblinka even appear on the scene in Poland.

Beate Niemann's mother dies in 1984, and that is when Beate Niemann starts searching for her father. She makes the rounds of more than a hundred archives in three countries, but the first traces of truth she finds among her mother's belongings and in the urban planning office in Berlin, right under her nose. She comes across a document that confirms how already in 1942 Bruno Sattler buys a house from a Gertrud Leon for the miserable sum of 21,000 Reichsmarks. To the purchase and sale agreement which Beate Niemann finds, there is attached a guarantee from Bruno Sattler in which he declares that he will spare Gertrud Leon from any possible transport, that he will guard her life, and that he will not allow anyone to move her anywhere or take her out of Berlin. Two weeks later Gertrud Leon goes off first to Theresienstadt, then from Theresienstadt to Auschwitz to breathe her fill of gas.

Beate Niemann then visits Belgrade. In Belgrade she meets Ljiljana Đorđević, who says, *Oh, yes, I remember S.S.-Major Bruno Sattler. S.S.-Major Bruno Sattler killed my father at the camp in Sajmište.*

So, how does S.S.-Major Bruno Sattler come to his end? In 1947 Russian agents pick him up in broad daylight on a Berlin street and take him off to an East German prison. Many years later, Beate Niemann goes to Leipzig, to the former Stasi prison then already abandoned, in order to peep into the cell her father had occupied. It is a small cell, in it twenty people slept on boards, they tell her, in that cell one could not walk, one could only lie. The walls were still filthy, ghostly, stained with various histories. Finally Beate Niemann learns that her father, S.S.-Major Bruno Sattler, died on 15 October, 1972, they say he was shot in the back of the neck. After that agonizing but greatly belated revelation, Beate Niemann begins her homage to Eastern Europe, seeking out surviving Jews, those who lived through the camps and all the torture and all the humiliation, and when she couldn't find *them*, because not many remained, she looked for their children, and to everybody she would say, to those who prevailed, to the *leftover people*, Beate Niemann would say, *Forgive me, forgive me, please forgive me.*

Then there's Monika Göth, the daughter of Amon Göth, the commander of Plaszow camp, the one from *Schindler's List* who loved shooting inmates from the balcony of his villa, and people wouldn't have known about him, they would have had no idea who he was, most people wouldn't have known who Amon Göth was had they not watched *Schindler's List*, but many did not see *Schindler's List*, they didn't *want* to see *Schindler's List*, because the theme of *Schindler's List* makes them nauseous, that's what they say, *We don't want to get upset*, they say, *all that is in the past now*, they say, and Monika Göth, who was one year old when in 1946 her father was hanged as a war criminal, Monika Göth, many years after, forty, fifty years after, also searches for surviving camp inmates tortured by her father and seeks their forgiveness, she roams the world and asks for forgiveness and to everyone she says, *I am not like him.* Every year Monika Göth goes to Auschwitz and in Auschwitz she pays her respects to the victims of her father, Amon Göth.

Then Peter Sichrovski, a journalist from Vienna, born in Vienna, who grew up in Vienna and who after the war played with the children of former Nazis, and who then, many years later, goes looking for them, for his street pals, in order to ask them, *What did your fathers do during the war?* and then records their answers.

Some of my kind ask me, *What does the child of a murderer look like? Is it obvious, is it evident that we are the children of murderers?* Oscar tells me that until their death his parents regretted that today no-one can force him to wear a pink triangle. We are all trapped, we, the children of Nazis. The prisoners of history. Those who grieve for their "tender" fathers who brought them souvenirs from Polish concentration camps and dandled them on their knees, and we who are trying to face our family truths. The woman who begs Sichrovski to take her paralysed father living in an old people's home for a short "walk", that pathetic, demented old man who still feeds on his Nazi faith, even if through a feeding tube, literally through a tube, she, too, is fucked up. *No matter what he was,* says this woman to Peter Sichrovski, *he is still my father, he loved me, I know he loved me,* says the woman in whose bosom a tornado must be raging. That frightens me. When in people who are monsters, butchers, slaughterers, perverse sadists we discover scraps of gentleness and frailty, I freeze in horror.

Hans, what do the children of murderers look like? some of my kind ask me.

Like us, I tell them, *they look like us.*

Helga Schneider I remember from Salzburg, then we met again at the promotion of her book in Bologna. Many of us write books, make films, hold photographic and video installations, paint the horrors we excavate from our own innards, monstrous worlds that remain mostly unintelligible and inaccessible. We are a lot unto ourselves, an ilk that has unhooked itself from Earth and now wanders through space.

We are little Helnweins and Bellmers in search of stars and meteors, of straggling heavenly bodies on which we could land, just to feel the ground beneath our feet, even if that ground is very far away. We do not believe in any gods, especially not in supernatural gods. In fact, we have no faith, because it is faith we do not believe in. Least of all do we believe in the Catholic faith, it has sullied itself the most, it has defiled itself.

Helga Schneider comes to Salzburg at the age of seventeen. I am ten at the time and I am already hanging out at Isabella Fischer-Rosenzweig's photography studio. Helga drops in during the afternoon, because she cleans Isabella's darkroom and mops the floors for pocket money. Helga takes me out for an ice cream.

By the time Helga Schneider tells me her story in 2001 I am already in frantic search of myself, I seek the dwarf who has resided in me from the time I was born, who breathes with me as I take each breath, who has been crouching for fifty-seven years in the dark, in the dark of my skull, in the gloom of my gut, who touches my bones and squeezes my heart with his little hands. Then I arrive at Helga's book launch in Bologna in 2001.

I was four in 1941, Helga said. *It was a cold autumn evening. She said, I am leaving. She said,* So, auf Wiedersehen, meine Kleine. *She picked up her suitcase and left*, Helga said. *She didn't kiss me. She didn't say where she was going, why she was leaving, when she would be back. My brother was still an infant, and he was asleep. We were left alone*, Helga said. *Then we cried, we howled, because our father was off fighting, I don't know where, all I know is that he was fighting for the Führer and the Fatherland. Then my father's mother came from Poland, Grandma Emma, whom we loved, but father remarried soon and he sent Grandma Emma back to Poland, and mama's name, Traudi, was never mentioned again in our household*, Helga said. *Traudi is dead, father said, dead, remember that, he said. His new wife didn't like me. She loved my brother. I got on her nerves*, Helga said, *so she dumped me in a reformatory, and afterwards sent me to a school for problem children, although I don't know why. I asked them, my father and my stepmother, Why am I a problem? What have I done? and they said,*

You're untidy. You're messy all over, especially in your head. I would see my mother again only thirty years later, in 1971, Helga said. But I did see Hitler. In December 1944 I was seven and still living at home and someone organized a visit to Hitler's bunker for children of high-ranking parents. It was festive. We were supposed to shake hands with the Führer. Special children of tried-and-true Nazis went, not just anyone, Helga said. *So we, my brother and I, went. The food was decorated beautifully. There was a lot set out to eat and plenty of colours. We could hardly wait for the handshaking to be over,* Helga said, *so we could eat. Then the Führer arrived, and he walked* terribly *slowly, dragged his feet, his footsteps slid as if snakes were slithering over the stone floor and hissing. Hitler walked hissing his feet,* Helga said, *all hunched over and grey, and while he was walking towards us, his head shook and his left arm hung there, swinging like a long, dead fish,* Helga said, *as if it were made of modelling clay,* she said. *He extended to me the other hand, the one that wasn't dangling and looked me straight in the eyes and I froze. I saw his pupils dancing,* Helga said, *and I waited for some evil little man to come leaping out of his eyes and drag me away with him. Hitler's handshake was soft, limp,* Helga said, *and the palm of his hand was moist. This is like holding a frog, I thought. And his cheeks sagged. Everything on him sagged. He had bags under his eyes. He was all flab. Only his moustache stood firm. Then he asked me, What's your name, dear? and I told him, Helga. I said only Helga, but forgot to add "mein Führer", which was a serious omission,* Helga said, *but my brother did not forget to say "mein Führer", my brother said it at least two, possibly three times, "mein Führer", "mein Führer". Then the hostess came and gave us each a bar of marzipan. We didn't get any of the lovely food, just a little marzipan bar each. Then the war ended,* Helga said, *but the hunger did not, and the great chaos became even greater. Father came back from the front. He decided in 1948 to take up residence once more in his homeland, Austria, which had reinstated its name and borders, which once again belonged only to itself. So we left Germany forever,* Helga said. *Things at home turned from bad to worse because of my stepmother, so one night,* Helga said, *I ran away and never went back.*

That's when I got work at Isabella's, she said, *and I also washed glasses at a Salzburg beer hall where it wasn't too bad. I could have lunch there, mostly sausages, and all the beer I wanted to drink. Then I finished secondary school,* Helga said, *and played little supporting roles in an experimental basement theatre, a* Kellertheater, *she said, and then I went to Vienna, and in Vienna I posed at the* Kunstakademie *for students and met Oskar Kokoschka. I rented two machines in Vienna: one for sewing, a hand-driven Singer (today that Singer is probably a museum piece), and one for writing, because I wanted to write about my life. I used the sewing machine to alter second-hand clothes I bought at the flea market for practically nothing, and on the typewriter I wrote a novel about my life that nobody was eager to publish. A publisher finally did offer me a small advance, however, and with it,* Helga said, *my friend and I went to Italy for a break, and in Italy I met a wonderful young man,* Helga said, *my future husband, and, to keep the story short,* she said, *we had a son. His name is Renzo. I worked as a foreign correspondent, I learned Italian, after many years everything was good, life in general, my* schöne Zeiten *have come,* she said. *When my son was born, my mother-in-law called him* il piccolo Austriaco *and those words stirred memories of my mother, and I thought to myself, Say, Helga, now you are a mother, but whatever happened to your mother? so I decided to look for her, maybe retrieve the mother I never had, my son would have another grandmother, that would be nice, ah, yes. I wrote to my father,* Helga said, *and asked if he knew anything about my mother, where she was, what she was up to, and he answered, I have no idea and I don't care, it would be best to forget her, he said,* Helga said. *Nevertheless I went looking for my mother, though I knew nothing about her. The only thing I knew for sure,* Helga said, *was that both of them, my mother and my father, were born in Vienna,* she said, *so my reasoning was that if she'd survived the war, she must have gone back to her city. I asked a Viennese friend, Susanna, to check the register of births, marriages and deaths, to search the phone books for everybody with the surname of Schneider, then I wrote to five women and one of them wrote back to say, It's me, that's me,* Helga said. *Then I told my husband, I've found my mother and now*

I'm going to Vienna and taking Renzo with me, so he can meet his grandmother. In Vienna I found a vigorous, good-looking, sixty-year-old woman who took me straight to her bedroom, showing no interest in Renzo, she just gave him a glass of milk and some biscuits, she took me to her bedroom, Helga said, *opened the wardrobe, pulled out some sort of uniform and said, Here, try this on, I want to see how it fits. I didn't understand,* Helga said, *I thought, that must be a theatre costume, I was totally ignorant, because at that point I knew nothing about my mother's life,* Helga said. *Then I asked her, Why? and she said, Just put it on, for years I've been wanting to see you in that uniform, and again I asked, Why, and she said, Because I wore this uniform at Birkenau. So,* Helga Schneider said, *after thirty years I had in front of me not a mother, but a monster. And this monster, this woman who gave birth to me, was standing there smiling and saying over and over, Es war so schön, so schön! I will not put on this uniform; it's soaked with blood, I told her,* Helga said, *at which point Traudi Schneider pulled out a handful of jewellery she had looted from the victims of Auschwitz and Ravensbrück and said, Here, take this. I grabbed Renzo and flew out into the street and realized that I have no mother, that I've never had a mother and that I will somehow have to get along without a mother,* said Helga. *Life went on. Renzo grew up, my husband died of cancer, and I dug around in the archives and dossiers and got to know the life story of this S.S. camp guard, this fanatical-unto-death Nazi, Traudi Schneider. Then in 1998 a letter in an ugly pink envelope arrived from Vienna. Your mother is in a nursing home, wrote a "close friend of Traudi Schneider",* Helga said. *Your mother is nearly ninety, wrote the friend. At times she loses her grip and she may die soon, she wrote, why wouldn't the two of you meet once more, she wrote, After all, she is your mother. I say to myself, she may be feeling remorse,* Helga said, *so I go to Vienna, I buy flowers and visit the nursing home. I find a thin old woman, weighing less than forty-five kilos, frail and neglected, and I feel sorry for her. I am your daughter, I tell her,* Helga said, *and Traudi Schneider shrieks, You are not my daughter, my daughter is dead, if you are my daughter, call me Mutti, children call their mothers Mutti, shouted Traudi Schneider, and then pinched me on the cheek, and I couldn't say Mutti, I couldn't utter that word Mutti, and then Traudi Schneider said, Just so you know, I was the strictest guard there, she said, I beat the inmates and they spat blood, she said.* Then she straightened up, Helga said, *and started describing the horrors of the medical experiments, and she said, Of course I was in favour of the Final Solution, why do you think I went there, for a holiday? And then she said, in those chambers, not everyone died at the same rate, she said, babies took only a few minutes, we'd pull out some who were stiff and bright blue, and sometimes there wasn't room in the crematoria, so we shot people in the head. We would line the Jews up along the edge of a huge pit and shoot, and they'd fall into the pit, all of them, men and women and children in the arms of their mothers, and I shot, of course I shot, I was a crack shot, said Traudi Schneider, smiling, O, schöne Zeiten, she said,* Helga said, *and once, Traudi said, two Jewish whores got into a fight over a crust of stolen bread and we saw it, we saw everything, those whores, and we took them off to be shot, naked, naked, of course, and torn up, with open gashes all over, because before that they had been lying in the punishment cell for fourteen days in the dark, with rats as fat as cats feeding on them, nearly eating them alive. That's why they were covered in wounds, and when we pulled them out, they were already mad from the horror and they could hardly wait to get a bullet in the head. I hated those damned Jews, ugh! A horrible race, a terrible race, believe me, revolting. And then I screamed,* said Helga, *I screamed, Enough, stop, I've read all your files, I already know all that, enough's enough, and I left, I went back to Bologna. I had terrible nightmares and my heart pounded as if Traudi Schneider were jumping inside it with a pistol in her hand and howling, Let me out! I'll shoot if you don't let me out, I'll kill you! And then the doctors gave me some pills and now my heart is as quiet as if it had died.*

Karl-Otto Saur Junior is still wearing his hair long to hide the bull neck he inherited from his father, the sturdy Karl-Otto Saur Senior, the last head of the technical office at the Armaments Ministry of the Third Reich, whom Hitler, in his crazy will of 1945, named as Speer's successor. Karl-Otto Saur comes through the Nuremberg trial with no conviction, because he agrees to testify against Krupp in the Krupp Affair. Karl-Otto Saur embarks on a better life in 1946, released from charges and guilt, even from the guilt of employing hundreds of thousands of Hungarian Jews in the production of weapons for exterminating the selfsame Hungarian Jews he "employed", which was evident, later, at the Wehrmacht exhibition in Berlin and cities throughout Germany, at which point I see many events much clearer, and because of this monstrous clarity I sleep less and nauseatingly badly. This same Karl-Otto Saur Senior, the one who opens up an engineering office after the war and then starts a publishing firm, which thrives today under the guidance of his elder son Klaus-Gerhard Saur, has descendants whose hair is unusually shaggy, reaching down to their shoulders, as if with their long hair his descendants will cover the possibility of history repeating itself, but they won't, with their long hair they'll cover nothing but their necks, so reminiscent of the neck of their father. We should probably be able to learn something from the repetition of history, *repetitio est mater studiorum*, but despite the fact that history stubbornly repeats itself, we are bad learners, and History, brazen and stubborn, does not desist, it goes right on repeating and repeating itself, *I will repeat myself until I faint*, it says, *I will repeat myself to spite you*, it says, *until finally you come to your senses*, it says, yet we do not come to our senses, we just grow our hair, hide and lie and feign innocence. Besides, for some of us, those of us who like Santa Claus lug sacks on our backs, sacks brimming with the sins of our ancestors, History has no need to return, History is in our marrow, and here, in our bones, it drills rheumatically and no medicine can cure that. History is in our blood and in our blood it flows quietly and destructively, while on the outside there's nothing, on the outside all is calm and ordinary, until one day, History, *our* History, the History in our blood, in our bones, goes mad and starts eroding the miserable, crumbling ramparts of our immunity, which we have been cautiously raising for decades.

At this point I, Hans Traube, do some research, and I learn that

Hermine Braunsteiner was born in Vienna in 1919, that she was raised in a strict Catholic family, that she joined the S.S. in 1939, and from then on worked as a guard at the concentration camps in Poland. I learn that the Austrian Court for War Crimes sentences Hermine Braunsteiner to three years in prison in 1948 and that she is released nine months later by that same court. I learn that until 1957 Hermine Braunsteiner works as a saleswoman in picturesque tourist towns in Austria, then meets her future husband, an American called Russell Ryan, and goes with him first to Halifax, Canada, then to the United States. I learn that Hermine Braunsteiner-Ryan lives in peace until 1968, when she is discovered by Simon Wiesenthal, and thanks to Wiesenthal is extradited to Germany and tried in Düsseldorf for the murder of "at least 1,181 camp inmates" and for being a co-perpetrator in the murder of another 705 persons. She is sentenced in 1981 when she is sixty-one and has many lovely memories, when she remembers her happy days, when she has grown children, American, who might cherish an affection for whips and high boots. Of course, these little histories that I research surface only after 1998, because until 1998, until Martha Traube informs me of the agonizing truth of my birth, I dig into nothing, into no past, just as many others never do, why should they, life goes on, look to the future, people tell themselves, tell them, tell us, everybody says so, at home, at school, on stage, parents say so, friends say so, and politicians, priests say so, and the Church. Then, when I least expected it, the Past jumped out at me in a flash, hop! like a carcass, like some rotten corpse, it draped itself around my neck, plunged its claws into my artery and it still isn't letting go. I'd like to shake it off, this Past, but it won't let me, it swings on me as I walk, it lies on me while I sleep, it looks me in the eyes and leers, *See, I'm still with you.* Like Hermine Braunsteiner's boots, the Past, my Past, our Past, presses up against my face, which, beneath it, contorts in a grimace like the grimace of a crazed detainee whose innocence or guilt has yet to be determined.

Listen, my colleague says to me, Tipura said, *this Stille Hilfe is a fairly repulsive organization and it is run by Frau Gudrun Burwitz,* who is actually Frau Gudrun Himmler, says my colleague, Tipura told me. So off we went to see what's what. Time has stopped for Gudrun, but on the other hand it hasn't. Gudrun's name is no longer Himmler but Burwitz, yet she behaves like a Himmler and dreams Himmlerian dreams, said Tipura. Gudrun Himmler Burwitz's daughter is neither a Himmler nor a Burwitz, women have it easier, they can always take their husband's name, right? said Tipura, though men can change their names too, when necessary, why not? There, in Gudrun Himmler Burwitz's house, we met her daughter, who was very upset by our visit, Tipura said. Gudrun Himmler Burwitz's adult daughter was completely beside herself when we came. She leapt at us, don't you dare air my mother's name in public, she threatened, Tipura said. None of my friends know who my mother is, cried Gudrun Himmler's daughter, even my husband doesn't know, she said, Tipura told me, which was remarkable information for me, Tipura said. What about Himmler's children born out of wedlock, the two Himmler had with his secretary Hedwig Potthast, who he moved into a newly furnished villa near the rest of Hitler's cronies so that everything would be as she wished? What about Helge Potthast Himmler, born in 1942, and his sister Nanette Dorothea Potthast Himmler, born two years later? wondered Walter Tipura. If they are alive, what do they tell their children and grandchildren? Do any former Nazis and their descendants suffer from post-traumatic stress disorder? Do they ever manifest symptoms of P.T.S.D., little hints suggesting that their soul is attacking their body and their body is burrowing through their soul? Katrin Himmler, the daughter of Heinrich's nephew, a 37-year-old scientist, married to a Jew (I no longer see this as coincidence), a Jew whose relatives disappeared in the Polish death camps, is beside herself: I dread the day I will have to tell my son that one half of his family exterminated the other half, says Katrin Himmler, Tipura told me. She dreads it so much that she started writing books about it, about Heinrich Himmler's brothers, about their children, who are her uncles, Tipura said.

I know that coincidences are rare, perhaps there are no coincidences, there is only our stupid and superstitious need to duck behind our own carnival life which prances by us. Our coincidences, which are actually our pasts, we bury under our family trees on which grow berries full of sweet poison. It is no coincidence that my friend Wolfgang, who works at the Austrian Documentation Centre for the Reparation of Victims of the War, pursuing the dirty past of the by now already senile murderers condemned to a quiet demise, and searching for stolen artworks in the well-concealed safes of their descendants, remembers how, after the war, the cronies and fellow fighters of his Nazi grandfather went to the Berlin Opera in a long line of black limousines, seeking respite from their memories. I know it is no coincidence that Wolfgang's mother, the daughter of a militant Nazi who after the war sat serenely in his loge at the Berlin Opera in blessed oblivion, focusing totally on the music that nourished his soul, that Wolfgang's mother married the son of a rebellious anarchist who met his end (by *secret* order of Stalin) in a Siberian backwater. It is no coincidence that Serge Klarsfeld, born in 1935 in Bucharest, whose father dies in Auschwitz, falls in love with Beate Künzel, born in 1939 in Berlin, the daughter of a member of the Wehrmacht, who learns more about the horrors of the Holocaust when she is in Paris in 1963. It is no coincidence that Beate and Serge become Nazi hunters and manage to drag the "butcher of Lyons", Klaus Barbie, from Bolivia to his Paris trial. It is no coincidence that there are so few random coincidences and there is so much repressed *ressentiment*. People wash themselves any way they know, heal themselves as best they can, find straits through which they navigate quietly, on tiptoe, to avoid, at all costs, meeting themselves. Who can keep track of all these branchings? No-one, because all those branches proliferate and proliferate, because families grow and spread, because families have a name (and behind every name there is a story). Unless those family branches interlace once and for all, just as that worm coiled itself around the eye of that frantic, unfortunate woman from a civilized European country, and unless, thus entangled, those branches penetrate into the centre of the pustule which becomes the axis of their silenced past, unless they reach the roots of their trees, their axis steeped in putrid pus, there can be no salvation for those who remain and those to come. The story lasts as long as the past, forever. Ah yes, that hurts, I know.

My father, said Tipura, *was born in 1929, and he grew up with a foster family, because his mother entrusted him to a foster family because his mother was only fifteen when she agreed, on 31 December, 1928, to go to the flat of a waiter who worked at a café at the hippodrome, a great aficionado of horse races, a fanatic gambler, who would, nine months later, become the biological father of my father, Norbert*, said Tipura. *As an adult, my father, too, became a fanatic gambler, a fixture at the horse races, I don't know how that happened*, said Tipura, *but now I, too, love horses and horse racing. My father*, said Tipura, *became head of the Munich branch of the* Hitlerjugend, *at home he had a large world map hanging on the kitchen wall and he pinned flags on it whenever the German troops, the* Wehrmacht *troops, captured a town, a region, a country, which then lost its name and became Germany. When the war ended, my father saw 1945 as a year of crushing defeat, rather than a year of victory. I was young, my father would later say*, Tipura told me, *and he often repeated, Lord, what would I have become had Nazism prevailed. But he did not dig deep, he never dug into the family shit, he only poked at it, smeared it around*, said Tipura. *His portraits of the children of Nazis are almost nostalgic flashes of the past, tender portrayals of helpless victims. And so, when I found my father's notebook, I set out on my own exculpatory journey, I looked for the same "children", for the ones my father spoke to forty years earlier, and I found elderly people clutching well-worn bundles of family history, bundles they baulk at unpacking, and when they do, everything inside is greyness.*

Martin Bormann Junior (a.k.a. Kronzi) was born in 1930, the first of ten children of S.S.-Obergruppenführer Martin Bormann, head of the National Socialist Party Chancellery and Hitler's private secretary, a stocky, muscular watchdog at the entrance to the Machiavellian Third Reich Hades, a hater of Christian churches, the fiercest anti-cleric among the Nazi officials, the man who sparked the Kirchenkampf, *who committed cowardly suicide in 1945, biting into a cyanide capsule after he had been wounded while fleeing Adolf's bunker. There is no help for Martin Bormann Junior, a dedicated young Nazi from 1940 to 1945, attending the Party Academy in Bavaria, who after the war embraces the Catholic faith and becomes a priest, so that he can repent the sins of his father, sins which spun around his body everlasting fibres, leaving him, Martin Bormann Junior, languishing for years like a squished caterpillar in a dark cocoon. Martin Bormann Junior is not helped by God or the Church or the fucking Our Father or "our trespasses, our trespasses", which he mutters into his beard. So after several wasted decades he bids the Church auf Wiedersehen! and marries a former nun who has also told the Church addio, bye bye, and the two of them start making the rounds of German and Austrian schools, where they tell children of the horrors of the Holocaust and the Third Reich. Then they go to Israel and bow to the victims of Martin Bormann Senior, and in so doing, coexist with the ghosts who sit at their table and crawl into their bed. Martin Bormann Junior told me he remembers the furniture and decorative lamps made of human bones and skin in the home of Himmler's mistress Hedwig Potthast,* Tipura said. *Bormann Junior does what he can to cure himself,* Tipura said, *but his sister Irmgard burns in her own hell, blinded by the flames of her diseased love for her "good and tender father, whom she would love and respect to her death",* Tipura said.

Arnold Schwarzenegger's father was a Nazi, Tipura said. *Gustav Schwarzenegger asked to join the National Socialist Party as early as 1938, before the annexation of Austria, but it was only in 1941 that the National Socialist Party drew him to its bosom. In his medical records from the time, one can read,* Tipura told me, *that Gustav Schwarzenegger was a quiet and reliable person, a person of average intelligence, not remarkable for anything in particular. From 1947 until he retires, Schwarzenegger works as a policeman – since, they say, he committed no war crimes. Arnold, however, during a time of peace and blessed Austrian forgetfulness, develops his physique by lifting weights, and in 1967, when he is twenty and before he becomes the Terminator, he wins the title of Mister Universe and looks like this:*

Today Schwarzenegger, who did not consent to speak with me, Tipura told me, *today Schwarzenegger says, My father was an ordinary soldier in the army of his country. My father fought in Belgium and in France and in Russia, and it is known, Schwarzenegger says, that my father did not commit a single crime, because the soldiers of the* Wehrmacht *did not kill, the soldiers of the* Wehrmacht *merely waged war, says Schwarzenegger who probably*  *did not attend the* Wehrmacht *exhibition,* said Tipura, *because had he attended the* Wehrmacht *exhibition he would have seen that even the ordinary German soldiers of the Third Reich committed appalling crimes, which was an insight that stunned the German public then, at that* Wehrmacht *exhibition, and perhaps that insight would have stunned him, Arnold Schwarzenegger, as well,* said Tipura.

I didn't need Tipura. I could have done without his stories and his discoveries. By 2000 I had amassed my own file of the "case histories" of Nazi descendants, the descendants of the first, second and *third* generation of Nazis, big and little, known and anonymous, regardless, the symptoms are more or less the same, and my file kept growing, getting fatter like a goose I was ruthlessly fattening until it keeled over. In nearly every case I studied there was a similar pattern: the children and grandchildren of Nazis rarely faced the history of their families and their own story. Nazis, many of them with blood-stained hands, some condemned to death, some sentenced to years in prison, a sentence they often didn't serve out, many who were never brought to justice, who went on working as physicians and judges, engineers and architects, living "distinguished" lives, these Nazis colluded in conspiratorial silence as weighty as a millstone under which life lies crushed beyond recognition and under which, by some inexplicable or, in fact, explicable miracle like Emperor Trojan's goat's ears, a grain of fragile truth would sprout here and there, truth that had a destructive, devastating power. It is incomprehensible that the children, the grandchildren, mostly asked no questions, that they still do not ask. But old photographs, unfinished manuscripts, hidden diaries surface; archives open, movies are made, books are written; the pebbles of history roll underfoot and in time our step grows less steady. Nazi, Fascist, Ustaša, Chetnik, regardless. Their germ has not been eradicated. Norman Frank understood this when he said, I will have no children, I want the vile Frank germ to disappear, then starts pouring milk down his throat, he drinks thirteen litres of milk per day, then dies. Norman's brother Niklas, however, is alive. A defiant and tireless demystifier, Niklas Frank writes and shouts, and at his unambiguous, defiant declarations, articles, books and projects, not to say performances (such as when, for a couple of years in his childhood, he used to masturbate to the point of orgasm on the anniversary of Hans Frank's execution), at every warning from him, the hypocritical and cowardly German public has been shocked for the last few decades, snarling at Niklas' uncomprising stand, wanting to sleep easy, as if a father were a sacrosanct being. But he is not. There are no sacrosanct beings. Even God is not sacrosanct, perhaps He least of all.

The truth is absolutely simple. Our fathers were criminals and murderers, so screw those platitudes about the banality of evil. There are no justifications, there is no valid relativization, there is no excuse. There is *no mercy* for the pathological debris of humanity, those tainted minds shouldn't have even been brought to trial, what miserable justice, what defence of which dignity, whose dignity, which pathetic Nurembergs, Stuttgarts, Dusseldorfs, Frankfurts, Munichs, Hagues, money wasted, time wasted, only dark, farcical performances after which not a single diseased mind has learned nor will learn a thing, all of them should have been executed after a summary trial the way the Russians and East Germans did in '46, '47 and '48, their germ should have been sent to seed so the new ones don't come along who keep coming and coming, they, too, should be swiftly done away with before they die in comfortable prisons playing chess or, worst of all, free, as heroes to whom monstrous monuments are raised, whose names bedeck city squares and airports, that scum ought to be *eliminated* so that the story wouldn't continue, elegantly and brazenly, inserting itself into reality and so that the malevolent Phoenix would once and for all stop hovering over our heads. That eternal and infinite *Herumgeschmuse* of the children of the murderers and criminals is becoming pathetic. Their "They were little Nazis" holds no water. There are no little Nazis. To begin (or end) with, to the children and grandchildren of the murderers and criminals I propose a verbal *Exerzier* and *exercitationes* of self-denazification, a *mea culpa* in the name of the second generation and the third. The fact that the descendants of the Nazis, Fascists, Ustašas, homeguard fighters, Chetniks, and so on and so forth, prefer not to recognize the crimes of their fathers and mothers, grandfathers and grandmothers, diminishes the overall crimes of the Germans and others, which were committed during the Third Reich. And this holds true, as well, for the descendants of former satellite Nazi-Fascist fabrications, formerly fascist countries. It applies across the board. And it applies to the Israelis today. I'm still waiting now for the Americans to bump off Morales, the silence has poured into a gigantic block of reinforced concrete, and the Catholic Church, this caricatured parade and more than revolting fabrication, this costumed theatre of transparent lies and empty promises should be done away with right now, once and for all, because the gatherings of the zealously blinded masses who bow down to the divine emissary are reminiscent of the ominous gatherings at which people shouted *Sieg Heil!*

Listen, says Bernhard, definitely Bernhard, *I was confirmed in my suspicion that our relations with Jesus Christ were in reality no different from those we had had with Adolf Hitler. When I went back to school after the war*, says Bernhard, *the school was called the Johanneum and it became a Catholic institution with a new name for the old building, which had been a National Socialist institution. The day-room, where we had formerly been instructed in National Socialism, had been turned into a chapel. In the place which had been occupied by the lectern, at which Grunkranz had stood before the end of the war and held forth about the Greater Germany, there now stood an altar; where Hitler's portrait had once hung on the wall, there was now a large cross, and in place of the piano at which Grunkranz had accompanied our singing of National Socialist songs like* Die Fahne hoch *or* Es zittern die morschen Knochen, *there now stood a harmonium. The room had not even been repainted. So, after the war, the colour of the ruling party was no longer Nazi brown, but once more the Catholic black it had been before the war. The gymnasium had always been and remained a strictly Catholic school, although after the war it was turned into a* state *gymnasium. After being subjected to the Nazi lie about history, I was now subjected to the Catholic lie. Both National Socialism and Catholicism are infectious diseases, diseases of the mind, but I succumbed to neither, since my grandfather had taken care to* immu-nize *me against them. Nevetheless I suffered* under *them, though not* from *them. Look at the Salzburg Summer Festival, which makes a hypocritcal pretension to universality, when so-called universal art is pressed into service to disguise this peverted denial of the spirit; and indeed, everything that goes on there in the summer is merely deceit and hypocrisy set to music and performed for all it is worth by various combinations of instruments. And all of it, the whole festival, was founded to temporarily mask the diseased, perverse and polluted being of that city, which does not greatly differ from numerous European Catholic cities that boasted of their National Socialism, or whatever it was then called.*

When in 2005 I said to my colleague Ian Buruma, *I must go to Sonnenstein, that's where my biological father, S.S.-Untersturmfuhrer Kurt Franz, began his career as executioner,* Ian said, *You won't find anything there, all traces have been removed. Several years ago I was in Pirna, at the time a neglected but unusual little town with beautiful nineteenth-century villas,* said Buruma, *and with some examples of late Gothic architecture,* he said. *I wanted to see the building in which the first gassings of mentally ill patients took place, I knew the building existed, I had seen photographs of that building, at the time the "origi-nal" extermination house for the "useless", in which more than 10,000 people were gassed with Zyklon B, but none of the tourist brochures* offered any information about it. I had trouble finding the place, Buruma said. *An old woman cheerfully sent me uphill, but I got lost, so I asked an elderly gentleman, Where did the Sonnenstein Institute use to be? and he said, Pardon? Where did what use to be? Again I said, the former euthanasia institute, and he asked, When was that? And I said, In Hitler's day, and he said, Sorry, I wouldn't know anything about that. Nonetheless, I finally found it, this former "institute"*, Buruma said. *I went over to a yellow-walled villa where there was a plaque that read,* SAUNA FOR THE ILL AND ELDERLY. *A young woman asked me what I was after. When I told her, she gave a start: Oh, no, that wasn't here. Here we work only with patients who require specialist therapy. You're looking for a different building, that one over there, where there used to be a factory of turbines, the young woman said*, Buruma told me. *The* building over there *was surrounded by a rusty wire fence, and the building itself looked quite forbidding. On it was a plaque commemorating an Albert Barthel,* OUR PARTY COMRADE WHO WAS KILLED BY THE NAZIS IN 1942. *So, I concluded*, Buruma said, *that the institute had not been in that building either. All the same I went into one of the rooms and watched some young men having lunch. It turned out that they were deacons who cared for mentally ill children. The former euthanasia institute? Oh, no, no, thank God, they said, that institute was not here, no, it was in the building* next to this one, said the deacons, Buruma told me. *I peered into the cellar of the neighbouring building, an elegant French-style villa. On it there were no plaques. Wild grass and weeds had grown around the door, latched shut. I heard birds chirping and the rustling of leaves in the mild breeze and thought about the pile of plush teddy bears I had seen in the hall of the deacons' building. Then I remembered Oskar Matzerath and his jazz music with Klepp at the elegant Zwiebelkeller in Dusseldorf and how the guests chopped onions and wept without restraint, how at last they were crying, how the tears gushed, even if they were artificial tears provoked by stinging onions, yet still they were tears that stung. Don't go to Sonnenstein*, Buruma said. *Sonnenstein is nothing but weeds.*

I met Niklas Frank at Thomas Bernhard's. I was taking pictures,

Niklas was interviewing Thomas for *Stern*. That was when Bernhard said, *We don't exist, we get existed. Never in my life have I freed myself from anything by writing. If I had, nothing would be left, there would be nothing to write about,* said Bernhard. *And what would I do with that freedom seeping into all the nooks and crannies of my life?* he asked. *I'm not in favour of liberation, of relief. The cemetery, maybe that's it,* Bernhard said, *but, no, I don't believe in the cemetery either,* he said, *because then there would be nothing left.*

Niklas' father, Hans Frank, was the King of Poland, the main man in the General Government, a lawyer with a doctoral degree, a tall, dashing dandy with a penchant for white suits and hats, for travelling to towns with old historical centres, for invaluable artworks displayed with finesse in the fancy villas where he stayed, a priggish *bon vivant*, a philanderer and closet homosexual whose pedantically detailed war diary in forty-three volumes became the most powerful evidence against him when he was finally tried at Nuremberg. On 2 June, 1943, Hans Frank notes in his journal, *Here we began with three and a half million Jews; of those three and a half million only a few that work in camps are left, the rest have – let us say – emigrated.*

Born in 1900 in Karlsruhe, Hans Frank enters the German Army at the age of seventeen, and later joins the extreme right-wing units of the *Freikorps,* which extorts politicians and frightens and kills people. Hans Frank is Reichsminister without Portfolio, leader of the National Socialist Association of Barristers, a member of the Reichstag, and, from 1941 to 1942, President of the International Chamber of Jurists. While he is serving as the Governor-General of Poland, his adminis-tration introduces death camps as a part of the design of the Final Solution. Millions of Jews, Roma and other "undesirables" disappear. Under Hans Frank's administration, the S.S. and Gestapo commit terrible crimes against Polish civilians, treating them as members of the resistance movement; they rape, torch towns, mutilate women and children and organize mass deportations to concentration camps.

Hans Frank, condemned for war crimes and crimes against humanity, is hanged in Nuremberg on 16 October, 1946. While in detention he returns to the Catholic faith, and sees his execution as a *partial* expiation for his sins, although he does not confess to all charges in the indictment. Hans Frank leaves the courtroom in the company of an Irish Franciscan, Father Sixtus O'Connor, and two weeks later enters the place of his execution with a smile.

Oh happy day
Oh happy day
When Jesus washed
When Jesus washed
Jesus washed
Washed my sins away
Oh happy day
La, la, la, la, la, la, la, la, la
La, la, la, la, la, la, la, la, la
La, la, la, la, la
La, la, la, la, la
Oh happy day

In 1946 Hans Frank is survived by five children and his wife Brigitte. Today, all except Niklas are dead. Niklas Frank was seven years old in 1946. His life until 1945 in the Wawel Royal Castle overlooking Cracow seems like a dream. While the "King of Poland" works to stamp out the Polish elite, claiming that *Poland must become a land of workers and peasants*, stripped of an educated class, while throughout the General Government he shuts down theatres, schools and universities, while he bans radio broadcasts, destroys libraries, proscribes the printing of books, and works towards eradicating the Polish language, while he sets the rationing of foodstuffs at less than starvation levels, the Frank family want for nothing, from provisions to servants to stolen artworks. Hans Frank hosts high-ranking S.S. officials, including Himmler, and while nibbling at caviar and sipping champagne he tickles the ivories, playing for them – oh, happy days – Chopin. Writing and talking about that time, Niklas mentions an outing with his nanny Hilde Albert to a place where a jolly man was persuading very thin people to mount a donkey, which bucked, throwing the thin people to the ground, and the very thin people struggled to get to their feet. *I watched the performance and laughed as if I were at a circus*, Niklas said. *But I was at a sub-camp of some nearby concentration camp*, he said. Niklas becomes a disreputable teenager and an avid hitchhiker, he roams throughout the western part of his divided country of Germany and takes its pulse. *As soon as I'd say that I was the son of a famous Nazi executed at Nuremberg, the driver would take me to lunch. During my many years of hitchhiking only one driver stopped, opened the door and said, Out!* says Niklas. At the Berlin Archive Niklas Frank studies his father's dossier. He makes the rounds of archives, pores over Hans Frank's diary entries, visits doddering Nazis, who at one time had been in touch with Hans Frank and his close associates, servants who worked for the Frank family in Berlin and Cracow, he goes to America to talk with Father Sixtus O'Connor, from whom Hans Frank sought the mercy of Jesus before his execution. *Did the noose over the black hood squeeze his neck enough?* perhaps Niklas Frank asks himself. *What was the snap like when they kicked away the chair? Was it loud enough?* he wonders. *I imagine myself biting into Hans Frank's heart while he screams violently, I thrust my teeth deeper and his howls grow louder and the blood spurts horribly and then his heart stops, empty and dead*, he says.

For a long time after the war, Germany was awash in collective denial of individual responsibility for the war, Niklas Frank says. *My father was a coward and a scoundrel and he is responsible for the deaths of two million people.* What Niklas Frank discovers in the course of his many years of research is transformed in 1987 into lifelong, obsessive loathing, a mission laced with fury because of the deafness which presses upon the earth, turning it into a Beckettian landscape in which, at the *end of the game*, the players are left with a few pieces and a *limited number of moves*. In the book entitled *Der Vater* – not *Mein Vater*, but *Der Vater* – Niklas Frank embarks on a dangerous duel, the outcome of which even Freud cannot decipher, and for which Greek tragedy has no response.

I was completely absorbed by my own investigation, obsessed by searching for information to confirm whether I am or am not what I believe myself to be, yet may not be at all, when Niklas' new book *Meine deutsche Mutter* came out in 2005. Niklas Frank is unrelenting. Niklas Frank is not giving up, so I won't either. The "Queen of Poland", Maria Brigitte Frank, unscrupulous, greedy, calculating and promiscuous, and dead for a very long time, passes muster no better than her "king". Niklas Frank continues to howl in a cosmos of deaf and dead silence. A small consolation which I keep, which I hold onto, so that it won't drop like overripe fruit onto muddy earth and rot.

I have arranged a multitude of lives, a pile of the past, into an inscrutable, incoherent series of occurrences. I have spent eight years probing these lives, these pasts, at the same time drilling into myself. I have dug up all the graves of imagination and longing I have come to. I have rummaged through a stored series of certainties without finding a trace of logic. Now I am standing at the door of the hotel room in Gorizia, watching the terrible mess I leave behind. A pile of dead witnesses with eyes that gleam like cold marbles, empty and weightless like dry, mummified heads impaled on two rows of stakes along the path that leads to my lair. On the bed, the chairs and shelves, on the floor are strewn letters and documents, books, testimonies, photographs, heaps of photographs, some of them mine, some of them taken by others, tepid loves, grey passions. All this lies before me in a deep swoon like tired, aged time that has descended from the sky to rest or pollute the atmosphere, either way. But it will suffice to blow a puff of air, open the window, and all these pasts will leap, fly, sucked up by a mighty whirlwind, a *tromba marina*, a *tromba d'aria* filled with the cacophonic voices of the crazed dead, and if I don't elude it – this vortex may sweep me up as well. The mess I have created can no longer be put back into order, nor can it be hung on a sturdy *Kleiderbügel*, a contemporary *Aufhänger*, to air.

I walk through Gorizia and I watch how a spent melody breaks off from its streets and the façades of its buildings. This melody drops onto my face like a mask, like a flattened sticky kiss that I do not wipe away. We know each other, this melody and I, so as I walk the two of us are silent and breathe shallowly. It is Monday, 3 July, 2006. At the Trattoria Piccola Grado on Via Morelli I order

Kaiserfleisch, or rather *costata di maiale affumicato cosparsa di cren fresco e accompagnata da gnocchi*, then I set off for Via Aprica 47. The door will be opened by a woman with strong hands and thick hair, about forty years old, wearing winter shoes without laces on bare feet. The woman will smile and say, *I told you, reality is boundless and indivisible.* The woman will introduce herself as Ada Tedeschi-Urban, Haya Tedeschi's niece, daughter of Haya's sister Paula. She will be the woman I met on the train, and in whose features I shall seek traces of my own, just as I still look with horror at the photographs of S.S.-Untersturmführer Kurt Franz, from whose boyish grin a fist leaps and squeezes my face into a rigid grimace, into fear that his grin might settle on my lips. In the room, by a tall window, an old woman will be sitting in a rocking chair. By her feet there will be a big red basket, and around the basket letters, documents, photographs, newspaper clippings will be strewn, a heap of lifeless paper, just like the one I left behind me. The old woman will rise and turn to me. We will stand there like that, I, tall and greyhaired, she, petite and greyhaired. I will think, This is good, I'm not bald like him and my eyes resemble hers. I will think, Did I become a photographer by chance? and then immediately I will think, My photographs are powerful, his are rubbish, and I will think, He is dead, I am alive. I don't like boxing, I'll think, I don't ride horses, I cycle. This will not console me.

When I write about the role of my mother in the universal history of infamy, I will not know who strolled around the San Sabba rice mill, who snapped pictures of San Sabba, my mother or I, who searched through the files of the officials of the Adriatisches Küstenland, she or I, who studied the details from the life of S.S.-Untersturmführer Kurt Franz, Haya Tedeschi or I, Hans Traube-Antonio Tedeschi, who was it that visited Treblinka. Together, we will drape ourselves in the histories of others, believing that those pasts are our pasts and we shall sit and we shall wait for those pasts to fall into our lap like a fat, dead cat.

We shall wend our way through a *Waste Land* and I will say to her

> *I think we are in rats' alley*
> *Where the dead men lost their bones,*

and she will ask

> *What shall I do now? What shall I do?*
> *I shall rush out as I am, and walk the street*
> *With my hair down, so.*
> *What shall we ever do?*

I will say

> *We shall play a game of chess.*

There will be more withered stumps of time upon the walls. Staring forms will lean out, and leaning out they will hush the room enclosed. Footsteps will shuffle on the stair. And I will ask her

>   *Do*
> *You know nothing? Do you see nothing? Do you remember*
> *Nothing?*

And she will say

> *I remember*
> *Those are the pearls that were his eyes.*
> *At my back in a cold blast I hear*
> *The rattle of the bones, and a chuckle spreads from ear to ear.*
> *The awful daring of a moment's surrender*
> *Which an age of prudence can never retract*
> *By this, and this only, we have existed*
> *Which is not to be found in our obituaries*
> *Or in memories draped by the beneficent spider*

And I will ask her

What is that sound high in the air?
Murmur of maternal lamentation, she will say.
What is that city over the mountains? I will ask her.
Unreal City, Od' und leer das Meer, a deserted and vacant sea.
Shall I at least set my lands in order? I will ask her.
Yes. You shall set your lands in order, she will say.
Ere the worm pierce your winding-sheet, ere the spider
Make a thin curtain for your epitaphs.

Then I will say
thank you
and servus,
now nothing matters.

Author's Note and Permissions

For this book I have been researching the historical archives in several countries, in a number of languages, for two years. In the spirit an established tradition of documentary fiction, I have incorporated the voices of many figures and the words of many distinguished writers. I have made grateful use of these published works and acknowledged as many of them as I could. If there is any writer whose work I have not acknowledged, I will make due reference in any future edition in whatever language.

The first part, the early life of Haya Tedeschi, is based on an account by Frank Gent of the life of Fulvia Schiff and her family ("My Mother's Story," 1996). In my book, the affair with an S.S. officer, and subsequent birth of a son, are fiction. In reality the Schiffs fled from Sicily to Albania in 1938 after the Nuremberg Race Laws, and lived there for six years until their return to Italy via Yugoslavia, Hungary, and Austria. Fulvia Schiff met a British soldier, Frank Dennis Gent, in Milan in 1945. She returned with him to England—where they still live—married, and had six children.

I make grateful acknowledgment to the following websites and organizations, from which I have taken and adapted text:

www.axishistory.com, by permission of "Schmauser"
www.xoxol.org/eichmann/eichmann.html
www.deportati.it/english-risiera_survivors.html
www.nizkor.org
www.deathcamps.org
avalon.law.yale.edu/imt/02-27-46.asp

My source for the list of transports and for some trial texts was www.holocaustresearchproject.org, and they are reprinted with permission of the Holocaust Research Project. I have also made extensive use of the Harvard Law School Library's Nuremberg Trials Project and the website of the United States Holocaust Memorial Museum.

D. D.

DAŠA DRNDIĆ is a distinguished Croatian novelist, playwright, and literary critic, born in Zagreb in 1946. She spent some years teaching in Canada and gained an MA in theatre and communications as part of the Fulbright Program, and a PhD on protofeminism. She is now an associate professor in the English Department at the University of Rijeka.

ELLEN ELIAS-BURSAĆ is the leading translator of Croatian into English and a South Slavic scholar who has taught at Harvard. Her translation of David Albahari's novel *Gotz and Meyer* was awarded the National Translation Award by the American Literary Translator's Association.